Praise for *The Impersonator*

"Miley shows a deft touch and sets a blistering pace in her debut novel, *The Impersonator*. Leah Randall/Jessie Carr leaps off the pages in this Roaring Twenties period piece that drips with bathtub gin, truck-size cars, outsize personalities, money, high stakes and enough twists, turns, and sleights of hand to keep one reading late into the night. It reminded me of *Some Like It Hot* but without the cross-dressing. Simply put, this book is FUN."

—David Baldacci, #1 *New York Times* bestselling author of *King and Maxwell*

"Mary Miley has delivered a tale that lures us into the dangerous underworld of Prohibition: rum smugglers, bootleggers, and the glamorous lost realm of vaudeville, ruled by troupers like Mae West, W. C. Fields, Eddie Cantor, and Jack Benny, a realm so real that we can almost smell the greasepaint. *The Impersonator* is an exciting debut that climaxes at the very tip of the rockbound coast of the Pacific Northwest, in a literal cliffhanger!"

—Katherine Neville, *New York Times* bestselling author of *The Eight*

"Add [Miley's] mastery of history to her fully realized characters—Leah/Jessie is especially appealing—and her shock-filled plot, and readers are treated to a lively debut and a welcome new voice in crime fiction." —*Richmond Times-Dispatch*

"The story is engrossing, the characters satisfyingly larger than life, and one can only hope for an encore from the smart, feisty, and talented heroine." —*Publishers Weekly* (starred review)

"Miley's clever historical debut successfully portrays an intricate puzzle featuring multiple cons. Her protagonist dazzles."

—*Library Journal*

"[A] spirited debut . . . Compelling characters, an engaging story line, and a heroine with lots of moxie make this a thoroughly enjoyable read."   —*Booklist*

"Historian Miley, winner of the Minotaur Books/Mystery Writers of America First Crime Novel Award, presents a colorfully detailed mystery . . . and a heroine whom readers will want to see succeed."   —*Kirkus Reviews*

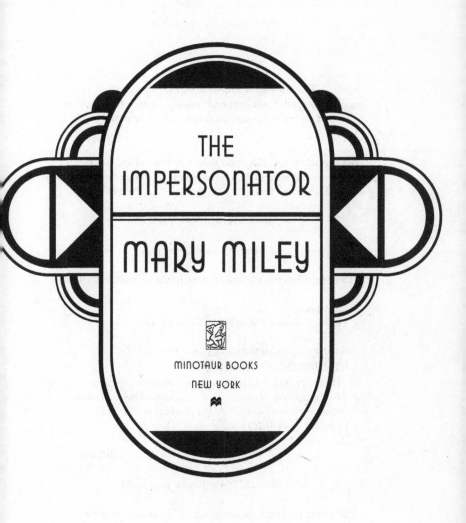

THE IMPERSONATOR

MARY MILEY

MINOTAUR BOOKS

NEW YORK

THE IMPERSONATOR. Copyright © 2013 by Mary Miley Theobald.
All rights reserved. Printed in the United States of America. For information,
address St. Martin's Press, 175 Fifth Avenue, New York, N.Y. 10010.

www.minotaurbooks.com

Designed by Anna Gorovoy

The Library of Congress has cataloged the hardcover edition as follows:

Miley, Mary.
    The impersonator / Mary Miley.—First Edition.
        p.   cm.
    ISBN 978-1-250-02816-7 (hardcover)
    ISBN 978-1-250-02817-4 (e-book)
    1. Heirs—Fiction.   2. Inheritance and succession—Fiction.
    3. Missing persons—Fiction.   4. Substitution of heirs—Fiction.
    5. Impersonation—Fiction.   6. Fraud—Fiction.   I. Title.
    PS3613.I532244I47 2013
    813'.6—dc23

                                                            2013013931

ISBN 978-1-250-05430-2 (trade paperback)

Minotaur books may be purchased for educational, business,
or promotional use. For information on bulk purchases, please contact
Macmillan Corporate and Premium Sales Department at 1-800-221-7945,
extension 5442, or write specialmarkets@macmillan.com.

D   10   9   8   7   6   5   4   3

THE
IMPERSONATOR

felt his eyes before I saw his face. A quick sweep of the audience
and I spotted him, the man from last night. On the aisle again,
row C, seat 1. A good choice—his bulk would have overflowed
the armrests of an interior seat and caused his neighbors to curl
their lips and lean away.

I am sensitive to being watched. Whenever someone's eyes
rest overlong on me, a prickly awareness flushes across my neck
and shoulders. It comes from a lifetime spent onstage, honing the
subtler tricks of the trade—the toss of the hair, the jut of the hips,
the flutter of the fingers—whatever pulls the audience's attention. I can throw attention too: a gasp and wide eyes will send them
searching for the cause of my surprise; my languid examination
of another actor will turn every head in the audience to him. I
know what I'm doing, and I know when I am doing it. At that
moment, I was doing nothing. I had finished my line and moved

stage right where I stood like a marble statue so as not to distract from Darcy's solo verse. I was doing nothing to draw the fat man's stare, yet he was staring.

Had he been young and attractive, I would have been pleased, but this man made me uneasy. He wasn't watching the act; he was watching me. Two nights in a row. I'd put it down to my great beauty, but I live my life close to the mirror, and I know better.

I missed my cue—something I'd hear about later. Hands on hips, I tap-danced back into the lights, caught up with Angie approaching from stage left, and the seven Little Darlings began to sing the final refrain.

> You've got to see Mama ev'ry night,
> Or you can't see Mama at all!

All eyes were on me now, and I blocked out any thought of the fat man in the third row.

2

Three bows. It should have been two, but "Mama" stole the last one, pulling us back onstage as the applause drizzled away, leaving us to slink off in silence. I was mortified, but no one blamed me, I was just a kid. So to speak. We got out of the way for the Kanazawa Japs.

Our dressing room was as small as a closet. Angie kept bumping my elbow as I wiped off the greasepaint. I snapped at her, then apologized. She was a good kid, wiser than her seventeen years, and a good friend since she'd joined the Little Darlings a couple years back. The closet wasn't her fault. Fact of the matter, it was better than most I'd seen growing up, with electric lights and heat and toilets in the basement. The Creighton, like all Orpheum Circuit theaters, was Big Time and pretty decent, all in all. But even a headliner's dressing room at the Creighton would have been seriously crowded with nine of us struggling to change to street clothes.

At last I escaped, my coat over my shoulders and Angie at my heels.

"Lordy mercy, I could use a drink!" she exclaimed—uselessly, since we both knew my bottle of hooch was empty and neither of us knew Omaha well enough to find a speakeasy that would admit two girls who looked fifteen. "Three shows! Whew!"

"Many's the time I've played four or even five shows a day," I said. "And in theaters without dressing rooms at all. We're lucky to have made Big Time."

"I know," she said, but she didn't really.

We threaded our way down the narrow passageway choked with crates, props, barrels, and paint cans. Angie caught her foot in a coil of rope and dislodged a rat. She smothered a scream as it scurried ahead of us and disappeared into the shadows.

"Yikes! Where's the Cat Circus when you need 'em?" I said, immediately regretting the little quip when I saw the quiver in Angie's lip. She was sweet on the young man who managed that act, and we hadn't shared a billing with him in many weeks.

"Button up," Angie said, as she squared her shoulders and threw open the heavy stage door. March in the Midwest has its pleasant days. This wasn't one of them.

"I'm going back to Mabel's," I told her by way of an invitation. "I snitched some rolls and chicken legs when no one was looking. Enough for two."

The alley was muddy and littered with broken glass. Old play-bills clogged the gutter. Ahead of us, a voice called out to someone, "Jessie!"

Angie and I tied scarves over our heads and made our way toward the main street, guided by the light of the single gas lamp that glowed in front of the theater. It was a nine-block walk to Mabel's boardinghouse where the Little Darlings were lodged this week. Tomorrow was our last night. On Sunday we'd jump to Tulsa, a day's train ride if we were lucky and there were no cows on the tracks.

"Jessie!"

I paid no attention. It wasn't my name.

Then I saw him in the lamplight. The fat man from the aisle seat. Waiting for Angie and me to come down the alley. Except I knew he wasn't waiting for Angie.

Nothing to worry about; I'd blown off men before.

He stood with his hands in the pockets of a cashmere top-coat, a Vandyke beard on his chin, and a fine fedora on his head. "Jessie! Jessamyn Carr!" he said as we came closer.

I gave an exaggerated look over my shoulder, shrugged, and attempted to walk past him.

"Wait! A moment, please. Just a moment. I recognized you from the audience, Jessie. You remember me, don't you? Uncle Oliver? Of course you do."

He didn't grab my arm or try to touch me in any way, and his round face was creased with what looked like genuine anxiety. Maybe, just maybe, he was legit—and I didn't want to be unkind. I decided to play it straight. "I'm sorry, sir. You've mistaken me for someone else. Excuse us, please."

"No, I can't be wrong. You're Jessie Carr. Even after all these years, I'd recognize you anywhere—the auburn hair, the eyes, the freckles." His sincerity was unmistakable, and I felt a stab of sympathy for him.

"Look, Mr. Oliver, I am sorry. But honestly, I'm not your niece. I've gone by a lot of names in my life, but Jessie was never one of them. I guess I look like her, but you know what they say: there's a double for every one of us somewhere in the world." His expression was almost comical with disbelief, and he seemed to grow smaller, like a round balloon with some of the air let out. I felt sorry for him. "Is your niece in vaudeville?"

"Oh, no . . . at least, not that I know of," he replied, peering hard at my face to watch for my reaction as he continued with his tale. "My late sister's child, Jessamyn Carr, disappeared seven years ago, in the summer of 1917. Ran away, no doubt. No one has seen her since. You look so much like her . . . those freckles . . . She would be twenty now, almost twenty-one. At first glance I thought you were too young, but after careful study, I realized you were older than the girl you play on stage. Are you sure there's no chance that you could be—"

"Well, I'm older than twenty," I said. His eyes widened in surprise. So did Angie's. I generally keep mum about my real age. Most people in the business figure I'm around seventeen, and they're amused at how much younger I appear, on stage and off. It's been the key to my success, really. "I've been in vaudeville since I was a baby, so I can't be your niece."

He gave a great sigh and rubbed his hand over his face. "I beg your pardon, young lady. I—I really thought . . . you are so like her, exactly as she would look grown-up. It's—well, it's uncanny. Excuse me."

He bowed from the waist like I was royalty, lifted his hat, and walked off in the opposite direction from Mabel's.

Angie arched her eyebrows in a silent question that I answered with a shrug of my shoulders.

"He seemed so sure . . ." She trailed off. I knew what she was thinking. Although we'd been in the same act for a couple years, she knew almost nothing about my life before the Little Darlings.

"I feel kind of sorry for him," I said as I watched him disappear into the night.

"He reminds me of Fatty Arbuckle," Angie said softly.

"I'm not his niece."

Angie giggled. "Maybe you should have said you were. Maybe he's fabulously rich and was going to leave you all his money!" And we laughed our way back to Mabel's.

3

Saturday's three shows went well enough. The Little Darlings hoofed it through their fourteen-minute musical routine with the flawless timing that comes from months of repetition. The audience applauded generously, and "Mama"—chastened earlier by the emcee—stole no bows. We'd been billed third this week and so finished by ten, a distinct advantage in my book since it left more time for celebration at the end of a long week. Angie and I waited impatiently for Sylvia, the assistant in the magician act billed after the Kanazawa Japs. Sylvia had played Omaha last year and knew of a blind pig that would serve us . . . if it hadn't been shut down by now. I hoped it had food too. I was hungry enough to eat a whole pig myself.

We wore our best. Angie and I had brushed the schoolgirl braids into pinned-up styles befitting sophisticated young ladies, and the new hat I'd bought at Younkers in Des Moines two weeks ago made me look at least eighteen. As soon as Sylvia joined us, we headed for the stage door.

The fat man was waiting for us by the gas lamp, dressed in a tuxedo.

"Excuse me, Miss—ah, Darling?"

I was in an end-of-the-week mood. "Uncle Oliver!" I exclaimed buoyantly. "I didn't see you in the audience tonight."

"I wasn't in the audience tonight." He doffed his homburg to acknowledge Angie and Sylvia, then turned back to me. His eyes took in my hair and outfit with a gleam that approved the transformation. "I came by the theater in the hope that I could persuade you to dine with me tonight. I would like to talk with you about a job, something I think will be well worth your while."

I'll just bet. Angie and Sylvia exchanged knowing glances. We'd each had our share of mashers on the make. The missing niece had been a ruse after all. I should have known.

"Thank you kindly, sir, but as you can see, my friends and I have plans for this evening."

"So that my intentions are not misconstrued, I was of course including your friends in my invitation. I have reserved a table at the Blackstone Hotel, reputedly the finest restaurant in the Midwest, where I will be honored to treat you and your friends to anything on the menu."

His gentle caress of the word "anything" would have made an actor proud. And who hadn't heard of the Blackstone? Only headliners could afford to stay there, and they raved about its luxury.

I had no idea if he knew how hungry I was at that moment or how poorly we'd eaten lately, but the memory of the fried meat, cornmeal mush, and peach preserves we'd been served for the past week at Mabel's made me drool for something better. Potluck at the blind pig was likely to be greasy sausages or nothing at all. A nod from Angie and Sylvia clinched the deal. Why not? The price for him would be high. The price for me was small: a curt refusal when he got around to making his "job offer."

"Thank you, sir; we'd be delighted to accept."

He beamed. Without turning his head, he lifted one arm and snapped his fingers. Before I had time to wonder, an enormous Pierce-Arrow hummed out of the darkness and a chauffeur leaped out to open our door.

The Blackstone Hotel lobby was a work of art with enough gold leaf to make Willie Sutton trade in his gun for a chisel. We gawked like rubes at the painted ceilings, fancy mirrors, and plush velvet furniture as we were ushered through to the Orleans Dining Room. A maid took our coats. A fawning maître d' bowed and motioned to a waiter, then led us to a table in the middle of the room.

It was a small table set for two. I waited for the maître d' to realize the obvious, but he maintained his expectant face as he held a chair for me. One look to my right and I caught on. The waiter was seating Angie and Sylvia at another table some feet away. The girls, as frozen with uncertainty as I, looked inquiringly in my direction. My call.

Seeing my mouth open to protest, my host said, "Surely you can have no objection to this arrangement. Your friends are nearby"—he smiled at them and waved his fingers—"and the waiter has been instructed to bring them whatever they desire. Our business is best discussed privately."

Neat. Very neat. And plotted well in advance, which meant he anticipated having to include my friends. I could pitch a fit, demand a larger table, and draw the attention of the entire dining room. Or I could shut up and sit down. I'd come this far. The girls were right there. It was a public restaurant. What was I afraid of? I closed my mouth and sat. Angie and Sylvia followed my lead.

Round one to Uncle Oliver. But I'd be damned if I'd help him out with charming conversation. He could jolly well talk to himself as far as I was concerned. Silently vowing to order the most expensive dish on the menu, I buried my nose in the hand-lettered menu and promptly forgot my resolution.

"Gracious! Lobster? Here? How do they manage that? And pheasant under glass! I always supposed that was made up." My stomach rumbled its appreciation. No wonder Uncle Oliver was fat.

"Would you like a cocktail? Or wine with dinner? Or perhaps both?"

Right out in the open? That was pretty bold of the Blackstone. "My word. Have they bought off the police, then?"

"No doubt. But they also take care to serve liquor in teacups so no one can tell what anyone is drinking. Should an emergency arise, one merely finishes one's tea. Quickly."

I was all admiration. "Could I have champagne?"

"You may have whatever you like, my dear." And he proceeded to place his order with a handsome young waiter for a martini for himself and French champagne for me. When it came in a porcelain teacup accompanied by a plate of pretty hors d'oeuvres, I couldn't help but giggle.

He was, I guessed, in his fifties, but his efforts to appear younger only made him seem older. A dapper gentleman of the Edwardian style, complete with malacca walking stick, mother-of-pearl cuff links, and white spats, he would have been attractive in the days before gluttony fattened his figure and age thinned his hair. To afford the dinner we ordered, he must be rich indeed. I decided that when the proposition was made, I would turn him down gently.

The courses came one after the other with baffling complexity as our conversation wandered from Omaha to Europe, where I had never been but longed to go. He had an urbane and natural wit and a boundless curiosity about my life, no doubt prompted by his need to douse that last flicker of uncertainty about my identity. I found myself talking more freely than I had intended.

"No, honestly, Darling is their real name," I said. "Jock and Francine. And Lizzie is their real daughter, and the boys, Darcy and Danny, are theirs too. I've been with them for several years and they're like family. Francine's the boss. And bossy. But we all get along."

"And now the act is seven children, like the Seven Little Foys."

"That was the idea. Anyway, the Foys broke up a year ago and we're still going strong."

"How long have you been on stage?"

"Twenty-five years, if you count the roles my mother played while she carried me."

His eyebrows shot up and he studied my face closely, looking for wrinkles, I guess. "Is your mother still living?"

I shook my head. "She died after a long illness when I was twelve. She was a talented singer—a headliner. I have her old playbills to prove it."

Talking about my mother brought back the hollow pain I always felt whenever I thought of her death. I was glad when he changed the subject. "What about your father?"

"He left before I was born." I thought he might ask if I was a bastard, which I most definitely am and would have said so to his face, but he did not. I guess it was self-evident. Everyone knew vaudeville people were immoral.

"So you literally grew up on the stage."

"My first role was Moses in the Bulrushes, and I'm told I made a good Baby Jesus later that year. By the time I was three I could memorize lines, so I began acting in scenes for kiddie versions of *Romeo and Juliet*, *Oliver Twist*, *Peter Pan*, and other vaudeville staples."

"I expect you have a good memory."

"A necessity in my business." I glanced over to Angie and Sylvia who were diving into a plate of prawns. Angie caught my eye and sent me a questioning look. I nodded back and smiled that all was well.

"Moving around like that, you could not have attended school. Did you have a governess?"

A governess! What fairy tale did this man live in? I thought of Marie Antoinette, who wondered why the breadless Parisians did not simply eat cake, and stifled a laugh. "Vaudeville kids don't have a schoolroom education but that doesn't mean they are uneducated. I learned to read from my mother, and I still read every book I can get my hands on."

"If Darling isn't your real name, what is?"

"My name's whatever role I'm playing. These days I'm billed as Carrie Darling, the second Little Darling. Angie over there is two inches taller so she's the eldest kid. Height trumps age in this business."

"But the name your mother gave you?"

"Leah. Why, I'll never know—she never used it. Usually she called me Baby."

"And your last name?"

"That depends. Mother's real last name was Pearson, but she dropped it when she left Ohio. Her family never spoke to her again after she went on the stage. She changed her name to Chloë Randall and stuck with that most of the time. But I seldom used Randall, or Leah, for that matter. During my Shakespeare period I was called Juliet, then Becky Jordan when I was one of the Jordan Sisters. During my Kid Kabaret years, I was billed as Sallie Angel—I *hated* that one!—and for a season I was Jo Baker with my twin brother Joey, and then Sophie Dale with the Dancing Dollies. I've done a little of everything, a bit of acrobatics, a dog act—I was even a magician's assistant for a while. The original jack-of-all-trades. Speaking of names, remind me of yours?"

He looked surprised. "I haven't properly introduced myself, have I? The name's Oliver Beckett, at your service."

"Pleased to meet you, Mr. Beckett." I slurped another oyster.

"What happened after your mother died?"

The pain that is wrapped around that question cannot be conveyed to a person who has not lost his only parent at a young age. I continued eating, as if the response didn't claw out my gut. "I didn't feel abandoned," I said with practiced bravado. "You have to understand, vaudeville is like one big family. In fact, there are a lot of families that tour together, like the Darlings. Mother fixed me up with a good kiddie act before she passed away. When that one crashed, I got other roles. I didn't grow much after twelve, so it was no trick to keep braiding my hair, accent the freckles, and avoid getting fat." Whoops. Too much champagne.

He ignored the gaffe. "You're vaudeville's version of Mary Pickford. She's well into her thirties and still playing adolescents in her films."

I nodded. Mary Pickford was my idol. She was playing eleven-year-old girls in *A Poor Little Rich Girl* and *Rebecca of Sunnybrook Farm* when she was my age, and she was nearly thirty when she played a young boy in *Little Lord Fauntleroy*. I'd sit through several showings of her films at one go, crouching under the seats each time the theater emptied so I didn't have to pay again, just to learn the tricks she used to help herself look childlike. What I learned from Mary Pickford about makeup, clothing, and youthful gestures I put to good use.

He asked more questions, and I made vaudeville sound like a pretty nice life. In many ways, it was. I was too proud to tell this rich man about the hungry times, the weeks of no work, the days I hung around the theater after the last show hoping someone would take me with them to get something to eat, the men who wanted a return on the money they'd spent, and the times I'd come out of the grocer's with more in my pockets than I'd paid for. I hadn't always played Big Time two-a-days. We were barely there now. Most of my life had been Small Time hardship, four or five shows a day, tawdry boardinghouses, promised salaries unpaid, and nights spent on a cold train to save the dollar the hotel room would have cost.

"If I may be so crass as to mention financial matters . . . what sort of money do you earn?"

"Enough to get by. The Darlings get $250 a week. They pay

hotels and food, and give me $20. The younger kids, Angie and the two boys, get $10 each." Here it comes, I thought.

"And how long is your contract?"

"A typical thirty-week run. Ends in May. It'll be renewed, though." We hoped.

"I have an unusual role I'd like you to consider." I braced myself and looked him straight in the eye. "I'd like you to play the role of Jessie Carr for a few years. For the rest of your life, if you like the part."

That was certainly not what I expected, but I was too well schooled to let my features betray surprise. At that moment, the young Adonis materialized at my shoulder to ask if I'd care for more tea. Dumbly, I nodded, and he left with my cup and saucer. I detected a flash of raw hunger in Oliver's eyes as they followed the waiter until he disappeared around the bar, and all at once I understood I had never been in any danger of an indecent proposition. Oliver turned back to the matter at hand as if there had been no interruption. "Before you say anything, let me tell you the whole story." Sure of his audience, he settled back in his chair and milked the pause before he began.

"Like you, my niece Jessie was orphaned as a child. Both her parents drowned in a sailing accident when she was eleven. She was sent to live in Oregon with her aunt and uncle and their four children. Have you ever heard the name Carr?"

Not in the way he meant it.

"Jessie's father, Lawrence Carr, was a very wealthy man. He inherited a family business that centered on logging and mining operations in a dozen states, and while he was not the sharpest knife in the drawer, at least he didn't run the business into the ground before he died. Jessie was his only child and sole heir. The business has been managed by a trust ever since—managed a good deal better than foolish Lawrence Carr would have done—and the fortune has grown considerably. I know little of the details but it seems to be worth somewhere in the range of ten million dollars. Jessie inherits everything the day she turns twenty-one. That day is September 30, 1924."

Six months from now.

It occurred to me that Uncle Oliver was not a nice man.

"Look, Oliver," I cut in. "If you think someone who looks vaguely like Jessie is going to convince her hotshot lawyers and all her relatives that she's the real McCoy, you're screwy."

"Jessie has no family left who knew her before she was orphaned. The lawyers and trustees met her once, when she was eleven and they were settling the estate after her parents were killed. Her aunt and uncle's family knew her only for the three years she lived with them. Jessie disappeared seven years ago. Memories dim with time."

"You really think someone like me, with no fancy manners, could fool rich people that I was one of them? Maybe for ten minutes!"

"Having just observed you eating your salad with the fish fork, I am well aware that certain training would be required in the realm of proper etiquette."

"And when the real Jessie Carr shows up on her birthday?"

"Jessie's dead."

He said it with such finality, I blinked with confusion. "I thought you said—"

"Oh, I don't know it for a fact—probably no one does. But it's been seven years this August. If she was kidnapped—something we all considered likely at the time—the kidnappers never asked for ransom. Or perhaps they killed her accidentally and had nothing with which to bargain."

"But you said she ran away."

"Sheer speculation. It's possible. If she ran away, she caught the Spanish flu and was buried in some potter's field. If she joined the circus, an elephant stepped on her. If she was playing a cruel trick on her aunt—something she was quite capable of doing, that child was bereft of decent feelings—she missed the pleasure of

shocking her aunt into a heart attack with an unexpected return." He turned up his hands in the universal gesture of helpless-
ness. "How do I know what happened to her? Except for the few
hours I thought you were Jessie, I've been convinced for years that
she was dead."

He glared at his water goblet while I swallowed my disgust. His
blunt words and cold manner made it clear that he had no genuine
affection for his poor niece. No, the girl had inconvenienced him
by going missing, and he resented the disruption. I could hardly
hide my contempt.

He reached into his breast pocket and took out a wallet. "Here,"
he said, handing me a small photograph. "Judge for yourself."

A familiar face stared back at me with an intensely serious
expression, and I felt a queer jolt of electricity tingling through my
limbs. I guessed she had been about twelve when it was taken.
She had my hair and my features, and I had to admit, the resemblance was striking—but it was the resemblance of sisters, not of
twins. Something about her touched me deeply though, something beyond superficial appearances . . . perhaps it was the connection of having been orphaned at almost the same age.

"I see now why you mistook me for her," I said, returning the
photograph.

"As will others. Now"—Oliver preened, unconscious of his
own outrageous conceit—"the key to the success of this plan is
myself. No one else could carry it off, even with an impersonator
as perfect as you. You see, I spent a good deal of time during those
three years with my niece's family. I visited their remote house in
Oregon quite often. My point is, I know the house, I know the
family, I know the servants, the pets, and all the little details of
everyday life that will convince everyone you are Jessie. I know
what Jessie knows and I know what she doesn't know. I can teach
you. It is simply another role for you to play."

"And you would help me pull off a trick like that so I could
claim the Carr fortune? How very generous of you!"

He twisted his lips into a serpent's smile that would give Satan the shivers. "Just so, my dear. You're so very clever, you realized some time ago where my interests lie. I have always had expensive tastes, and sadly, I find myself unable to continue in the manner to which I have become accustomed without regular infusions of cash. I am not, however, a greedy man. I also realize that transferring large amounts of money to my name would be impossible without alerting the trustees, lawyers, and bankers who are all vigilant minders of the Carr fortune."

Now I was curious. "So how would you get the money?"

"Leave the details to me. I am the soul of discretion and, never fear, there is plenty to go around. We won't be taking the money away from anyone—not really—we'll just be sharing it among a broader group of people."

I didn't need to think this one over. Not for a moment. What Oliver was proposing was anything but a simple acting job. It was a crime—a serious crime, and fraught with peril. Punishable by a who-knows-what-length prison sentence. With millions of dollars at stake, no lawyers or relatives were going to smile sweetly, congratulate me, and hand over the dough without exhaustive background checks and a thousand sneaky little tricks designed to trip me up. One slipup with the pony's name and I'd be breaking rocks in Sing Sing. Not to mention the hold dear Uncle Oliver would have over me should I ever object to his pulling my strings. Thanks, but no thanks.

Oliver continued, "Jessie Carr, vaudeville star, has come home for her twenty-first birthday. It will be the easiest role you've ever played. You need invent no tales about where you have been for the past seven years. You merely tell the truth. The private investigators who will be hired to verify your story will find everything you say is true." He wet his lips as two large servings of baked Alaska were placed before us. "You must see that it's perfect."

Perfectly absurd. As soon as the waiter had stepped away, I burst his bubble.

"Thank you, Oliver, for your kind offer to make yourself rich. Sadly, I am booked for the foreseeable future with the Little Darlings, whose ironclad contract prohibits me from taking on other roles."

I expected him to erupt in a great rage or at least continue to argue his point, but nothing, it seems, could divert this hedonist from the task before him. Into the mound of ice cream and meringue he plunged, inhaling it with such gusto I wondered whether he had even heard me. I looked in the direction of Angie and Sylvia's table, but they were too engrossed in flaming cherries jubilee to notice that I was itching to leave.

When the plate was clean, Oliver sat back again, wiped his mouth on his napkin, and gave me a smirk I did not like at all. "Quite all right, my dear. I understand completely. Think on my proposal. If you should change your mind, you'll know where to find me."

I hadn't a clue where to find the wretch. And that was fine with me.

Angie and Sylvia had finished their desserts. We stood up, and they followed us out of the dining room, back to the gilded lobby. Oliver took my coat from the maid and guided my arms into the sleeves as the woman helped the girls with theirs. He bade us good-bye at the hotel entrance, summoning the Pierce-Arrow to take us wherever we wanted to go next.

4

I t was two days past my twenty-fifth birthday before I realized the date had slipped by me unobserved. Just as well. I needed no reminders of my advancing age. The example of Mary Pickford buoyed me up. Like her, I would play kiddie roles until my hair turned gray or lumbago made me hobble with a cane.

The Little Darlings killed 'em in Lincoln and Topeka, and we were jumping to Tulsa when the letter reached Francine. Our agent had earned his five percent and renewed our contract with Orpheum—hip, hip, hooray! Another thirty weeks and a slight rise in pay. I had never been happier.

The Darlings had become the family I had never had, the family I had always longed for. We celebrated that night with a meal at a decent hotel, then Jock went back to the boarding-house and drank himself to bed. We were big time for another season. Audiences were not sitting on their hands. The act was good and getting better. The real reason was Darcy.

At five, Darcy was a born entertainer with a sterling silver future. Although his brother Danny was a year older, Darcy was the more sophisticated in every way. Danny sang like a child; Darcy crooned like a seasoned pro. Danny could hoof it a little; Darcy's stair routine would make Bojangles Robinson sit up and gape. Danny could repeat a joke and get a chuckle; Darcy's instinct for timing and facial expressions made audiences fall out of their seats laughing. I was already imagining their future as a musical comedy act as they grew older, with Danny playing straight man to Darcy's lead. The Darling Boys, or maybe the Darling Duo.

We had a great week in Tulsa. Angie struck gold—the Cat Circus finally shared our billing again, and her young man was still making goo-goo eyes in her direction. It should not have surprised me at all, but it did, when Angie came to our room in the boardinghouse on Friday evening while I was getting ready to head over to the theater.

"I got some news," she said, twisting her hands. Her face turned fiery red and she stammered a little. "I—I was just upstairs telling Francine and Jock. After them, you're first to know. I'm leaving the Little Darlings. I'm joining Walter's Cat Circus."

"Why, Angie!" I had no idea the romance had progressed so far so fast. "Why, that's . . . that's . . . oh, my goodness, that's wonderful news . . . are you—well, are you sure?"

She nodded fiercely. "I'm not leaving the act high and dry, don't worry. I'll stay on through Oklahoma City to give the Darlings time to train a replacement. Walter and the cats are billed there with us next week, then he goes to Canada and the Little Darlings are for Kansas and, well, I just couldn't bear it, being separated from Walter again."

True love. I'd caught it myself a couple times and knew its pleasures and its pains firsthand. I had my doubts about Walter's staying power, but heck, I wasn't about to rain on her parade. I collected my wits and said all the right things. I'd miss Angie.

Change is the only thing you can count on in vaudeville, my mother used to say. So I was prepared when on Saturday night after the last show, Francine and Jock sent Darcy to fetch me to their room.

"We need to talk about the act," Jock began. He was standing at the fireplace, his hair still wet from his bath. One hand fiddled with the change in his pocket, the other drummed on the mantel. Francine's hands were folded serenely in her lap and, as she occupied the only chair in the room, I perched on the edge of the bed.

I agreed with him. The addition of a new person to an act was a good time to make changes. I had some ideas to contribute.

"We've been thinking about this for some time. Angie's leaving makes it come about a little quicker than we had planned but it's where we were going anyway. We've decided not to replace Angie."

Bad move, I thought. Everyone knows dancing acts need an odd number to look right on stage. Three, five, fifteen, whatever. Odd numbers allow for greater versatility in the choreography. I was about to say so when Francine spoke up.

"We've been working up some different routines, ones that play up to Darcy," she said.

"I couldn't agree more. That boy's got the makings of a real star."

Francine beamed. What mother doesn't enjoy hearing her child praised? "Robert's family wants him to come home," she continued. At eleven, Robert played the third oldest Darling, the stair step down from me. He had been with us a year and a half. A nice boy, but he could be replaced without much difficulty. "His father is doing poorly," continued Francine, "and his mother needs him on the farm more than she needs the money we pay him. He's going home next Saturday." She cleared her throat delicately. "And we've found a place for Stanley with an acrobatic act. He's always been so limber. He'll do well there."

Oh, my God, she was breaking up the act! A sick, hollow feeling I hadn't known in years settled in my stomach like a cold rock. She couldn't be dumping me too? Surely they would keep me?

"And me?" My voice cracked on the question. I cleared my throat to cover up my rising panic.

"We've been keeping an eye out for something for you too," said Jock without meeting my eyes. "We care about all four of you, and you've been with us a long while. You're like real family."

Not quite. Real family wasn't being cast off. "So the Little Darlings are going to go on, but with only three kids?" I asked, hardly able to breathe.

Jock found something interesting about his fingernails.

"I see." And I did. With Darcy taking on a bigger role, they could do as well or better with three kids as with seven. And the $50 a week they wouldn't be giving me, Angie, and the boys would translate into a big raise for them. It was obvious. So obvious it made me want to throw up. How had I not seen this coming?

The betrayal cut into me like a dull knife. In my whole life, I had been with no act longer than the Little Darlings. I had practically raised Darcy and Danny, and I loved little Lizzie and her antics. Francine and Jock were only five or ten years older than me, and I thought of them as a brother and sister. In a flash, I saw how stupid I had been to let myself care and how gullible to think I was ever anything more than hired help.

Orphaned again. Why did each time feel like the first?

I got up off the bed, swallowing hard, determined to die before I let them see me cry. I didn't want to hear what they had in mind for me. I didn't need Jock and Francine. I could find my own jobs. Lord knows, I'd done it before. I'd been in this business a lot longer than they had, and I had friends. A lot of friends. And some money saved. There were loads of opportunities for someone with my talents. Right now, I just wanted to escape to my own room where I could be alone before my eyes spilled over.

"I know this has been a shock . . ." Jock began.

"Not at all," I lied, swallowing hard. "I'll find something else."

"It's just business. Nothing personal. No hard feelings, hon?"

"None at all." I lifted my chin and left their room.

5

You can find the location of any act in big-time vaudeville simply by looking in the pages of *Variety* or *Billboard*, weeklies that list who, where, and when for the Orpheum and Keith-Albee circuits. The lesser circuits—the Pantages, Western, Interstate, and such—print similar broadsides, not as accurate but serviceable. So it was simple for me to write the larger kiddie acts and request an audition. From Oklahoma City, I sent word to the Darlings' New York agent—agents are often the first to learn of vacancies—and had a polite reply. This was a particularly bad time for singles to try to break in, he advised. Stick to groups or a double. He'd keep me in mind. It was a good start.

I didn't limit myself to juvenile. A versatile performer like me can fit into almost any routine. I could sing, dance most styles—ballet, tap, clogging, folk, or ballroom—play a little flute and clarinet, and act in comedies, tragedies, or musicals. I set out to find something good, something long-term. Someone with my talents could afford to be choosy.

Right away I was called to Denver to audition for a part with a troupe that specialized in Gilbert and Sullivan operettas. I adored Gilbert and Sullivan and knew most of their songs by heart. I'd performed "Three Little Maids from School Are We" when I was ten, dressed in a beautiful green silk kimono Mother had made for me. I did that number for them, minus the kimono. They needed two players, and I was certain I would be offered one of the spots, but I lost out.

In late May in St. Louis I tried for several roles, one with a kiddie song-and-dance troupe, one with the Russian Dolls, an ensemble that specialized in Russian folk dancing, another that put on famous scenes from Shakespeare, and a Wild West show that needed a cowgirl who could sing and do ropes. My rope twirling was weak, but I assured them I was a quick study. I think I'd have gotten that role if I'd been able to shoot a bow and arrow. I finally accepted an offer to assist the Great Adolfo, who seemed impressed with my previous experience in magic. Three days later I walked off—without pay—after it became clear that I was expected to perform in bed as well as on stage.

By then I was in Memphis where I picked up two weeks of work substituting for a girl who had gone home for her mother's funeral and another week helping behind the scenes with a chicken act, getting my arms pecked bloody while rounding up those nasty creatures when they would try to escape into the wings. I auditioned for a Hawaiian song-and-dance act and was rejected.

I had my mail forwarded from Oklahoma City to Memphis, where I rewrote fifty letters to see whether anything new had opened up in the past few weeks. Friends sent their best wishes and said they would let me know as soon as they heard of a good lead, but most didn't respond at all. You can't bank warm wishes, and my money was running low, but I told myself there was plenty of time.

Even out of a job a while, I wouldn't starve. Working with magicians had taught me enough sleight of hand to feed myself for free at any grocer's. In my younger years, after Mother had died and no one was paying me much attention, I'd been a passable thief, stealing from department stores so vast that what I took was never noticed. Except once, when carelessness earned me two nights in a slop-bucket cell with roaches coming out of the cracks faster than I could squash them. I'd learned my lesson. I never stole anything ever again unless I was one hundred percent certain that I wouldn't get caught.

In Minneapolis in June I teamed up with a man who had lost his female partner to another act. It was a routine full of silly patter where he delivered the straight lines and I provided the zany misunderstandings. We opened at the Hennepin in the dreaded number two position, which I blame for our meager applause. After our first matinee, the manager came backstage and handed us our publicity photos, brusquely uttering the most feared word in vaudeville: "Canceled." We changed our name twice and tried again at a couple small-time theaters, but no dice.

I told myself my luck would change in Toledo. But Bert Earl and Girls auditioned only tall dancers and my range wasn't high enough for Hanson's Double Quartette. I filled in for an usher at one theater and sold tickets at another to pay my room. A roper hired me to give some sex appeal to his cowboy routine, but he figured on going into burlesque and I figured I'd be wearing nothing but a holster, so we parted ways. I worked one-night stands on the "death trail"—five shows a day—with a Polish ethnic act until they finally gave up and went home to Cleveland. I went with them to audition for a job as a song plugger selling sheet music, but they didn't think I looked the part.

Late July found me sick from bad chili, sweltering in a fifty-cent Akron hotel with seven clams to my name. The bed was set in four pans of oxalic acid, which kept the ants from getting into the sheets but did nothing to discourage the fleas that were already safely tucked in. The god-awful flocked wallpaper on the ceiling was losing its battle with gravity, curling at the seams. With every step in the room above, a delicate shower of dried flour paste snowed down on my sheets.

I was not finished with vaudeville, but vaudeville was finished with me. Even small-time spots I'd gone for had bombed. At every kiddie audition, I had lost to a kid. Why hire a woman to play a girl when they could hire the real thing and pay her less? I was not Mary Pickford after all. The same talents that had seemed so precocious in a ten-year-old turned out to be stunningly average in an adult. It dawned on me that, but for the kindness of the Darlings, I'd have washed up years ago.

Jack-of-all-trades, I had called myself. There was another side to that coin: master of none.

My self-confidence shattered, I examined the options. If not vaudeville, what? How could I make a living? I knew nothing beyond the stage. I had no idea how the civilian world worked. No one would hire me as an office clerk or a telephone operator or a shopgirl with the taint of vaudeville on my skin. Performers are toasted and admired as long as they are onstage. Offstage, we are not respectable, like gypsies or immigrants.

I had no money, no prospects, and no family to turn to for help. The only world I knew had turned its back on me. I felt so sick and alone I wanted to die.

Come on, Baby, don't give up. I heard my mother's voice in my head as I often did, as clear as if she were standing beside my pillow. *We've been here before. Remember Cincinnati and that awful stage manager? Remember that winter in Albany? You've been through worse than this. Think about what you've got going for you. There's always another job just around the corner.*

In point of fact, there was a job for the asking directly across the street. An inner voice forced me to the window where I looked through the grimy glass at the brothel that faced my hotel. A man walked out and paused to light a cigarette. Curtains moved in an upstairs window. Another man went in. There had been a brothel a few blocks down from my hotel in Toledo. There had been a brothel on the corner near my rooming house in Cleveland. And now, here was a brothel across the street. Suddenly, I saw what was happening, and my heart raced. They were getting closer. How much longer before they reached me?

Panic squeezed my chest. "No!" I said aloud.

An attack of chills drove me to dig my winter coat out of my trunk. Shivering in the summer heat, I slipped my arms into the sleeves and my hands into the pockets. In the right pocket, my fingers closed around a business card. Oliver Beckett must have placed it there without my knowledge back in March.

An omen? I'd once helped fleece gullible people at séances. Was that so different from helping to con a wealthy family out of their money by playing the role of an heiress? Another town, another name, another role. It was just a job, and for once, a well-paying one. No one gets hurt; no one is left destitute. I glanced down at Oliver's card and saw in my mind the photograph of the poor little rich girl who looked like me, and I couldn't help wondering, *What really happened to her?*

Firmly I pushed that thought aside. Never mind the heiress. I was in this for the money. Thoughts of the real Jessamyn Carr dimmed, like a fade-out at the end of a sad moving picture.

6

A faint knock at my bedroom door. A creaking noise. The ruddy round cheeks of the housekeeper peeping in once again. Yes, I was awake. Yes, I could see Mr. Oliver Beckett. "As soon as I'm dressed, I'll come—"

But he was right behind her.

I pushed myself up against the pillows and yawned as Oliver lumbered into the room. I didn't care. Oliver had no interest in women. Besides, I was swathed from neck to wrist to ankle in a maidenly nightgown supplied by the housekeeper herself after I had arrived at the door of the Beckett mansion four days earlier, feverish, incoherent, and "without suitable nightclothes." As Oliver had promised, an army of servants and two doctors mobilized to wait on me. And I let them.

He beamed. "I came as soon as I could, my dear. I trust everyone has been taking good care of you?"

"The heir to the throne could not have received better care, thank you very much. I've been bathed, brushed, spoon-fed, and pampered like a French poodle." The sickness that had started with something I ate had taken a detour through fever territory, keeping me in bed for several days, but I felt better today. I stretched my lips into a smile. No matter what I thought of Oliver, I was going to have to work with him.

Oliver snapped his fingers at the housekeeper, who bobbed her head and backed out of the room. He smiled at me. "Let me have a good look at you," he said in a jovial voice, sweeping open the draperies to the four o'clock sun. "I've been quite worried about you."

A shame if I were to die and ruin his only chance at a fortune.

"I'll make it. Lucky you have a house in Cleveland. I was so sick, I don't believe I could have managed a longer trip."

I had come, as he instructed, on the train from Akron, arriving at Cleveland's Union Terminal an hour after we had exchanged telegrams. A uniformed chauffeur had met me on the platform, lugged my luggage and me to the car, and drove us west along the Gold Coast of Lake Erie. The trip was a blur.

"But this is not my house! Did you think that? No, it belongs to a dear chum, Randolph Stouffer, who is traveling in Europe. When I realized your dire straits, I thought through my list of pliable friends for one close to Akron. Randy came first to mind. He was delighted to lend me his home for as long as we want it. Keeps the servants out of mischief, he said."

So *that* was how Oliver lived—mooching off rich friends in the best four-flusher tradition. Nice work if you could get it. He pulled a chair over beside my bed and sat. We pretended not to notice the protesting creak.

"While you have been recuperating, my dear, I have not been idle. I have drawn floor plans and family trees, made lists of what you'll need to learn, and gathered information and photographs to help you."

A pretty young maid stopped at the doorway and cleared her throat. "Excuse me, sir, miss. Mrs. Wisniowolski is wanting to know if you'd care for tea?"

Oliver barely noticed her. I told the girl we would love tea. And some of those dainty bread-and-butter sandwiches I was unable to stomach yesterday. "So that's how you say her name," I mused when the maid was out of earshot. I repeated the unfamiliar sounds softly.

"Surely you, of all people, are accustomed to foreign-sounding names. I thought vaudeville was full of Polacks, niggers, kikes, and other . . . well, immigrants." And he could look down his nose at them because his grandfather had come over on an earlier boat. I had known snooty people like him before.

"Yep, and they always seem to be the most talented performers too. But on their way through the stage door, they usually trade their originals for something catchy the public will remember. Years ago, when I was in the Kid Kabaret with Eddie Cantor, he told me his real name was Israel Iskowitz. Who's going to remember that, let alone spell it? I could give you dozens of examples like that."

No need. Oliver was all business at hand.

"What made you change your mind?"

It was a question I had wrestled with during the past few days as I lay in bed. Why had I changed my mind? The easy answer, of course, was that I had been sick, scared, and desperate enough to snatch at any way out. In my fevered state, Oliver Beckett's card in my coat pocket represented the solution to all my troubles. Penniless and alone, I had few options. And yet . . . it wasn't that simple.

My mother would have disapproved. *Well, you're not sick anymore,* I could hear her say. I'm still very weak, I protested. *So wait a few days and then tell him you can't go through with it.* But I can't find work. *You can sell tickets at a box office in Cleveland until a suitable act passes through.* I'm not good enough. Anything I got would be Small Time or "death trail." *Nonsense, you've more talent than that.* I'm just trying the part on for size. I can always back out. *It's dishonest.* No more than most. We're not cutting the family off, you know, just spreading the wealth a bit further. It's really no different than what those spiritualists do, taking money from people who can afford it and making them happy by contacting their lost loved one. No harm done. *It's dangerous.* No one will get hurt.

Mother came to me every night in my dreams, but I wouldn't listen to her. Vaudeville had beaten me down and humiliated me beyond recovery. I couldn't go back for another punch in the face. I wasn't as talented as Mother thought. As I myself had once thought. And I *had* found work, I argued. I had taken a role in Oliver Beckett's production of *She Stoops to Con,* and if I played the part well, I had a shot at real money, a comfortable life, and something else. Something money couldn't buy. Suppose they were happy to see me? Suppose I really could take Jessie's place in Jessie's family?

And then there was that feeling I could not quite put into words, even to Mother. The sense that this was what Jessie wanted. From the moment I saw her photograph, I had liked her, and I suspected she liked me. We had something in common, Jessie and I, something more than just our looks, as remarkable as that resemblance was. Something beyond our shared status as orphans. But what? I was no threat to her, and she knew it. If she were still alive and returned home, I'd exit stage left faster than you could say "Jack Robinson." If she were dead . . . but she felt too alive to be dead.

To be sure, masquerading as an heiress would be tricky. I'd been impersonating people all my life, but this was a tougher gig than any I'd ever had, being on stage every waking minute. The challenge roused me from the melancholy that had held me down for weeks. I could do this. I could do it well.

I looked at Oliver. I had anticipated his question. Still, I cocked my head to one side and paused so my reply would not sound rehearsed.

"Jock and Francine decided to shrink the act to genuine Darlings. I had a lot of offers—good ones—but, to be honest, nothing appealed. In twenty-five years of vaudeville, I've played every part the circuit has to offer. I want to see what it's like to live somewhere for longer than a week. I want to wear clothes that aren't costumes and makeup that isn't greasepaint. I want to see the Leaning Tower of Pisa and the Eiffel Tower before I die. I want some money."

"You realize you are going to have to work hard?"

"I've always worked hard, Mr. Beckett," I said in a tone that would freeze water.

"And it involves a good deal of risk. More for me than you."

He was right about that. In a pinch, I could disappear into anonymity with little lost, since I came into this escapade with nothing but my face and my acting talents. Somehow I couldn't picture portly Oliver hopping a boxcar with a cardboard suitcase and making for Mexico. It was an advantage I had over him, something I could use if he became too domineering and started treating me as rudely as he treated Randy Stouffer's servants.

"Will you be ready to begin tomorrow morning?"

Some of my old self-confidence had returned with my health. Like a soldier coming home from the war, I'd been wounded in battle and shaken to the core, but I had survived with a more realistic notion of my worth. I had accepted a job, and I would handle it like the professional I was. Still, the notion of me waltzing into high society without anyone noticing I didn't belong there rattled me more than I wanted to admit.

"I'm ready this evening, if you like."

Oliver stood. "Get dressed, then, and meet me in the study. I'll tell the girl to bring the tray down there."

I had to poke about a while before I found the right room, one that was lined ceiling to floor with fine leather books. My host, magnifying glasses on his nose and thin hair combed across his bald spot, was busy at a large library table, shuffling papers like a croupier. The maid was busy at the tea table, dealing cups and plates of tiny sandwiches. I sank into a soft leather sofa and poured.

"We'll start with you, Jessie," he said as soon as the maid had departed, and from that moment forward, I became Jessie. Jessamyn Beckett Carr, born on September 30, 1903, in London to American parents who spent more time out of their country than in it. He had a dozen pictures of myself to show me.

"Look, here you are at four, with your nanny and your mother, Blanche," he said, placing on the table several silver- and gilt-framed photographs he'd acquired for the occasion. "Dear Blanche." He sighed. "I was very fond of my little sister. And here you are at ten, with both parents in Paris."

Oliver's photographs brought that same tingle of electricity I had experienced the first time I saw his small image of Jessie at our dinner in Omaha. Like that one, these portrayed a serious girl, a girl who did not smile often, a girl whose eyes looked through the camera with an intensity far greater than her years, almost as if she were trying to reach into the future to people who would view her photograph and make them understand. Unconsciously, I touched the glass. I wanted to understand.

I went up to my room and retrieved my collection of publicity photos from the bottom of my trunk. Oliver and I compared the kimono-clad ten-year-old who sang "Three Little Maids from School Are We" with Jessie's Paris portrait, taken when she was about the same age. My eyes were larger than hers and my eyebrows straighter, she had more freckles. Naturally, I was thinner—I hadn't had the benefit of three meals a day all my life. I peered hard at her later photos until Oliver grew worried. "What is wrong?"

"I'm trying to see Jessie's teeth."

"Teeth?"

"Mine are pretty straight. Were Jessie's crooked or gapped? Had she lost any?"

We squinted at the various pictures until we decided that Jessie's teeth, if not perfectly straight, were not remarkably crooked either. "And they might have straightened as you grew older," he added lamely.

"What about other mannerisms?"

"You bit your fingernails, but you grew out of that disgusting habit." He wrinkled his forehead in thought. "I can't think of any others. Oh, you purposely annoyed your aunt by whistling. She thought it vulgar." That made me smile. When I was younger, I too had annoyed people with my shrill whistle.

"Any other identifying marks? Moles? Scars? Birthmarks?"

"None that I know of. It's always possible."

We pored over family photos while Oliver lectured me about my relatives, dead and alive, starting with my mother's side. The Becketts were few—all I had left was Uncle Oliver, a confirmed bachelor, and his widowed mother, whom I called Grandmother. Grandfather had died of a heart attack years earlier. He and Grandmother had raised three children: Oliver, the eldest, was the only one still living. Oliver's younger brother, Clarence, had succumbed to meningitis years ago while working in England; Oliver's sister, Blanche, and her husband, Lawrence Carr, perished in the sailing accident that orphaned Jessie.

The Carr family was only slightly more numerous. There was my widowed aunt Victoria, whose late husband, Charles Carr, had been disinherited by his parents long ago for riotous living. "I'll wager there was no love lost between those two brothers," I remarked.

Oliver nodded grimly. "They despised each other. Not that Lawrence was any more virtuous than Charles. Both were . . ." He shook his head as words failed him. "But Lawrence was the older brother and more discreet where his behavior was concerned. Charles and Victoria's four children, Henry, Ross, and the twins, Valerie and Caroline, grew up resenting their father's exclusion for their own sake as well as his, since it deprived them all of their rightful share of Carr Industries."

Most of the pictures Oliver showed me had been mailed home by Blanche Beckett Carr to her mother from the Carr residences in London, Florence, Paris, and New York. Oliver had procured picture books of those cities for me to study so I could hold forth convincingly about climbing the tower of Notre Dame Cathedral or buying trinkets on the Ponte Vecchio. He knew little about the Carr family travels because, in spite of his fond recollections, he and Blanche had grown apart. No surprise there, considering his opinion of the man she married.

"There was nothing wrong with Blanche that a good husband wouldn't have cured. Unfortunately, she married a shallow prig with an intellect the size of a grape. Her idea of travel was shops and balls, his was casinos and racetracks. Neither would have been found within a hundred yards of the Uffizi Galleries or the Louvre; any cultural attractions you experienced were due solely to the efforts of your governesses."

"What if an investigation should dig up one of my governesses?"

"Then we should be sunk faster than the *Titanic*, my dear, for I frankly know nothing of governesses or your life during those years. However, I calculate that the odds of finding one of them in Europe are slim. If they were all as young as this one"—he stabbed a pudgy finger at the nanny in the photo—"it is my fervent hope that they are married now and have changed their last names."

Swell. First day on the job and prison loomed large. I did not voice my concerns. I could always walk away from this if the odds started to tilt against me.

We talked culture until dinner, Oliver frowning pointedly at my notebook to let me know I wasn't writing down enough of what he was saying. I ignored him until he snapped, "Don't you think you should take this a little more seriously, Jessie? We don't have time to review again and again." Twenty years of memorizing Shakespeare plays, Gilbert and Sullivan lyrics, Coleridge poetry, and Cohan songs had given me a memory like a sponge. I rattled off the last dozen things he had told me, repeating the same words he had used. He did not apologize, but he did back off.

The butler announced dinner in the small, informal dining room, and I had my first real meal in many days. It was also the first of many lessons in posh table manners—how to distinguish between the bouillon spoon and the creamed-soup spoon, how to eat European style by holding the fork in the left hand with tines pointing down when bringing the bite to the mouth, how to break bread with the fingers and butter it properly, how to use a finger bowl, and how to participate when a toast is proposed. That night, I ate sparingly and skipped the alcohol, at least until Oliver treated me to a monologue on the medicinal value of red wine. After watching him finish both his and my apple brown Betty, we returned to the library to resume our lessons.

The butler offered after-dinner drinks. Oliver ordered port and helped himself to one of Randy Stouffer's cigars. Mindful of my health, I asked for hot milk. We discussed the various Carr houses in Europe. "No one should be able to trip you up with specific questions about a particular house because no one on either side of the family except Mother was welcome to visit, and her mind is wandering. Should the subject arise, it should be easy to convince her that the fault lies with her memory rather than with you. Otherwise, you'll just have to say you were too young to recall."

I shook my head. "That won't work. Any child over four remembers her home."

Ad-libbing sounds most convincing if one gives details that are plentiful but vague, specifics that could apply to virtually any circumstance and be modified if challenged. It isn't as hard as it sounds. Time for a test.

"That house in Paris, yes, of course, I remember it . . . although I wasn't very old . . . let me see . . . we stayed there when I was quite little, and again when I was older. I remember the house, though. It was very elegant, tall, three—or maybe four—stories with a sweeping staircase and lots of windows that gave out over a large area where there were many interesting goings-on to watch when my lessons got boring. And it had tall ceilings, a beautiful floor where I used to try not to step on the cracks, and lovely crystal chandeliers that needed a ladder for the maids to clean. And I had a doll with French clothes—"

The expression on his face brought my routine to a screeching halt. "What is it? Am I overacting?"

"No, no, my dear, you are perfect. I am speechless with admiration." He began to chortle. "If anyone had been to the Carr house, your description would fit, I am sure. It fits every house in Paris I have ever seen. How on earth . . . ?"

I took a slight bow. A professional doesn't give away all her secrets.

C atastrophe struck at breakfast. "Oh, dear," blurted Oliver, troubled enough to pause his fork halfway to his mouth. "Do you ride?"

"Horses? Gracious, no!"

This was a serious deficiency. Evidently Jessie had been quite the equestrian. Nothing I could say would persuade Oliver that a person could forget how to ride after seven years.

"Nonsense. It's like swimming or riding a bicycle. You never forget. By the way, you do swim, do you not?"

I told him yes. Well, it was almost true. I had thrashed about in swimming holes once or twice without drowning. And I'd learned to ride a bicycle from the boys in the Monkey Business act. But now I would have to learn to ride a horse. I had never been around horses, and the idea terrified me.

There was no reprieve, not even a short delay to allow me to become accustomed to the idea. Later that same morning, Oliver and I drove west along Lake Road past a string of bloated mansions that peered out over the crystal waters of Lake Erie, until we reached a stable where a patient young groom with puppy-dog eyes introduced me to the largest, most ferocious beast this side of the Mississippi River.

"Her name's Candy," said the boy. "Pat her nose. She's gentle as a lamb. Candy, old girl, this is Jessie."

I reached out fearfully, as if I were putting my hand into a flame, and touched its nose with one finger. The animal shook its head angrily, eyes blazing, and snorted a warning. I gave a cry of alarm and stepped back so it couldn't stomp me with those massive hoofs.

"That nod of her head is a greeting. She likes you."

Sure. And couldn't wait for me to climb aboard so it could buck me off and break my neck. I watched in horror as the groom picked up a mess of leather straps and metal drawer pulls, pried open the beast's mouth, and shoved most of it between the biggest, meanest teeth I'd ever seen. One easy bite could take off my head.

"This is the bridle that controls the horse," he began patiently, pointing to each part and giving it a name. "This is the bit; these are the reins. You'll be able to do this yourself in no time."

I not only had to learn to ride, I also had to touch the horse and learn how to rig it out with all the trappings? I nearly fainted.

The groom kept talking, softly and gently so as not to frighten the animal, as he put a blanket on its back and a heavy saddle on top of that, and then he tightened the belt under its belly. I figured all that tight lacing must be making the horse really angry, and I was sure it would start to buck and snort any minute now, like I'd seen in the cowboy pictures. My knees turned to jelly.

"Now up you go, little lady," and before I could back off, the groom put my left boot in the stirrup and slung my right leg over the horse's back. Trembling like a cornered rabbit, I clung for all

I was worth to the handle on the saddle as the boy took the reins and walked us over to a ring. That's all we did that day, walk around and around that damn ring, me clutching the handle, and the wild beast thinking up ways to buck me into the dirt as soon as the boy let go of the reins. After a century had passed, the boy helped me climb down. I was just easing away when he handed me half an apple.

"Here, she's been a good girl, give her this treat. Hold your hand flat like this, so she doesn't accidentally nip your fingers."

Oh, my God. Those enormous teeth weren't within six inches of my hand when I snatched it back, tumbling the apple to the ground. The horse just bent its neck and ate the apple, dirt and all. I knew it was laughing at me.

Every day thereafter, we returned for another lesson, progressing from the ring to open fields and even low jumps. I learned to control my fear, but never conquered it. I hated riding. My sore thighs hated riding. My stiff shoulders hated riding. But I learned to ride.

"Thank God Jessie didn't play the piano!" I remarked one day, brushing off my jodhpurs after a particularly grueling session in the ring. "I couldn't possibly learn that in a couple weeks."

"No," mused Oliver. "But a broken finger would keep your hand in a cast for many weeks." I'd wager he'd be willing to break it for me too. I wondered—and not for the first time—whether I had underestimated Oliver's potential for causing me real harm.

For three years, Jessie had lived with her Carr cousins and her aunt—or rather, they lived with Jessie in the mansion Jessie's father, Lawrence Carr, had built on the cliffs high above the Pacific coast of Oregon. Oliver had visited them many times during those three years, and he could recall almost everything he had seen or heard. He possessed a remarkably observant eye as well as the ability to pull the smallest of details out of his mental file cabinet. I learned about pets, I learned about favorite colors, I learned about toys and games. I learned about the servants and the governess who was hired to tame the Carr cousins. I learned about Jessie's uncle Charles Carr, who with his wife Victoria had been persuaded by the trustees to raise the orphaned Jessie along with their own four in exchange for a generous stipend and their use of the house in Oregon. But Charles's poor health had made him a minor presence in all their lives. His weak heart had finally given out a year after Jessie disappeared—I can't say I was sorry since it left one less relative for me to worry about.

The cousins were my biggest concern. The twin girls were a few years younger than Jessie, not nearly the threat that the two boys would be. I imagined Henry was too much older to have much to do with a younger girl cousin, but his brother, Ross, was the same age as Jessie. There I smelled danger.

"What about the Carr governess?"

"Miss Lavinia did her best, difficult as you all were. She stayed on after you disappeared until the twins turned fifteen, then she moved to San Francisco, where she was tragically run down by an automobile while crossing the street." Thank you, Fates! "But you don't know that," added Oliver, "so you will be very surprised and sad when you learn of her death." My, yes.

Oliver coached me in some rudimentary Italian and French so I could pronounce the basics that Jessie probably learned from her European governesses. *Enchantée de faire votre connaissance*, I said, and *Che ora é? Uno, due, tre, quattro, cinque.* He had even acquired some Italian and French money, curious bits of paper and light, thin coins that I studied so they would feel familiar in case someone passed francs or lira my way and asked what they were. One day we visited a studio in Lakewood to have my photograph taken. "You'll send it along with your letter when you notify the family of your return," Oliver directed. "That alone should go a long way toward convincing them."

"By the way, did Jessie keep a diary?"

"If she did, we never found it."

"Did she have any hobbies?"

"Hobbies?"

"All girls collect things. Dolls, seashells, foreign stamps, coins?"

Oliver scowled as he considered the question. "There is one thing. She used to spend a lot of time walking on the beach at low tide, looking for colored rocks. And two or three times, she found one of those green glass balls that wash ashore, do you know them?" When I shook my head, he explained. "Japanese fishermen use them as floats for their nets. Some get lost and ocean currents wash them east. I expect it takes them years to travel all the way across the Pacific."

"How can they get that far without breaking?"

"Doubtless some do break. Others don't. Your aunt put them in a shallow planter in the parlor, here." He pointed to a spot on his floor plan. "You showed them to me once. Each one has an indentation on the bottom."

"What's that?"

"Mouth-blown glass has a rough spot on the bottom where the piece connected to the glassblower's pipe. You can smooth it away on fine pieces, but no one troubles with workaday fishnet floats."

It was a good detail. One I could use. Oliver was full of such tidbits.

"There's someone we are forgetting in all this rehearsal," I said one day. "The most important person of all."

"And who is that?"

"The one who is being deprived of the Carr fortune. Our greatest antagonist. Who would inherit if Jessie never returned?"

"I haven't forgotten. I take exquisite pleasure in the knowledge that they will be cut off. Next in line are your cousins, Henry and Ross Carr and the twins. Henry is a sanctimonious dilettante, sailing in regattas and hobnobbing with swells. Ross is a pompous ass. The girls are of no concern. Actually, they come into the inheritance indirectly, through your father's brother, Charles."

"Sounds like the succession to the British throne. Why didn't they inherit before now?"

"Because you were missing, not dead. The law says missing persons can be declared legally dead seven years after their disappearance. That would be this month, August, which is why your arrival on the scene is so fortuitous. I have no doubt the trustees are busily preparing the paperwork that names the Carr children as your legal heirs. During the past seven years, the trustees have continued to manage Carr Industries in your name, as they would have done until you turned twenty-one in September. So it is the cousins who forfeit your father's fortune at your return. A fortune they do not merit, I might add."

Nor do you, Uncle Oliver, I did not say.

8

Tuesday, August 19, 1924. Opening day for *The Return of Jessie Carr*, a sensitive drama about a young woman's return to the bosom of her family after years as a vaudeville sensation. The curtain was about to rise on the role of a lifetime.

I gave myself a critical once-over in my room at the Grande Hotel in Sacramento. I had twisted my thick auburn hair into a large chignon, then encouraged a few tendrils to escape around my face like a picture frame. It gave me a wistful, ingénue look that was complemented by my blue sailor-collar dress with its drop waist, crisp pleats, and matching white straw hat and gloves. Youthful but not juvenile. I had done my makeup with a light hand, blushing my cheeks for a little nervousness and applying just enough kohl and lipstick to add poise. My changeable eyes sparkled more blue than green today, persuaded by the color of my dress. I looked the part. For the first time in my life, I was the headliner.

With confidence that comes from years on the stage, I straightened my shoulders, lifted my chin, and walked out of the hotel like a duchess at court. The weather was sunny and fine as I made my way along the sidewalk past the gleaming white dome of Sacramento's capitol building. My destination, the law offices of Smith and Wade, was four blocks distant on Ninth Street, where I had been summoned to meet with the trustees of Lawrence Carr's estate. Bankers, accountants, lawyers, and one Methodist minister—an audience of eight old men—all waiting to meet me, hear me, watch me, test me, judge me.

There was still time to turn back, but I knew I would not. Easy Street was just around the corner.

Once Oliver became confident that I had thoroughly absorbed my role, we had parted, I to Akron where I took a room at a decent hotel, he to his mother's house in San Francisco to wait for the inevitable call from Victoria Carr letting them know of my resurrection. I mailed my aunt Victoria the photograph and a penitent letter informing her I was alive and coming home, and begging her forgiveness for the anxiety I had caused her when I ran away. A stiff reply had come, not from Aunt Victoria, but from Mr. Severinus Wade of Smith and Wade, one of the trustees of the Carr estate, who suggested it would be wiser for me to meet with them in Sacramento before traveling north to the Carr home.

That was not the plan, but as in vaudeville, flexibility is everything.

"Good morning," I said.

A sensibly dressed spinster with an iron-gray hair knot looked up, stuck a yellow pencil behind her ear, and examined me hat to toe. She nodded a crisp reply.

"I'm Miss Jessamyn Carr, here to meet with Mr. Wade and associates."

"I'll let Mr. Wade know you are here, Miss Carr. Won't you have a seat?"

I elected to stand. One rarely sits onstage for more than a moment—standing was the better pose and I wanted every advantage.

The clerk came back into the reception room. "They are waiting for you in conference, miss. Right this way, please."

My heart beat faster as it always does when I am in the wings, about to go on. The curtain rose. The clerk held open the door and motioned me to enter. I almost expected her to give my fanny a pat the way the emcees do when they send children onto the stage.

Eight chairs scraped the oak floor and eight men stood as I entered the conference room. The man I had pegged as Mr. Severinus Wade offered me his hand, not to shake but to hold, and for a moment I thought he was going to kiss it.

"Good morning, miss."

The absence of my name was no accident. He and the others were pointedly withholding its bestowal until they had made their decision. The pleasantries took several minutes. I was introduced to the other seven men, offered a glass of water, and given a chair at the head of a polished mahogany table. Eight places had papers and files before them. My place had no such prompts. I was pleased to note that the eight were all old enough to be my grandfather; three were positively ancient. Old men make an easy audience.

I smiled.

We sat.

Everyone looked expectantly at Mr. Wade, who had obviously been chosen to lead this effort. It was not a role he relished. He removed his cheaters, took out his pocket handkerchief, and wiped the lenses deliberately. I waited, my hands folded demurely on the table. It was not I who had called the meeting.

Mr. Wade asked if my hotel was comfortable. I said it was. He asked if my breakfast had been satisfactory. I said it had been very good. He asked if the train trip from Ohio had been difficult. I said it had been quite uneventful. He asked if I thought Sacramento was a nice city. I said it was charming. Fearing we would all remain trapped in this limbo forever, I departed from plan and spoke my lines.

"Mr. Wade, gentlemen," I began, letting my eyes linger on each man's face in turn as I spoke. "It has been many years since we last met, and I confess I do not remember you at all. I was only eleven at the time and quite dull with grief. You cannot remember me well either, and I suspect I have changed far more than you."

This prompted a dry, nervous chuckle that fluttered around the table like wind through dead leaves. I had seized control of the interrogation.

"I quite understand why you have asked me here, and I am completely in agreement with your intention to make sure that I am, indeed, the same Jessie Carr who ran away seven years ago. Of course, I am not really the same. I am older, wiser, and more appreciative of my home and family than I was as a spoilt child. I am quite ready to answer your questions so I can prove to you beyond the shadow of a doubt that I am not an impostor."

There was a satisfied muttering at this speech. One man pulled out a photograph of thirteen-year-old Jessie from the folder in front of him and compared her features to mine before passing it to his right.

"When and where were you born?" asked a man who looked older than Methuselah. A sadly unimaginative start, but I responded graciously enough.

"Who were your parents?" asked another. "How did they die?"

"Where did you go to school?" asked the minister, and I noticed they seemed to be taking turns clockwise around the table.

"Where did you grow up?" I elaborated a little on that one, although I knew full well embellishment was tempting the Fates.

Stick to the questions, Oliver had stressed. No more, no less. Oh, all right.

One of the lawyers spoke out of turn. "I visited your parents at their home in Florence in 1911," he said. Uh-oh. That was unexpected. Oliver had been sure no family members had visited the Carrs, but he hadn't known about business acquaintances.

"I'm sorry, sir, I don't remember you. I would have been only seven or eight then."

"Exactly. A precocious little lady, too, if I might add. But the house. You remember it?"

"Certainly."

"What do you remember about it?"

"Let me think. It was in the Via del Corso close to a pretty church, and there was a park very near where we would walk and play outside whenever the weather was fine. I remember that the house itself was quite old. Or so it seemed to me. It had lots and lots of rooms, and stone floors that were cold on bare feet where the rugs didn't cover them. All the walls had old paintings on them, all of strange people and places I didn't know, and the ceilings were very high. There was a grand staircase and so many crystal chandeliers I couldn't count them all. The maids needed a ladder to clean them! I had a lovely room upstairs next to the schoolroom, and my governess was next to that." I went into eloquent detail about my own bedroom and the kitchen, as it was certain no visitor had been in those parts of the house. My wide-eyed sincerity charmed them. "The entrance hall had a large table with a tall vase for fresh flowers—usually roses, my mother's favorite. And there were lots of statues of naked people."

"Ahem, yes." He coughed to cover up his embarrassment at my use of the word "naked." "Nude" was acceptable in polite conversation but not "naked." I had done it on purpose of course, to fluster him enough to change the subject, and it worked. "Now then, my dear, why did you run away from home?"

I gave a deep, pained sigh at the recollection. "At the time,

I could not have told you the reason. I hated everyone. I thought everyone hated me. I took what money I had and caught the train to Portland, thinking only about having a good time for a few days, shopping and seeing shows. A real adventure. The first night, I went to a theater and loved the show so much, I joined a dance act and never looked back. I think if I hadn't been hired so quickly, I'd have come home when I ran out of money."

"Why did you neglect to contact your family? Why did you let them worry so, thinking you were kidnapped or dead?"

"I suppose I was punishing them for the pain I felt. Oh, I know now it wasn't their fault. I blame my loneliness and my orphaned state. My cousins had parents—I had none. Life seemed unbearably unfair."

"Tell us about the past seven years."

Truth is easy, but nonetheless, I had rehearsed my response to this question as well. As two of the men took notes, I recounted my travels with the various acts, ending with the Darlings. I pulled playbills and theatrical photos from my handbag, described my roles and as many of the cities we visited as I could recall, and told them how to address mail to any act in care of the theaters listed in *Variety*, current examples of which I thoughtfully provided for them—a disarming tactic I thought of myself. They planned to hire a Pinkerton or two to run down the details, and this would help their investigation immensely. I professed myself happy to oblige.

Like all civilians, they were intrigued with my tales of vaudeville life, and I deliberately dropped names they were likely to know, all carefully vetted to include only those I had met during the past seven years.

"I got to know Benny Kubelsky, a violin and patter man who has changed his name several times. Now it's Jack Benny." A few nods. Some had seen Benny in San Francisco. "I played on the same stage with little Milton Berlinger—you may have seen him in several pictures with Mary Pickford, where they cut his last name in half. And I've shared billing with Mary Jane West—you know her as Mae." To a man, they scowled and feigned disapproval, but I knew better. No male of the human species who had seen Mae West perform didn't silently lust after her and wish his own wife possessed some of her brassy charm.

When we had passed a cheerful hour, there came a knock at the door behind me. All heads turned as a petite lady with white hair, about eighty years of age and dressed in widow's weeds, stepped into the room. She smiled at me, and all heads turned again, to watch my reaction.

"Jessie!" She breathed my name in a melodramatic sigh often used by amateurs.

It took me all of two heartbeats to figure out what they were up to. A shame Oliver wasn't there to appreciate my agility. I had studied enough photographs to know Jessie's grandmother's every wrinkle. I merely stared at this stranger, my face a mask of bewilderment.

"Well, Jessie," prompted Mr. Wade. "Don't you recognize your grandmother Beckett?"

Now, really.

Timing is everything, so I counted to five before I turned my wide eyes toward Mr. Wade. "I am certain I would recognize my grandmother if she were to walk into this room, sir. That nice lady is not my grandmother."

At that, the room broke into a hullabaloo, with little Jessie's eyes demurely cast down as the interrogators shook hands all around, exclaiming their apologies for the dastardly trick. Only one of them—the youngest of the old men—remained in his seat, eyeing the others as if they were sums on a ledger sheet that were not quite adding up. I heard him clear his throat and say something about a governess to the man next to him.

But the show was over. There was no turning back now. Ring down the curtain. Applause, applause for Jessie Carr.

9

That milestone was but the first on the road to riches, and while gratified by my success, I knew it was not yet time to pop a champagne cork.

I returned to the Grande Hotel to find my room had been searched during my absence. The signs were subtle but unmistakable to someone who had prepared for it. I dropped my hat and gloves on the bed, kicked off my shoes, and surveyed the premises. The two drawers I had left not quite closed were shut tight, the clothes hanging in my closet had shifted as pockets were searched, and the suitcase I had positioned in the corner precisely between two purple flowers on the carpet now sat directly on top of one of those blossoms.

The intrusion caused me no alarm. The trustees had hired someone to scour my belongings for clues while I was away. He had found nothing. There was nothing to find. Only one thing could harm me, one item that would, in the wrong hands, utterly destroy our plans. My most precious possession—the collection of publicity photos and playbills from my mother's career and my own early years.

I knew back in Cleveland that I should destroy the lot, but I could no more have done that than I could take an innocent life. They were all I had of my mother and of my childhood. I knew I could not keep them with me. Nor could I give them to Oliver to hold. I dared not even remind him of their existence. He was not above destroying them himself if I refused to.

Finally, I had separated out the playbills and pictures of recent vintage to serve as props for my charade, and wrapped the others in plain brown paper. On the front of the package, I wrote a note that read, "Treasured photos and personal papers belonging to Leah Randall. Do not throw away! Please hold until she returns to claim them." Before leaving Randolph Stouffer's mansion in Cleveland, I placed the package in a bottom drawer of the desk in his study, a desk that looked as if it hadn't been disturbed by Mr. Stouffer in years. With any luck, no one would even see the package until I was thoroughly ensconced in my new life and could return to claim them without fear of exposure. I regretted the risk, but life was risk and I was a player.

The trustees had advised me to alter my plans, to go directly to San Francisco to visit my grandmother. As matriarch of the Beckett family, she deserved my first allegiance. From her house I could proceed to the Carr estate near the coastal town of Dexter, Oregon.

My first reaction had been to ignore them. Our plan was for Oliver to stay as far from me as possible so that even the most suspicious mind could find nothing to link us, but a little reflection brought me around. The most difficult part of this deception would be convincing those who knew Jessie best—the aunt and the cousins—that I was Jessie reincarnate. How much stronger would my claim be if I arrived having already won the recognition of the trustees as well as my grandmother and uncle? I would appear at the Carr estate a veritable fait accompli.

So I had dutifully deferred to the trustees and accepted Mr. Wade's offer to send a wire to my grandmother and arrange a short visit to San Francisco the next day. That was when Mr. Wade informed me that my uncle Oliver happened to be staying with her.

"I'll be glad to see Uncle again," I said. "He used to visit the house in Dexter often and brought me presents."

"I'm sure a reminder of some of those presents will convince him of your true identity," Mr. Wade offered. I thanked him for that excellent idea and for his offer to send a train ticket to my hotel this evening. I had no money, but Mr. Wade seemed disinclined to part with cash.

The afternoon was fine, and I had no desire to spend it cooped up in my room. I would do some window-shopping, enjoy a nice meal at the Grande Hotel, and have a long, hot bath before retiring.

No sooner had I stepped out onto the sidewalk than I felt hostile eyes on my back. It took only a few adjustments in my pace and direction to determine the owner of those eyes—an ordinary-looking man in a brown sack suit and fedora who resembled every other businessman in the capital that day. He was following me.

This gave me the willies. Searching my room was fair play, but I did not appreciate the trustees setting a bloodhound on my trail. I ducked into a lingerie shop, left by a rear door, and continued my stroll in peace. But I was not surprised that when I returned to the hotel a couple hours later, he was there waiting for me, leaning against a lamppost across from the entrance. For all I knew, he intended to follow me to San Francisco, perhaps to Oregon. That I would not tolerate.

I reminded myself that I was trying to appear trustworthy, not arouse anyone's suspicions. I would have to lose Brown Fedora in a subtle, natural manner. Returning to the privacy of my room,

I had my hot bath and ordered up a lovely dinner. After the sun had set, I packed my valise. At the front desk, I found the promised train ticket—a first-class reservation on tomorrow's 1:10 to San Francisco. Making sure Brown Fedora was still out front, I left the hotel by a side entrance and walked the distance to the train station under cover of darkness, my valise in hand.

A glance at the departures board told me there were no trains to San Francisco tonight.

"Good evening," I said to the ticket clerk. "I'd like to exchange this ticket for an earlier train. And make it second class, please."

I left with a reserved seat on tomorrow's 9:35 A.M. and a couple of bucks' refund—enough to pay for a room at one of the cheap hotels that cluster around every train station in America. I crossed the street, checked into the nearest one, and fell asleep.

The following morning I spent my last few coins on a cup of coffee, a cold roll, and a copy of the morning *Sacramento Union* to read on the trip. It wasn't until the train had left the station that I looked at the front page. My original hotel, the Grande Hotel, had caught fire last night. They were still counting the bodies.

10

I arrived at the Southern Pacific station in San Francisco where I found a line of taxis waiting outside the Third Street entrance. I knew the city from having performed in several of its theaters as a child with my mother. I remembered it as a brash town that wore its gaudy glamour on the surface like greasepaint on an actor's face. Mother and I had not stepped far beyond the theater district, so the San Francisco I was about to experience—the tame residential portion—was entirely new to me.

Fog had not yet drawn its curtain over the city as we drove through the privileged neighborhood of Pacific Heights. Its streets were lined with mansions built to outdo their predecessors on Nob Hill in size and luxury. I gaped at the exuberant architecture, the widow's walks, turrets, bulging bay windows, French chateaux, columned porticos, and fanciful Victorian gingerbread, some of which I recognized from Oliver's picture books.

"Here we are, miss," said the driver as he stopped the car. He carried my valise to the door and waited for the maid to fetch my fare.

My grandmother Beckett's modest house reminded me that it was the Carr side of Jessie's family that had been blessed with money, not the Becketts. A plain, older Victorian home squashed between overweening upstarts, my grandmother's house sat back from the curb, a proud survivor of the horrendous San Francisco earthquake of 1906 and a remnant of a less ostentatious era. I remembered Oliver saying that the old lady was all that stood between it and the wrecking ball.

As Oliver had instructed, I called her Grandmother. She was as he had described, cold and inscrutable. I didn't mind a bit. The very idea of having a grandmother intrigued me. I thought she was fascinating.

She gave me a searching look before presenting her cheek to kiss. It was dry and powdery and smelled of lavender. Her white hair wound in a bun on the back of her head. She looked me over slowly and silently. Her face was like a plaster death mask. I could read nothing from it. Had I passed her inspection?

"Do come into the parlor, Jessie. Ruth will take your things upstairs."

"Will I have the usual room?" I asked, eager to prove myself.

She looked puzzled. "Which room is that?"

"The blue room in the back. Where I used to stay when I came with Mother and Father."

"Oh, did you? Yes, that's right . . . the blue room . . . No, dear, Oliver is in that room. You may have the guest room on the third floor. Your young legs will manage the stairs. Ruth, take Jessie's things up and then ask Delia to bring tea into the parlor. Be sure she includes some of those scones that Oliver likes."

"Is there any of Delia's queen's cake? It was always my favorite!"

"Don't try so hard, Jessie. I would not mistake my own grand-daughter, even after seven years. We believe you. Ah, here's Oliver."

At last! I desperately needed some time alone with Oliver to tell him about the hotel fire, but Grandmother showed no sign of leaving us alone, even for a minute. We had a touching reunion where he exclaimed over the lovely young lady I had grown into, and I remarked how the years hadn't changed him at all. We retired to the parlor where I blinked in surprise to see several of the photos I had studied only last week displayed on tables draped with Irish lace. There were so many framed photographs, I understood how Oliver had managed to borrow some of them without his mother noticing. I vowed to examine them all carefully as soon as I had some time to myself. I wanted to learn everything I could about Jessie, and the simplest way seemed to be through her photographs.

Warmed by a cheerful fire, I covered up my impatience with a calm outward manner. We spoke of the weather and the approaching elections. Coolidge had received the Republican nomination for president last month. The Democrats had chosen an obscure West Virginian. "No one I have talked to has heard anything about John Davis," said Oliver, who expressed his assurance that President Coolidge would win a second term. "You will be twenty-one by the time of the November election," he added. "I trust your first ballot will be cast for a Republican?"

I said I hadn't given it much thought. "Politics is not a game vaudeville plays. Performers are constantly on the move, and without a permanent legal residence, they can't register to vote."

"Now that you have a permanent home, you'll want to break that tradition," Oliver said. "Decent people need to cast their ballots, or the democratic process will be overwhelmed by the self-serving votes of the ignorant rabble."

I assured him that I would vote as he did himself, putting the welfare of the country before personal, selfish interests. His eyes narrowed in warning.

Grandmother made clear her disapproval of female suffrage,

granted only four years ago. It was not ladylike to vote, and she would not demean herself by pushing into an election hall crowd to cast a ballot for some man she hadn't even been introduced to socially. Oddly enough, she encouraged me to do that very thing. "Voting is for young people who have a stake in the future."

It seemed like hours passed before Grandmother retired for her afternoon nap. Finally, I could tell Oliver about events in Sacramento!

"How did it go?" he asked as soon as his mother was out of earshot.

"I killed 'em," I said smugly.

"Don't get overconfident. Tomorrow I'm going to suggest that Mother go with you to Dexter and stay a week with Victoria and the children. I think she'll agree if I accompany her, and I'll allow myself to be persuaded after a little arm-twisting. With the trustees' backing, and Mother's and mine, you'll walk into that house with a presumption of legitimacy."

"There's been . . . Something's been worrying me. I was staying at the Grande Hotel." Quickly, I filled him in on the room search, Brown Fedora, and the Grande Hotel fire. Even unflappable Oliver raised his eyebrows at that last bit.

"And you think all this was the work of the same man?"

"I don't know what to think. Who else but the trustees would have had my room searched? That made sense, and we expected it. But the shadow? Maybe he wasn't tailing me to see where I was going; maybe he was trying to find a quiet alley where he could knock me in the head."

"Maybe he was trying to protect you."

"From what?" Oliver turned up his hands in the universal gesture that meant, Who knows? "So maybe this fella burned down the Grande Hotel. What I can't figure out is why Mr. Wade or one of the trustees would want Jessie dead. And no one else knew where I was staying, so it had to be one of them. You didn't know, did you?"

He shook his head. "Severinus Wade has played this close to the chest."

"No one else knew."

"Au contraire, my dear. All the trustees might have known, not to mention anyone who worked in Wade's office. Let me think."

He stared into the fireplace for several minutes until I grew impatient and interrupted the silence. "I asked myself, why would the trustees want to kill Jessie? If they thought I was an imposter, they would have called the police. But no, they believed me. They were delighted I'd come home."

"They damn well should have been. They've made fat fees for the past seven years managing Carr Industries, and when Jessie inherits, they'll be able to continue their service. The Carr brothers were certain to terminate them and run the company themselves, but you couldn't do that."

"Why not?"

"A woman can't run a big company," he said sneeringly.

"What if one of the trustees has been skimming funds and needs to cover up his crime?"

"By killing Jessie? Hardly. The truth is, all of the trustees are probably helping themselves to extras. So what? You aren't equipped to expose them. They aren't worried about you."

He considered the circumstances a while longer, then pronounced his conclusion. "The fire was a coincidence. A lucky break for me—you might have been killed if you hadn't checked out. The newspaper said it started in the kitchen, a logical place. There was no mention of arson. The man following you was probably the same one who searched your room, by order of Severinus Wade, as a precaution. Could even have been a Pinkerton. You said yourself that they were going to hire Pinkertons to investigate. But they know you've come here, and they know you're going to Oregon, so if they want to shadow you, it won't be hard. We'll watch for it, but I don't think it will be a problem."

A coincidence. That was the only logical explanation.

As vaudeville lingo would have it, I had killed 'em at a one-night stand in Sacramento and jumped to San Francisco where I played to a small and easily satisfied audience. Coming off rave reviews, I jumped to Portland, a tougher venue but one where, if opening reviews were positive, I could look forward to an engagement of as many weeks as I cared to perform. From there I envisioned long holidays in Italy, southern France, Greece, or wherever the climate was endlessly sunny, the food fresh and plentiful, and the people welcoming. This dream, nurtured by the travel books Oliver had given me to study, kept me focused on perfecting my role.

I had twice in my life played Portland, Salem, and Eugene, a trio of Oregon cities that adored vaudeville. That made it easy for Jessie's story to hinge on having joined a vaudeville act in Portland instead of returning home after her runaway adventure. I had some hazy recall of Portland's rivers and bridges and a large mountain hovering nearby, and some pretty clear memories of the theaters we'd played, should anyone ask.

Never mind that I had spent so much of my life on trains that I sleep better sitting up than lying down, our trip north to Oregon brought a surprise. Grandmother, Oliver, and I rode the six hundred miles from San Francisco to Portland in two first-class compartments that came with berths and a lanky Negro porter whose only job was to think up ways to make our journey more comfortable.

Dusk had arrived by the time we reached Portland, but low-hanging clouds made it seem more like night. It took two taxis to ferry the three of us and our luggage from the station to the opulent Hotel Benson in the heart of the city. As we approached the intersection of Broadway and Oak, our driver turned to Oliver. "Looks like some parked cars are blocking the main entrance, sir. I can pull up beside them or half a block ahead, whatever you like."

Oliver peered out the window. "There isn't much traffic this time of day," he said. "Just get as close as you can to the awning, boy, so my mother doesn't have too far to walk."

The driver double-parked in front of the main entrance and our second taxi followed suit. No sooner had we alighted than a bellhop scurried out to take charge of our luggage. A doorman swung wide the front door for Grandmother who made her way slowly toward the sidewalk on Oliver's arm. It was pretty quiet for downtown. On the opposite side of the street, a couple strolled hand in hand and a man walked his dog. Gaslights glowed in the evening gloom and two motorcars drove past, giving us a wide berth.

The hotel building was boxy and tall—at least a dozen stories—and I craned my neck to make out the striking roofline as I stood beside the taxi, waiting for the drivers to unload all our belongings. A motorcar started up in the block behind me, its engine getting louder as it came closer, but my attention was on a lively party that had just spilled out of an unmarked speakeasy across the way. All at once, several of that group were shouting and pointing to a car bearing down on us. And there in the street beside the double-parked taxi in the midst of our luggage, I stood . . . directly in its path.

"Watch out!" called the bellhop as he leaped to the safety of the sidewalk. I dove between two of the parked vehicles a split second before the speeding car roared past, coming so close that I felt its bumper slap the hem of my skirt. So close I could see the driver's squint eyes and big nose over the steering wheel. Never slowing, he rounded the corner with an earsplitting squeal of tires on pavement, scattering our luggage, smacking sloppily into the opposite curb, and scraping against a gaslight. Had the driver of an oncoming vehicle not slammed its brakes and honked, there would have been a serious collision as well.

One of the taxi drivers swore. "You all right, lady? I never seen such crazy driving in all my born days."

"That fella must've been drunk," agreed the other. "He was all over the road."

Oliver rushed to my side. I tried to assure everyone that I was fine, but I had to take several deep breaths to steady my racing pulse. "I'm not hurt. And it was partly our fault. We shouldn't have been unloading here in the middle of the street."

"We don't let cars park here at the entrance," said the bell-man. "I don't know who let 'em park here. That's what caused the trouble. I'm going to call the police to come give 'em what for. And a ticket."

The three men scrambled to collect our bags, battered but not broken, while Oliver guided me toward the lobby. "Maybe the Prohibitionists are right after all," I said to him, only half joking. "I hope that idiot gets home before he kills someone."

I looked around for Grandmother. She hadn't moved from her spot at the hotel entrance where she had had a front-row view of the mishap, and she was staring, unblinking, not at me but at the corner where the drunk had disappeared from view. Then she gave me a long, measured look. I knew what she was thinking. Before she could speak, Oliver gently took her arm, breaking her concentration. The three of us crossed the threshold together.

As Oliver paused to speak to the desk clerk, Grandmother drew me aside.

"You could have been killed," she said in a low voice.

I nodded. "Accidents happen."

"Accidents can be made to happen."

"I wondered the same thing," I admitted. "But only for a moment. No one knew when we were arriving, or even which hotel we would choose. And no one could predict that our taxi would unload in the street, or that I would stand near it. It was an accident."

Accident. Coincidence. The words taunted me. If Mr. Wade had spoken of our trip to others in his office, news might have leaked. It was no secret that I was traveling to Oregon and there were only so many train possibilities. But the rest? Staging that drama with all the cars would be no easy task. Was someone trying to kill Jessie? Or scare her away? Was it because they thought I was Jessie, or because they thought I wasn't Jessie? I reassured myself that at the first sign of real danger, I would skip town, change my name, and return to the safety of vaudeville. I could always find something there. If there were any more coincidences in Dexter, I'd cancel the charade and do a flit. But I'd give it a couple more days.

"It was just an accident," I reassured Grandmother. She didn't look convinced.

Still, I would be glad to reach the Carr estate in Dexter where I would be safe.

Years of living in cheap hotels and boardinghouses had not prepared me for the luxurious Benson, a veritable palace built by Simon Benson, lumber baron and friend of Jessie's father. Oliver had procured for us the Presidential Suite—no president had ever darkened its door but it was ready and waiting should one stroll by. Remembering my fondness for champagne, he arranged for the chef to send up a meal of sautéed salmon on delicately herbed rice at our arrival, along with a chilled bottle of bubbly. What a life!

"The story goes," said Oliver, gesturing toward the polished paneled walls and massive columns that stood in the lobby like tree trunks in an enchanted woodland, "that this rare figured walnut came all the way from the czar's forests in Russia, and when the bill arrived, it was so immense that Benson fainted when he saw it." If he was trying to take my mind off the close call, he did not succeed.

"Will I faint, like Simon Benson did, when I see our bill?" I asked idly after we had settled into our suite and Grandmother was out of earshot. I had speculated that Oliver was up to his usual mooching ways with some friend at the hotel. Silly me. The rise in Oliver's standard of living had already begun.

"Don't bother your pretty head about expenses, my dear. This is how the heiress to the Carr fortune is expected to travel. Must travel, in point of fact. I don't concern myself with mundane matters of money; I simply forward the bills to Severinus Wade."

Somehow, I had imagined that Carr cash would not start flowing until I reached the magic age of twenty-one. But no, Oliver had turned on the spigot and money was gushing like water from a broken main. This heiress gig was nice work.

Unless it got you killed.

12

The next morning, after an extravagant breakfast, Grandmother, Oliver, and I left to catch the train for the short trip
west—seventy-five miles or so—to Dexter, a small town on a
small bay tucked behind a spit of land that formed a natural harbor all but invisible to passing boats. The town had prospered for
decades, first from gold mining and salmon fishing, then lumber-
ing. It was the last business that brought Jessie's parents for a visit
during the early years of their marriage. Lawrence Carr loved the
hunting and fishing and his wife found the cool summer climate
delightful and the town quaint, so on a whim, they ordered a
summer cottage built overlooking the ocean on one of the highest points of land on the west coast of America. They lived long
enough to visit it once.

My heart beat faster in anticipation. My mind's eye conjured
up a tender family scene—Aunt Victoria, Henry, Ross, and the

twins, Caroline and Valerie, gathered on the platform to greet me as we arrived at the Dexter station. I'd rehearsed my little speech, a longer version of the one I'd given the trustees in Sacramento, along with a heartfelt apology for the worries I'd caused and a promise to make it up to them. I would acknowledge their doubts and encourage their questions so I could prove myself quickly. I expected a trick or two, something along the order of the fake grandmother, and braced mentally for the challenge. With luck, I'd be a genuine member of the family by the end of the evening.

We disembarked that afternoon onto a wooden platform at Dexter's train station. Our porter deposited the bags in the shade of the eaves, and we joined them there just as a thin bald man ambled over and introduced himself. His name was Clyde. I had no idea if I should know Clyde or not. Oliver had not mentioned him in the lecture on servants, so I waited with bated breath for a cue from Clyde himself.

"Welcome home, Miss Carr," he said unhelpfully, lifting his hat to Grandmother and me.

"Clyde, is it?" Sir Oliver rode to my rescue. "Have we met? I have visited a number of times but am sorry I don't remember you, my good man. I'm Oliver Beckett, Miss Carr's uncle."

"No, sir, Mr. Beckett. We've not met. I've been driving for Mrs. Carr for a few years now, but I didn't live in Dexter when Young Miss was here. The flivver's over there," he said with a jerk of his head toward a spanking clean Ford sedan. "It'll hold you folks fine but I'll have to come back for the luggage."

I had little chance to take stock of Dexter other than to notice that the main street was planked and the others were dirt. Soon we had left the city limits, and were heading south on a narrow macadam road that led through a woodland of tall firs and spruce trees. The air was cool and clean. I filled my lungs with the citrus-and-spice fragrance of the forest that grew almost to the edge of the pavement, like dark green walls lining a long passageway. For a moment the trees cleared on my side and I was startled to see how high we had climbed. I glimpsed Dexter far below, looking like a child's toy village smothered with spun glass. Then the evergreen curtain closed and it was gone.

We turned a bend in the road and nearly ran down two children.

I yelled "Stop!" at the same moment that Clyde smashed his foot on the brake, yanked the brake lever, and skidded to the right, missing the boys by inches. With a mild oath, he threw open his door as they descended upon us, eyes wide with fear, gesturing frantically and yelling.

Both youngsters shouted at the same time, their words tangling together so that nothing could be understood. They pointed toward the woods with their fishing poles . . . something about a woman. A dead woman.

"There! Over there! In there!" The boy, no older than ten, with a runny nose and grimy face, gestured but would not leave the road to show us.

We couldn't see anything from the road. Clyde and I climbed out of the car. He hesitated a moment at the edge of the pavement before stepping into the tall grass. "Stay here," he ordered.

I followed.

It took all of five steps to find her.

"Maybe she's not . . ." I offered hopefully.

But she was.

If she had been wearing red or yellow, someone would have seen her from the road before now, but her faded clothing was brown and the grass was knee high. Her body was crumpled like one of Marchetti's Marionettes, carelessly cast into the wings after the show was over. Dark braids did not obscure her face, which was so black with dried blood that her own mother would not have recognized her. Stage blood, I noted, was a lot redder than the real thing. The woman's neck bent at an impossible angle and flies swarmed on the blood. My first thought was that she had been walking with the boys, been hit by a car, and thrown into the woods by the force of the impact.

"Holy Mary Mother of God," said Clyde.

I felt sick and turned away, nearly colliding with Grandmother. Oliver was not far behind. "Don't look," I said, but it was too late.

"Two days. Maybe three," she said in her matter-of-fact way.

I knew what she meant. "How do you know?"

"There were corpses everywhere after the quake in aught six, and we knew exactly how long they'd been there."

My eyes returned reluctantly to the gruesome sight. This time I noticed the strings of small shell beads around her broken neck. White, yellow, and blue. And something else. "Look, Grandmother. Her hair." One of her plaits was neatly finished with beads tied to the ends. The other, shorter plait had none. The beaded tip had been cut off.

"Get in the car, boys," I ordered. "Clyde, where is the nearest police station?"

Oliver got into the front while Grandmother and I squeezed together to make room for the boys in the back. Within seconds, Clyde had turned the car around on that narrow road and was heading downhill, back to the planked main street of Dexter. I took a few deep breaths and Grandmother surprised me by squeezing my hand.

"You're not going to be sick, are you?" she asked me quietly.

"No. But I admit I'm shocked. I haven't seen a lot of dead people in my life. Certainly not murdered ones."

"It's a terrible thing," she agreed. But she remained composed, and I thought, what a tough old bird! How could Oliver think that her mind was wandering?

At the police station, Officer Wainwright worried his moustache as the boys delivered their garbled accounts. I added that she looked Indian. He noted all our names, then sent the boys home before picking up the telephone. "Millie, honey," he said to the operator, "get me Doc Milner, there's a good girl." After a short exchange, the two men arranged to meet at once on the south road about two miles out of town.

Wainwright followed us in the police car, back to the place where the girl's body lay.

"Yep, she's Indian all right. Looks like some redskin on the warpath drank a little too much firewater and beat up his squaw," he said with a rueful twitch of his lips after he had seen the corpse. "Sorry you ladies had to see that. But we'll handle everything now." A sedan approached and a gray-haired gentleman in a dark suit and fedora climbed out. His black bag left no doubt as to his identity. "Here's Doc Milner now. You all go on home. We'll be in touch if we need to ask any questions, but I don't think that will be necessary." He turned his back on us as he led the doctor into the grass.

Over his shoulder, he said, "Not a very nice welcome home, is it, Miss Carr?"

13

When rich people say "summer cottage," they don't mean a shack in the woods that brings you closer to nature. The Carr summer cottage stood three stories tall, with wings forming three sides of a square, and every board of it made of Oregon timber as befitted the home of an Oregon lumber baron. Except for the stone chimneys on each end, the entire mansion was painted banana yellow and white—a celestial invitation perhaps, for the sun to burn through the clouds that so often overstayed their welcome along this coast. Located near the edge of a cliff, the place even had a name—Cliff House, what else?

Clyde transported us in silence to Cliff House and deposited us at the foot of a flight of limestone steps where I saw how generously Uncle Oliver could tip with other people's money. As Clyde turned the Ford around and headed back to the station for our luggage, I quietly pulled off my gloves, reached into my pocketbook for the dog biscuit I'd brought, and rubbed it on my fingers and under my nails. Something I'd learned from Al Gordon and his Comedy Canines.

At that moment the front door flew open and Aunt Victoria Carr bustled down the steps.

"Jessie! Oh, Jessie, Jessie, Jessie!" was all she could say as she pressed me to her gardenia-scented bosom and wept genuine tears. She tore herself away long enough to greet Oliver and Grandmother, then ushered us into the house, her arm tight around my shoulder as if she would never let me go again. I pushed aside the twinge of conscience I felt at deceiving her. I couldn't afford scruples in this gig.

As Oliver had instructed, we refrained from mentioning the dead Indian girl, although she was certainly foremost in all our minds. There would be time for that later, he'd said in the car. It was a delicate subject. He would break the news to Aunt Victoria when they were alone and let her decide whether or not to tell the twins. She was very protective of the twins, now sixteen years old.

A lively fire in the parlor fireplace chased the chill from the air. Someone had filled a fat cinnabar vase with bloodred roses.

"Luncheon will be served momentarily, but you must be thirsty after that long journey," said Aunt Victoria, fluttering her fingers at a maid who correctly interpreted the gesture and ran off. Her voice was cultured and her dark eyes steady as they examined me. "Jessie, Jessie, Jessie. Let me look at you! My, you have grown. Or . . . actually, you haven't grown very much, have you? But you do look older, and so very pretty! Oh, my, I can only think of my dear sister-in-law Blanche at this moment, with that beautiful auburn hair!" She lifted a strand of my long hair and admired it. "You look so very much like her. How she hated those freckles! Oh, but of course they look utterly charming on you, dear."

Aunt Victoria was a pleasant woman, neither plain nor beautiful, neither tall nor short, neither fat nor thin. Her light brown hair had been braided German-style into two side plaits that she had wrapped over the top of her head like a halo. It made me think of the German peasant act, Holstein and Schmidt, the one that had prudently gone Dutch during the Great War.

I made the right responses. It was good to be home, I had come to miss the family, I was glad to—

The girls tumbled into the room, saw me, and froze.

Valerie and Caroline were identical twins bent on denying the obvious. What they couldn't disguise—their impossibly long legs, their light brown hair, and their hazel eyes—they did their best to camouflage by accentuating their differences. Caroline had cut her hair into a boyish bob that cupped at the chin; Valerie, the more traditional one, let hers ripple down her back in soft, feminine waves. They had not dressed alike today, and I was soon proven correct in my supposition that they never did: Caroline preferred bright primary colors and straight waist cuts while Valerie tended toward flouncy florals, lace, and pastel hues. Perhaps once upon a time they had been provoked to the edge of insult by the inability of others to tell them apart.

From the way they stared, I might have been a sideshow freak. Aunt Victoria gave them a parental nudge.

"Manners, please, girls. This is Jessie's grandmother, Mrs. Beckett. And you remember Mr. Oliver Beckett—he used to visit with us quite often in the old days, when Jessie was young." They bobbed curtsies to Grandmother, acknowledged Uncle Oliver with a hello as flat as old soda water, and turned back toward me.

"I suspect we've all changed in the past seven years," I began. "But I'd recognize you two anywhere. You're taller, and almost grown-up, I see."

"Were you really an *actress* all these years?" Valerie blurted, making the word sound like a synonym for "prostitute."

"Not exactly. I was a vaudeville performer. Sometimes I acted in short plays, but more often I danced or sang. Once I was a magician's assistant."

Valerie whispered something into her sister's ear, and they giggled. Maybe it was my makeup. No one here wore any at all.

"Do come in and sit down, girls," Aunt Victoria said as the maid appeared with a tray of lemonade.

We perched on friendly chintz furniture in a room that could have come straight off the set of Oscar Wilde's *Lady Windermere's Fan*. A large Coromandel screen in one corner balanced the grand piano on the opposite side of the room. A stack of magazines lay on the coffee table, and a dainty French writing desk by the largest window took advantage of the light. Several potted ferns and a great many china ornaments provided decoration. A canary chirped from his cage in the corner. I had never seen a lovelier room.

As Grandmother was settling herself into a Martha Washington chair by the fire where she could doze unobserved, a cocker spaniel ambled into the room.

"Oh, look, it's King! Hello, King, darling, do you remember me?" I dropped to my knees on the rug and prayed he wouldn't bite my outstretched hand.

King sniffed and licked my fingers, his tail wagging enthusiastically until he figured out I was all scent and no food and moved on to the hearth rug. His performance lacked a certain enthusiasm, but it passed muster.

The planter by the window caught my eye. Amidst a tangle of philodendron leaves were several glass balls of varying sizes, hollow, green, and handblown. "Did I find all these?" I wondered aloud. "Or have you added to the collection in the last few years?" Without waiting for a reply, I picked one up and found the rough glassblower's mark. "Look! My thumb still fits!"

Out of the corner of my eye, I saw Uncle Oliver's shocked expression and slack jaw. Before I had time to wonder what horrible mistake I had just made, my attention was directed behind me to the doorway where the two young men of the family were standing.

The photographs I had seen of the Carr brothers were several years old but there was no mistaking these two. Henry was not only the firstborn of Aunt Victoria's four children, he was the tallest, the strongest, the handsomest, and probably his mother's favorite. Athletic as a youth, he now had a thickening middle that revealed a bad case of rich man's belly in the making, and I imagined him growing in girth over the next few years until he matched His Rotund Highness, Uncle Oliver Beckett.

Now he stood at the threshold, pale as paste, with one foot planted in the hall and the other in the parlor like some gangster ready to make a quick getaway the second the shooting started. I had the distinct impression that he was afraid of me. Why? What had I said to frighten him like that? I pushed the absurd thought aside as I replaced the green globe. "Hello, Henry," I said carefully, waiting to see what he was waiting for.

The silent standoff was broken by Ross, who pushed past his older brother and entered the room, hands clenched in the pockets of his baggy oxfords and lips curled like a man confronted with a bad smell. With his saddle shoes, baggy cuffed oxfords, crisp shirt, and bow tie, he looked like an actor playing the part of a college student.

"Well, well," he said at last. "It's Jessie, is it?" Like a casting director at an audition, he scrutinized my every feature without bothering to conceal his disparaging expression.

"Yes, it is," I answered firmly. "It's good to see you again, Ross."

A head shorter than his brother, Ross was, at twenty-one, the runt of the litter. He must have taken after his father for I saw nothing of Aunt Victoria in his dark curly hair, green eyes, and thin face. He was the only member of the family to wear spectacles. Thick and round they were, set in dark frames too large for his nose, and I sensed he was hiding behind them, keeping his thoughts safely obscured. If so, he was mistaken—the lenses worked both ways, magnifying whatever emotions he would rather conceal—and I was shaken for a moment at the rage I saw simmering deep inside those emerald pools. He looked like he wanted to strangle me.

"I'll bet it is. Hello, Mrs. Beckett, Mr. Beckett." He held out his hand. The action jolted Henry out of his trance and into a weak semblance of verbal etiquette but he still didn't speak to me. No one did.

I lifted my chin a fraction and took a deep breath. "Since we are all together at last, there is something I'd like to say." Ross glowered. Henry's hand shook as he rubbed his glistening forehead and leaned weakly against the doorjamb as if his legs would give way. Oliver met my eyes but made no outward sign of encouragement.

"I know my return has been a shock to you all," I began, offering my heartfelt regret for the pain I had caused by running away. Apologizing is easy when it comes on behalf of someone else, but I had the advantage of sincerity. I meant every word. I *was* sorry these people had suffered through the disappearance of a child. Anyone would be. "Some of you may have lingering doubts about my identity, which I do not resent in the least. I hope those will be overcome when the trustees' investigation proves everything I have said is true beyond the shadow of a doubt. I understand how awkward my return is, but it need not cause you any material worry. Life will go on just as it has since my parents died. All my family, the Carr side and the Becketts"—here I looked pointedly at Uncle Oliver—"are welcome to live at Cliff House for as long as they like, and I hope you, Aunt Victoria, will continue to manage the household as you have done so capably over the years."

Of course I knew this pretty speech would not mollify the brothers who had just seen several million dollars run through their fingers like water, but I expected it would reassure Aunt Victoria and the girls that they would not lose their home or income. Only my aunt seemed pleased. She smiled with quivering lips, pulled out a lace handkerchief and dabbed her eyes.

"Thank you, Jessie dear." Oliver spoke first, deliberately using my name to set a precedent. "You are your mother's daughter."

The Swiss mantel clock pinged once. Aunt Victoria stood. "You'll want to freshen up before we eat," she said. "Henry, why don't you and Ross help Mrs. Beckett to her room? And you'll have your usual room, Oliver. Yours is the same too, Jessie. We never gave up hope that you would return."

"Thank you, Aunt. I'll go now and wash up."

Up the stairs, turn right at the split landing, then right again at the top. Go to the end of the hall and take the last room on the left. Simple enough. Grandmother was protesting that she wasn't an invalid and didn't need two boys to help her up the stairs, but they and the twins followed along, no doubt to see if I could pass the first test—finding my bedroom.

I could. Opening the door, I stepped confidently into the room where Jessie had slept for three years of her life.

It was exactly as Oliver had described, a corner room with three large windows, but no stage set I had ever seen prepared me for such luxury. Everything matched, as if it had been bought all at once. Lavender and yellow draperies were tied back at the windows to let in the light. Coordinating fabrics dressed the canopy bed and soft chairs. Floral wallpaper covered three walls and a plush yellow carpet covered the floor. Even the roses were yellow, dozens of them, and they filled the air with a fragrance that made me hungry.

The late summer sun streamed in through the window, illuminating a large patch of dust on the floorboards between the rug and the wall, something I thought odd because there was not a speck of dust on any other surface in the entire room. An audience of four watched from the hall with breathless anticipation as I dropped my hat on the settee and examined the room.

The silence was deafening. I felt like I had forgotten my lines and the whole theater full of patrons were at the edge of their seats, waiting to see if I could recover. To stall for time, I walked to the window and looked out, thinking hard.

"Beautiful view," I remarked, but my eyes were blind to the gardens below and the distant sea. Something was up and I needed to figure it out fast. My heart raced. *Think!*

Turning slightly, I let my eyes sweep the room again. This time I noticed two dents in the deep pile rug where heavy furniture legs had recently stood. No one in the audience so much as blinked.

"Excuse me," I said, walking through the cousins into the hall toward the bathroom that I knew was situated at the end of the corridor. "I'll go wash up now. Oh, and Ross, if you don't mind, could you and Henry move my furniture back? I prefer it the way it was."

Even a lady of Aunt Victoria Carr's social accomplishments found lunch a tough slog. Henry stared at his uneaten food as if he were going to be sick, while the other young Carrs maintained a sullen reserve. Grandmother, always quiet, murmured an occasional "How lovely" to show her approval as each course was laid. From the far end of the table, Uncle Oliver, fidgeting with his fork, sent a barrage of furtive glances my way that made it plain I had blundered worrisomely during the opening scene in the parlor. Fortunately, Aunt Victoria had been raised in an era when conversational skills were as important as good bloodlines, and could converse with a potted palm if the occasion required. She prodded the conversation along, lobbing questions back and forth, until I was reminded of a tennis instructor gamely serving balls over the net and waiting for their return.

When she wanted to pause for a bite of poached fish, she aimed a long shot at one of her children.

"Tell Jessie about your studies, Valerie," she commanded, starting with the most biddable. Aunt Victoria was cleverer than I had first judged.

It seems the girls had a tutor, a Mrs. Applewhite, who went away in August to visit her daughter's family in Seattle. She would return shortly to start their final year of algebra, geometry, literature, French, Latin, and history. A music teacher, a china painting instructor, and a riding master came from Portland once a week to "round the girls out." I silently vowed to make myself scarce on riding lesson day.

Once she had the twins speaking to me, the boys could hardly do otherwise without seeming churlish. "Henry, darling, fill Jessie in on your activities since she left," Aunt Victoria directed next, saving the most truculent, Ross, for last. "We are so proud of Henry," she confided, as if he were not sitting inches away. "He's our public servant, or will be after November's elections. Even as a youngster, Henry took an interest in politics—that and sailing were his favorite pastimes, as you remember, no doubt. Why, Henry! With Jessie here, you'll have another vote!"

Henry's favorite subject was himself, and his mother's request pulled him out of his stupor. He warmed to the subject, glossing over his studies at Stanford University and going into greater detail about his many Portland political connections. "Our legislator is retiring at the end of this term, and the party is supporting me for his seat. I've come to know everyone of importance in the state, and they recommend this as the usual way to begin," he said, adding modestly, "Then after a term in the state legislature, I'll step up to governor or perhaps take the national route and become a senator."

"Or president." Aunt Victoria beamed. Oliver choked on a piece of bread.

I smiled and nodded, thinking I'd mark my ballot for Genghis Khan before I'd vote for this smug young man. I'd known Henry only an hour and already I shared Oliver's aversion.

"And what is it you've been doing since you graduated from Stanford?" I asked. The trustees sent money regularly to Aunt Victoria for maintenance of the house and for the family's living expenses, but there was no stipend to keep a grown man in funds over the years.

"I didn't graduate. After three years, I realized there was nothing more they could teach me and I left. One scholar in the family is quite enough."

"Yes, Ross is our future professor," agreed Aunt Victoria. "Tell Jessie what you're doing, Ross."

Using the longest words he could manufacture, Ross outlined his years at Stanford—"magna cum laude," interjected his mother—and his quest for a master's and ultimately a doctorate in history. "I plan to become an academician," he told me, addressing Oliver so as to avoid meeting my eyes. "I've completed the mandatory course requirements for the master's degree and am currently working on my thesis. As soon as I've accomplished those prerequisites, I'll embark on the doctor of philosophy degree."

"Do you want to stay at Stanford to teach?" Oliver asked.

"Yes, and I am quite intent on that. I've mapped my future and feel Stanford is the best place to pursue my ethnographic research into the native tribes of the Northwest."

"It sounds like the perfect career for you," I said. "You look just like a professor." I meant it nicely, but it seems I missed the mark. He glared at his fish knife.

"Now Jessie, turnabout's fair play," said Aunt Victoria. "I know the girls are famished for details of your vaudeville days."

Finding the dead Indian woman had robbed me of my appetite, so it was no trouble laying aside my fork and folding my hands in my lap. "I've been involved with several acts during the past seven years," I began. "Most recently I was with the Little Darlings. It was—well, it still is—a family act that combines dancing, singing, and short comedy routines into a fourteen-minute program. Until I left, there were seven Little Darlings plus Jock and Francine, the parents. Only three of the children were theirs, the rest of us were paid. I was Carrie Darling, the second child."

"You mean they *said* they were all one family, but they weren't?" Valerie made it sound as if the Darlings had been caught robbing banks. She seemed quite the infant for sixteen.

"That's common in vaudeville. Most acts are formed to maximize talent. The Seven Little Foys are all genuine Foys, but that's rare."

"You're almost twenty-one! How could you play a little girl?" wondered Valerie.

"That was my specialty. My size gives me a young appearance anyway, but the right makeup, clothing, and braids make me look positively juvenile, especially from a distance."

"And you sang songs and danced in front of hundreds of people?"

"You get used to it. If you like, I'll teach you a number one day and we'll perform for the family."

"Oh, no! I couldn't!"

"I could!" Caroline chimed in. Ah, the dramatic one in the family. I could make use of that later.

Once I had started, the twins couldn't get enough of vaudeville. The boys feigned boredom, but I noticed they were listening as attentively as their sisters. And I knew why. They were looking for something that would trip me up.

"The two youngest Little Darlings are brothers," I told the girls. "Just five and six."

"You don't say! Imagine such babies performing onstage! I wish I could see them sometime. Where are they now?"

"I don't honestly know . . . probably in the upper Midwest this time of year . . . but it's easy to find out. You just buy a copy of

Billboard or *Variety* or one of the vaudeville newspapers on sale at any theater or hotel and you can read who's playing in the two-a-days all over the country. We could check to see if they are scheduled to come to Portland again, then go see them."

At that remark, some of Uncle Oliver's water sloshed out of its glass, but only I noticed. I couldn't explain to him that the statement was a safe bet. The odds of the Little Darlings playing in Oregon in the next couple of months were slim to none, and by autumn we'd both be Somewhere Else. Even so, it seemed I had strayed from the approved script once again.

"What are two-a-days?" asked Caroline.

"Sorry, that's just vaudeville talk for Big Time. It means the good theaters where you only have to perform twice a day. Usually a matinee and an evening show, or sometimes two evening shows. Playing Small Time can mean four or five or even six."

Aunt Victoria stood, signifying the end of luncheon. "Well, I see there will be no dull conversations at mealtime in this house! Jessie, why don't you take your grandmother for a turn in the garden? I'll join you in a jiffy."

"Yes, Jessie, you remember the garden," said Ross, taking off his eyeglasses and wiping the lenses with his handkerchief. "One of your favorite places to take a book."

Without his cheaters in the way, Ross's eyes rivaled Valentino's for dreamy beauty. A girl would die for those long sooty lashes that curled at the tips. I was not, however, so distracted that I missed his trap.

"I don't remember being much of a reader," I replied. "The garden does look lovely—I caught a glimpse of it from my bedroom window—but you had only the trellised roses along the chimneys when I was here, isn't that right, Aunt Victoria?"

"Exactly so," she agreed. "I had the wall built shortly after you left—that alone took six months, then it took three more years before the plantings were finished. Not that I could ever call a garden finished. Gardens are works in progress, your uncle Charles used to say." At the mention of her late husband, she gave a sigh. "Dear me, I do miss him."

"The trustees told me, of course, that Uncle Charles had passed away. I am so sorry. They said it was about a year after I left."

"On December 9, 1918, at 2:14 P.M., his spirit left him for a far better world," she said, placing one hand on her bosom in the dramatic fashion of an old-time actress preparing to recite. "He'd been ill for so many years, it was hardly what you could call a surprise, but . . . well, I find one is usually surprised at death even when one expects it."

Grandmother and I exchanged a long glance. Death had certainly surprised us a few short hours ago. I wondered what had become of the corpse by now. Poor girl. I could only imagine her family's grief.

"Would you like a turn in the garden, Grandmother?"

"I believe I would."

I was headed upstairs to fetch her shawl when I heard a hiss. There, lurking in an alcove below the staircase was Oliver, gesturing wildly. Mindful of his warning that we not be seen talking alone, I looked about to make sure we were unobserved.

"What is it? Whatever is the matter? You needn't worry about the Little Darlings showing up in Portland, and I don't know what I said wrong in the parlor when the boys walked in."

"Who told you that?" he demanded. "Who told you about putting your thumb in the glass mark?"

"My thumb? Uh, you did, of course. You told me about the green glass floats and how they were made in Japan. Don't you remember?"

"Yes, yes, but not the thumb!" he rasped. "I never told you that. I couldn't have told you. I didn't remember it myself until you came out with it. I'd completely forgotten that Jessie used to say that."

"Well, I wouldn't make something like that up out of whole cloth. Are you sure you didn't tell me?"

"Of course I'm sure," he said, eyeing me warily.

"Stop looking at me like that! I'm not Jessie!"

"Then how did you know?"

"Coincidence. It's a natural progression of thought. Pick up the glass ball and your thumb fits in the sealing mark. Anyone would say it. Calm down, you're overreacting."

Oliver pulled out a handkerchief and dabbed his brow. "Maybe." Then his face took on a crafty look, and his puffy eyes narrowed to slits. "Just don't get ahead of yourself, girl. We're playing this by my rules, not yours."

I held up my hands in innocent protest. "Of course."

"I've invested too much time and money in you to have this endeavor fall short. Oh, I know what you've been thinking all along, that if things get rough or you don't like the way the game is going, you'll just slip away clean as soap. Well, think again, my precious niece. We're in this to the end, and you'll dance to my tune for as long as I play it. Succeed and I can be generous. Fail or leave me and I'll send a copy of your pretty new photograph to *Variety* and the rest of those weeklies with a notice about your criminal activities and no one will touch you with a ten-foot stage hook. You'll never work again."

Too numb to respond, I walked away, no longer very clear about why I was going up the stairs but very much aware of Oliver's eyes boring into my back at every step. Never mind how, he knew, and with one simple threat had blocked my exit. He had understood all along that I could change my mind about this swindle and leave him high and dry. So he had devised a way to keep me in the game by cutting off my only escape route. With one stroke, he could prevent me from ever working again in the only business I knew. I was trapped.

15

"Oliver is telling your aunt about the dead woman," said Grandmother, her shoes crunching along the marl path that led around the west side of Cliff House toward the garden gate. "Finally. She won't want the twins to know."

"She can hardly expect to keep that sort of thing a secret. Surely it will be in the newspapers and discussed all over town."

"Those girls seem quite sheltered. She's concerned the news will frighten them."

"I don't know why it should," I said, holding the gate open for Grandmother. "It has nothing to do with us."

Someone had built the garden wall by taking thousands of flat rocks and laying them one upon another, fitting them together like pieces of a jigsaw puzzle so skillfully that no mortar was needed to hold them in place. Standing on my toes, I could peer over the top and see a wall of another sort, a forest of young trees that formed a barrier between the garden and the edge of the cliff. Beyond lay the Pacific Ocean.

The rhythmic wash of waves on the beach might have penetrated the woods or the rock wall, but not both. Only the birds chirping and the splashing of a nearby fountain broke a heavy silence. It struck me as odd that Jessie's parents would build a house on the edge of the world to overlook the ocean, and Aunt Victoria would devote years to blocking both its sound and view. But Lawrence and Blanche Carr had died in a boating accident, so perhaps the association was unpleasant for her.

Some of the garden had been divided into trim flower beds, but a good deal of the space was given over to flowering bushes and trees. I recognized the roses—one sees plenty of roses at opening or closing performances—but the rest of the garden was as much a mystery to me as the stock market. Grandmother and I meandered along one pathway for a while.

"Those boys are going to give you the devil," she said abruptly. "But it won't last. The oldest doesn't spend much time here and the puny one will return to Stanford soon."

And I thought she'd dozed through the meal. It was comforting to have someone on my side. I breathed deeply. The scent was unfamiliar, an intoxicating mix of roses and other blossoms. A chorus of bees hummed their one-note tune.

"You can't expect them to be pleased by my return. I'm sure Henry had big plans for Father's money. Probably intended to finance his political career that way. I can't imagine such an officious prig appealing to voters, though, can you? And did you notice he avoided answering my question about what he does for a living?"

She gave a sage nod. "Makes you wonder how such a young man came so far so fast, doesn't it? But the other one . . . Ross . . . I'm wary of deep thinkers. I wouldn't turn my back on him in the dark." The path took us to a fancy fountain planted in the hub of the garden like something from Versailles. Our arrival frightened a dozen small birds away from their bath. "What will you do?" Grandmother asked.

Most elderly women are sentimental, even maudlin. Not Grandmother. She was plainspoken and kept any emotions hidden behind a placid expression. So it was odd that I could sense her thoughts. I knew exactly what she was asking.

"I've not yet decided. But I think, after my birthday, I'd like to travel a bit, return to Europe and see some of the places we lived when I was a child."

"You'll probably live there."

"Perhaps."

"It would be best." It would? I wondered why she thought that, but before I could ask she went on. "You were smart to stay away until you came into your inheritance. I still have your last letter."

"Oh?"

"You remember what you wrote in it?"

"It's been a long time . . ."

"You said your cousin had tried to kill you."

16

There you are," called Aunt Victoria, striding toward us, a Kashmiri shawl thrown over her high-collared white shirt-waist. Ramrod posture gave her an elegance that was heightened by her loyalty to the fashions of her youth, long before the Great War years had conspired to shorten skirts, banish corsets, and bob hair.

"Oliver has just informed me about your gruesome experience on the road. How perfectly dreadful for you! I am certain the police will have identified the poor woman by now, and will soon have her killer in custody. Don't mention it to the girls, will you? No need to frighten them unnecessarily. Tsk-tsk. What is the world coming to? Dead girls on the side of the road! Well, maybe it was a fall that killed her after all. Or a heart attack. Still, it must have been an awful shock."

The effort of pretending away murder while I carried on this introductory charade had exhausted me, dulling my mind so much that I could scarcely wrap my thoughts around Grandmother's latest revelation. One of the cousins had tried to kill young Jessie seven years ago? If Oliver knew about this attempt, he had not seen fit to mention it to me. But why would he have known what was in Jessie's letter to her grandmother? It seemed there were more gaps in Oliver's knowledge than I originally thought.

"I suppose we'll read about it in the newspaper eventually," worried Aunt Victoria. "I do hope they don't mention your names. That would be too dreadful." Then, remembering her duties as hostess, she smoothed her brow and adopted a cheerful tone, saying, "Well now, do let me show you around the garden."

"The flowers are splendid," said Grandmother. "Decent gardeners are impossible to find in San Francisco."

"Ours is a Chinaman. A real jewel, even if he is foreign. I hired him to start a kitchen garden—those Orientals are so good at growing herbs and vegetables—and you see what has come of that in only five years!" Catching no glimpse of the Chinaman, she continued, "Chen must be working around back in the kitchen garden today. The tennis court is back there too. Maybe you remember when we were planning it, Jessie, just before you left?"

I nodded in a vague way. Which cousin had tried to kill young Jessie? Henry or Ross? Surely not one of the twins. How was I going to find out what was in that letter?

"Vegetables on the south side," commented Grandmother. "You need lots of sun for vegetables."

"And rain. As you can imagine, we get plenty of that. We grow most of our own herbs and vegetables now. The squash we just ate was grown right here."

"I've never seen asters this tall," said Grandmother.

Aunt Victoria preened as if she did the work herself, taking as much pride in her gardens as she did in her children. "I wanted purple in that spot. I tried lavender but this climate proved too wet for lavender. However, the fall asters thrive there."

Around the south side of the house lay the vegetable garden with its neat rows of staked tomato vines and string beans, lettuces, lacy carrot tops, and a dozen herbs whose names I had never heard. For a lifelong city girl whose closest look at crops had been from a train window, this was all very intriguing. I'd never admit in a million years that I hadn't realized carrots grew underground.

Chen the Chinaman rose from his knees in the herb patch to present us with a solemn bow. I hardly saw his face beneath the wide coolie hat woven from tough grass, but I noted the absence of a queue. Male Chinese performers I had known on the circuit—Fong and Tang, the Chinese Flowers, Shanghai Circus, the Mandarins—had all worn queues, something I thought their religion or culture required. Evidently not.

As the ladies rhapsodized over the vegetables, my mind circled back to Grandmother's letter. Had Jessie been seriously at odds with Ross or Henry, I wondered, or was she just upset about some childish prank that got out of hand? What could they have done that she would make an accusation like that? Shoved her off a swing? Surely it was just roughhousing or tough talk. Then I wondered uneasily just *when* Jessie had written this letter. A year before she had disappeared or a week before? If it had been a short time before she went missing, it put an entirely different light on the matter. Had Grandmother mentioned this at the time of the search? Could it be linked to her disappearance? Had one of the boys threatened Jessie or frightened her away? What exactly had she said in that letter? And more to the point, was she prone to melodrama or exaggeration? I was stuck. I could hardly ask Grandmother Beckett about a letter I had supposedly written myself.

We spent an hour meandering about the gardens, pausing for rest on wrought-iron benches, chatting like old friends about the price of beef—I had little to contribute here—and the difficulty of finding and keeping servants who didn't rob you blind—ditto there. But I knew how to listen and cluck in dismay at the right time. Playing a civilian was turning out to be a manageable role. It was the sinister undercurrent of death that made me wonder whether this charade was going to be as easy as Oliver had promised.

17

My first night in Jessie's soft bed, now pushed back against the interior wall where it had always stood, was a restless one. Visions of the dead Indian girl, crumpled up and thrown away like so much trash, kept me at the edge of wakefulness all night. When I finally dozed off, I slipped into a disturbing dream where young Jessie was standing next to my bed, talking to me. I couldn't understand her because her voice was miles away in some clammy, dark place, even through she herself was quite close. I thought when I saw her that she was dead too, just like the Indian girl. Then Jessie was the Indian girl; then she wasn't.

I woke knowing I was dreaming, not seeing a ghost. With Jessie occupying my every waking moment, it was no surprise that she had started sharing my dreams as well as my routine. I had heard of a Broadway actor who, after playing the same role on stage for years, began to have trouble distinguishing his character's personality from his own. Eventually he abandoned himself to the role and became the person he portrayed on stage. It didn't seem as incredible to me now as it once had.

I was becoming Jessie and living her life. But I couldn't shake the feeling that she wanted me to know something about a dark, damp place. A cellar? *Hurry*, I sensed she was saying. *Hurry*.

I gave up trying to sleep when a young girl with a likable face and a tray of coffee and warm cinnamon bread knocked at my door. Lorraine, her name was, and she was newly hired. My own maid! Grandmother had one too. This was the life of Riley, I thought, propped up against a pile of pillows like a harem girl and drinking my coffee with thick cream and sugar while Lorraine looked through my valise for something suitable for me to wear this morning.

Five weeks until I could return to Sacramento to sign off on my inheritance. Five weeks and one day until I could leave for a long tour of Europe. I wiggled my toes and stretched against the cool linens. During those weeks, this city girl would spend her time reading some of the books in that lovely library and exploring the countryside. Starting today. Shoving the real Jessamyn Carr out of my head, I reminded myself sternly that I was in this for the money. I couldn't back out now. A brand-new life. Security forever. The fate of the missing heiress was none of my concern.

Coffee and rolls was not breakfast, mind you, it was just to tide one over until the morning repast in the dining room, served buffet style in the English tradition. Meal consumed, I was planning to fetch a sweater and head to the cliff when Caroline—short hair—asked, "Do you want to come to the stables with us, Jessie? Val and I are riding this morning."

No danger there. Jessie's pet horse had died a couple years ago. My eyes had grown misty last night when Valerie—long hair—told me about it. Yet I sensed the girls were up to something.

"Certainly," I said gamely, figuring it was best to get these little incidents out of the way so I could relax in my role.

Uncle Oliver did not ride and had never set foot in the stables, so he knew nothing of the animals or the groom except his name. "Since Anton was hired fairly recently," he told me, "you needn't worry about him." So I was not worrying as I followed the twins to the stables.

The path led through a patch of woods thick with ferns, down a hill, and over a tiny stream we crossed with a single leap. As we approached, I could see the groom in a paddock brushing down one of the horses, his powerful arms sweeping across the animal's flanks with a sense of confident familiarity I could not achieve if I lived to ninety. His back was to us, but I could see he was fair and tall, a powerfully built man. We were quite close before he heard us and turned.

"Buster!" exclaimed Caroline. "What are you doing here today? Where's Anton?"

Buster's grin revealed a number of missing teeth. Dropping the brush, he wrapped his arms around his own broad shoulders in a happy hug. "Hey, Miss Caroline. Hey, Miss Valerie," he said, his voice low and his speech deliberate. When he looked at me, the grin grew to a mile-wide smile. "Hey, Miss Jessie. I heard you come back." And as I met his eye, he gave me an exaggerated wink.

It was not a lascivious wink; it was a friendly one that begged for a response. Not knowing quite why, I winked back. "Hey, Buster," I said in a conspiratorial tone of voice.

"How is my darling Star today?" Caroline was crooning and kissing her horse's nose as she threw a question over her shoulder. "Where's Anton? This isn't his day off."

Buster thought long before answering. "Anton sick. I heard Miss Jessie come back. I knew you come back, Miss Jessie. I knew it."

Success in vaudeville depends on quick reaction to every unexpected turn of events, so dealing with a sudden script change was nothing shocking. I considered my next move. Buster was not the regular groom, Buster was simpleminded, and Buster had known Jessie. Slow didn't mean stupid. I needed to tread softly.

With a noisy clatter, the girls began hauling bridles and blankets out of the tack room and, with Buster's help, outfitted the appropriate beasts. I was introduced to Star, who had a white patch on her forehead, Socks, who had two white feet, Lady, a placid mare with a back as wide as a Windsor chair, Blackie, a black gelding, and Chestnut, who was reddish brown. Excessive imagination did not seem to be a Carr family trait.

The girls' plan was transparent—to test whether or not I could ride like Jessie.

"Won't you come with us on Mother's horse?" Valerie asked with a sly look at her sister. "We could saddle him while you run back to the house and change." Ah, the little angels were going to try to pass off one of the friskier geldings as their mother's horse when it was obviously the mare.

I declined with regret, citing my lack of riding habit. "I'm looking forward to taking a walk along the cliff on my first day home. I haven't seen the ocean in a long time."

"I don't suppose you'd fit into your old riding habits?" asked Caroline.

I looked bewildered.

"Your clothes are all still in your room. Mother wouldn't throw anything out. Didn't you look in the wardrobe and drawers?"

"It never occurred to me. But I shouldn't think anything would fit. I may not have grown much but I have grown." I could postpone this but not sidestep it, so I decided I might as well make it happen to suit myself. "I'll try to come up with something so I can go with you another time."

"Jessie, have you heard of Anastasia?" asked Caroline.

"Who?"

"The Grand Duchess Anastasia of Russia, who was murdered by the Reds at the end of the Great War with the czar and her whole family."

"Oh, yes, of course. Very sad. What about her?"

"She came back, you know. She says she wasn't really dead,

only wounded. A soldier rescued her. She reminds me of you. She says she is Anastasia but not everyone believes her. Some people say—"

I finished for her. "They say she's just after the money."

"Henry and Ross say you're not Jessie."

"And what do you think?"

Each girl looked at the ground and waited for the other to reply.

"You will all know for certain when the trustees complete their investigation."

"When will that be?"

"Soon, I hope. I'd rather my cousins believed me, as do my grandmother, my uncle, and your mother. Anastasia's case is quite different. She has no near relatives left who can identify her or ask her questions that only the real Anastasia could answer. They were all killed by the Reds. I can prove I'm Jessie because I know things only Jessie would know."

"Like what?"

"Like your eighth birthday present was a pony you named Muffin. And that your Mother used to read to us from the Oz books at bedtime. Caroline's favorite was *Ozma of Oz*. I forget your favorite, Valerie."

The twins gaped like carp. "How did you know that?" Caroline gasped.

"Only one way," I said. Buster was standing next to Star with one huge hand cupped to give Caroline a leg up. He hoisted her into the saddle as if she weighed no more than a kitten. "Now go on, have a good ride. I'm going for a walk."

Still speechless, the girls took off at a sedate trot. I waited for them to get out of earshot before I turned to Buster with an encouraging smile. Time to find out what he knew.

"It's good to see you again, Buster."

"I knew you come back." He gave a broad wink as he began collecting the currycombs and brushes.

I winked back. "You're still working here," I said.

"I come Sundays. And sometimes Anton sick."

"I'm glad you're still here."

I followed him inside. It was a spacious building with eight stalls, five horses, a tack room, a tiny apartment for the groom, and a loft. He pointed to an empty stall.

"She gone."

He meant Jessie's horse. "Yes, I heard. I was very sad."

"Old."

"Yes. Did you bury her?"

"In the field. I love them."

The horses. "Yes, I know. They love you."

"They love me." A calico barn cat wove in and out between his legs, purring contentedly. "I knew you come back." He bent to stroke the cat, then looked up at me with a frown. "I kep' the treasure safe."

"You did?"

"You want to see? I kep' it safe."

He showed me to a small corner room furnished with an iron bed and washstand. The walls were not finished, just studs and outside clapboards, but Buster reached up to a spot just below the ceiling where a board had been nailed between two studs, creating a hidden pocket. Without a crowbar or anything but his bare hands, he wrenched the board away. Behind it was a box about the size of three books, coated with seven years of dirt.

The sudden motion also tore off a wasps' nest that had been concealed in the compartment, releasing a swarm of furious insects bent on revenge. Buster snatched the box, and we made a dash for the stable door, swatting at our attackers as we ran. Outside at last, we lost them.

I collapsed on the grass, panting. "Did they get you?" I cried, taking stock of my own injuries. "They got my arm twice. And my ankle, right through my stocking."

Buster crouched beside me, holding out the box for me to take. His hands revealed several stings.

"Stay here," he said. "I know what to do." And before I could caution him, he headed back to the stables.

Left alone, I opened the clasp on the box. It was full of agates—blue, green, red, pink, white—all collected, I presumed, by Jessie and Buster seven or eight years ago. There were also several large glass beads of a kind I had never seen. Clear with tiny, multicolored flowers inside, they seemed an artistic miracle. Beneath them all was a lock of auburn hair tied with a scrap of ribbon.

Just then, Buster emerged from the stables carrying a tin cup in one hand and a toothbrush and an orange box of baking soda in the other. "They all gone now. I know what to do."

"The agates are so pretty," I said, as he stirred some baking soda into the water with the end of his toothbrush until he had a thick paste. "And these colored beads are beautiful!"

"Bennis beads."

"Bennis beads?"

"You said they are Bennis beads."

"I don't remember," I said.

"I remember."

The big man stopped stirring and sat beside me on the grass. Wordlessly, he set the tin cup between us and began smearing the paste on his hands. I did the same, dabbing it on my arm where one of the wretches had gotten me but good. To reach the sting on my ankle, I removed my shoe and rolled down my stocking. Buster's eyes followed my every move, locking onto my bare foot and growing wider and wider as I applied the baking soda.

I guessed he didn't see a lot of female bare feet. "One of 'em got me good here," I said, but Buster remained awkwardly silent. I glanced up at his face. His mouth hung open, his eyes bulged. He looked at me like I had some awful disease.

"You're not Jessie. You're not Jessie. Where is Jessie?"

"What do you mean, Buster? Of course I'm Jessie."

"You're not Jessie." He scrambled backward like a crab, repeating the words over and over, louder each time. I nearly panicked, fearing he would leap up and run to the main house, shouting all the way that I was an imposter.

"Wait, Buster! Wait! Don't go! Tell me why I'm not Jessie."

He paused and squinted down at my foot. It was something to do with my bare ankle.

Finally he pointed and said, "Jessie has red on her foot there. You're not Jessie."

"Oh, that. The red place. It went away."

"You're not Jessie. I want Jessie to come home."

Here it was my first full day, and I'd blown the con. Jessie had some sort of red mark on her foot. A birthmark probably. Oliver would never have known. Buster knew. He must have walked barefoot with Jessie along the shore, hunting these very agates. He knew about the birthmark.

And if he went up to the house now and blabbed, the whole swindle was over.

"Wait! Wait, Buster. Come sit here beside me and let me tell you the secret. You can keep a secret, right? You kept the treasure secret all those years."

"Jessie's treasure." Glaring at me, he snatched the box out of my hands and clutched it to his chest, but at least he didn't run off.

"Sit with me, and I'll tell you the secret."

Slowly, he lowered himself to the ground.

I took a deep breath. "You're right, Buster. I'm not Jessie. I couldn't fool you, could I? But I'm pretending to be Jessie, so I can find her. You could help me find Jessie, if you would. You'd like that, wouldn't you?"

He did not respond.

"I'm trying to figure out where Jessie went. You knew about her treasure. You might know where she went. Did she tell you where she was going? Did she give you her treasure to keep until she returned?"

Buster pulled up bits of grass and let the wind carry them away. He did not look at me.

"You love Jessie, right?"

His eyes filled with water, but still he said nothing.

"I love Jessie too. Maybe together we can find her."

Just saying the words released a weight from my soul. After weeks of pretending that Jessie's fate was none of my concern, I had admitted the truth. Maybe it was because we shared the pain of being orphaned at a young age; maybe it was the way I had immersed myself in her life. Whatever the reason, I despised the way Uncle Oliver waved his niece aside like an unpleasant smell. So she wasn't sweet and demure; she was scrappy and tough. I liked her all the more for it. In vaudeville, they'd say she had heart. I wanted to know what had happened to Jessie.

"Buster, did Jessie tell you she was leaving?"

He shook his head mournfully.

"Tell me about Jessie. Did you hunt agates together?"

He squeezed the precious box against his chest and nodded. "We go in pirate caves."

"You and Jessie loved horses."

He nodded. "We go on long rides. Just me and Jessie. The twins are too little to come."

"Long rides? Where?"

He waved his arm carelessly. "Long rides. Picnics. We hunt gold in the river. We visit the Indians. We build forts."

"Indians? There are Indians living nearby?" He waved his arm again. "What kind of Indians?"

"Indians."

"Did you and Jessie have Indian friends?"

He nodded.

I had wondered about Jessie running away. She was unhappy and alone. If she had run away, how did she go? She hadn't taken her horse that day. Maybe she went on foot. If she had friends nearby, would she not have gone there first? Had the dead Indian girl come from that community? Had she been Jessie's friend years ago? Did it matter?

"Could we go riding one day? Could you take me to the Indians?"

He nodded.

I stood. "Remember, Buster, this is our secret. Like the treasure box. Don't tell anyone about our secret, or we won't ever find Jessie. Promise?"

He squinted up at me and slowly handed me Jessie's box of agates. I took it as a gesture of trust. I hoped I was right.

"Thank you, Buster. I'll keep them safe in her room." Then I winked, but Buster didn't wink back.

retraced my steps through the woods toward the house. Henry's fancy Packard Phaeton was sitting in the driveway. As I walked by, its owner came out the front door and ambled down the steps. Bad timing. There was no skirting him now.

"Good morning, Henry," I said pleasantly, holding Jessie's box out of sight in the folds of my skirt.

"And a good morning to you, cousin," he replied sarcastically, mocking me with the last word. "What, not riding with the twins? Let's see, it couldn't be because you can't ride, could it?"

"I haven't ridden in years, but I don't believe one forgets such things. Sorry, Henry, I'm afraid it's because I have no riding habit."

"A good excuse, but it won't last long. And neither will you. Enjoy playacting while you can. The trustees' investigation will soon expose you for the fake you are, and as added insurance, I've launched my own inquiry into your background. I have friends in many places, high and low."

I shrugged to show how little I cared. "Suit yourself. It doesn't matter to me how you spend your money, as long as it *is* your money and not my father's."

That barb struck sharply. His handsome face reddened. "Carr Industries is mine! And Ross's. It should have come to us to begin with. Our father didn't deserve to be cast aside like he was. Uncle Lawrence was sure as hell no model of virtuous living. He just managed to conceal his indiscretions from his parents." Then his features relaxed and he chuckled merrily, switching on the charming smile. "Look at us, scrapping like naughty children. And you're certainly no child, are you?" He treated me to a once-over that I'm sure he thought was debonair. "Let's be honest here. I know you're not Jessie, and it's only a matter of days until you're exposed. You'll be left with nothing but a long prison sentence when we charge you with fraud. Why not let me make your life easy? I'll give you a handsome settlement to disappear." When I made to walk past him, his hand shot out and grabbed my arm. "No, hear me out. This charade of yours is all about money. So I'll give you money. Just name the amount. I'll set up a bank account for you wherever you like, all legal, proper, and risk-free. You'll be amply repaid for all the trouble you've gone to in impersonating my cousin. You can leave safely, and we'll all live happily ever after."

I jerked out of his grasp and nearly dropped the treasure box as I entered the house, taking the steps two at a time. I was pretty sure he wouldn't follow me inside—but not so sure that I didn't check over my shoulder. His offer rattled me more than I cared to admit. Had I been alone in this, I might have been tempted to consider it.

I carried Jessie's box up to my room. I wiped off the dirt and set it on the dressing table. On an impulse, I rummaged through her jewelry drawer until I found a simple gold chain. A moment later, the beautiful Bennis beads were around my neck. The necklace would be my amulet. I wasn't superstitious, but a good-luck charm couldn't hurt. It was something of Jessie's, something that would protect me. I felt absurdly pleased to have it on.

I glanced out the window before going back outdoors. Henry and the Packard had gone. I was relieved no one had witnessed our little contretemps. At least, I didn't think so.

King caught sight of me and bounded up. "Hello, sweetheart." I patted his head. "I'm going for a walk. Do you want to come?" His tail wagged furiously. "All right, let's go!"

Just past the garden wall we plunged into the fantasy forest with its neat lines of lean, young trees planted six rows deep and offset like squares on a checkerboard. When we emerged from these sheltering boughs, the ocean panorama struck me full force.

The sea wind whipped my hair out of its pins and stung my eyes as I squinted up and down the desolate coastal highlands, then west to a fog bank far out to sea. A hundred feet in front of me, the land dropped out of sight as if cut by a giant knife and sliced into the sea. Every now and then as the ocean heaved, I could make out jagged black reefs lurking just beneath the foam. Offshore, massive boulders as tall as the cliff on which I stood jutted from the ocean floor like sentinels guarding the coast from marauders, preventing any ships from coming near this rough stretch of coastline. Eons ago, before the sea had torn them away, those boulders had been attached to the land under my feet. It made me wonder how long before storms and surf cut off the slice I was standing on.

The sound of waves against a pebbly beach pulled me toward the edge. King barked a warning that I could barely hear over the wind in my ears. Without getting too close—who knew if this was the morning for the edge to crumble away?—I looked down into turbulence, a sheer drop greater than the distance between the highest catwalk and the stage floor, to where a not-so-pacific ocean showed off its muscle.

To my right, a thicket of bent coastal pines hugged the edge of the cliff. A path into the middle of it suggested the way to the beach and a better view of the northern coastline. King and I followed the trail as it led to the edge of the cliff and from there, down to the beach and the sea caves I had heard about from Oliver. The caves Jessie and Buster had enjoyed exploring. I was about to descend when I felt eyes on my back.

I wheeled around.

Ross stood not six feet away, his eyes blazing.

It seemed imprudent to stand between a cliff and someone who would inherit a fortune at my death. I stepped away from the edge.

"What are you doing here?" he demanded, stuffing clenched fists inside his trouser pockets as if they couldn't be trusted with freedom. The wind tousled his curly hair, making him seem younger. I could see exactly what he had looked like as a little boy. It wasn't reassuring.

"I'm taking a walk. Does that meet with your approval?" He couldn't miss the sarcasm.

There was an awkward moment before he spoke again, gruffly this time, like a father to a wayward child. "Don't get too close to the edge."

"Why, thank you for those words of caution, cousin. I wouldn't have realized the danger myself." Ross shifted his glare from me to the ocean. "Never mind," I continued, pretending he had apologized. "You nearly gave me a heart attack, sneaking up on me like that, but it wasn't your fault. I couldn't hear you coming with the wind in my ears, and of course King wouldn't bark at you."

"You shouldn't be out here alone where no one can see you. It's dangerous. The edge of the cliff is always crumbling away. Something could happen and no one would know you were here."

I didn't bother to point out that if I were to fall into the ocean in a rockslide, an onlooker could hardly save me. I guessed the dead woman had set him thinking about death. "You heard about the body on the side of the road?"

"Yes." He looked thoughtful. "Mr. Beckett told me yesterday. No doubt we'll be treated to the gory details in the newspaper."

"Dexter has a daily?" I regretted the slip too late. But maybe Jessie had been too young to be interested in the newspaper, or perhaps Ross thought I was asking whether Dexter had a daily *now*, because he answered with no indication of having caught me out.

"Just the weekly. It isn't much. Still just a few pages of school awards, Ladies' League minutes, and some old prospector turning ninety and reminiscing about the gold rush. A murder will be front page. Things like that don't happen in Dexter."

In the short time I had been standing there, the fog had moved toward land, fingering a distant promontory that curved out into the water to the north of us where moments earlier sunlight had sparkled. It would reach us soon enough and the morning would be ruined for exploring.

"It's a treacherous place," he said finally. "Out there, I mean. As I well know. You remember how much we used to sail?"

If this was a trap, I thought I could handle it. Oliver had mentioned that the boys spent a lot of time on the water—in truth, sailing was a Carr family passion—so I could reply with confidence, "Yes, and I hated it because I got seasick so easily. But I thought you just sailed around the bay?"

"We were supposed to stay inside the bay, but we used to slip out and sail along the coast. We had some close calls."

"That was unwise, especially considering what happened to my parents."

"You're right, of course. They don't call this the Graveyard of the Pacific for nothing."

"There were that many shipwrecks around here?"

"Untold numbers, all along the Oregon coast. This area"—he swept the air with one arm—"this part of the West Coast was first explored by Sir Francis Drake during his circumnavigation voyage in 1579. Did you know that?"

I wouldn't admit my ignorance and so said nothing. He didn't seem to notice. The lecture continued.

"The Europeans were certain that there was a water route to China through North America, the Northwest Passage, which, of course, there isn't, but Drake thought he'd found it at the Juan de Fuca Straits. That's the waterway between Vancouver Island and the United States."

"I know where the straits are."

"That's right, I forget you've traveled a bit," he said condescendingly.

"I've even read a book or two."

He didn't miss the testy tone of my voice. "Well, you can't blame me for wondering. You haven't had any education in the past seven years."

"I didn't need a classroom to learn. Besides, there are lots of important things schools can't teach."

Ross was not one to let my peevishness ruin a good lecture. He continued as if there had been no pause and, to be honest, what he said was interesting.

"There were probably no other Europeans hereabouts for two hundred years until Captain James Cook in the HMS *Resolution* mapped the whole coast from California to Alaska. When he left North America, he returned to Hawaii where he was murdered by the natives in 1779. You know what I like most about Captain Cook?"

"What?"

"He died trying to stop a fight between his men and the native Hawaiians. Not many people try to put a stop to the illtreatment of the natives. No one around here."

An odd comment. Curious to hear more, I plopped myself down on the grass next to King who was stretched out at my feet, a move designed to encourage him to continue and continue he did.

"Not much happened around here until gold was discovered in 1849 and hundreds of thousands of get-rich-quick dreamers poured into California and Oregon from all over the world. The problem was that suddenly there were thousands of people— mostly men, lots of Chinese—and no law enforcement except a gun. The Indians got the worst of it."

"The real Wild West."

"There were dozens of tribes in Oregon before the white man came—the Killamook, the Tututni, the Coos, the Nestuccas, the Kalapuyan, the Umatilla, and so forth. They lived in villages along the rivers. Unfortunately, that's also where the gold was. When they resisted being run off by greedy miners, they were slaughtered. Most white men subscribed to the belief that the only good Indian was a dead Indian."

It began to make sense to me now, why Indians all over this country were treated so badly and lived in such miserable places nowadays. They had occupied all the best land and were driven off to the worst. I thought of the dead Indian girl. "Are there many Indians left in Oregon today?"

"Not a lot," Ross said as he sat down beside me. "Those that weren't murdered died of white man's diseases, like smallpox or measles. In the 1850s, after the Rogue River Wars, local tribes were forced onto reservations for their own protection, or so said the authorities. But these reservations were located on land that would not support them, so they starved to death."

He sent a furtive glance in my direction to make sure I was paying attention before he delivered the coup de grâce. "As a matter of fact, in the course of my research, I discovered that we are sitting on what was once part of the Grand Ronde reservation where local Yaquina and Alsea Indians were squashed in with a dozen inland tribes marched here at gunpoint. Originally Grand Ronde's population was about four thousand Indians. By the turn of this century, there were fewer than five hundred left."

"How did my father come to own reservation land?"

"In 1887, the federal government decided to allot individual Indians with specific acreage rather than have the land owned communally by the tribe. Once that happened, they were easily cheated out of most of their land. Then in 1901, the government declared the remaining reservation land surplus and sold it to the public. Over the years, the reservation shrank from seventy thousand acres to about four hundred."

"So my father swindled the Indians?"

"Not directly. He bought this land from a speculator in 1910. The speculator swindled the Indians."

I reminded myself that Lawrence Carr wasn't really my father, but I still felt like a thief. I didn't want to own land that had been stolen from its rightful owners. "This is the topic of your research, isn't it?"

"Obviously."

"And where are the Indians now? Nearby?"

He began tossing pebbles over the cliff and the motion focused my attention to his hands. I couldn't help but notice an unusual band around his wrist, a thin bracelet made of leather and beads. White, yellow, and blue beads, like those the dead woman wore. A shiver ran down my spine. Had Ross known the girl? His fingers were long and slender, his nails short and neat. Strong hands, and capable. Capable of what?

"Grand Ronde reservation still exists, southeast of us. A few Indians live there. Others live at the edge of towns like Dexter where they work in packing plants shucking oysters or canning salmon. Some weave baskets. I talk to the ones with the longest memories about the old days."

I did some quick subtraction in my head. "If the first prospectors came in the 1850s, someone seventy-five years or older might remember that."

"Several do remember. And some can relate what their parents had to say about life before the white man came, before the wars and relocations to the reservations. I am incorporating those first- and secondhand accounts into my thesis, which is about the cultural changes of the local tribes in the initial years of contact. The Indians old enough to provide eyewitness accounts won't be around much longer and their knowledge will be lost forever unless I record it now."

"The dead woman had black braids and shell beads. I think she was an Indian."

He eyed me with interest. "She was. That's why no one is much bothered about her death. No one in town, that is. She has family on the Grand Ronde reservation."

"Oh, dear. How—"

"I went into town and talked to some Indians I know. The girl had come to Dexter a few months ago to find work. She must have found something because she sent money home a couple times, but no one at the cannery knew her. She may have been headed home when she was killed."

"You mean she got into trouble and was running back to the reservation for safety?"

"Possibly. Some Indians trust me enough to talk to me, but this stuff is touchy, and when all's said and done, I'm still white."

So that's how he knew. He'd been playing detective, poking into places the local constabulary should have been investigating. Did he have more than a scholar's interest in the Indians?

"Did you know the dead girl?"

He gave me a queer look. "Why do you ask?"

"Just wondering."

"No."

I had the feeling he wasn't telling the truth, but the lecture had come to an end. We sat a while without speaking, the air around us alive with nature's own voice. Cormorants soaring effortlessly on updrafts called to their mates nesting in the cliffs below, crickets warned of the oncoming fog, and the endless rhythm of the surf washing the shore provided the backdrop for our thoughts. Life could be unfair in vaudeville too, but overall, it was better than in the civilian world where hotels didn't rent rooms to Negro or Asian or Indian performers and many eateries and speakeasies refused to serve them. I'd been turned away from places myself when my group included someone the owners found objectionable.

"Are there any books about this Indian history?"

"None written in words of one syllable."

I stood and brushed the grass off my skirt. "Have it your way, Ross. I'm through trying to be nice."

"Acting nice isn't going to convince us you're Jessie."

"Has it occurred to you that I don't have to convince you? My grandmother and uncle are convinced, and the trustees will give their final approval as soon as their investigation is finished. That's all that matters, although I admit to being pleased that the twins and your mother believe me."

"You've misjudged my mother if you think that polite façade reflects her true feelings."

Only then did I notice how close the fog had come, its first wisps blowing across the cliff edge toward us. Getting caught inside that thick white cloud with Ross would be the height of folly. "I'm heading back," I said, turning toward the house.

Ross stood and surveyed the distance. "Good idea. Fog is disorienting. You could easily become confused and walk over the edge of the cliff." I could hear him phrasing it just that way: "She must've become confused in the fog and walked over the edge of the cliff." As Grandmother would say, *Time to watch your back.* Cave exploration could wait for another day.

At the thicket, I paused to let Ross go first. I was more comfortable walking behind him, and I had long ago learned to obey my instincts where men are concerned. We pushed through the thorny tangle of berry vines, single file, until we came to the tiny stream. Suddenly—so suddenly I bumped into him—he halted.

"Oh! Excuse me!" I said.

He crouched down and pointed to a flower. "Look. A cobra lily."

It wasn't much like the lilies I'd seen at funerals. I peered over his shoulder at a stem that bent like a shepherd's crook with a bulbous center and a reddish protruding forked leaf.

"And another one!" Excited, he began searching the ground intently like a woman looking for a lost earring. In a moment he found what he was hunting for. A bug.

"It's carnivorous. Watch." He upended the flower and dropped the doomed insect inside. It struggled against the hairs and slippery sides of the interior until it slid out of sight into the guts of the flower. "Its name comes from the shape of the plant. Doesn't it look just like a deadly cobra ready to strike its prey? And this leaf part looks like the serpent's forked tongue, doesn't it? The flower doesn't strike its prey like a cobra; it lures insects inside with its scent and its colorful leaf."

Mother once told me about a religion in India whose followers thought all life was sacred so they walked with their heads down watching the ground to avoid killing even a single ant. That's not me. I've slapped my share of mosquitoes, squashed plenty of spiders, and stepped on more cockroaches than I care to remember, but Ross's undisguised glee in sending the hapless insect to its certain death made me queasy. He knew it too, looking up at me with a sly innocence and saying, "There's a lot of death around here, isn't there?"

The little bug did not die in vain. I returned to the house disturbed enough by Ross's behavior to know I wouldn't rest until I had taken care of an important chore.

Grandmother and Aunt Victoria were in the garden, Oliver had retired to the library, Henry was out on his yacht, and the twins were playing tennis. Glancing around to make sure none of the servants was watching, I skulked up the stairs and into Grandmother's bedroom.

"I still have your last letter," she had said yesterday. Of course I knew that did not necessarily mean she had brought it with her to Oregon, but some people, especially old people, carry precious letters around with them. I had a hunch that Grandmother was one of those.

She was! In the bottom drawer of the jewelry box left open on the dressing table, beneath her pearls, I found a packet of a dozen letters, all with U.S. stamps in the corner except the one with Queen Victoria's profile facing left, tied together with a frayed bit of blue picot ribbon. A quick shuffle through the envelopes brought me to the only one addressed in a round, childish hand. It was from Jessie and dated April 25, 1917, about three months before she went missing. Her careless, juvenile handwriting and frequent mistakes would have made her governess blush.

Dear Grandmother,

I hate living here more than ever. Why cant I live with you. I want to go back to Paris. Everybody here hates me and I hate them. The stupid twins broke one of my china cats so I smashed in their favorite dolls faces but only I got punished. Henry is mean all the time but not so much any more since I found out something and I'll tattle on him if he's mean again. Ross pretends like Im not here he doesnt talk or look at me even when [blotchy smudge]. He says he wishes I was dead and locked me in the cellar Wensday so I would die and I would have died down there and my bones rotted except for Cook needed some potatoes. I tattled but he wasnt punished very hard. No one ever punishes him.

Yours truely,

Jessie.

Holding Jessie's letter in my hands gave me the willies. It was as if she were talking directly to me. Or as if I were talking to myself in my young stage voice. We even made our *j*s the same way. Goose bumps pricked my arms all the way up to the nape of my neck.

Twice through was enough to commit the contents to memory. I slid the ribbon around the letters and replaced them exactly as they were, tucked beneath the string of pearls. For an alibi, I picked up Grandmother's paisley shawl before I opened the door. One of the housemaids was coming down the hall, barely visible behind a stack of starched linens. When she had passed, I went to my own bedroom. I needed to think about Jessie.

Now I understood why Grandmother had been so easily persuaded that I was Jessie. She must have almost expected Jessie to run away, pushed by unhappiness or fear. So she would have expected Jessie to return before her twenty-first birthday to claim her inheritance.

And I was starting to understand what a troubled, unhappy child Jessie had been. Hostile, even violent, and difficult to handle—that much was clear. I found myself rising to her defense. The poor thing had been neglected by hedonistic parents and handed off to nannies and governesses. She had led a lonely, seminomadic life for eleven years with no siblings and few friends her own age. When she was orphaned, her troubles grew like weeds. Living with her relatives was, if anything, worse. Aunt Victoria spent those years devoting herself to a bedridden husband, leaving their four children essentially unsupervised—never mind the ineffectual governess, the late Miss Lavinia. Jessie did not fit in. She had lashed out, hating everyone and everything. No wonder she had run away. She had no one to love, and no one loved her. I was angry at her treatment. I wished I had been there to defend her.

I wondered too what she had discovered about Henry. He would have been seventeen then. Had he been sailing his boat outside the bay? Smoking in the shed? Fondling the housemaid in the closet? Drinking in the laundry room? Bootlegging? No, Prohibition wasn't in effect back in 1917; it didn't start until 1920.

Now that I was aware of the history of dislike between Jessie and Ross, his current hostility made more sense. Jessie must have provoked the boy beyond his self-control. That cellar—my dreams had been so strong, yet so vague. Ross had locked her in the cellar once. Could he possibly have become so angry that he would . . . ? Dread crept to the edge of my consciousness. What had happened to young Jessie?

Suddenly, seeing the cellar became an itch that could no longer go unscratched.

Thanks to Oliver's house plans, I knew exactly where the entrance to the cellar was located, beside the pantry in the kitchen. I opened the door and turned on the light.

"What is it, Miss Jessie?" Marie spoke over her shoulder as she stirred cream into a pot of leek soup. "Is there something you're looking for?"

"I thought I'd look through the wine for something special for dinner. I don't mean to bother you." It was feeble, since I knew nothing about wine other than it came in red and white, but what other excuse could I come up with for wandering into the cellar?

Too busy to be suspicious, Marie said, "No bother, dear. You call if you need some help."

The cellar was cool, aggressively clean, well lit, and organized with shelves full of bottles, jars, tins, and boxes—so many liquor boxes that I knew Prohibition wouldn't arrive at Cliff House for decades. Last night, Aunt Victoria had made a point of saying, rather apologetically, that they were just drinking up old supplies, but these boxes looked like recent arrivals. I looked about, then closed my eyes, trying to feel something, anything that would make me think of Jessie. Nothing. The cellar was not scary or damp, and there was no place to hide a dead mouse let alone a dead body. Jessie had not died in some forgotten nook in the cellar. I felt foolish. Finding a corpse on the side of the road had fed my overactive imagination and fired up my dreams.

At the top of the stairs, I nearly collided with my maid, Lorraine.

"There you are, miss," she said brightly. "I was wondering, did you want me to unpack your things now?"

"No, I—yes! There's hardly anything to unpack, but the twins told me all my old clothes are still in the closet. I can't imagine that anything will fit me after seven years, but I thought it would be worth my while to make sure." I didn't say that what I was really after was a pair of britches. What I had dreaded most had become an urgent need—to go riding.

I had learned growing up that there were two types of clothing: costumes and day clothes. Good costumes were essential to a successful act so performers naturally put their money there. Consequently, I had little enough to wear offstage, and what there was fit comfortably into one valise.

Together we ransacked the closet, the wardrobe, and the chest of drawers that I had not even thought to open yesterday, piling everything on the bed. Then we went to work unfolding, shaking, examining, trying on, evaluating, taking off, and refolding every item Jessie had owned at thirteen. It was all top quality and custom made. I, of course, pretended to recognize everything, why, I'm not sure. Lorraine was a stolid girl, eager to please but not the sort to look beneath the surface of things.

"Do you know what we need, Lorraine?"

"What's that, miss?"

"Cartons. Are there any cardboard boxes downstairs?"

"Boxes, miss?"

"Yes, to put these clothes in. Doesn't the grocery delivery come in boxes?"

"I don't think so, miss. Or, it does, but the boy takes them back."

"I know—liquor boxes."

"Liquor, miss?"

"You know, wine and port and whiskey." Prohibition be damned, the Carrs had enough bottles of wine and liquor to open their own blind pig. "Go to the kitchen and ask Marie if there are any empty liquor cartons in the cellar. If not, empty some of them."

"Yes, miss. I'll be right back."

Against the east wall stood a tilt-mirror dressing table clad in an eyelet dresser scarf and matching skirt. I sat on the stool and examined the contents of the drawers. Inside the center one I found a beautiful sterling silver brush and a comb engraved with Jessie's initials: *J B* and a large *C* in the middle for Jessamyn Beckett Carr. I turned over the brush and saw strands of Jessie's copper hair still tangled among its bristles. Suddenly Jessie was painfully real to me—an unhappy girl who had just brushed her hair a moment ago, who had just stepped out of the room, who would be right back, who would laugh, and talk to me, and marvel at how much we looked alike. This brush was Jessie. The real Jessie.

I pulled out some of the loose hairs and held them up to my own. Indistinguishable. I began brushing my hair with Jessie's brush—long rough strokes—and when I stopped, a little breathless, our hair was entwined in the bristles. And no one, not even I, could tell the strands apart.

Lorraine clattered in with three empty Seagram's VO boxes, and I quickly stuffed the brush and comb back in the drawer. "Careful, miss," she said. "There's chalk on some of these and it gets on your clothes. But it brushes off." A few quick whacks of her hand took the green dust off her black uniform.

I felt queasy, as if I had been yanked out of a deep trance.

"Now," I said brightly, trying to shake the queer mood, "we'll sort these clothes as we go. Anything too small—and that's most of this—we'll put in the boxes. Do you know anyone who might fit these clothes?" She looked baffled. "Someone who is about this size." I held up a blouse to illustrate.

This unexpected generosity flummoxed Lorraine, who evidently had never been on the giving end of charity. "Well, there's . . . the church. First Presbyterian. They give away clothes. My mother got a coat there last week. Nearly new."

"Fine, then, if we can't think of anyone in particular, we'll give them to the church to distribute," I said, folding a lime-green cardigan that was too short at the wrists for me. "This is so pretty. A shame it won't fit me."

"Might I . . . might I take that one, miss?" She reddened at her own boldness. "Green is my little sister's favorite color."

"Why, of course! Will it fit her, do you think? How old is she?"

"Thirteen, miss."

"Why ever didn't you say so? Won't all these things fit her?"

Lorraine looked confused. "So much to one girl, miss?"

"All of this probably won't fit your sister, but surely she has cousins or friends? I know! She could invite her friends to come to her house and try things on, and everyone could have some new clothes." Heck, this bounty could outfit half of Dexter's thirteen-year-olds. Hand-me-downs of this quality were seldom seen.

"That would be very kind, miss."

We continued sorting until not one but *four* riding habits turned up. With pounding heart I pulled my legs into each pair of jodhpurs, heaving a frustrated sigh when all proved too short. Determined to ride tomorrow, I chose the largest pair.

"Do you know where I can find a needle and thread?" I asked her. "I need to move these buttons."

"Oh, miss, I'll do that for you."

"Thank you very much. Move them as far as possible."

As I folded the last of the skirts and laid them in the box, I asked, "Lorraine, don't I remember some caves in the cliff below this house?"

"Caves, miss?"

"Sea caves. On the beach below the house. I was thinking about following the path down to the beach."

"You can find agates on the beach, miss," she said, closing one full box and tying it with twine.

"Yes, I remember. Aren't there caves as well?"

"You shouldn't go in them. They're dangerous when the tide comes in. And they're haunted."

"Haunted?"

"Some say it's the spirits of sailors shipwrecked and washed up into the caves to die."

"Have you been in the caves below this house, Lorraine?"

"Not me, miss. That would be dangerous. And—and, miss . . . Lorraine is my name for sure but no one calls me that. Everyone calls me Rainy. If it's all right, miss, I'd like it if you called me Rainy too."

"Why, of course—it's a lovely nickname! And an appropriate one considering Oregon's coastal climate. And you must call me Jessie."

"Oh, no, miss. That wouldn't do."

"Of course it would."

"I'd be in heaps of trouble with the others."

"Not if you told them I insisted."

She shook her head stubbornly. "No, miss, it isn't right. They'd say I was putting on airs and you was beneath your dignity. Some things just aren't proper."

Professional standards were something I could understand—vaudeville had plenty of unwritten rules developed over time to reduce the friction of working with so many different types of people. Evidently the servant class had its own professional standards and I was trying to breach an important one. Know when to fold 'em.

"Okay, I'm sure you know best about that sort of thing. I haven't had much experience with servants."

"Oh, but surely when you used to live here before, you had a maid?"

"Umm, well, I meant in recent years." I could have kicked myself. I was getting careless. Especially with people I liked. Sternly I reminded myself that I was onstage and could not afford to relax for even one moment.

By the time we had finished, Rainy and I had filled eleven large boxes with dresses, coats, shoes, sweaters, skirts, blouses, socks, underclothes—even a couple of rabbit fur muffs. And I emerged

with several new additions to my wardrobe—loose-fitting clothing like nightgowns and cardigans, things that had probably
been too large for Jessie to begin with—as well as a new friend
who thought I hung the moon.

What in the name of all the gods in the Pantheon had possessed me to agree to come to church with the family? I had allowed myself to be persuaded when Aunt Victoria pressed me last evening, but in the clear light of day, I regretted my compliance. Church could very well turn out to be a two-hour walk through a minefield.

In my entire twenty-five years, I'd never been to Sunday church. Mother had jettisoned her strict religious upbringing along with her name, and few in vaudeville spent their one free day hunting down a local church of the correct flavor. Those who did make the effort spoke of pointed looks, lips pressed tight, and whispers behind fans. A few weddings and funerals had given me a grasp of the fundamentals, but until we were climbing into the car the next morning, it did not occur to me that I was heading toward catastrophe.

I gathered from the way Aunt Victoria bit her lower lip when I came down the stairs that my best dress and gloves were not up to the mark. Caroline had lent me one of her white lace squares and I pinned it in my hair as she and Valerie did, but it seemed that the rest of my clothing did not meet Carr standards.

Six of us rode into Dexter that morning in Henry's Packard. Grandmother had pleaded a headache. Oliver made no excuse at all; he just stared at me with a horrified expression that told me, too late, how badly I'd blundered. Religion was not a subject we had covered back in Cleveland.

I kept my eyes glued to Aunt Victoria, very much aware that Henry and Ross were keeping their eyes glued to me, waiting for the Good Lord to strike me down with a lightning bolt. Aunt bobbed a curtsy before she entered the pew; I did the same. She knelt; I knelt. She recited mumbo jumbo; I faked it. It wasn't really much different than following a dance routine, and I had had plenty of practice there, so I suppose I acquitted myself well enough. Nonetheless, I heaved a huge sigh of relief when it was over. I vowed to take a page from Grandmother's script and cultivate headaches for the next four Sundays.

At the conclusion of the service, the congregation trailed into an adjacent social hall for hot tea and warm shortbread—and a close-up look at the lost-and-found heiress. It was dangerous ground, and I knew it. I kept close to Aunt Victoria whose good breeding required her to smooth every social introduction with prompts.

"Good morning, Eleanor," she said in her unfailingly gracious way. "Won't you help welcome Jessie back to Dexter? Jessie, dear, you remember Mrs. Gaskin, don't you?" I made suitable remarks, watching Ross and Henry warily out of the corner of my eye.

To my surprise, neither one paid much attention to me. I thought they'd be trying to trip me up. Instead, Ross was deep in conversation with the minister, discussing the dead Indian girl, and Henry was busy working the crowd. With the panache of a

seasoned performer, he circulated around the room, exchanging
a kind word with each lady, shaking hands respectfully with each
older man, slapping the backs of the younger ones, and accom-
plishing it all without a shred of pomposity. As I sipped my tea, I
watched him pat the head of a darling blond girl, flirt with two
plain young women who looked like sisters, and nod gravely over
an old man's opinion, pausing only to scoop up a tiny tot running
away from his mother, lift him like an airplane and fly him back
to her arms. Everyone chortled fondly. It was enough to make me
doubt my own judgment. Who had replaced the self-important
Henry Carr from Cliff House with this utterly charming Henry
Carr, a man so affable that he might very well win his election
after all?

"Jessie? A moment, please?" Henry motioned at me from across
the room. The two plain sisters were beside him, and I tensed,
expecting a trap. "Jessie, you probably don't remember Mabel and
Roxanne Laughton, but a more talented pair you will not find in
all of Dexter. Our Jessie, you know," he confided to Mabel, "spent
the last seven years on the stage and she's become quite musical.
Mabel is a fine pianist and Roxanne sings like an angel." Right
on cue, the girls blushed, giggled, and protested the compliment.
"You girls will have to let Jessie teach you some of her vaudeville
songs."

Finally, after everyone in the hall had had the opportunity to
look me over and say a few words, Aunt Victoria herded us home
where Marie had a simple three-course dinner waiting. Out of the
spotlight, Henry dropped the charming behavior, putting me in
mind of those protean acts—some call them transfigurators or
quick-change artists—who can change their clothing and transform their characters in front of the audience with lightning speed.

We ate mushroom soup followed by a spicy chicken dish with
whipped potatoes, fresh corn, and salad, and finished with black-
berry pie and ice cream—my first opportunity to demonstrate
my skill with an ice cream fork. Sundays were a day of rest and

reflection, and since that precluded outdoor activities like my expedition with Buster, we gathered in the parlor after the coffee cups had been cleared. A long afternoon loomed.

Ross opened the gramophone cabinet and lifted out a stack of records.

"I expect radio will be the death of records," said Oliver, stuffing his pipe with a fragrant tobacco. "Why pay for records that shatter so easily when the radio will bring you the music for free?"

"Oh, my," exclaimed Aunt Victoria with an anxious flutter of her fingers. "Mr. Beckett, I am dreadfully afraid . . ."

"Ah, yes, my apologies," he said, returning the pipe to his pocket. "I almost forgot. The asthma hasn't improved, then, Ross?"

"Regretfully not, sir. However, there is a new medicine that is a great help whenever an episode strikes."

"As for radio," Aunt Victoria resumed, pulling her needlepoint from a wicker sewing box, "I will always prefer my recordings because I can select what I like to hear rather than what the radio offers. Play the Chopin first, Ross, dear."

"There's not much danger of having to choose between the two," replied Ross as he shuffled gingerly through the fragile discs. "Portland just got a radio station two years ago and I doubt Dexter ever will, not this far away from civilization."

"Radio is like vaudeville—entertainment for city folk. What do vaudeville performers think of radio, Jessie?" asked Oliver. Always so careful to avoid drawing suspicion, he would not speak directly to me unless others were around to hear our innocent conversation.

"They don't like it at all. Personally, I don't think radio will ever threaten vaudeville. People want to watch their entertainment, not just listen. You can sing over the radio or tell jokes, but try listening to Houdini's escape tricks or Bojangles's stair dance or W. C. Fields's juggling act. The Venetian Masqueraders are nothing if you can't see their fabulous costumes, and I can't imagine listening to a performance of the Cat Circus," I said, experiencing a pang of homesickness as I wondered what Angie, Walter, and the felines were doing at this very moment. "Vaudeville is so much more than sound. Radio will never compete."

Grandmother nodded over her poetry book as the conversation swirled around her.

"Are you reading *my* fashion magazine, Caro?" demanded Valerie.

"Oh, pooh, fashion." She tossed it back. "Who cares? Let's play cards!" Valerie was willing, and together they badgered their brothers into joining them for Hearts. I was about to excuse myself to my room when Aunt Victoria foiled my escape.

"I'm sure Jessie would like to play too," she said.

"Oh, no, thank you, I have to—"

"Nonsense! Ross, a chair for Jessie," she commanded.

Silent count to three, then Ross straightened up like a man headed for the gallows and carried a fifth chair to the table. I tamped down my annoyance and sat.

"Do you know the rules?" Ross inquired coldly.

"Yes."

Henry poured himself a full glass of Seagram's VO over ice and began shuffling cards, showing no trace of his earlier geniality. I tossed my head and pretended I wasn't the least disconcerted by the repeated shifts in his manner. No one else seemed to notice it at all. No doubt they were used to Henry's mood swings.

Hearts doesn't take much concentration and I wasn't giving it any when an odd movement made me look twice at Henry's hands. I thought I saw him deal his own card from the bottom of the deck. Certain I was mistaken, I watched more closely without seeming to, thinking perhaps he was cheating to lose as many adults do when playing with youngsters.

But no, the sap was cheating to win. He peeked at cards passed to him before discarding his own and kept a close eye on the twins, waiting for them to turn their hands enough for him to catch a glimpse of their cards. He was a reasonably good cheater. Good enough to cheat at poker or one of the more lucrative card games. That I could understand—cheating for profit. But cheating one's younger siblings for the pleasure of seeing them lose?

I said nothing. Henry won every hand he dealt as well as half the others. Perhaps that was how he funded his comfortable life away from Cliff House.

"I believe I'll go upstairs and lie down for a while," said Grandmother when we reached a break in the game. "Jessie, will you help me up to my room?"

"Yes, of course, Grandmother. Please continue the game without me," I said to the cousins as I stood up from the card table and took Grandmother's arm. With me on her left side and the banister on her right, she managed the steps quite easily. When we reached her room, she let go of my arm and closed the door behind us.

"He was cheating, you know," she said, settling herself on the overstuffed chaise lounge.

Taken aback, I said, "I did know. But I'm surprised you could tell."

"My eyes are sharp for distance; I only need these for close work," she said, indicating the magnifying glasses she wore on a chain around her neck.

"I didn't mean that. I meant that I'm surprised you recognize cheating when you see it. Most people don't. Unless they've had a lot of experience with card playing."

"And you don't think your old grandmother knows about cards?" Every wrinkle in her face deepened with her wide smile. "Come sit here by me, girl, and I'll tell you a tale no one alive today knows. When I was young, before I married your grandfather, I worked some months in a saloon." She paused to see the effect of her pronouncement on me—I nearly fell off my footstool—and when she was satisfied that she had shocked me to the core, she went on.

"It was back during the Civil War—although out where I

lived in California, that was just a war to read about in the newspapers. I took a job for a few months at a saloon in Stockton, serving drinks to the miners. Sometimes I did some singing and dancing. Hard to believe, looking at me now, but I had a pretty face and was light on my toes back then. Besides, there were hardly any women in town, so even the plain ones looked good to those prospectors. I met your grandfather in Stockton. We married and moved to San Francisco where we had three children—now Blanche and Clarence are gone and only Oliver is left—and we got too respectable to ever mention Stockton again. What do you think about that?"

I was dumbfounded. It took a lot of imagination to transform this frail old lady in a high-necked, rose silk dress into a young girl in low-cut flounces entertaining a room full of rowdy gold miners. "I'm flabbergasted! Was there a stage? Were you part of an act? What did you sing?"

She chuckled, pleased she had caught me by surprise. "No, no, it was nothing like vaudeville. There was no stage and no act, just a piano that was always out of tune and a vegetable crate beside it to raise me up. I sang 'Buffalo Gal,' 'Darling Clementine,' 'Yellow Rose of Texas,' and anything else the men called out, even if I had to make up my own words. Sometimes I danced with the men."

"And you learned how to spot card cheats."

"That was over sixty years ago. Seems like another lifetime. I hadn't thought about Stockton in years. Not until I heard you had come home and had been working in vaudeville. Your grandfather was ashamed that I had entertained the miners, and he made me ashamed too, but all of a sudden, I got to thinking, just what was so bad about a little singing and dancing with some lonely men? It never went further than that. Your years in vaudeville made a lot of sense to me, because I'd done something like that when I needed to earn my own way. I thought to myself, maybe she got that from me, that little spark of talent and the gumption to show it off. Maybe we have more in common than some think."

"Seems we do."

"There's something else I learned in Stockton. I learned how to take the measure of a man pretty quick. I learned not to look at a man's face or his clothes, but to watch how he treated others. There's no better way to judge. And I can tell you this, I'm wary of men who cheat at children's games. Why didn't you call him on it?"

"I don't know. Somehow, it just seemed smarter to hold back that I was on to him."

She gave me a measured look and patted my hand. "You *are* smart, Jessie. You think before you act. That's a rare enough trait in young people. Well, now I'm going to lie down a bit. But I'll be keeping my eye on Henry and Ross Carr. I don't like them, and I don't trust them."

21

n o one was awake but the servants when I left my room the following morning wearing my too short, too tight riding britches. I made for the kitchen where Marie packed a picnic for Buster and me. It didn't seem right to go visiting empty-handed, so I helped myself to several Mason jars of preserved fruit and some of Marie's scones. I told her that Buster and I were going to spend the day riding, and she promised to let Aunt Victoria know.

Just then, Aunt Victoria appeared out of thin air. "Good morning, dear. You're up with the sun," she exclaimed brightly, almost as if she had been expecting me. "Oh, look! You're wearing your Venetian beads!"

I touched the five bright beads at my throat—Buster's "Bennis" beads were Venice beads! Souvenirs from Jessie's years in Italy.

"You know, after you left, I searched your room, hoping for

a note of explanation," she said, unable to keep the note of reproach out of her voice.

"I know, Aunt, I should have—"

She held up her hand. "No, no. What's past is past. What I meant to say was that I didn't see your Venetian beads then and thought you must have taken them with you."

"Actually, I left these in a box of agates in the stables with Buster. We used to call it our treasure. And that's why I'm up so early this morning. Buster and I are going for a long ride, like in the old days. It's all right if I take Lady, isn't it?"

"Of course you may take her any time you wish. But"—and now she took in my ill-fitting jodhpurs—"you can't go dressed like that."

"It's all I can manage for the moment."

"What about a jacket and boots?"

"I don't need a jacket, and these shoes have a little heel."

"Oh, dear, what if someone sees you? Oh, dear, what will they think?"

"No one will see us. We're just going in the woods."

"You must have riding boots, my dear. I could lend you mine, although they'll be far too large for your foot. And my jacket, but you'll swim in it. And no hat either!" She came closer and fingered my long curls. "You have such pretty hair, just like Blanche's."

Uncomfortable, I stepped back out of reach. "I'll be fine like this."

"Well, my dear, I can't forbid it, but we must go shopping right away. You need so much!"

When I reached the stables, Lady and Chestnut were saddled and ready. I was grateful that my first time on Lady would occur without any of the family watching. By the time the Carrs saw me ride, Lady and I would be old friends.

Buster led me east into a forest noisy with morning birds, and within minutes, I was hopelessly lost. Sometimes he followed a narrow trail, but mostly we picked our way through the woods, cantered across meadows, and forded shallow streams, stopping twice to stretch our legs and let the animals drink. Lady was a sweetheart, so placid and agreeable that I could actually relax and enjoy the scenery.

My nose told me we had reached our goal several hours later when it picked up the scent of a campfire. We broke out of the woods into a clearing where a few rude huts clustered between neat fields and a river. At first glance, the family farm seemed deserted except for some chickens, but I felt more than a few eyes trained on me. Dismounting, I called a cheerful, "Hello! Anyone home?"

A bent-backed old man appeared at the doorway of the largest cabin. Dressed in blue work pants and a clean checked shirt, he looked like every farmer in America except for the way he wore his hair—long and tied in the back with a strip of leather. His lips did not smile but his wrinkled eyes sparkled in recognition when he saw us.

"Welcome, daughter. It is good to see you after so many years. Welcome, brother." I knew from Buster that this was Tom Mercier, one of the elders who used to tell stories to us children.

"Seven long years," I said.

"We wondered why you did not come. Later, we learned you had run away. I was not surprised. You were very unhappy."

"I am happier now."

In my role as Jessie, I could hardly ask him whether Jessie had sought refuge here when she ran away. Fortunately, I didn't have to. His conversation told me that she had not.

"You have had a long ride. Will you rest a while and honor us by sharing our meal? My grandson has caught two large fish this morning."

I looked at Buster, who nodded eagerly. I was hungry too. "We can share," I said, pulling out Marie's scones and chicken sandwiches. "We'll have a feast!"

A woman of middle years came out of a nearby hut carrying a

skillet. Quickly she added fuel to the fire, and in no time, the fish and cornbread were sizzling away. A few more people appeared, but none approached. Buster walked to the woodpile and picked up an enormous log as if it weighed no more than a stick, setting it beside the fire for the two of us to use as a seat. I continued to talk with the old man while the younger generations went about their chores.

"How is my friend Hattie?" I asked, mentally blessing Buster for his phenomenal memory.

"My granddaughter is well. She lives across the river now, with her husband's family near Old Grand Ronde. She married a good man. They have four children now."

My hand flew to my mouth. "Four!" As he described each youngster, I could feel the pride behind his words reaching through the generations, binding every member of the family with fetters of love. I envied that connection to others. It was something I would never know.

"And Luke?" I asked.

"That grandson works as a logger."

The fresh air and exercise had made me ravenous, and I nearly wolfed down the odd assortment of food. When it seemed Tom Mercier would not bring up the subject of the dead Indian girl, I was forced to ask. "When I came home last week," I began cautiously, "I heard about an Indian girl who was killed. Was it someone from the reservation? Did I know her?"

The old man finished his bite and took another, chewing slowly, as if he had not heard my question. I knew enough to wait. Finally he said, "You knew her. She was my late sister's grandchild, Lizzette Petit. She was older than you, but still very young."

"How terrible. I am very sorry to hear it. Do the police know who committed this awful crime?"

He shook his head. "It was not an Indian, although my niece's husband says the white sheriff thinks it was. He only says it was an Indian so he does not have to trouble himself to find her killer. My niece's husband says Lizzette was working in Dexter, but he cannot learn where. She sent money home." He heaved a great sigh. "The priest from St. Michael's buried her yesterday at the tribal cemetery."

As Buster and I began the long ride home, I thought about Lizzette and Jessie. One dead, one missing. Lizzette was older than Jessie—did they know each other well? Had they both stumbled into danger? It was beginning to look more and more like Jessie was dead. If she had run away, she had not taken her horse, nor had she done the logical thing and fled to her Indian friends. Yes, she could have walked into Dexter and hopped the train to Portland, but why not ride and leave the horse tied up at the station?

Uncle Oliver had told me that everyone first suspected Jessie had run away, until a search of her room revealed she had taken nothing with her. With her horse safe in its stall, a riding accident was ruled out. A dozen people combed the grounds and seaside to no avail. Only then did they notify the police on the chance that she had been kidnapped. When no ransom note came and no body was found, she was listed as a runaway. Some huge number of Pinkertons worked the case for years with no results. Jessie had vanished.

It was, of course, impossible to investigate Jessie's disappearance when I was impersonating Jessie. But I could look into the Indian girl's death on the chance that they were somehow related.

And there was another possibility. Maybe, just maybe, Jessie was still alive and on her way home at this moment, in time for her twenty-first birthday.

22

B eing onstage fourteen or fifteen hours a day makes for a tough gig. The daily routine kept me in full view of my audience for long periods without any breaks between acts, and I found myself heading for the privacy of the Great Outdoors at every opportunity.

"Oh, checkmate! I win! I win!" Caroline exulted from the game table while Valerie glowered. Aunt Victoria looked up from the latest *Time* weekly and made a gentle remark about being gracious in victory.

We were a feminine group that afternoon. Grandmother sat in her favorite chair by the fire, her nose buried in the *Reader's Digest* and so quiet that it was easy to forget she was in the room. Ross passed his days in the study hovering over the hired typist—a little blond looker—as she pounded out the final draft of his thesis, though Aunt Victoria assured me Ross was only interested in dark-haired intellectuals. Henry had left for political activities. I soon realized that he was seldom in residence at Cliff House, preferring his apartment in Portland or his yacht in Dexter's harbor.

I recalled the day I'd arrived and first met Henry and Ross. Henry's fear and Ross's belligerence had vanished, replaced by a cautious tolerance that could only mean they were waiting for the trustees' report to demolish my story. Although their behavior now was civil, it was far from friendly, and I did not believe either one had accepted Jessie's return and the loss of all that money. I just didn't know when the next attack would come.

"How about a card game?" I said, bored to desperation. "What do you like to play besides Hearts?"

"Slap Jack . . . umm . . ."

"Do you play poker?"

The twins shook their heads.

"I can teach you. It's easy."

At the word "poker," Aunt Victoria's nose came out of her magazine. "Perhaps you know another game, Jessie dear. One more suitable for young ladies."

The twins grimaced. "Oh, Mother!"

"Certainly," I said. "Let's see now . . ."

"What about Go Fish?" Aunt Victoria suggested. "That's always been a family favorite."

"Sounds great," I said. "Remind me of the rules, Valerie?"

Half a game of Go Fish and I was watching a housefly crawl across the windowpane for excitement. As I looked about the room for inspiration, my eyes came to rest on the coffee table where a crystal bowl of saltwater taffy called to me.

Mother used to say that if squash were called something nicer—a pretty word like "sassafras" or "calliope"—children would eat it up without complaint.

"Look, I've thought of a good game. It's easy to learn. It's called Give and Take." A spark of interest lit the girls' eyes, so I continued. "We'll start with the basic form. Valerie, you shuffle the deck and deal seven cards to each of us, facedown. Caroline, you take this taffy and divide it into three equal piles." I took a sheet of paper and a pencil and started making an ordered list: royal flush, straight flush, four of a kind, and on down.

"Now," I said, setting the empty crystal dish in the center of the table, "here is the pot, and these are the rules."

In no time I had created two little bluffers whose guileless expressions could have cleaned out Doc Holliday and Wild Bill Hickok without those gentlemen ever seeing beyond their angelic innocence. Gradually I introduced more rules and strategies, and soon we were shrieking with laughter as the taffy traveled back and forth across the table.

Finally, Aunt Victoria could resist no longer. "Can four play?"

"The more the merrier!" I said. "Grandmother?" She shook her head and sent me a look that told me she knew exactly what I was doing. The girls briefed their mother on the rules and we had a gay time before they started squabbling over whose turn it was to deal.

"Let's take a break and go outside for a while," I said. "Grandmother?"

She accepted the invitation and reached for her shawl. The twins opted for a game of tennis and ran upstairs to change clothes.

As soon as we were out of range, Grandmother began, "I hope that when you come into your fortune, Jessie, you can do something for those girls. They live boring lives in this isolated house. Young people need more activity—school, parties, friends."

I was ashamed I hadn't given it much thought. "I suppose when the governess is here, they spend a good deal of the day with their studies."

"No doubt. But what a lonely existence. Their mother means well, but she sees only what she wants to see. I'm afraid she is the sort who would do anything for her children except let them grow up."

We found Chen squatting in the flower bed, shaded by his grass hat, wearing grass shoes and mud-stained trousers, weeding vigorously. I gave him a perfunctory "Good afternoon" with no expectation of a response.

He stood, stretched his back, and smiled at us warily. "Good afternoon, miss, madam," he said with an accent so slight most people would not notice it at all.

"Oh! I didn't realize . . . You speak English?"

"Yes, miss. I was born in this country. My name is Chen Xingen but in English I am John Chen."

"Oh, excuse my mistake. I thought . . . well, the other day . . ."

"It's a natural mistake. Most Chinese immigrants speak very little English. But those born here, like me, grew up speaking English as well as Cantonese."

I tried to guess his age. It was impossible. His skin was leathery from a lifetime of hard work out-of-doors and his face, lined with deep wrinkles that fanned out from his eyes and cut around his mouth, looked old, yet when he straightened up, there was nothing crooked or frail about him. He had the strong hands and powerful shoulders one expected in a common laborer and the sharp, intelligent eyes one did not.

"Well, I am delighted to know you do—now you can tell me something about all this. I'm afraid city girls like me know very little about gardening." Grandmother perched on the nearest bench where she could soak up the sunshine.

"I will be happy to teach you. Most flowers have finished blooming for the year and will not come again until next spring. These"—he gestured to where he had been kneeling—"are hydrangea. They are great favorites in China and in America because they bloom from spring until fall."

Of course I knew at some level that all flowers had names, but the idea suddenly intrigued me, and I looked about with new interest, like a stranger curious as to the identity of the guests at the party. Within moments Chen had introduced me to the prolific pink hydrangeas and rows of tall, happy-faced zinnias of every color in the crayon box.

"These roses are native to China," he said, pointing to some bushes thick with small white roses. "Over there are traditional European roses, larger and more fragrant, but China roses bloom longer, as you can see. They will continue to bloom in this sheltered garden until early winter. America has welcomed many Chinese plants." Chen pointed to a bed of bright flowers planted against the far wall. "Those have Chinese origins as well."

"Daisies!"

"I regret to say they are not, although their petals do resemble those of the daisy. They are a type of chrysanthemum."

"They are very pretty, aren't they?" I threw my arms wide. "Do you take care of all this by yourself?"

"Now, it is not so much work and I am alone. In the beginning, about six years ago, Mrs. Carr hired four to build the wall and lay out the garden. And plant the red alder trees."

"Oh, is that what they are? Why ever did she want them there, do you know? Most people pay money for an ocean view, and she has blocked it with trees."

He nodded his understanding. "Erosion is a problem all along the coast. Little by little, the cliffs crumble into the sea. Some believe tree roots will help prevent that."

So that was it!

"What do you think?" I asked.

He shrugged. "The earth is weak; the ocean is powerful. The outcome is not in doubt, but perhaps the trees will delay it a short while." He must have seen the look on my face, for he hastened to reassure me, "The house is in no danger, miss, not for many, many years. Maybe never. You mustn't worry. The weak part of the cliff is south of here where the rock is softer. A large chunk broke off and fell into the sea just last month."

I had walked north along the coast a few days ago. Chen was pointing in the opposite direction.

"Perhaps I'll walk that way and have a look."

"Take care, miss. There are many cracks in the ground."

"I certainly shall."

"You must go now, if you like, Jessie," said Grandmother, adding that she was perfectly satisfied to sit in the sun while I went to see the landslide.

As happened before, King appeared at my heels the moment I stepped outside the garden walls. Together we threaded our way through the red alders and turned south. Almost at once the ground began its downward slope out of sight of the house. A five-minute walk brought me to a point of land where I could see that the cliffs ahead of me were only half the height of the ones beside the house. Lawrence Carr had situated his summer house at the highest point in the area. To the north of the house, the ground descended to Dexter and the bay; to the south, it sloped more gently to a vulnerable, crumbling coast that was uninhabited and uninhabitable.

My progress was slowed by several large cracks in the earth—like miniature fault lines running parallel to the coastline. All at once I came to a macadam road which was, I realized, the continuation of the one from Dexter that brought us to Cliff House and then snaked south, linking Oregon's remote coastal towns to the outside world. Few cars came this way, and I saw none today. I did see a discarded wooden A-frame lying on its side with an old pulley, a wooden handbarrow, and some other junk that looked like it had been left behind after the construction of the coastal road a dozen years ago. King and I followed the pavement until it veered away from the ocean.

It didn't take a geologist to spot the recent avalanche. The new face of the cliff was freshly exposed where a slab of weak rock had collapsed into rubble on the shore, revealing an artist's palette of earthen colors striped horizontally across the exposed area. As beautiful as it was, nothing could erase the sense that the earth was holding its breath, waiting to release the next landslide.

With King leading the way, I took a slightly different route back. Rounding a large boulder, I spotted him poised at the edge of the largest crevice I had yet seen, sniffing suspiciously. This one must have been three feet wide and a good deal longer; like the rest, it ran parallel to the cliff edge a hundred feet away. I wondered when this chunk of high land was destined to meet the sea. In a hundred years? A thousand? Next week? I peered cautiously into the dark hole and saw nothing but black. Cool, fresh-smelling air drifted into my face. It would be very easy to fall here, and no one would be the wiser. Someone could trip in the dark, or the earth at the edge could collapse. Could Jessie have stumbled that day she disappeared seven years ago? The fall would probably prove fatal. Had they searched these crevices when she went missing? Oliver would know. But then I remembered that Jessie had vanished during the day, not at night, so toppling into a crevice wasn't a likely theory.

Being pushed, however, did not depend upon daylight or darkness.

"Don't get too close, King," I warned, looking around nervously. "Come!" I snapped my fingers and motioned to him to follow.

Chen was where I had left him weeding the flower beds, with Grandmother nearby. Briefly I told him about the large crevice and my idea to rope it off. "There are many such in that low ground," he said over his shoulder. "No one can put fences around them all. No one goes there."

"You're probably right. Do you have some scissors? I think I'll cut some of these pretty things for my room. Chrysanthemums, did you say?"

He looked around at the other flowers. "Why not pick some roses?"

"My room is full of roses. They are beautiful and quite fragrant, but these chrysanthemums are so cheerful, I think I'll put some in a vase by my bed."

I thought I saw him scowl as he bent over his basket. "There are black-eyed Susans over there." He stood and pointed to a bed of exuberant yellow blossoms several feet away. "See? They are very nice, with tall stems. Rather like daisies. Some call them brown-eyed Susans. You can decide, brown-eyed or black-eyed."

"Perhaps I should get permission from Aunt Victoria first, is that what you mean?"

"No, no. She would be delighted for you to pick whatever you like. Here." He handed me some clippers. The sun slipped behind a cloud, and the drop in temperature sent Grandmother back into the house. I snipped a couple dozen chrysanthemum blossoms, choosing the tallest stems. To please Chen, I picked a few of the black-eyed Susans as well and left him to his weeding. In the kitchen, Marie gave me a vase and I arranged them carelessly.

Aunt Victoria passed me on my way to my room. "There you are, dear," she said cheerily. "Henry just called saying he was bringing a guest to dinner tonight. Oh, how lovely!"

"I hope you don't mind, I've raided your flower beds." I held up my vase for her inspection.

"Mind? Gracious no, dear, I'm thrilled to find someone who shares my interest. The girls don't care a fig for gardening and the boys—well . . . You must give instructions to Chen whenever you like. Change anything. Variety is the essence of a pleasure garden. Although," she said, peering closely at the flowers, "I am surprised Chen let you pick those."

"I thought I imagined his reluctance."

"Oh, the silly man. He didn't want them in the garden at all, but I insisted. In China, chrysanthemums are thought to bring bad luck. What a superstitious lot those Orientals are!"

"Bad luck? How can a pretty flower bring bad luck?"

"The Chinese think chrysanthemums symbolize death. They use them for funerals and on graves. To give them to someone would be to wish them dead."

Vaudeville harbors some peculiar superstitions—peacock feathers bring bad luck and whistling in dressing rooms courts disaster, while touching a humpback's hump or wearing your undershirt inside out guarantees good fortune—but when she was alive, my mother had no patience for such silliness. Neither did I. Defiantly, I set the lovely daisy-faced flowers square in the center of my dressing table.

23

Continuing my exploring, I decided to see what the rooms above me looked like, and I headed to the door at the end of the hallway. At first I felt like an intruder. Then I remembered it was my house, and I strode up the stairs with all the confidence ownership imparts.

According to Uncle Oliver, the third floor had never been used. Intended for large house parties, it consisted of a ballroom across the front and numerous guest bedrooms in each wing. Had Blanche and Lawrence Carr lived, they would no doubt have hosted weeklong affairs throughout the summer season, where society swells would sail their yachts into Dexter Bay and spend the week hunting, fishing, riding, and gossiping. But the Fates had decreed otherwise. The vast ballroom echoed eerily as I walked through.

I had descended the stairs to the second floor just as Henry and his dinner guest came through the front door. Hand on the railing that overlooked the entrance hall, I paused to watch the scene unfold from a balcony vantage point.

The two men entered quietly and hung their hats on the hat rack. The guest stood as tall as Henry but lacked Henry's paunch. They seemed roughly the same age. "I'll get her," I heard Henry say and I assumed he meant his mother. Before he could move, Ross entered stage left and shook hands with the newcomer. Hearing voices, the twins poked their heads around the corner. I decided the scene looked harmless and began to descend.

"Ah, here she is," said Henry as he caught sight of me on the landing, "your prodigal sister home at last! I've brought your brother home for dinner tonight, Jessie."

My legs exhibited a will of their own and continued their slow descent, but the rest of my body tensed with alarm. Relax, keep going, said some part of my brain. It's just another trick. If Jessie had a brother, Oliver would have told you. If Jessie had a brother, he would have inherited before the Carrs.

"Well . . . your prodigal *half* sister, I should say." Henry smirked. "Hasn't she grown up grand?"

At that moment Aunt Victoria swept into the foyer. She took one look at Henry's guest, stifled a gasp, and turned crimson. Henry, clearly put out by his mother's reaction, nudged his guest forward just as I reached the bottom stair.

"Hello, Jessie," the stranger stammered. "It's been a long time. You're looking very grown-up." He blushed furiously.

What we had here was another, rather pathetic version of the Fake Grandmother ploy. No doubt if Henry had known that particular trap had already been sprung by the trustees, he would not have set it a second time. Yet something was off. Aunt Victoria did not quickly correct Henry as I expected her to. She knew this person. She was biting her bottom lip with indecision. Henry had somehow ensnared his mother as well as me.

The "brother" himself looked monstrously ill at ease. His full lips were pressed into a tight line, and he shifted his weight from foot to foot like a performer caught before a hostile audience. Clueless as I was, I felt a moment's sympathy for his predicament.

"What game are we playing now, Henry?" I sighed dramatically, my eyes locked on the stranger even as I spoke to my cousin.

"Well, naturally I thought Jessie would enjoy seeing her half brother again—"

Why was Aunt Victoria silent? Why did she not correct Henry? Could this man really be Jessie's half brother? If so, why had Oliver not warned me? With no idea which way to go, I decided my only recourse was to throw a tantrum.

"I have lost patience with you and your silly tricks!" I said forcefully. "I meant it when I said I could prove I was Jessie, and I can. I can tell you things only Jessie would know." I warmed to my theme, turning to the family one by one as my voice grew more strident with each example. "I can tell you which room Uncle Charles used for his sickroom, I can tell you why Santa left lumps of coal in Ross's stocking, I can tell you the name of Henry's dog buried under the big tree out back, I can tell you how mad Ross was when I tore out the last pages of his Tom Swift books, I can tell you why I smashed the girls' favorite dolls—" I skidded to a halt and addressed an aside to Valerie and Caroline: "I'm very sorry about that, by the way. I should have known you two didn't break my china cat on purpose." Ignoring Ross's open mouth, I turned back to Henry and resumed my tirade. "Nobody but Jessie would know these things. Well, get your childish tricks in now because I won't be here much longer. I am leaving as soon as the trustees submit the results of their investigation, which I hope will be soon because I am sick, sick, *sick* of this!"

While I'd been raving, Uncle Oliver and Grandmother appeared at the top of the stairs, probably in time to overhear everything. Aunt Victoria found her composure at last and sidled up, draping one arm around my shoulder. "There, there, Jessie, we believe you." She glared at Henry, who wasn't looking the least

bit penitent, and took a deep breath. "And may I have the plea-
sure of introducing you to David Murray. He is your father's son.
I'm afraid none of us knew of his existence until last March when
Henry met him in Portland. Mr. Murray, may I present Jessie
Carr?"

"Pleased to meet you," he mumbled without quite meeting my
eye.

So that was it. My, my. Lawrence Carr's bastard boy. That
explained Aunt Victoria's shock at seeing him in her house and
her mortification at having to introduce him socially. Well, there
was a bastard in every family. I was proof of that.

I examined him during the introductions. Perhaps it was as
well that I hadn't noticed the family resemblance at once because I might have made the wrong choice and fallen for Henry's
trick, pretending to know someone Jessie could not have known.
I drew a deep breath to steady my nerves. It had been a close call.
This David fellow did look remarkably like the Lawrence Carr
I remembered from his wedding photo—handsome, fair-haired,
with blue eyes, but this man was rugged where Lawrence Carr
was soft, and tanned by the sun where Lawrence Carr was pale.
David hadn't had the easy life of a rich man. Bastards never do.

"And my daughters, Caroline and Valerie," Aunt Victoria was
saying, "and Jessie's uncle, Mr. Oliver Beckett, and his mother,
Mrs. Beckett. And you have met Ross."

I glanced at Oliver. He looked as if his heart had stopped.
And I knew why. Another heir to worry about.

"How is it no one ever told us about Jessie's half brother?"
Caroline whined. "We never get to know anything!"

"It wasn't any of your concern." The twins exchanged exas-
perated glances and Aunt Victoria was forced to continue. "He
was born before your uncle Lawrence married your aunt Blanche.
Before they had even met."

"So? He's still our cousin, isn't he?" continued Caroline, like a
dog with a bone.

"In a sense . . . distantly . . ."

Valerie—smarter than her sister if not as bold—turned to David with a perplexed crease in her brow. "Then why isn't your name Carr, like ours?"

Aunt Victoria hastened to interrupt any reply the bastard might have made.

"It was a different sort of marriage. Not entirely legal. Those children usually take their mother's last name. Now, enough of this rudeness, prying into other people's personal matters! Since we're all present and accounted for, we may as well go into the dining room . . . Ross, would you please select a wine from the cellar? I'll go tell Marie to put dinner ahead." Poor Aunt—convention wouldn't permit her to dine with a bastard and manners wouldn't allow her to throw him out. "Jessie, darling, you sit on my left and Mr. Murray, you on my right, please." And she marched toward the kitchen, sending me a look that promised to reveal all at a later time, if only I would cooperate for the present.

As we filtered into the dining room to take our assigned seats, Henry made a show of gallantry, holding my chair.

"Round two to you, Miss Fraud," he said, bending close to my ear. "That was quite a performance in there. You may have bamboozled some people but not me. I know you're not Jessie, and I'll prove it, sooner or later." I murmured something to Valerie on my left and pretended I hadn't heard him.

The only person at that table more uncomfortable than Aunt Victoria was the bastard himself, who must have realized he'd been set up as much as I. He sat quietly through the first course, eyeing the others to see which spoon to use and speaking only when spoken to. Henry carried on gaily as though nothing untoward had occurred. Oliver had regained his composure once he understood David was illegitimate and therefore no threat. Aunt Victoria valiantly led the conversation through several thoroughly dull but socially acceptable topics, but even she grew alarmed after we had exhausted the best sort of books for Dexter's new lending library and the main course had not yet appeared.

"What's happening in Salem, Henry?" she asked, counting on Henry to step up to the political podium with the faintest encouragement.

"Well, they're appealing that new compulsory education act to the U.S. Supreme Court."

"I saw that in yesterday's newspaper," said Uncle Oliver, earning his keep in the time-honored manner of upper-class moochers by serving in the role of Chief Conversationalist and Social Asset. "What is the objection?"

"It's a good law," Henry continued with what sounded like a rehearsal of his campaign speech. "Passed by referendum last year, thanks to strong support from Governor Pierce. It's about time we closed down those foreign Papist schools with their anti-American values. All children deserve a decent, patriotic, American education, not some hocus-pocus religious indoctrination from the nuns and priests at the Academy of the Holy Toenail. With Governor Pierce leading the way, we should be able to make real improvements in the everyday lives of genuine Americans and shut down the flood of Bolsheviks and colored races into our land. We're looking at the dawn of a great awakening of American pride and power!"

Aunt Victoria beamed. I wondered how she could employ Chen if she were so intent on barring the door to foreigners. "Speaking of tutors," she announced, "Mrs. Applewhite returns next week!" The twins groaned on cue. "Oh, fiddlesticks! You'll be happier without so much time on your hands. You've worn out those poor horses with all that riding."

"I've worn out my riding habit," complained Caroline. "Val too. We need new ones. And so does Jessie. She can't ride at all until she gets some proper clothes. We should go shopping before Mrs. Applewhite returns."

Aunt thought it an inspired idea. "We must go into the city

for a shopping trip. Jessie, you need suitable clothing for church too, and some nice daywear as well. Not that your wardrobe isn't lovely, my dear, but it isn't very extensive, is it?" she said delicately. "And nothing in your closet fit, of course. Never mind, even if it had fit, it would have been out of style. Let's see now . . . we'll go day after tomorrow and come back Saturday evening. One night should be enough."

Overnight? Only then did I realize a shopping trip meant Portland. Dexter's population supported a couple general stores but evidently nothing that passed for fashionable.

"You'll stay at the Benson Hotel?" asked Oliver.

"We always do. Simon Benson was such a dear friend of Lawrence and Blanche. And it's so close to the better stores. Why, it's right around the corner from Meier and Frank."

Valerie clapped her hands. "We'll be there for Friday Surprise!"

I looked agreeable, as if I knew what a Friday Surprise was.

"Perhaps Mother and I might accompany you," said Oliver. "We've enjoyed our stay immensely but it's high time we started the long trip back to San Francisco."

After much exclamation that surely dear Oliver and his mother were not thinking of leaving so soon, that everyone had hoped they would stay through Christmas, the protests faded away. I was a little rattled by Oliver's proposal, although I'd been expecting his eventual departure. It would be hard to lose my only allies. I'd miss Grandmother far more than Oliver. Having her sharp eyes watching out for me was a comfort. But honestly, all I had to do was keep out of trouble's path until the trustees' report arrived, and I was home free.

There was no chance of the private investigators finding anything amiss with my story. I had worked it out too carefully. I had told the trustees nothing but the truth about my past seven years. There was nothing they could find to hurt me. Four years with the Little Darlings, one with Jo & Joey Baker, and short stints with several others. I knew for a fact they would not run down Jo & Joey Baker—I was Jo and my "brother" Joey's real name was something I'd long forgotten. I'd heard he'd quit the stage when his father inherited a dry-goods store somewhere in Texas. Even if they found him, he'd have as little to say about me as I would about him. I didn't make a point of telling people my real age, and no one in vaudeville sat around blabbing about their civilian lives. The theater is a closemouthed business. If Pinkertons could trace people who changed their names and their acts at the drop of a hat and traveled the United States and Canada with no permanent address, they were genuine magicians.

They could trace only the names I had given them, the stage names I had performed under for the past seven years. They would meet only the people I had performed with during those years, and none of them went back far enough to have known my mother or anything substantive about my past. And the investigators wouldn't find all of those people anyway, for some had dropped out of vaudeville for God knows where, and the rest changed their acts and their names as often as their undergarments. Still, the slim chance that some old codger might walk up as the investigators were flashing my photograph and say, "Gee whillikers, that's Chloë Randall's girl, isn't it?" kept me from sleeping soundly.

I saw Uncle Oliver eyeing me thoughtfully during the meal, and I knew exactly what he was thinking. I would disabuse him of the idea when I had him alone. I was not another of Lawrence Carr's bastards. My mother had never talked about the man who fathered me, but I had picked up enough to know he was a drifter. She well knew the dangers of dallying with rich dandies and would never have given Lawrence Carr the time of day. What she hadn't known was that men were all the same, regardless of social class. They said what you wanted to hear, had their fun, and left. No doubt there were exceptions to the rule, but I hadn't met any.

Someone else was watching me closely during dinner. I looked up just as dessert was being served and caught Aunt Victoria staring at me with such hostility that I blinked in astonishment, thinking I'd imagined it. Sure enough, on second glance, her expression had resumed its usual vague affability, with the corners of her lips drawn up in a bland smile. She nodded genially in my direction before turning to speak to Oliver.

I said nothing to David Murray during the entire meal, although I sat across from him, and he excused himself so quickly afterward that I didn't realize he had left the house until Aunt Victoria motioned me to follow her.

"My dear, what can I say? That was dreadful for all of us. No doubt Henry didn't realize how awkward that would be."

"It makes no difference, Aunt. Don't trouble yourself about it."

"I didn't think there was any reason for you to know about him. I didn't want your father's image tarnished in his daughter's eyes."

"How long have you known about him?"

"When your father and mother died and Charles went to the trustees, he learned about his brother's, ahem, indiscretion. Charles later told me. Lawrence had known this Murray woman before your mother, dear, so you mustn't think there was any unfaithfulness during their marriage, and young men, well, they need to sow their wild oats, but you won't know about such things."

Oh, I knew more than she thought about such things. I'd been the recipient of a few wild oats myself and had learned a proper wariness of handsome young men with glib tongues and smiles.

"Lawrence had arranged for money to be sent every quarter to Mrs. Murray, as she called herself although she never married, so he did support the boy, which was quite decent of him, really. Dear Blanche knew nothing about it, of course, and for that, I'm most grateful. When that awful accident took them both from us, the trustees stopped the payments."

"Why?"

"There was nothing in Lawrence's will about Mrs. Murray, so they had no authority to continue. And Charles said they didn't approve of the payments in any case."

I did the calculation. David would have been about sixteen when the money stopped. Tough life, but at least he'd had a father's financial support during his early years. My own father had left Mother with me in her belly and ridden into the sunset. My opinion of Lawrence Carr—never very high—rose a notch. He may have been a worthless cad, but at least he took some financial responsibility for his offspring.

"I'm glad to know the truth, Aunt, never worry about that."

She squeezed my arm. "Dearest Jessie, you are such a joy to me. I can't tell you how proud I am to see the fine lady you've become . . . if only your mother could see you now. I blame myself for your unhappy years and wish I could have been a better substitute for dear Blanche but I was so preoccupied with Charles's final illness that I failed you utterly and I've never ceased to regret that—"

"No, no, no. You were not to blame for my running away. You were more than I deserved and I was too young to appreciate it. But I do now, and I am very grateful for your love and devotion after all these years."

She pulled a lacy handkerchief from her sleeve and dabbed at a tear at the corner of each eye. "Now, Ross has retired to his study and Henry took David Murray into Dexter for the train, so how about you and I and the girls play a few rounds of Give and Take?"

Later that night I lay awake in bed at the very edge of sleep, unable to rid myself of the image of Aunt Victoria's hard glare. What Ross had said at the cliff edge ran through my head, how a polite façade masked his mother's true feelings. And I thought back to the day in Cleveland only a few weeks ago when I had asked Oliver who would inherit if Jessie never returned. The four cousins, he had replied. They had the most to lose by our scheme.

But that no longer rang true. Who had the most to lose now that Jessie had returned? Not Henry—he could continue in crooked politics funding his way of life with bribes and favors. Not Ross—academia would pay enough to keep him in books, which was his chief concern. No, the one who had the most to lose was the one who did not stand to inherit, not directly anyway. It was Aunt Victoria, whose passion in life was her children. Would her daughters make brilliant marriages if they were not wealthy? Would her sons reach their highest potential without the Carr fortune behind them? Would she need to find another husband to support her? Was there anything she wouldn't do for her children?

After I heard the clock strike two, I got up and, in desperation, headed down to the kitchen for some hot milk. As I passed the parlor, the decanter of sherry called my name, and I took a full glass upstairs. As I drank it, I thought about the Carrs and their ambitions, one by one, then looked long and hard at Chen's bad-luck chrysanthemums and threw them in the wastebasket. Only then did I fall asleep, and I slept undisturbed by dreams for the first time since my arrival at Cliff House.

24

Learn something new every day, my mother used to say, so I decided I'd learn to drive a motorcar. In my current line of work, a skill like that could come in handy if a sudden change in script required a quick getaway.

Aunt Victoria did not drive; she had Clyde at her daily beck and call. Clyde brought the Carr mail from the post office every afternoon, along with the groceries Marie telephoned in to the A&P. I had taken to watching for his Ford flivver, hoping for the Pinkerton report from Smith and Wade. I waylaid him that afternoon after he had deposited the grocery box inside the kitchen door.

"Any mail, Clyde?"

"None today, miss. Sorry."

Instead of screaming with frustration—what in heaven's name was taking those wretched old men so long?—I took a deep breath and said dismissively, "Never mind. It's nothing important. By the way, I know how busy you are, but I wonder if you would have the time to teach me to drive?"

His expression said that old Clyde didn't hold with women driving, but he was too much the gentleman to voice the opinion. "You want to learn now?" he asked doubtfully.

"If you have time."

"I got time." He opened the car door and motioned me behind the wheel. "That there round pedal'll start 'er up," he began, pointing to a button in the center of the floorboard close to the seat base. I pressed with my right heel and the engine coughed to life. "Now to go forward, push this brake lever all the way toward the front while you press the left pedal all the way in, engage low—that's it—and advance the throttle here another few notches." With the car moving forward in low, I released the left pedal, shifted into high, and we were off on our trip around the house.

For the next half hour I was enmeshed in a battle between my hands and my feet. When I approached it as I would learning a dance routine, it got easier. An hour later, I cruised triumphantly into Dexter with Clyde beside me, most of the way in high gear with no feet at all, bought us sodas at the drugstore, and drove home to Cliff House with only a few lurches bad enough to make Clyde wince. This was freedom like I'd never known.

When the twins saw me drive up, nothing would satisfy them but to learn to drive as well. At that moment, Ross joined us, giving Clyde the interruption he needed to recall some urgent business back in Dexter. I assured the girls their chance would come soon.

"And Clyde," I said as he was leaving. "I'd like to buy a car for myself. A Ford will do fine, but a roadster, perhaps, or a runabout. Do you know of one for sale in Dexter, or must I send to Portland?" Clyde promised to have a look-see and let me know in a day or two.

A sudden frown spoiled Ross's features, telegraphing his disapproval. As Clyde drove off and the twins melted away, I turned to go inside. I wasn't fast enough.

"Who do you think you are?" he demanded, his voice deadly quiet. "That money's not yours."

"It soon will be. And I have no doubt the trustees will approve that purchase in advance of my birthday," I said, continuing up the steps. Aunt Victoria appeared, effectively shutting off any further nastiness. Instead, he raised his voice so his mother could hear.

"I trust you'll be careful, Jessie," he said, sounding like an anxious father. "The danger for a woman driving a car is not to be underestimated. All sorts of accidents can happen on the road." I was sure he'd be more than happy to provide one.

"What's this I hear about Jessie driving?" asked Aunt Victoria.

"I've just had my lesson from Clyde."

"She plans to buy her own car," said Ross.

"Oh, my, well, you must do whatever you think best, Jessie dear, of course, but Ross's concerns are not misplaced. No indeed. Driving is very dangerous, especially for ladies." She cast a fond glance at her youngest son.

"I'll be careful, Aunt."

The cheerful day, clear, sunny, and warmer than the previous few, made me feel adventurous. After taking the precaution of telling Grandmother where I was going, I set off for the beach to visit the caves, eager to see where Jessie and Buster had played out their pirate fantasies.

At the top of the bluff, I faced into a mild sea breeze. The hat brim shaded the sun from my eyes as I scanned the coast for miles north and south, then a distant bark turned my attention to the beach where I saw I would not be alone. Someone was moving slowly along the strand, picking his way around the piles of tree litter, stooping now and then, and putting something into a shiny tin pail. The distance was too great to identify the person's face, but his conical straw hat was clue enough. Leaving my sweater on a large rock, I set off through the thicket.

The path to the beach did not make a difficult descent, and five minutes later, my shoes crunched the pebbles that the Pacific currents had deposited on Carr property thousands of years before it was Carr property.

"Hello, Chen!" I called loudly over the sound of the waves.

King bounded over to greet me, stopping to bark at a dead jellyfish. I caught up with Chen and peered into his bucket. He nodded but did not smile.

"Oh, agates. I thought you were collecting seashells for the garden."

"No, agates and jasper. After rough weather, the beaches around here are full of them." As if to prove his point, he stooped and picked up a dark green stone with red flecks in it.

"Ooh, that's beautiful. They're shiny when they're wet, aren't they?"

"They show up better too."

"Is this one?" Chen peered at my find and nodded. I dropped it in his pail. "What are you collecting them for? To put in the garden?"

He didn't answer for so long, I wondered if he had not heard me. All at once, a sick sense of horror drenched me. Jessie had collected agates on the beach. Jessie would never have asked, *Is this one?* I had just ruined the entire scheme. No wonder Chen was silent; he was reflecting on Jessie's odd reaction. He would repeat his doubts to the family. I was sunk.

Finally Chen spoke. It was not the question I expected. It was not a question at all. "These are not for the garden. But I don't take time away from my work to search. I work longer to make up for the time."

My knees almost buckled with relief. How had I forgotten? Chen hadn't worked here when Jessie lived at Cliff House. Chen hadn't known Jessie or her interest in agates. The lengthy silence hadn't indicated Chen's suspicion, it had been Chen's concern about his new employer's opinion. Now I just had to hope Chen didn't say anything to anyone about my ignorance about agates. And why would he? The Carrs didn't fraternize with the help.

"I beg your pardon, Chen," I said, grateful for the reprieve. "I didn't intend to pry, and I certainly wasn't suggesting anything about your work. I only came down here to visit the caves." I pointed to the two gaping holes a short distance ahead of us and noticed as I did so that a third one was barely visible farther south in the cove beyond an outcropping of jagged boulders where the cliffs were not as high. While the first two caves were readily accessible, reaching the third would require climbing a rough patch of rock or swimming around it. Above us, dark-feathered birds dipped and called out with raucous voices, plunging into the water for fish, then flying up to their nests in the cliff. I wondered whether there were babies in the nests this time of year. Birds were like gardens—subjects I knew nothing about. I leaned over to pick up a lovely agate with green and purple bands, dropped it in Chen's pail, and started to move away toward the largest cave.

"Those caves are dangerous," he said, reeling me back to his side with his words.

I looked around. Modest waves slapped the shore. The sun shone, the air was crisp and clear, shorebirds skittered across the pebbles, and King sniffed at some menacing driftwood. A more tranquil scene would be hard to imagine. "I'm sure during a storm the waves get violent, but now it seems quite peaceful."

Chen walked a while with his brow furrowed, considering, I think, how to answer without contradicting.

"Storms, yes. They can be violent. The last storm brought waves as high as that." He indicated an outcropping and a twisted bush clinging to the edge of it about halfway up the cliff. I could see the marks. I was about to say I had no idea the waves could get that high when he added, "Other times, the spray comes as high as the top."

I craned my neck to see the top and tried to imagine an ocean swell that could reach that height. The idea was more than a little frightening.

"Now it is low tide. But twice a day, high tide brings the sea to the cliff edge, and there is no place to walk. Then the water rushes into the caves through the openings. Anything inside will be dashed against the rocks and washed away."

"But it's safe for the moment."

"Safe enough. But even on fine days like this, the water can be very strong. Don't think of bathing here. People can wade in up to their ankles and be knocked down by a strong wave, then dragged out to sea by the currents."

No doubt he was exaggerating to make his point. "Well, these waves look tame as a trained bear," I said.

"Even a trained bear can turn on its master."

"I'm just going to have a quick look inside." I left him at the water's edge. Nothing was going to dissuade me from a visit to the caves. It was time to understand what it was that caused Jessie to spend long hours on the beach and in these caves. I felt drawn to them because of her connection—and my dream. Going inside might provide me with some sort of clue to her character or her disappearance . . . an absurd notion, really, since Chen had just told me they were completely washed out at every high tide.

As I reached its mouth, the loose pebbles underfoot gave way to rough rock and slime. My thin soles fared poorly on the jagged floor. The cavern itself was larger inside than its narrow mouth suggested, about the size of a theater stage, and as high, with starfish decorating its walls and crevices. I called to myself and my own voice answered in the emptiness. I picked my way about halfway in until I could see the back wall, then turned back into the sun. No clues there.

The cave next door was so small there was no need to enter it. Its wide mouth funneled down to a rock room no bigger than my bedroom. I wondered what Jessie had found so interesting about empty caves.

I turned to see the third cave some distance to the south. Scrambling over the rocky outcrop would ruin my shoes, and considering how little of interest there was in the first two, my curiosity flagged.

By now Chen had turned and was retracing his steps along the wet strand, his head down and his walk measured. I caught up with him. Without speaking, I matched his pace and fastened my eyes to the beach. "Here's a beaut," I said after a while, crouching to sift through the stones with my fingers. "They are so pretty, they could be jewelry."

"That is what they will become. I collect these for an old man. He polishes agates and jasper until they sparkle like gemstones. It takes a very long time in a rock tumbler, but they become brilliant. Then he makes beads and necklaces and other jewelry from them. It is the only work he can do. His poor health lost him his cannery job, and this work allows him to feed himself and his grandson."

"Is he a relative of yours?"

"Not the way you mean it. But in a foreign country, all Chinese are related."

"Vaudeville works the same way. Doesn't the boy have parents?"

"His father is in prison. His mother, the old man's daughter, was murdered. Without the jewelry making, they would be beggars."

"How horrible for a child to have a father who killed his mother!"

"No, no, excuse me. I am not clear. The father was sent to prison some months before his wife's death. She did not come home one night. The next day, her body was found on the wharf. She had been strangled."

"Did the police catch the murderer?"

He gave me a pitying look. "A Chinese girl out at night is

presumed to be a lady of the evening. And her husband was a known criminal. There was no investigation."

"When did this happen?" I asked, thinking of Lizzette's death last week. "That Indian girl . . . she was strangled too."

"This was several years ago, in the fall of 1918."

"So there's probably no connection. Still . . . no doubt the police will investigate now, after a second killing."

Chen's snort told me his opinion on the likelihood of that.

I pulled up suddenly, as if my mind had tripped over something. "You know what, Chen? I really love these agates. I might like to buy some of those beads. Would you know how I could do that?"

"I will ask the old man and bring you some if he agrees."

Leaving him to finish his search, I started up the path with King at my heels, absorbed by thoughts of the violent deaths of the Indian woman and the Chinese woman. Could there be any connection between the two unsolved murders, coming as they did six years apart? Both young, both strangled. Both foreign looking, with dark hair. One with the tip of a braid cut off, like a trophy. What about the other?

The climb was steep, like ascending a staircase where each step was a different height, and King bounded ahead when I paused to catch my breath. At irregular intervals, gnarled branches provided handholds as I climbed. Finally, my heart pounding hard and my head down to watch each step, I reached the top.

When I lifted my eyes, I was staring at a pair of highly polished black boots, so close to my nose I could see my reflection in their shine.

I froze. To my right, the path dropped away to the stones far below. Instinctively, my left hand tightened its grip on an exposed root.

"Well, well, if it isn't Miss Fraud," taunted Henry. "Don't you know it's dangerous to play around cliffs?"

I nearly jumped out of my skin. Henry Carr was the last

person I wanted to see towering above me next to a sheer drop onto sharp rocks. He was supposed to have been out sailing. Unable to speak, unable to move, unable to breathe, I could only lock eyes with the man who would inherit a fortune at my death.

"I'm afraid you wouldn't survive a fall from this height." He took a step closer and reached down to me, his mouth open and his breath coming in shallow, rapid pulses. I could see the hatred in his eyes and something else—the triumph of the hunter who has cornered his prey. He was going to pull my hand off the root and drop me over the side. And he was going to enjoy doing it.

Beside him danced King, wagging his tail happily, oblivious to the "accident" that was about to occur.

I found my voice. "Chen is right behind me," I lied, praying it would come true. "Chen!" I shouted, unable to keep the hysterical note from my voice.

Miraculously, Chen's reply came from around the corner, a few feet away. "Yes, miss?"

Henry straightened at once. His face tightened and went blank.

My knees nearly gave way with relief, and I gulped a ragged breath of air. "Henry is here to greet us."

Chen appeared behind me and Henry stepped back from the edge. "There you are, Chen," he said sternly. "That last storm eroded some of the ground here and it's become quite dangerous. Miss Jessie almost fell over the edge. See that you get some iron rods and chain and make the path safe again."

C lyde judged $350 a fair price for a Ford runabout, so I con-
tacted Smith and Wade and they consented to advance the
money, something I took as a sign that all was quiet on the
investigation front. Before you could say Jack Robinson, two boys
delivered my new car from Colvin's in McMinnville. And none
too soon. Being stuck in one place—and such a remote place at
that—was starting to turn me screwy.

Aunt Victoria and Grandmother asked for a ride in the new
vehicle, Uncle Oliver had to take it for a spin, and even Ross
deigned to give it a glance. Poor Caroline was confined to bed
with a cold—the Portland shopping trip had to be postponed—
and I tried to lessen Valerie's disappointment by letting her drive
around and around the house, practicing shifting gears until she
nearly ran the tank dry.

"I need to drive into town for more fuel," I announced. "Maybe

I'll see if I can give Chen a ride home, as long as I'm going that way."

"Always so thoughtful." Aunt Victoria smiled. "Just like your mother. Tell them at the station to put the gasoline on our tab."

Chen was wrapping green tomatoes in newspaper in the back-yard. I offered him a ride home.

"You'll be risking your life with a new driver," I said, clutching my handbag, "but if you would be so kind as to show me where the old man lives, I'd like to buy some of his jewelry."

He gave me a measured look, then nodded and wiped his hands on a rag.

I think Chen knew what I had in mind. Ever since he told me about the Chinese girl's murder, I hadn't been able to get the similarities of the two deaths out of my thoughts. Two young women strangled in one small town—an unlikely coincidence, surely. October 1918 and August 1924—six years apart. Would anyone but me wonder about a connection between the two? Was that what had happened to Jessie? Could there have been three young women murdered, starting with Jessie in August of 1917? Had she really run away, or was her body out there somewhere, waiting to be found?

Mr. Tang's home was no more than a hovel among rows of hovels clustered near the cannery. Chen left me to wait in the runabout at the end of the filth-clogged alley, saying he would bring the old Chinaman and his wares to me. In moments he returned with a stooped, gray-haired man carrying a frayed carpetbag. He spoke no English, but bowed to me as I stepped out of the car, then squatted on the ground to spread his wares on a piece of newspaper. Several passersby eyed our impromptu marketplace.

The beads were lovely. He had a couple dozen strands, shiny black, red and green, and multicolored mixtures. I fingered them one by one as I planned my questions in my mind.

"How much does he want for a strand, Chen?"

The two men exchanged words. Chen replied, "Fifty cents."

I counted the strands. There were twenty-three. "Ask him if he'll take twenty-five dollars for them all."

Chen showed no surprise as he translated. The old man nodded.

"Tell him I am very sorry to have learned about his daughter's death, all those years ago."

Chen translated. The old man said nothing as he picked up the beads, one strand at a time, methodically rewrapping them in the newspaper. I looked at Chen for support, but he wouldn't meet my eye.

"Ask him if it is true that she was strangled."

"It is true," said Chen.

"Ask him anyway." He did. The old man nodded.

"Ask him, when they found her body, was there anything unusual about her hair?"

Chen gave me a sharp look before translating. The old man said nothing for a long while, and I feared I had strayed beyond the boundaries of decency, but then he said, in perfect English, "Why do you ask these questions? The police did not ask."

Chen vanished behind an expressionless face. No help there. "Because another young woman, an Indian girl named Lizzette, was strangled a couple weeks ago, and I think the murders might be connected."

He gave my explanation long consideration before answering. "My daughter was not a dutiful girl. She went out of home often and would not tell me why. She was working for some Americans. She would not tell me more. I begged her to stay home and care for her son, but she wanted money. I could not get enough for her. The women who washed her for the funeral said some of her hair had been cut off on one side, here." He put his hand to his chin to show the length.

"Thank you for telling me, Mr. Tang. And thank you for the

beads. I have a grandmother, two cousins, and an aunt who will be delighted with them."

He bowed. I left Chen near his home, filled the fuel tank, and drove up the winding road to Cliff House, elated with my discovery. My hunch had been correct. The same person had killed both women and commemorated the deed with locks of their dark hair. Since both were poor and neither was white, the authorities wasted little time on the cases. Could these two deaths have any relation to Jessie's disappearance? My sixth sense told me they did, that Jessie had been murdered too, but intuition without evidence would get me laughed out of the police station.

Halfway home, a sick feeling came over me, so strong I had to pull over to the side of the road. I remembered Jessie's treasure box. The one Buster had saved for her for seven years. The one with a lock of auburn hair inside. Could Buster be involved in this? I wouldn't believe it. Buster loved Jessie. He was her only friend. *And yet* . . . he was big and strong and didn't always realize his own strength. What if it had been an accident?

No, if Buster had somehow been involved in Jessie's death, he would not have believed, even for a minute, that I was Jessie. And until I had taken off my stocking, he had believed. Breathing deeply, I guided the Ford back onto the road and back to Cliff House.

I could no longer avoid talking to Oliver.

I found him in the library writing a letter. His eyebrows arched in surprise as I closed the door and came to stand on the other side of the desk.

"A few days ago, I walked along the cliff south of the house. When Jessie went missing, did they search all those crevices along the edge?"

"Naturally. They even lowered lanterns to the bottom of the deeper ones. Why do you ask?"

"I think Jessie's dead."

"I told you that in Omaha."

"I think she was killed."

"A distinct possibility," he said carelessly. I hated him.

"I think she stumbled into something criminal and was murdered, like the Indian girl."

"Are you going gaga on me? That dead squaw has nothing to do with Jessie. It was some tribal feud."

"That's just what the lazy sheriff said to avoid an investigation."

"And how do you know that?"

"I talked to some of her people on the reservation a few days ago. I rode over with the stable boy."

His eyes narrowed as he contemplated that. "You've been snooping?"

"A Chinese girl was also strangled a few years ago along Dexter's waterfront. Her father believes she was involved in something illegal. I talked to him this afternoon. I'm sure these two murders are related, and I think Jessie's disappearance is too. Dexter is a pretty small town to have three young women killed in a seven-year span. It can't be coincidence."

Oliver hoisted his bulk from behind the desk and transported himself to my side. His face grew mottled with the effort of controlling his rage, and his breathing became uneven. "You unspeakable little tramp. How dare you traipse around playing detective? Your job is to impersonate my niece, not to stir up trouble all over town."

Without warning, he slapped me. Twice. Hard.

"I don't give a tinker's damn about who's dead and who's not, but I know someone who is going to be dead very soon if she doesn't play the part she was hired to play."

And when I'd finished playing that part, when Oliver's pudgy fingers were securely wrapped around a large chunk of Carr money, would he decide that a dead accomplice was safer than a live one?

26

O ne, two, three, turn. Left, step, left, step. Tiny steps, now
circle left in four counts—no, Valerie, left."

It was to have been a simple song-and-dance routine,
performed by the twins and me for the family on a rainy day, but,
as theatricals are wont to do, the play ran away with us. In no
time we were the Carr Cousins with plans for half a dozen short
acts, including two poetry recitations that their governess, Mrs.
Applewhite, agreed to supervise, plus magic tricks, a twin act, and a
song and dance for the three of us: "Three Little Maids from
School Are We," what else? Nothing but the third-floor ballroom
would do for our theater, and the twins and I spent every spare
moment working on the show—there were costumes to plan and
sew, scenery to design and paint, lyrics and dance steps to memorize, and magic tricks to practice over and over again.

The redoubtable Mrs. Applewhite had moved back into her

suite on the second floor. I liked her at once. Short, plump, and energetic, she had returned to Cliff House the previous Sunday with her arms full of mind-improving books and a last-chance resolve to muscle as much knowledge as she could into her charges' heads. But she also had a rare ability to work lessons into everyday life, and she saw our theatrical production as an opportunity for learning.

Caroline was quicker to master the routines, unencumbered as she was by modesty, but Valerie had the better voice—if I could coax her to use it. Coordinating the two of them proved harder than I thought. The fancy oak Victrola provided the music. I had sent for several records from Portland, so all we had to do was sing along. I demonstrated the song and dance from Gilbert and Sullivan's *The Mikado* that my mother had taught me when I was a little girl. If I live to a hundred, I will remember those steps.

Three little maids from school are we
Pert as a school-girl well can be
Filled to the brim with girlish glee
Three little maids from school.

"Stop!" shrieked Valerie. She caught a glimpse of Ross peering into the ballroom from the hallway.

"Come on in, Ross," I called as he scuttered away. "You can critique us."

"No!" Valerie protested. "I can't practice with someone watching!"

"Never mind." His voice came from around the corner. "My eyes are shut, and I didn't see a thing. I don't want to interrupt you."

"Come in," I insisted. "Sit there and watch. We've got the first part down. Come on, girls, it's good to practice in front of an audience." I put the needle on the record, and the music forced them to begin the routine.

Aunt Victoria came up the stairs. "Girls, it's two o'clock and Mr. Tyndall has arrived. Time for your art lesson."

"But we're rehearsing," protested Caroline.

"We need a break," I said, "and maybe Mr. Tyndall could help with some ideas for the design of the *Mikado* backdrop. While you're working on that, I'll dash into town and buy some canvas and paint."

It was a plan. They trooped downstairs, and I headed for my new Ford.

"Would you like me to come with you?" asked Ross.

I was instantly alert. "What for?"

He shrugged. "I can help carry paint cans and canvas." I looked around, realizing I had not seen Henry since lunch. "I sent my thesis off yesterday, and I'm not doing anything."

The abrupt change in demeanor put me on my guard. He wanted to help with the production? Had he turned a corner in his doubts about my identity? I needed to find out. What else could I say except, "Well, sure. I'll put you to work. Come along."

We headed to the shed where I kept my car out of the elements. I expected him to demand the key, but to my surprise he climbed into the passenger seat.

"Doesn't it make you nervous to ride with a woman?"

"If you don't mind, I'll wait and see how you handle this bronco before I answer that."

"Most men wouldn't care to be seen with a woman driving," I said as I steered down the long driveway.

"Long as you miss those trees and keep the wheels on the road, I'll keep my opinion to myself. Did you get your permit?"

"Not yet, but I sent in the quarter and it should arrive in this week's mail."

"Caroline and Valerie look like they're having the time of their lives with this show. When do you think you'll be ready?"

"That's hard to say. We just started, and there's a lot to do."

"Maybe I can help. I don't thread a needle, but I'm steady with a paintbrush and pretty good at rigging things." He gave me an apologetic glance. "I've really nothing else to do but wait for word that my thesis is accepted." Waiting was something I understood all too well. The trustees' report had still not arrived and I was getting antsy.

I'd been over it a thousand times in my head. Three days was all it should have taken. In three days a Pinkerton could catch the train for Milwaukee where *Variety* placed the Little Darlings, have a nice visit with Jock and Francine about the time I'd spent with their act, and return with a pretty report, neatly typed, paper clipped together in a leather presentation folder. Three days. Four if they were incompetent. What had gone wrong?

"To tell you the truth, we could use a man's help with the backdrop. If I can get what I need in town, we can start on that today. Maybe . . . if everything goes well, we could shoot for a performance in two weeks."

"Great."

"By the way, what's the latest on the Indian girl's death?"

"What?"

"I mean, have the police made any headway? Any suspects?"

"Don't be silly. I told you there wouldn't be any investigation once the sheriff decided it was some tribal vendetta. Which it wasn't. I finally persuaded one of the younger Killamook men to tell me that the girl had been involved in something illegal. What, he wouldn't say or didn't know, but to my mind, that means prostitution, smuggling, bootlegging, or maybe theft. We'll never know. No one cares what happens to an Indian girl."

"You do."

He shrugged his shoulders.

"Because of your research?"

"My research?" He gave a thin smile. "Maybe just because I like dark-haired women."

I took the sharp turns carefully and reached the bottom of the hill without once seeing Ross press his foot against the floorboard or reach for the wheel. As we approached the town limits, I opened my mouth to ask which way to go to the hardware store when my predicament slapped me square in the face.

Jessie would know where the hardware store was. I didn't even know its name.

Think!

"Oh, dear." I sighed audibly. I took several deep breaths, inhaling through my nose and exhaling through my mouth. It took a few repetitions; he wasn't very perceptive.

"Is something wrong?" he asked finally.

"No, I . . . yes . . . oh, dear, I think I'd better stop before—" I pulled over to the gravel edge of the road and got out of the car, clutching my stomach.

"Are you all right?"

"I'll be fine. Just give me a moment. I think it's this winding road. I'm feeling rather seasick."

"Maybe I'd better drive?"

Bingo. I handed him the keys with a look of regret, and after a few moments climbed into the passenger seat, still breathing deeply.

"Shouldn't we wait a while longer? I wouldn't want you to be sick in this nice new car."

"No, I'm better now. I just needed to settle my stomach, and the curves are done. Go on." I sat limply beside him and looked out the window as we entered town and turned left, then right, and onto the planked main street that paralleled the wharf, passing by the Polly Anna Bake Shop and Café on the right and the Cozy Corner Confectionery across from it. On Dock Street, Ross found room to park the flivver up against the wooden sidewalk in front of the rain barrels outside Berkeley and Son Hardware, and we got out.

Across from us fishing boats and pleasure craft were tied up at several piers. A cannery stood at the end of the point and warehouses and shops lined the street. It was a busy time of day with fishermen cleaning their shiny catches on tables at the edge of the water to the delight of a squadron of gulls that dove for the fish guts tossed into the bay. The cannery shift was changing and workers, mostly Chinamen and Indians, trudged down the street, lunch pails in hand, heading home. The moist air smelled of ocean, fish, and tar.

Ross and I wound our way past the casks of nails and coils of hemp rope to the back of the store where the owner was struggling with a parcel of rakes.

"What can I help you with, Mr. Carr?"

"Miss Carr needs some things." Ross had his faults, but at least he wasn't one of those superior-minded men who always try to take over from women.

"I'll need the biggest muslin or canvas sheets you have, the sort painters use for drop cloth would do. Three of them. And half a dozen cans of paint—black, white, green, and the primaries—with assorted brushes and turpentine and some—"

"Pa! Pa!" A tousled-haired boy of about fourteen burst through the screen door, letting it fly shut with a bang. Panting and sweating, he pulled the cap off his head and pushed the hair out of his eyes. "There's a coroner from Portland going t'come identify the bones!"

"William! Hold off, son, I'm with a customer! Excuse me, Miss Carr, but—"

"What bones?" I asked, seized by a premonition of disaster.

"There was a warehouse fire last night," said the storekeeper. "You know the empty Kelsey building back of us on Second Street? It half burned down before the volunteers could put it out, but they found a body—or the remains of a body—inside."

"It was hidden," said William, flush with the importance of a boy who knew something the adults didn't. "Under the stairs to the loft was a room . . . not a room, a closet, a little place with a door that was locked. They hacked into there with their axes and found a body. Doc Milner said it was a girl with a broken neck.

Deader than a dodo's grandfather. Not killed by the fire. He said she'd been dead five or ten years. Nobody knows who it was, and Doc Milner's not a real coroner, so they called for a real coroner to try to tell who it was."

The bones in my knees dissolved. Ross slid a stool behind me not a second too soon.

They'd found Jessie.

have never suffered from stage fright and refused to start now. Finding Jessie's body required ad-libbing and steady nerves, like the time the orchestra played Offenbach instead of Gershwin, or Darcy upchucked on stage, or the costumes went to St. Louis while the show went to St. Paul. My cue card said "Exit Stage Left." Not in some panic-stricken flight but calmly, in a dignified manner. The circumstances were so dire that even Oliver's threat to ruin my career no longer deterred me. Unemployment was preferable to prison.

To be honest, part of me was relieved the charade was over. Another part felt a sense of grim satisfaction that Oliver's grand scheme had failed. I'd have loved to see his reaction when the news hit, but I'd be long gone by then.

There was no need to rush. Coroners don't issue same-day rulings. It would be days, weeks perhaps, before his medical investigation was finished and he presented his findings to the police. He would correlate the details of the girl's remains—hair, clothing, jewelry perhaps—with the list of young females missing between roughly 1914 and 1919. The authorities would note that the reappearance of Jessie Carr involved some initial doubts as to her identity, and they would put two and two together. By the time they reached four, I'd be gone. Toronto, I thought. I had already chosen my new name. I should have gone straight to Oliver to warn him that the game was up and that I would be leaving soon, but the scene in the library had cost him any loyalty I might have owed him.

My conscience pricked. In the short time I'd been at Cliff House, I had come to care for the girls, and I would miss Aunt Victoria's peculiar mixture of flightiness and competence. Grandmother's protective love felt better than a warm blanket on a cold night. Pretending they were family had started to make it seem so. They would be hurt when they learned about my deception, then angry at having been suckered. Henry would crow. Ross would say he knew all along I wasn't Jessie.

The gig was up. Professionally speaking, I think I would have succeeded had not fate lit a fire in an old warehouse. I would miss the ironed sheets and swell food. But the worst would be never knowing the whole truth about what had happened to Jessie. I had come to think of myself as her stand-in, her understudy, called up to take the part she couldn't finish. Jessie had crept under my skin. I cared for her. I wanted to know who had killed her. I wanted someone to pay for the crime.

On the drive home, the possibilities ran unbidden through my head. One, Jessie had crawled into the space below the stairs to hide from someone, been accidentally locked in, and starved to death. I gave that low marks. It didn't explain the broken neck. Two, Jessie had been the victim of a kidnapping gone wrong. Oliver had expressed that opinion when we first met. The theory had one glaring defect—kidnappers kidnapped for money. Killing the kid benefited no one. Perhaps her death was accidental—she had stumbled down the warehouse steps trying to escape and broken her neck before the kidnappers had had the chance to send their ransom note. Well, it was a possibility.

Three, someone strangled her and stashed her body in an abandoned building, where, absent the fire, it might never have been discovered. The same Jack the Ripper madman who had killed the other girls?

The young Chinese woman had died on the docks just a couple blocks from the warehouse where they found Jessie. The incidents had to be related. Surely Lizzette and the Chinese woman had been killed by the same person—someone who strangled first and then cut off a lock of hair as a keepsake. If the coroner's report on Jessie's body showed a lock of hair missing, that would clinch it.

But an heiress's murder is unlikely to be the result of random violence. The first thing to ask is who stands to inherit. Jessie's death shifted the Carr fortune to Jessie's cousins. Could the late Uncle Charles, the invalid, have hired someone to kidnap Jessie and kill her so his children would inherit what he had been denied? It was all too preposterous. People didn't murder children for money.

And then I remembered Shakespeare's *Richard III*.

There was a fourth possibility. Anticipating their own eventual inheritance, Henry and Ross could have arranged Jessie's death. But although my close encounters with Henry and Ross at the cliff edge left me in no doubt that they would kill me today if it could be made to look an accident, their killing Jessie seemed unlikely. Henry would have been only seventeen and Ross fifteen—surely too young to actually murder a young girl cousin.

I remembered Jessie's last letter to Grandmother. Was there another reason Henry might have wanted Jessie out of the way? What was Henry's secret? What hold did Jessie have over him? Something serious enough to make him kill her? And Ross. He had tried to lock her in the basement once—but surely that was just a childish act of intimidation. Wasn't it?

I cast back to our first encounter and replayed that scene through my head. That pasty pallor. The ready-to-run stance. Henry had been terrified that Jessie really had returned. I was certain of it, then and now. If he or his father had caused Jessie's death, he'd have known I was an impostor, yet, at least initially, he had showed doubt. Days later, at the dinner table with David, he'd said, "I know you're not Jessie." At the time, I hadn't given his choice of words much thought, but looking back, the significance of the verb crashed over my head like thunder. Not "I *think* you're not Jessie," but "I *know*."

All at once, I knew what had happened.

Henry hadn't physically killed Jessie, he had locked her in the warehouse closet and left her to die. When I showed up seven years later claiming to be Jessie, he had to face the real possibility that Jessie had somehow escaped and run off. That day I met him, he was expecting me to rat on him and was ready to high-tail it out of Oregon the moment I accused him of attempted murder. When I didn't accuse him of anything, he was pretty sure I was an impostor. So he went back to the scene of the crime to check whether Jessie's body was still in the warehouse. It was. So now he *knew* I wasn't Jessie, as he said to me at dinner that night. By setting the building on fire, he made sure Jessie's remains would be found. As soon as the body was identified, I would be exposed. He'd be rid of me. He and his siblings would reclaim the Carr fortune.

That was the worst part, that they would get Jessie's inheritance. They would win. She would have hated that. And I hated it too, more for her sake than for mine.

Word of the body spread faster than the fire, reaching Cliff House before Ross and I returned with our supplies.

"It's horrifying," proclaimed Aunt Victoria as we carried our paint cans up to the ballroom. "Simply horrifying. Soon we'll all

be murdered in our beds! A nice town like Dexter and two murders in two weeks!"

The ever-practical Ross pointed out that the murders were
separated by many years. "The woman in the warehouse was probably killed before we ever moved to Dexter, Mother." I refrained
from adding anything about the strangled Chinese girl. No need
to add to my aunt's anxieties.

Henry was absent from the dinner table that night, which
meant we could skip the speechifying. Aunt Victoria, who had
kept all news of the body in the warehouse away from the
twins, kept up an inane prattle designed, I was sure, to divert
our thoughts. I was toying with my food when she resurrected the
shopping trip to Portland. Caroline's cold had mended, she said
brightly, and the original plan was back on schedule. It made my
flight simpler.

"We'll catch the first train tomorrow morning. Jessie can drive
us to the station and leave the runabout there overnight, can't
you, dear?"

"We'll all go," said Oliver. "Mother and I have outstayed our
welcome"—he held his hands up to ward off the vehement protes-
tations that they were welcome at Cliff House until Doomsday—
"and we can catch the train to San Francisco the next day."

As long as I was leaving, it didn't matter who was coming
with me as far as Portland. Once I got there, I'd say I was going to
stay an extra day and then disappear.

I spent my last night at Cliff House wishing I didn't have to
leave. The worst of it was, I'd let Jessie down. Like everyone else
in her life.

28

The next morning Aunt Victoria put her foot wrong and slid down three steps in the cellar, spraining her ankle. Dr. Milner hurried over, wrapped it in stiff bandages, and gave her aspirin for the pain and swelling.

"No trips for you, Mrs. Carr," he pronounced.

"I'm terribly sorry, girls," she said sadly. "Our shopping trip seems cursed! The doctor says I must sit with my foot raised for several days to rest this sprain. How silly of me to be so careless. We'll go next week, I promise!"

But the twins, in a now-or-never frame of mind, whined that it wasn't really for them, it was for poor Jessie who was growing weak from lack of exercise, and if she didn't go shopping for a riding habit and a tennis costume soon, she would have to take to her bed.

"Why don't Mother and I supervise the girls?" asked Oliver.

"We'll ride into Portland tomorrow morning as planned and stay the night with the young ladies at the Benson. The next day, Mother and I can leave for San Francisco and the girls can return home."

"Yes, yes!" The twins were ecstatic. Aunt Victoria graciously consented, and the trip was back on.

I walked Doc Milner to his sedan so I could snatch a private moment.

"Any developments in the death of the Indian girl?" I began.

"Nope."

I could hear Ross telling me, "No one will care."

"Do they know who she was yet?"

"Some girl off the reservation. Killamook, someone said. Strangled, and her head cracked by a club or something."

As if she were stunned first and then throttled. I winced. "Have they found her killer?"

He shook his head. "And they never will. It was probably a lover's quarrel turned ugly. Or tribal vengeance. The Killamooks hate the Umpquas or the Chinooks, or maybe it's the Chinooks who hate the Killamooks. I can't keep track of such folderol."

"I heard about the body they found yesterday," I said to him.

"You and everyone else in town. A shame good news doesn't travel as fast."

"I suppose it will be a long while before the coroner rules on the cause of death. Any idea who she is?"

"No one from these parts, that's for sure," he said. "Unless I'm badly mistaken, however, the girl's death was caused by strangulation. Her neck was broken, which doesn't happen in strangulation unless the violence is extreme. As for who she was, no one can name any young woman with dark hair who's gone missing in the past few years."

"Dark hair?" I blurted, my heart in my throat. Dear God, it wasn't Jessie after all! It couldn't have been Jessie, not with dark hair! Only my grip on the stair rail kept me from melting to the ground.

A great wave of relief washed over me when I realized what this meant. I was safe. I could stay. I was still Jessie.

"Yes, dark brown. Why the surprise?"

"I—well. I heard different, that's all." I was flabbergasted almost beyond speech. "And . . . and someone said you put her death at five or ten years ago."

"That was my first thought when I saw the remains, judging from the state of decomposition. Now I think her death took place in late September of 1919."

"How on earth did you arrive at that?"

"For one thing, the color and weight of the fabrics did not suggest spring or summer, and there was no coat, which would have suggested winter, so that leaves autumn. But before you admire my Sherlock Holmes powers of observation, let me confess that when the remains were taken up later that day, there was a scrap of a Portland newspaper in her handbag dated September 17, 1919. Makes me wonder if she wasn't from Portland."

"Was there anything strange about her hair?"

"Not that I noticed," said the doctor, "but I did not conduct an examination. Her hair was in disarray." His bushy eyebrows met in disapproval. "You sound like the sheriff with all these questions."

Before I had to respond there came a shout from the front steps. "Hey, Doc!" It was Ross. "Hilda just telephoned to tell you Mrs. Beazley's baby has started to come and to meet them at the house."

"Damnation," he muttered. "Six weeks early . . . and Dexter with no incubator. I was hoping she—never mind. Now you keep your aunt off her feet or that ankle will never mend."

My explanation for Jessie's death was so much horse manure. The flaws in my theory had been right in front of me all along. For one, why would Henry have waited so long to check the warehouse? Why not do it before I had even arrived at Cliff House, instead of attempting to expose me with tricks and delaying for a couple of weeks? And the warehouse girl had been strangled, so there could have been no uncertainty about her death that would have drawn Henry back to check. No, Henry hadn't killed Jessie. I didn't like him, but that didn't mean he'd killed anyone.

And why was I so certain Jessie was dead? Could she not be waiting until her twenty-first birthday to return home? What made me think she'd come to Dexter at all? The Smith and Wade office in Sacramento made more sense. Perhaps she was there now, and they were getting ready to spring the trap on her impersonator.

29

On Friday morning as we were making ready to leave for Portland, Grandmother had a sudden change of heart. She would stay at Cliff House a while longer. She was having a lovely visit and saw no reason to cut it short. She would remain until Jessie's birthday, then she and I could ride the train south together when I returned to Sacramento and the trustees.

No one was more surprised at this turnabout than I. Grandmother had spent her days at the fringe of activity, saying little, dozing often, arranging a vase of flowers now and then, and attracting no attention—but she was an acerbic old woman, and she was keeping an eye on Henry and Ross for me after I told her about the two menacing incidents on the bluff. I was delighted that she would stay. She was my only ally, the only person who genuinely cared about me, and I felt safer with her watching my back. Uncle Oliver, on the other hand, needed to leave. His past visits to Cliff

House had never lasted so long, and he feared deviation from the pattern could bring unwanted speculation. Besides, an old friend was sailing into San Francisco soon and Oliver wanted to be on the dock to greet him.

So Oliver, the twins, and I climbed aboard the early train to Portland, and before the clock's hands pointed north, we had deposited our valises in a commodious suite at the Benson Hotel, with Oliver in a bachelor's room down the hall. Like puppies pulling at a leash, the twins were wild to reach the stores and the Friday Surprise.

"I'll meet you girls in the dining room at eight," Oliver said to me. "Do try not to deplete the entire Carr fortune in one afternoon." Oliver was becoming quite possessive of the Carr fortune. For the hundredth time, I wondered how he planned to get his hands on it without attracting any notice. I could hardly write him a big check without arousing questions.

This week's Friday Surprise involved silverware, men's hats, and ice cream, only one of which interested my young cousins, but the electricity generated by the sale crackled in the air along Sixth Street before we had even reached the entrance. Our plan was to look over all the finer retailers on Friday and return to buy on Saturday, however, Friday evening found us still at Meier & Frank's.

"This is awful," wailed Caroline at the dinner table, attacking her beef Wellington as if it had caused the time to fly. "The last train leaves at two o'clock tomorrow. We won't have enough time for Eastern Outfitting or Roberts Brothers or that little dress shop or anything!"

"Why don't we stay another night?" I asked, masking my own eagerness to extend the trip. Coming home Sunday afternoon would mean another day in the stores, but my real interest lay across town. The Portland theater district was calling my name.

I'd been seized with an attack of homesickness the moment we arrived in the city. The inescapable pull of vaudeville was growing by the minute, and I knew how the ancient Greek sailors felt when they passed the Sirens, hearing their bewitching songs and leaping off their ships. It would be prudent for me to keep in mind their fate—death on the rocks. But in my entire life I had never been parted one day from vaudeville, and today marked the sixth week of our separation. I missed it, suddenly and with a sharp desperation that made my stomach ache and turned the food in my mouth to sand. The sound of the audience settling into their seats, the smell of flop sweat and greasepaint on players in the wings, the sense of anticipation that makes the pulse race with excitement as one's act is announced—I wanted it all and I wanted it now. I needed it now. Intense longing for that heart-thumping moment when the curtain rises, the music bursts out of the pit, and the heat of the spotlight meets the skin made my breath come faster, and I twitched with impatience to get to the hotel's front desk for a copy of *Variety* to see who was in town this week. But I could not do any of this with Oliver clinging to us like a Spanish duenna to her maidens, so my chief goal became his departure tomorrow. If he knew I was planning a visit to the theater, he'd lock me in my room.

"I'll telephone your mother," I said, "and persuade her to let you stay another day." If she wouldn't agree, I'd bundle the girls onto the train and stay the extra day myself.

"Oh, yes, Jessie, you can convince her! I know you can!" said Caroline. "She likes you."

"Whatever her response," I said, "you needn't delay your trip south, Uncle Oliver."

He dabbed his lips on the napkin and gave me a needle-sharp look. "It would not be inconvenient for me to stay another night, my dear. Propriety and all."

"I appreciate the sentiment, but I've been taking care of myself for seven years now, and I think I can manage one more night in a luxurious hotel . . . with two mature cousins for company," I added for their benefit. "We'll see what Aunt Victoria says."

Aunt Victoria needed little persuasion, especially when I let it be understood, without precisely saying so, that Oliver would remain close at hand. "I'm sure you're a more competent chaperone than I could be, Jessie," she said. "And the stores are all so convenient to the hotel, I don't worry about you straying into undesirable parts of town."

When we retired to our suite to plan Saturday's assault on Portland's retail houses, I tucked a folded copy of *Variety* under my arm.

The next morning we bade farewell to Uncle Oliver at the train station and then hopped the streetcar for Tenth and Washington—Eastern Outfitting's five floors of clothing and household goods. By early afternoon we had returned to Meier & Frank's to be fitted for riding habits. Mine was a soft fawn color that made me almost look forward to an outing on Lady's back, theirs in darker shades carefully chosen to look different from one another. I found a ready-made tennis costume—pleated bloomers, very stylish—and proper shoes to go with it, several day frocks with the new-fashion drop waist, five becoming hats, some ritzy evening wear, a couple of cashmere sweaters, several scarves, and six pairs of shoes, some with ankle straps and comfortable low heels, and art silk stockings to wear with them. I topped it off with a crystal bottle of jasmine perfume that smelled good enough to eat. On instructions from Aunt Victoria, who had pointed out that the girls' wrists were protruding from their winter coats, we bought new ones all around as the twins sighed over the latest shawl collars and wrap-over fasteners.

We rode the elevator to the sixth-floor music section where I chose a number of records I thought would prove useful in the days ahead, and to the luggage department where the staff insisted that a Hermès was the only leather valise worthy of Miss Carr's wardrobe. At every step of the way, syrupy salesladies swarmed like honeybees to ripe pears, measuring our waists, recommending flattering colors, producing ropes of matching beads, suggesting smart

hats and gloves, offering their honest opinions—and charging it
all to the bottomless pit known as the Carr account. Alterations
would be performed by Chinese tailors sewing into the wee hours,
then everything would be brushed, ironed, boxed, wrapped, and
delivered to the train station in the morning. I never knew shopping could be so much like a magic act.

"What do you think, shall we have an early dinner and go to
the eight o'clock show?"

"You mean *vaudeville?*" Caroline asked incredulously.

"The Egyptian Theater is pulling at me like a magnet," I said
recklessly. "I checked *Variety* to see who was on the bill and I know
a couple of the acts playing there this week." That was an under-
statement. One of my oldest friends was onstage this week—
Benny Kubelsky.

The twins exchanged a silent, wide-eyed message. "We've
never seen a vaudeville show," said Valerie, hesitating a little.

I wasn't aware there was anyone over the age of six who hadn't
seen a vaudeville show, but these girls had been wrapped in cotton
wool for their entire lives, so I shouldn't have been surprised. "Well
then, the Egyptian is the place to start. It's brand spanking new. I
haven't been there myself, but I've heard it's a spectacle. Are you
game, or shall I go alone?"

"We'll go!"

"Good. Then keep hold of one of your new frocks and we'll
dress up for the occasion—your first time in a theater and my first
time to pay for ducats. We'll get box seats, seventy-five cents each,
the best in the house. No dime gallery for the Carr girls!" I said
gaily, trying to reassure the niggling voice inside my head warning
me that a vaudeville theater was the last place I should venture at
this stage of the game.

30

The Union Street Egyptian Theater hadn't been built when the Little Darlings last played Portland in '22. Back then we'd been booked at the Nob Hill, and when I was much younger, I'd performed at one or two of the Foster Road theaters, but the Egyptian outshone everything else Portland had to offer. Freshly painted with lotus-flower motifs, slathered with decorative pyramids and colorful urns, it was one of many such theaters built during the King Tut craze that had seized the country ever since archaeologists had stumbled upon the boy pharaoh's tomb. Egyptian architecture, Egyptian furniture, Egyptian wallpaper, Egyptian jewelry, even Egyptian-looking eyes made up with dark mascara and plucked brows . . . anything Egyptian was all the rage.

A boy handed us programs and another ushered us to our box, leaving us time to watch the audience settle in.

"Backstage right now," I told them, "a stagehand is calling time. He calls half hour—that's when all the players are supposed to be at the theater, then fifteen minutes, five minutes, places, and finally overture. You watch your own time after that."

At last the orchestra struck up a jaunty "Ain't We Got Fun," and the emcee strode on stage with the confidence of a seasoned veteran, greeting, welcoming, announcing, and introducing the first act.

"The first act is always a dumb act, with no speaking parts," I said, leaning across Valerie so Caroline could hear me too. "That's because of the noise in the theater as latecomers get settled. No one would be able to hear the words anyway. The last act is usually a dumb act, too, for the same reason." Sure enough, the first group on stage was the Fearless Flyers, eight young tumblers who performed astonishing feats of agility and strength. I had heard of them, but didn't recall ever sharing a billing. They were followed by the versatile boy-and-girl dance team of Freda and Anthony whose ten-minute medley of tap, tango, waltz, and Charleston was executed without a single pause for breath. Next came the vocalist, ten-year-old Baby Sylvia, billed as the "Little Princess of Song." I knew she wouldn't remember me from four years ago when we had played the same theaters together for three weeks in a row, but I recalled her as a spoiled brat. Baby Sylvia was followed by a sinister one-act play based on Oscar Wilde's *The Picture of Dorian Gray*. The fifth spot went to the headliner, Adam Berlitz, a swell pair of pipes who delighted the audience with a smooth blend of song and funny stories. After loud applause we broke for intermission.

Valerie fanned herself vigorously with her program. "I'm thirsty," she said.

We made our way to the lobby where I bought iced lemonade for three. Red-vested boys held open the front doors, hoping to coax a little of the evening air inside without letting freeloaders sneak in, and we stepped outside to cool off.

"So what do you think so far?" I asked, as if their shining faces didn't tell me the evening was a hit.

"It isn't risqué, is it?" asked Valerie. "Mother says vaudeville is risqué and not appropriate for ladies."

"That's not true!" Criticism of vaudeville always feels like someone is maligning my family. "She's confusing vaudeville with burlesque. Burlesque theaters feature women who are scantily clothed and men who tell blue jokes—"

"What's a blue joke?" asked Caroline.

"One that uses profanity, sex, or toilet words. But vaudeville has always been family entertainment and always will be. I've seen performers fired for using a vulgar word."

"Really? Like what?"

"Like liar, slob, son of a gun, devil, sucker, or damn." Two pairs of eyes widened at my naughtiness.

"Do you know any of the performers here tonight?"

I nodded. "The Little Darlings shared the stage with Baby Sylvia some years ago, but I doubt she would remember me. I have a particular friend in the second set. Someone I got to know in the Midwest when our schedules overlapped for an entire season." I pointed to a line on my program. " 'Jack Benny, Aristocrat of Humor,' it says here, although that's a new name for him. It used to be Benny Kubelsky, then for a while it was Ben K. Benny. He's a patter and violin man. And here's another group I love. The Highland Fling. They're talented singers and dancers, and they also play bagpipes. You'll like their costumes. Scottish men wear skirts, you know."

They didn't. What the twins didn't know would fill an encyclopedia.

Deep inside the theater, a gong signaled the end of intermission. Slurping the last of our lemonade, we turned to go inside, and I happened to glance toward the street. My eye caught two men coming out of the burlesque house down the block. Two men I recognized at once—cousin Henry and half brother David.

Instinctively I drew back into the doorway where I could watch without being seen. They were both dressed to the nines, something that surprised me because I didn't think David could afford that sort of clothing. They descended the steps and paused, blocking the sidewalk and talking earnestly as people swirled around them like water around rocks. As I looked on, Henry took his wallet from his breast pocket, peeled off several bills, and handed them to David. Settling a debt? Payment for a job well done? Charity for the family bastard? With a grim look on his face, David took the money and abruptly turned my way. I ducked inside and caught up with the twins.

The second half opened with Claude Delaney, a ventriloquist whose dummy recited familiar poetry that had been reworded into amusing ditties. A woman singer followed—she was such a "fish" that I suspected it was her first week onstage. And likely her last. Finally my Scottish friends made their entrance, and I pressed my tongue against my teeth and let loose a whistle that made the twins jump sky-high. "Sorry," I smiled. "Very uncouth, I know." And I whistled again as the bagpipes struck up their plaintive wail. For thirteen minutes the six Scotsmen sang folk songs, danced the Highland fling, played the pipes and bodhran drum, and climaxed with a dangerous flaming torch and sword dance, perfectly executed. Thundering applause escorted them from the stage and brought them back two times. I was as proud as a parent.

The next-to-last act was Jack Benny, whose straight face and knack for timing brought laughter to the simplest lines. He screeched when he played his violin, not from lack of skill but on purpose to add humor to his act. Many's the time I'd heard him play his old instrument better than any pro in the pit. His gags flopped, but I whistled and applauded like a madwoman. Never mind, I'm sure he could tell from the tepid audience response that tonight his routine was off. Cats and Rats ended the show, astonishing the audience as rats rode peacefully on cats' backs around a track, crossed tightropes, and for the finale, walked across a raised platform carrying miniature American flags.

"However do they teach them to *do* that!" exclaimed Valerie as we worked our way out of the box and down the side steps.

"They stuff the cats and starve the rats," I said bluntly. "Come on."

I could find my way backstage at any theater in the world blindfolded, with nothing but my sense of smell to guide me. The wings teemed with performers dodging in and out of dressing rooms, musicians packing up their instruments, and stage crew hauling down lights, sweeping floors, and repairing scenery for Monday's new lineup. Shouts, scrapes, crashes, arguments, and warning calls—"Watch out! Heads up! Coming through!"—surrounded us. Boys who worked for free to see the show trotted alongside electricians, scene shifters, and carpenters like young apprentices eager to help. Everything was confusion and noise. It sounded like home.

I saw the Highlanders at once. "Scotty, you old rascal! How are you?" I threw my arms around his neck and hugged him like a long-lost father.

"There ye are, lass. I ken ye were out there the moment I heard the unholy whistle. Let me swatch at ye," he said, holding me at arm's length. "My, an' don't ye swatch bonnie as a picture! I heard about yer good fortune. Word travels, it does."

I introduced the twins who bobbed a quick curtsy and giggled as Scotty bowed low and kissed their hands.

"Ah, lass, it's been a while, hasn't it? Since . . . last September, I think, in Denver, eh?"

I nodded happily. "You were wonderful tonight. Better than ever. And such applause! You killed 'em."

"Thank ye, lass. The lads are working hard. Now, tell us about yerself, lass. How's civilian life treatin' ye?"

"Well enough, really and truly. But I'm a little homesick. I—" And to my horror, tears sprang into my eyes. I blinked them away quickly, but not before Scotty saw. He put an arm around my shoulder.

"There, there. I miss the Highlands somethin' fierce at times, but you can't go through life lookin' backward. Life is guid when you've got kith an' kin, and you've got both now, eh?"

I nodded. "Everything's good for me now."

He heard the lack of enthusiasm and chucked me under the chin. "Don't go romancin' the past, lass. Every path ye follow goes some rocky, some smooth. Find yerself a guid man and have some bairns. Them out there"—he jerked his head toward the empty rows—"think it's glamorous, but ye an' I ken the truth of it. Ye don't have to leave vaudeville—you can aye be part of the audience. Now . . ." He planted a loud buss on both my cheeks. "It's the end of a fine week an' me an' the lads are headin' out to see a man about a dog. I'd ask ye to come wi' us but these two fillies ye have in tow don't quite fit in wi' our plans."

"That's all right, we need to get back to the hotel soon. But first I need to find Jack Benny."

"Ah, Benny. He's had a rough week, he has. Almost got canceled on Wednesday." Scotty started to say something else but the lads hauled him away as I blew kisses at them all.

"What does that mean?" asked Caroline, pointing to a sign that read, DO NOT SEND OUT YOUR LAUNDRY UNTIL AFTER THE FIRST MATINEE.

"Oh, that. It's a reminder not to tie yourself down until the manager has seen your first act, which is the matinee. If he doesn't like it, he'll hand you your photos and you're out." I turned toward Valerie and bumped squarely into Jack Benny, who was heading out of his dressing room, his violin case in one hand and his hat in the other.

"Benny!" I cried, giving him a hug while his hands were still full. I should have called him Jack, but when we were first onstage together, before the Great War, his last name was his first. Under cover of the hug, I whispered in his ear, "Don't ask me any questions!"

No one ad-libs better than a vaudeville pro, and Benny was certainly that. "Well, well, if this isn't a wonderful surprise," he said mildly. "I heard you had retired a few months ago and gone home." He chose his words carefully, and looked pointedly at the twins as he spoke.

"Yes. I'm using my real name now, Jessie Carr. These are my cousins, Valerie and Caroline Carr. Girls, this is Mr. Jack Benny."

Although the girls hadn't been overwhelmed by Benny's act, they were round-eyed at meeting yet another handsome young man.

"How's my second-best girl?" he asked me.

"Does that mean you are still seeing Mary Kelly?"

He smiled and nodded. "Yes, she's a great girl, but I'm afraid—well, did you know her brother's a Catholic priest, for crying out loud? Her father doesn't approve of shiftless vaudeville performers, especially Jewish ones."

"You have a great future ahead of you!"

"Only a dear friend would say that after watching tonight's show."

"So you had an off night; what's new about that? You'll bounce back next week."

A swarthy young man passed us and Benny called to him. "Oh, Rodrigo! There's something I'd like you to do, if you have no objection to showing pretty girls around. Rodrigo is stage manager here at the Egyptian, and he's very good at giving backstage tours of this enchanting new theater, aren't you, Rodrigo?"

Rodrigo professed his love of escorting attractive young ladies backstage, and the twins were whisked off for a lesson in stage props before they could blink an eye.

"Can we talk now? What's this I hear about investigators?"

"What did you hear?" I asked carefully.

"That a Pinkerton caught up with the Darlings in Milwaukee and was nosing around. The word is, you're in line to inherit some money from some distant relatives. Is that so?"

"More or less," I said, steering carefully between truth and fiction.

"You're not in any trouble, are you? What's going on?"

I had worked out ahead of time how much I would tell Benny. I hated having to lie to him. I had been hoping that he hadn't heard anything at all about me. My throat tightened, but I had to go on.

"It's perfectly all right, Benny. I've come into some money and the lawyers just wanted to make sure I was the genuine article. The Pinkertons are looking up the acts I worked with over the past few years. Won't find many of 'em, the way things change in this business, but it will make them happy to have tried."

I've never been a good liar. A good actress, yes, but acting is pretending, not lying, and it's done in front of people who are willing participants in the deception. No one in an audience ever really believed I was Romeo's Juliet or a Chinese schoolgirl or any of the characters I played. Lying is different. Lying to people I know is hard. I don't think I do it very well.

Judging from the penetrating stare Benny fastened on me, I was right. I turned the conversation away from myself with a question.

"Where are you playing next week, Benny?"

"Salem. A quick jump, one week. Then it's on to San Francisco for a longer stint at Pantages. Do you live in Portland now?"

"No, the family home is in Dexter, a small town on the coast a couple hours from here by train. We just came into the city for the weekend to shop."

"Are you happy?"

"Sure! Everything's wonderful."

His wry look told me I was losing my touch. Picking his words with the care of a man writing a telegram and paying for every word, he said, "You miss the business. It's in your blood."

"I guess so."

"I understand, doll. We all understand. They don't."

"Look, Benny, there is something else. I can't explain every-thing right now, but I need to ask you a favor. I really need some help, and I thought you might do something for me tomorrow, on your day off. Just take a trip to the police station and ask a few questions for me. Do you mind?"

Worried eyes searched my face. "You *are* in some sort of trouble!"

"No trouble. Well, not really. Not me, I mean. I just need some information, that's all, and they aren't going to give it to a woman."

His nod told me to continue.

"Tell the police you're from Canada, a Mountie or a Pinker-ton—do they have Pinkertons in Canada?"

"You let me worry about the cover story."

"Wear a disguise, in case they recognize you from the theater. Tell them you're investigating a woman's murder in Canada somewhere, and you want to know if there have been any similar murders in Portland since 1916. Any unsolved murders where a young woman was strangled and some of her hair cut off."

Benny gave me one very long look before he said, "And if they tell me of one, what do you want to know?"

"I want to know everything about that file that they'll let you copy. Name, date, and any details about the victim."

"How can I reach you?"

"Send a letter to Jessie Carr at Cliff House in Dexter."

He gave it some thought. Benny wasn't one to make prom-ises he didn't intend to keep. "My train doesn't leave until three in the afternoon. I can do that for you at noon and then leave town."

"Thank you, Benny. I owe you."

He took my arm and we walked to the theater door. "Oh, Rodrigo," he called over his shoulder. "Time to return the little lambs to the shepherd." And turning to me, he said quietly, "If you can't tell me the truth, I won't press you. We go back too far for that. But you know how to find me if you need to."

I hugged him hard. "It's been so good seeing you again, Benny. Good to breathe some two-a-day air."

He gave me his tight little grin and a kiss on the cheek, then tipped his hat to the twins and turned to go. Watching his back disappear down the dark alley made me feel quite alone in a very big world.

"He's handsome, isn't he?" said Valerie. "Was he your beau?"

"Oh, maybe he was, once, a long time ago. But then he became something even better—my friend."

31

The twins and I had planned to return to the hotel for dessert after the show, but as we headed toward the streetcar, Caroline spotted an ice-cream parlor on the corner. "Oh, look, Jessie! Can we go there instead?"

"Why not?"

The theater crowd had already filled the ice-cream parlor to the bursting point, but a boy showed us to a round table for two, dragging a third chair over from the corner for me. With a full house, it was twenty minutes before he delivered our banana split and two sundaes. We were busy dissecting the various acts we'd just seen when Caroline suddenly gasped. "That looks like—it is! Look over there. Under the street lamp. See him? It's that David Murray!"

It was David again all right, hands in his pockets, rocking back and forth from heel to toe, obviously waiting for someone.

"Maybe we should invite him to join us?" suggested Valerie, a bit tentatively. "He's really very good-looking, isn't he?"

"Don't get any ideas; he's our cousin."

"Hush up, Caro, I wasn't getting ideas! I was just saying he's good-looking. I'm allowed to say someone is good-looking if I want to! Isn't he good-looking, Jessie?"

"Lower your voices, girls. People are staring."

"Shall we invite him inside?" whispered Valerie.

"There isn't room at the table," I said.

"But—"

At that moment, David caught sight of someone he knew. A few long strides took him out of our view.

"Why didn't Mother want us to meet David?" persisted Valerie. "He seemed nice at dinner, even though he didn't talk much. And he is our cousin, even if it's only halfway, isn't he? Oughtn't that to count for something?"

"Your mother didn't want you to meet him because he's a bastard," I said.

Valerie gasped. Caroline's hand flew to her throat. "You shouldn't say swear words!"

" 'Bastard' isn't a swear word."

"Yes it is. I've heard Henry use it, when I was hiding in the parlor one time, behind the Coromandel screen. He was telling Ross that he called someone a you-know-what and they got into a fight."

Mentally noting the possibilities of the Coromandel screen, I replied, "Well, some people use it as an insult, but it isn't a swear word." I looked at them both, their fresh faces devoid of makeup and their eyes wide with an earnest innocence, and I knew the answer before I asked. "You do know what a bastard is, don't you?"

"Of course. Mother explained it the other day. Someone whose parents had a marriage that wasn't exactly legal."

Geez, Louise. These two girls—sixteen years old—had no idea how babies came into the world. It was hard for me to believe, growing up in the circumstances I did, that anyone over the age of ten could be unaware of sexual relations between men and women, but their world had been more sheltered than mine. They'd been kept close to home, tutored by governesses, with few friends their own age and no babies to help care for, so it had been easy for Aunt Victoria to keep them entirely innocent of things she did not wish them to know. David's appearance at dinner had jeopardized her conspiracy of silence. She wasn't ready to let them grow up . . . if, indeed, she would ever be ready.

I thought of my friend Angie, almost the same age as the twins yet epochs apart. On her own since she was fifteen, living with Walter at seventeen, Angie might be in a family way by now, even married. Whatever happened, Angie could take care of herself. The twins were helpless as newborn kittens. And for women, helpless was dangerous.

Maybe I wasn't the best biology teacher, but five sentences later, Valerie and Caroline had a rudimentary grasp of the difference between male and female anatomy and how the two fitted together. The information struck them dumb.

Feeling as old as their mother, I waited for them to digest what I'd told them. After an agonizing silence, I continued. "Most people enjoy it, so much so that they don't always wait to get married. They fall in love and can't help themselves. A bastard is the child of two people who were never married."

"So David Murray is . . . I mean, Uncle Lawrence, I mean, your father had . . . oh, my goodness . . ."

"He had an affair with David's mother before he was married to my mother, your aunt Blanche. For some reason they didn't marry, probably because his parents didn't approve of her. Your mother didn't want you to know about that, which is why she was so dismayed when Henry brought David home."

"She doesn't like bastards?"

"Some people snub bastards, but it's hardly their fault, is it? I think your mother believes you are too young to understand about sexual relations, or maybe she was too embarrassed to explain these private matters to you, so having David arrive unexpectedly like that threw her off balance."

"You're not embarrassed."

What could I say? I'd come to grips early on with my own parentage, or lack thereof, but as Jessie Carr I could hardly say that. People were pretty frank about sex in the theatrical world. Little was said outright, but you'd have to be blind and addlepated not to notice men and women coming together and breaking apart as often as the various acts merged and split up. Heck, sex was the cause of many acts breaking up! Then there were the men who preferred men and the women who preferred women. No one talked about it, but there was a tacit understanding that as long as people led honest lives and were good at what they did, they were welcome in vaudeville. Performers didn't make a practice of probing into anyone's privacy, something I was thankful for now that the trustees and their Pinkertons were rummaging about in my past. They would have little to show for their efforts.

"Me? Why should I be embarrassed? Sexual relations are a normal part of nature. All human beings have sexual relations. So do animals and insects and even plants, sort of, or their kind would die out. Gracious, doesn't Mrs. Applewhite teach you any biology?"

"Did you ever—ouch!" Valerie glared at her sister as she rubbed her arm. "What? I wasn't going to ask that! I was going to say, um . . ."

"I'm glad you weren't going to ask, Valerie, because it's very impolite. In fact, if you mention any of this conversation to your mother, it will be the last time she allows any of us to go for a walk in the garden unchaperoned."

"Do you think Henry and Ross know about this?"

"Yes," I said firmly.

32

There was no excuse now. I had the bowler hat. I had the linen jacket. I had the jodhpurs. I had the boots. My prayers for rain were answered with blazing sun. It was ten o'clock on Monday morning. Time to climb onto that beast and look like the avid horsewoman I was supposed to be. The ride to the Indian village with Buster had been quiet and unobserved. Today all eyes were on me. Buster gave me a broad wink and held out one huge hand to give me a leg up. I took a deep breath, stretched my lips into a smile, and swung my right leg over Lady's back.

"You girls look so smart in your new habits," said Aunt Victoria. She stroked Lady's nose as I mounted. "That color highlights your hair, Jessie. You have such lovely hair, my dear. Now Lady, none of your lazy, plodding ways today—you give Jessie a good time."

"I wish you would come with us, Mother. We'll take it slow. Jessie could ride Blackie or Chestnut."

My worst nightmare. A spirited horse that was seldom ridden. I took a deep breath and swallowed hard, trying to keep the panic in my stomach. If I threw up now, all would be lost.

"Thank you, dearest," replied Aunt Victoria, "but my ankle would prefer a few more days of gentle treatment. I'll stay home and keep Ross company."

Ross had suffered a particularly severe asthma attack that morning. When he discovered he had run out of his regular medicine, Dr. Milner had been summoned to administer an ephedrine injection, and now Ross was resting quietly on the sofa. I was grateful for his absence. He was far more observant than the girls, and I couldn't afford his sharp eyes on me.

Confidences usually inspire trust, and what I had told the girls at the ice-cream parlor paid big dividends. Jessie was the Font of All Knowledge, the source of honest information that others had conspired to keep from them. Jessie treated them like adults when others considered them children. I relaxed a bit, knowing there would be no further sabotage from that direction. The boys were my only detractors now, and working on the show seemed to be bringing Ross around. The most I could hope for with Henry was that he would keep his distance until I could make my getaway to Europe.

"We'll pick Ross some wildflowers," offered Caro.

"Pick them for me, dear, I think we should keep flowers away from Ross for the time being."

"All right, Mother. Let's go!"

And we were off. The slow walk led to an easy canter through the woods along a well-traveled bridle path that led beneath low branches and over rocky streams until it opened on a meadow spread before us like a tablecloth embroidered with daisies, buttercups, and bachelor's buttons, and edged with Queen Anne's lace. The scene would have been enchanting if I hadn't been concentrating so hard on looking happy.

Two hours later we were safely back at the stables. All had gone smoothly. I had worried myself sick over nothing.

"Now let's play tennis!" said Caro.

"Good idea," Val answered. "Come on, Jessie. You'll play too, won't you?"

"What, no lessons today?" I asked.

"Mrs. Applewhite's headache excused us for the whole morning."

"How do three people play tennis?"

"Oh, it can work. We'll show you."

"Remember, now, I don't know how to play. The tennis court wasn't here when I left."

"I know," replied Val. "But you have that smart new tennis costume, and that's what's important."

Mrs. Applewhite didn't come down to lunch, so we continued in the afternoon with our rehearsals and scenery painting. Aunt Victoria let Ross take the velvet curtains from the parlor and rig them across the back of the ballroom where we planned our stage. We hung our painted backdrops on the wall. I tried not to be suspicious of Ross's motives as he became nicer and more helpful.

And all the while, I fretted.

It had been twenty days since I had left the Sacramento offices of Smith and Wade. Twenty days since the trustees initiated their investigation of my story. Twenty days since they'd sicced their Pinkerton dogs on vaudeville to sniff out evidence that would corroborate the facts I'd fed them. What in the name of Sam Hill was taking so long? For their investigation to take twenty days, the Pinkertons must have heard something from the Darlings that didn't ring true. I imagined the worst—they had stumbled on someone who remembered my mother and all they were waiting for was to close in on me. To hedge my bets, I packed my smallest valise with the basics and left it under my bed. Some cash would have been helpful but not essential. I knew how to ride trains without a ticket. I knew how to eat without money.

I was trying to stay busy. Ross had been stunned to silence when I popped my head in his library one morning and asked for

a book about Oregon's native Indian tribes. Chen was more welcoming when I presented myself for work in the garden. He taught
me how to deadhead roses, let me pull onions, and showed me
how to distinguish herbs from weeds. Working in the dirt was
tonic for my frazzled nerves. Grandmother instructed me in the
art of flower arranging. Every day after lessons the girls and I
slipped up to the third floor to practice our acts. But my anxieties
had grown, and by Tuesday my nerves were strung tight as a high-
wire act. I would not have slept at all without the relaxing effect
of a glass—or two—of bedtime sherry.

The only vaudeville person who knew about Oliver and his
scheme was Angie. I had forgotten about Angie until recently. She
had been on the scene when Oliver mistook me for his niece.
She had joined us for dinner at the Blackstone Hotel, and she and
I had talked quite freely afterward about his preposterous proposal. Had the Pinkertons stumbled across Angie? Not likely.
They had no reason to look for the Cat Circus. But what if the
Darlings mentioned her name and told them she and I were
friends? They'd go looking for her then, wouldn't they? The Darlings knew she had joined Walter's cat act. They might have
mentioned it. I reminded myself that Angie distrusted cops,
Pinkertons, teachers, preachers, heck, anyone in authority. Surely
she'd clam up if anyone started asking questions. Wouldn't she?

I had a dream that night. Another Jessie dream. She was collecting agates on the beach, then all at once I saw her huddled in
a cave this time, not a cellar, and her feet were wet. My feet were
wet. I was there beside her, saving her agates from the grasp of
the sea, moving farther into the cave as the water rose. I felt her
urgency. *Hurry.* Then the water receded and she was on the
beach again, a beach that sparkled with agates and precious jewels
as big as robins' eggs. Rubies, emeralds, diamonds so plentiful you
could hardly straighten up between them. Buster put them in a
pretty treasure box and hid it where the cousins wouldn't find it.

I refuse to believe in ghosts. This wasn't a ghost; it was nothing more than a dream brought on by my own guilty conscience. I had taken Jessie's name. I had taken her room, her house, her clothes, and her relatives, and I was fixing to take her fortune. No wonder I was plagued by dreams!

I didn't believe in ghosts, but I did believe in my mother. Ever since her death a dozen years ago, she had come to me in my dreams and spoken to me in my thoughts. She was always close by. It seemed so normal, never spooky or eerie. Perhaps these dreams of Jessie were something like that. If only she could talk to me once! If only she had kept a diary. Oliver said she had not, but diaries, like boxes of treasure, were secret. Could she have hidden a diary?

Dawn's glow seeped around the edge of the curtains. I got up and threw a robe over my nightgown. Jessie's pink robe. I pushed deep into the closet. Rainy and I had emptied it of clothes, but there were still some boxes in the back, heavy boxes of books that we hadn't emptied. A diary was a book. Where better to hide a book than in a box of books?

I pulled the boxes out, one by one, and emptied each.

Books, yes, but there were also school papers and photo albums and postcards of European sights and miniature porcelain animals wrapped in tissue paper and pictures in tarnished silver frames and games and jigsaw puzzles and shell fossils and a Number 2 Brownie camera with no film and a leather pouch full of foreign coins and colored pencils and a collection of silver demitasse spoons and some paper butterflies and . . . and no diary. But each keepsake had a story; each offered a glimpse into Jessie's life. I studied them all closely to see what I could learn about her. The postcard of Notre Dame Cathedral told me she had climbed the tower stairs to the rooftop to see the gargoyles up close. The jigsaw pieces spoke of her patience and her determination to solve the puzzle—a characteristic we shared. The camera said how much she had loved taking pictures of her pony. I turned page after page of her album until overcome with the sheer loneliness of the images. Plenty of photographs of prim European nannies in starched uniforms, but no friends, no family, no parents. I had no photographs of my parents either, but it wasn't due to lack of love. At least I had Mother's playbills.

I shoved the last of the boxes back into the closet. No diary. No answers.

It was not until Wednesday night as the family, minus Henry, sat down to dinner that Aunt Victoria remarked, "Oh, Jessie. I keep forgetting to tell you—I received a letter a few days ago from Mr. Severinus Wade. It seems the agents he dispatched to investigate your past finally turned in their report. Of course, it supported your own information exactly."

"A few days ago?" I didn't mean to sound accusatory, but I couldn't help it.

"Oh, my, I'm sorry, dear, I didn't realize you were so concerned about it. I should have told you right away, but it came while you were in Portland, and I forgot about it. All it says is that you should return to their offices on your birthday to sign some papers, but you already knew that, so I didn't think it was important."

"I wasn't concerned," I lied. "I just wanted Henry and Ross to know." And like a smart-alecky twelve-year-old, I blessed Ross with an I-told-you-so smirk.

"If you like, I'll write a letter to Henry with the news . . . or maybe you can tell him yourself. Isn't he supposed to be home this weekend, Ross, darling?"

"He may not make it, Mother. The election is only eight weeks away, after all, and he's busy kissing babies and pretending to know something about farming."

"Yes, I suppose it is a tremendous amount of work, getting elected. He's so busy. And he has so many friends." Her vapid smile was starting to grate on my nerves.

Later that evening Grandmother came to my bedroom and told me she had overheard Aunt Victoria talking with Henry on the telephone, informing him of the trustees' report.

"I could tell from her side of the conversation that he offered to make amends by inviting David Murray to stay at Cliff House for a few days. He thought you'd like to get to know your half brother better. Victoria said it was a lovely gesture on his part and suggested the guest room with the cabbage-rose wallpaper. He's coming tomorrow." She waited for my reaction and, getting none, added, "A lovely gesture is not something I would expect from Henry."

Me neither.

33

T he next day I became a modern woman. I drove into Dexter, found the beauty parlor, and had my long hair bobbed.

Back home, I slipped upstairs to change for dinner and paint my fingernails dark red. Rainy helped me out of my day dress and buttoned me into one of my new silk dinner frocks, the coppery one that matched the color of my hair, fussing all the while over my short locks as I applied a little rouge to my cheeks and drew a dark red bow on my lips.

"Oh, miss, your new hair is wonderful, but it was so beautiful and wavy, all long down your back. Don't you miss it?" Her hand went to her own long hair, pulled into a bun and topped with a white cap, as if to check that it was still attached to her head.

"To tell the truth, Rainy, I'm glad to get rid of it." I blotted my lipstick on a handkerchief. "For so long, it was schoolgirl braids or curls tied back with ribbons. Now I am free of all that, I can look my age. And wear those chic cloche hats!"

A sound from the open door behind us turned our heads.

"Excuse me," said David Murray, knocking politely on the door-jamb. Evidently he and Henry had arrived while I was in town. "I was on my way downstairs and heard you talking . . . and I just wanted to say hello. If I'm not disturbing you?"

I looked at him warily, this pawn of Henry's.

"I'll take this down to the laundry to brush the dust off," said Rainy as she ducked out of the room.

"You've bobbed your hair," David said. "I knew something was different."

"Just today, as a matter of fact. I wanted to look older."

"You look swell."

"Thanks. Aunt Victoria cried out in horror when I walked through the front door. She's crazy for long hair."

"Most older women are. But that makes me wonder why she let Caroline bob hers."

"She didn't. The story I heard was that Caro hacked off her own hair and made such a mess of it that a bob was the only way out."

"I knew that girl had spunk!" David chuckled. "And I'd say you accomplished your goal. You really do look young for your age, and this gives you a more sophisticated appearance."

"Well, thank you for the compliment. But I can't complain about looking young. After all, it was my living for many years. Won't you come in?"

"No, I'll just say what I have to say from here." Reminded of his mission, he swallowed nervously and wet his lips. "I just wanted to say that I am sorry as heck for the trick we played on you. I would never have done it, but Henry told me you were an impos-tor that he needed to flush out. I know that's not true now, and I am ashamed I was so gullible to believe everything he said. That's not me, not usually. I don't judge people before I get to know them. I should have met you myself and made up my own mind. And now I hope you will forgive me and we can start fresh."

There wasn't an ounce of guile in this man. I couldn't help liking him, even if he did pal around with Henry.

"Of course I forgive you. Henry can be . . . well, never mind Henry." Maybe he saw only Henry's charming half.

"It's just that I'm not used to having blood relatives. Until a few months ago, I thought the only living person in the world related to me was my mother. Then I met Henry by accident, learned who he was, and found I had four cousins and a half sister. I don't mind saying it about bowled me over."

And he had gone a little too far trying to please his newfound cousin. I understood him quite well, though I couldn't say as much. I was as alone in the world as he. More so. I think I'd go giddy if I were to discover I had one living relative, let alone half a dozen. My eye fell on the silver gilt picture frame on my dressing table.

"Have you ever seen a picture of our father?"

He shook his head.

"Here's a picture of him with my mother when they were married. He was about thirty then, a little older than you, but the resemblance is there, don't you think?" David picked up the photograph and looked at it for a long time before setting it gently back down on the dressing table. "You can keep that if you like."

"I'll tell you straight, I don't think much of him. My mother wasn't good enough to marry, and I wasn't good enough to meet. But no one's all bad, I'll hand you that. Maybe you can tell me some things about him that would make me see his better qualities."

"Does your mother ever speak of him?"

"Never."

I sighed. It sounded all too familiar. "Well, to be honest, I didn't know him very well either. He was away from home even when he was home, if you know what I mean. Spent most of his time with friends in casinos or at racetracks, and sailing in regattas. I was only eleven when he died. My lasting impression is of a man in formal dress heading out the door. It wasn't so much that he wasn't interested in *you*, it was more that he wasn't interested in children. I think his better qualities were that he was young, handsome, rich, and the life of the party."

"You're a remarkable person."

"Am I?"

"Most people wouldn't have anything to do with an illegitimate brother, yet you don't seem the least ashamed."

"Me ashamed? Why on earth? I had nothing to do with it. Nor did you." The clock pinged. "Come on, that's the signal," I said.

He gave me his arm and we descended the stairs.

Nine at the table made for a noisy meal. Aunt Victoria sat at one end and Grandmother opposite, with David placed between the twins on one side and Mrs. Applewhite, Henry, Ross, and I opposite them. The awkwardness that had plagued us at David's first meal with the family had receded, now that he had been acknowledged and, to some degree, accepted.

"Henry says you're a cowboy," began Caro, before the soup course was even served. "Tell us about your ranch."

"If rounding up cows makes a man a cowboy, then I plead guilty as charged," said David with a wide smile that brought a dimple to both sides of his mouth. I realized it was the first time I'd seen him smile. "Although I'm afraid I don't have the ranch any longer."

"Why not?"

"Sold it."

Aunt Victoria shot Caro a reproving look to warn against personal questions, but she was not easily reined in. "Why?"

"My mother was ill, and I couldn't take care of her from Montana. It wasn't much of a ranch anyway, so I sold it last year and came back to Portland."

"Is your mother better?"

"Yes," he said, but the response lacked conviction.

"Where was your ranch? Was it big?"

"It was a little bitty ranch, just a few thousand acres near the Little Bighorn River."

"I know that!" said Val. "Custer's Last Stand! You must have been sad to sell it."

"Not so sad as you might think. It's awful lonely out there, and the living is too rough for a woman, so it was best all around for me to sell up and come back home to Portland. I left when I was sixteen to make my way in the world, so here I am back again after ten years." The significance of his age when he left Portland struck me. Aunt Victoria knew as well, but I didn't think anyone else understood that it was the same year the trustees had cut off Mrs. Murray's allowance. David had left school to find a way to support himself.

The girls' tutor, Mrs. Applewhite, joined the questioning. "What are you doing with yourself in Portland these days?"

"Well, ma'am, my mother has a store"—he looked at me when he said the word, and I realized Lawrence Carr had something to do with that store—"and I help with that. Merchandise in, merchandise out. Not too hard a life."

"What kind of store?" asked Val. "Is it near Meier and Frank's?"

David shook his head. "No, it's on the other side of town. Just a small dry-goods store."

"Oh," gasped Caro, "that makes me remember! Do you remember, Val, when we were at the ice-cream parlor in Portland, and we saw him? We saw you out the window, David! Across the street from the theater. And I wanted to invite you over to join us but Jessie said the table wasn't big enough."

I felt the need to explain. "And you were gone before we could even think about another chair."

Plainly, this was unwelcome information. David looked at Henry with a frown, and neither said a word. Aunt Victoria broke the silence.

"How is the campaign going, Henry, darling?"

Never one to turn down an invitation to dominate the conversation, Henry responded with vigor. His campaign was going brilliantly. His speeches were excellent, his wit much admired, his popularity rocketing like a Chinese firecracker in the night sky. Hardly anyone even knew the name of his opponent.

"Would that be Conrad Livingston?" asked Mrs. Applewhite innocently. Henry grunted. "You're running as a Democrat, are you not?" Another grunt. "Mr. Livingston has a reputation in Portland as a respected lawyer. You may not find him so easy to beat."

"A Democrat?" I asked, ignorant of party politics.

"Democrats have dominated our state legislature for years now with the support of the Ku Klux Klan," said Henry, "and their influence is starting to pay off. Last year they barred the Japs from owning land and banned private schools. This year we're following up on Congress's immigration bill, the one Coolidge signed in May, to keep out undesirable foreigners and Communists. 'One hundred percent Americanism' is our motto. Not that we're against foreigners, mind you. They're fine as long as they stay in their own country."

Angel food cake was served. Mrs. Applewhite used the change of courses to look across the table at me and ask, "What are your plans for the future, Jessie? Will you be staying in Dexter for the time being or perhaps moving to Sacramento to work for Carr Industries?"

Henry took refuge in his linen napkin, laughing so hard he nearly choked on his food.

"You find that amusing, young man, that a woman would hold a position of responsibility in a business?"

"No. No, ma'am, not at all," he said with his napkin to his face, pretending his laughter was really a coughing spell. "Ahem, let me just say . . . ahem . . . some women make wonderful secretaries or switchboard operators." He gave up and collapsed with laughter again. This time Ross joined him until they were holding their sides. Aunt Victoria pursed her lips and shushed to no effect. "If they hired Jessie," Ross gasped, "they'd get a gal who can't file or type or write a letter, but man alive, can she tell jokes and cut a rug!"

"Henry, Ross, one more word from either of you and you'll leave this house at once. Do you hear?"

"Yes, Mother," they said in unison.

"I am mortified by your behavior. Apologize at once."

They mumbled something. I nodded my head to accept it, but only for Aunt Victoria's sake.

"Now then, Jessie," said Mrs. Applewhite. "Do tell me about your future plans."

"I'd be delighted. I'll be going to Sacramento to sign papers on my birthday, and then I'm planning to sail to Europe to visit the places I lived as a child."

"Oh, no!" exclaimed Caro. "How long will you be away?"

There was nothing to be gained by telling them I was not coming back. "Several months, probably. I might try to look up some of the people I knew, some friends of Mother and Father, if they are still in the area. You girls must take care of my car while I'm away." They brightened a little at that. "And you must come visit me after I'm settled."

The moment the words left my tongue, I knew I had blundered. Oliver's plan had been for me to take legal control of Carr Industries and then go someplace far away where my contact with the family would, forever after, be limited to an occasional postal card. Now I'd have to find an excuse to withdraw the invitation. My increasing fondness for the twins had come in the way of good sense.

Oliver was right. Being around Henry and Ross was too unnerving, and Henry's rapidly growing political power would afford him too many ways to make my life miserable. I needed to be out of reach, someplace where the men of the family couldn't find me.

I glanced up at Henry, who had gone very still. He was

watching me with a fierce speculation that brought goose bumps to my arms. I much preferred the mocking Henry to this serious one.

"We must have a party for you, Jessie," said Aunt Victoria. "A bon voyage party! Or—why didn't we think of it sooner? A birthday party to celebrate your majority! It's been ages since there's been a real party at Cliff House!"

I managed not to cringe. The girls loved the idea, but all I could picture were scores of people who knew Jessie Back When, asking questions and reminiscing about those Good Old Days. I put on what I thought was a convincing smile.

Then I saw Henry's narrowed eyes and knew there was one person who wasn't convinced at all.

34

s there anything else you need, miss?" Rainy gave my dress a brisk shake, hung it in the wardrobe, and gathered up my underthings for laundering. I climbed into bed.

"No, thank you. It's late. You go on to bed too." The house was as quiet as midnight although the clock had not yet struck twelve. I threw back the blanket. "My word, that bath made me hot. Would you open both windows, please? A cool breeze would feel good."

"Certainly, miss. You do look flushed."

I felt flushed. And my heart was beating hard, as if I'd been running a long way on a hot day.

"Mercy! I think I need some cool water . . ."

"Stay in bed, miss, I'll get it."

I heard the water streaming through the pipes to the sink in the hall bathroom. By the time Rainy returned, my heart was galloping like a runaway horse.

"You're very red." Rainy gave me the water and then, her face wrinkled with worry, a hand mirror. My cheeks looked like boiled beets.

I fell back onto the pillows and saw myself from a dizzying height, as if I'd been leaning over the balcony rail of a large theater. My arms flailed weakly. I watched my bed begin to tilt, then spin, slowly at first, then faster. My mouth opened but no words came out.

I clung to the sheets so I wouldn't fall off the bed. Rainy was beside me. Rainy was gone. Rainy was back, seconds, minutes, hours later, with the gardener, of all people! She really wasn't very bright. I lay on my back, unable to speak, watching with curious detachment as the bedside drama unfolded.

The words Rainy and Chen exchanged were drowned out by the blood pounding in my ears. Chen was gone. Chen returned. Chen held a bowl to my lips.

As much of his nasty brew dribbled down my chin as my throat. Chen kept insisting more, a little more, more, until suddenly I pushed his hand away and doubled up. Rainy stood beside the bed, ready with a large basin, and I heaved the contents of my stomach.

Sweating like a horse, I lay back as Rainy bathed my face and neck with a cool compress. I could hear her voice from miles away.

". . . oysters tonight . . . or the fish sauce . . ."

Chen eyed my almost empty glass of sherry. He picked it up and stuck his finger in it. How rude.

Exhausted, I slept.

When I woke, the clock on the mantel said eleven. Gradually I became aware of Rainy in the room with me, knitting as she sat in the Martha Washington chair by the fireplace. She'd been there all night.

"I didn't know you could knit," I said stupidly.

She set her work aside. "How do you feel this morning, miss?"

I touched myself in a few places. My skin felt tender, like that of a person who had the influenza. Holy smoke! Influenza! That deadly disease had killed millions when it swept around the world after the Great War. I hadn't heard much about it in a couple years, but it had never disappeared entirely.

"I told them you were under the weather, miss, and would stay upstairs today. Chen says would you call for him when you're fit?"

"I certainly will," I croaked. "I need to thank him for his medicine."

"I thought of it!" she said proudly. "I had a bad stomach last week, and Chen gave me that drink of his, and it was cured like a doctor did it. Better than a doctor."

"I'd vote for that."

"You ate sumpin' bad, miss. And threw it up, praise be."

"I remember that much."

"You looked bad, miss."

I shuddered, remembering my red face in the mirror. "I did at that."

"Now can you drink some tea—no milk, just sugar—and maybe take a bite of toast?"

Aunt Victoria came by to make sure I was improving. "No matter how much better you feel, I've called the doctor," she fussed. "I'm sure Chen's herb medicine did no real harm, but I'll not rest easy until a real doctor has looked at you."

By late afternoon, I felt strong enough to leave my bed, if not my room. Rainy went outside to ask Chen to come upstairs. Grandmother came in too.

"I heard you were sick last night," she said, settling into the overstuffed chair.

"Horribly sick. Something I ate. I'm fine now. Aunt Victoria insisted on ringing for the doctor, but I don't really need a house call."

Chen appeared at the door to my room and bowed low. "I am so glad to see you well."

"Thank you, Chen, come in. It's all your doing. I'm very grateful. How did you happen to be here last night?"

He entered and bowed low to Grandmother.

"It is a long walk to town. I have fixed a little space in the shed for myself whenever I want to stay the night. Mrs. Carr knows of this," he added, a bit defensively. As if I were likely to disapprove!

"What was that you gave me to drink?"

"Boneset. A strong dose usually causes vomiting."

"Thank heaven it worked. Was no one else sick? Did I get the only bad oyster?"

Black eyes looked directly at me for the first time, then at the floor. "I do not believe it was a bad oyster. I believe it was something in your glass."

No shock there. Prohibition had brought a profusion of ills, one of which was the proliferation of bathtub gin. It wasn't always gin, and it wasn't always made in a bathtub, but it was everywhere. Anyone could fashion a still with a copper boiler, some pipe, and a few gadgets from the hardware store, and people breaking the law tended not to be fussy about recipes. White lightning, rotgut, moonshine, panther sweat—it had a hundred names and as many unpredictable ingredients, like embalming fluid or creosote. Everyone knew of someone who had gone blind, been paralyzed, or died from drinking bathtub gin. Even a smuggled-in foreign bottle with a fancy French label was no guarantee as labels could be counterfeited and the booze adulterated.

"I've been sick before on rotgut but never that bad."

Chen shook his head. "Not rotgut. What was in your glass?"

"Sherry."

"Something in the sherry. Did you pour your own drink?"

I nodded. Chen glanced nervously at Grandmother, then back at me.

"There was a piece of white in the bottom of your glass. It tasted bitter, like ma huang. I think there was ma huang in your bottle of sherry."

"What the devil is ma huang?"

Anticipating my question, he pulled from his pocket a cluster of bright green spindly stems. "Ma huang. I don't know the English name, if there is one. It is a bush I grow in the garden, useful for many things, especially colds or hay fever. But many herbs that are good in small amounts are deadly in large amounts."

"What are you saying?"

"What was in your glass is not my ma huang. I cannot make white pills. Someone made ma huang into a white pill that would dissolve in liquid. But there was so much, it did not dissolve all the way."

My mind refused to follow.

"Did others drink the sherry?" he asked.

I shook my head.

"Who knew you drink sherry?"

"Everyone, I suppose. I have a glass before bed every night. It's no secret."

"Someone wanted you to become sick. Maybe worse. Be very careful." He looked pointedly at Grandmother, then bowed again to both of us and left the room.

Someone wanted me dead? That was nothing new. The Carrs stood to inherit at my death, so they were the obvious suspects. But that's what made it so very unlikely that they would try to poison me here.

Before I had time to think this over, Aunt Victoria came bustling down the hall. "Dr. Milner is here, Jessie. He would have been here sooner but he was setting Lem Stoner's arm. Right this way, Doctor. Here's our little patient, looking much better this afternoon."

Doc Milner gave his "little patient" a perfunctory examination, looking down my throat and listening to my chest. "Food poisoning," he intoned. "Probably a bad oyster from last night's dinner." He prescribed bed rest, tea, and toast. Useless man. He bade us good day, and Aunt Victoria showed him out.

A message flashed between Grandmother and me, and we waited until their footsteps disappeared down the hall before taking up our peculiar shorthand conversation. "It could have been the oysters," I said lamely.

"A remarkable coincidence that the only bad oyster graced the plate of the wealthiest person at the table."

"Doc Milner's a real doctor."

"Chen is a real doctor to the Chinese. And the one who saved your life."

"Well, there's no way to know for certain. Rainy cleaned up everything last night after I threw up. Henry and Ross aren't fools. If I had died, that glass would have been right here on the table and everything would point straight to them." The thought made me sad. Henry was an ass, but I rather thought Ross was coming around to my side.

Grandmother continued, "Ross is the smart one around here. You can see his brain working through his eyes. We'll return to San Francisco tomorrow. You'll be safe there."

Would I really be safe, or would it just be easier to stage an "accident" in a big city where the blame would not fall on either of them? A random criminal act would arouse no suspicion in the city. Both Henry and Ross knew San Francisco very well from their years at Stanford. And Ross would be back at school soon, very close by.

I'll admit I was pretty shaken by the poison idea, but there was another reason I didn't want to leave Cliff House, one I couldn't explain to anyone. I needed to solve Jessie's disappearance. I couldn't leave her now, without knowing what had become of her. If she had been murdered, I needed to find out who did it. I owed her that much, in return for her name, her family, and her money. But there was more to it than repaying a debt. I cared about Jessie. I understood her. Apart from Buster, I think I was the only one who did. We shared more than a name. She was rich, I was poor, yet our lives had taken many of the same turns and our fates seemed eerily intertwined. I couldn't investigate Jessie's death when I was supposed to be Jessie, but I could continue to investigate the deaths of the other girls without any interference from Oliver.

"No, Grandmother, I think I'm as safe here as anywhere. It's not for much longer. I'm warned now, and you know the old saying: 'Forewarned is forearmed.' I'll make sure I'm never alone with Henry or Ross. I'll be careful."

Slowly she nodded and rose to her feet. I heard her going down the hall toward her room, taking each step with care. In a few moments, she was back.

"I meant to give this to you earlier," she said, handing me a purple velvet pouch drawn tight with a gold cord. I pried the knot open and dumped the contents on my lap. Pearls, diamonds, colored gemstones, and gold, like the contents of the treasure chest in *The Pirates of Penzance*. Only these were real.

"The remains of your mother's jewelry. I am sure she had a lot more—I wasn't that familiar with Blanche's finery, but I remember once admiring a ruby bracelet she had been given for her birthday, and it isn't here. Neither is the diamond tiara she liked to wear. No doubt some enterprising maid helped herself before the lawyers got there to take inventory."

Speechless, I held up a strand of lustrous matched pearls so long it would have reached my knees.

"You know what they say about pearls? You must wear them or they turn dull and lifeless. It's been ten long years since anyone young and pretty wore these baubles. Enjoy them. Or sell them or give them away. I don't care. They belong to you."

Waving off my stammered thanks, she retired.

I lay on my back, staring at the dragonflies frolicking among the yellow and lavender flowers on the wallpaper and feeling like a heel. Blanche's jewelry! Geez Louise, the poor woman was probably turning over in her grave knowing some vaudeville fake had her mitts on her precious jewelry.

I decided to play my hand with greater care from now on, not showing any cards, letting the food poisoning diagnosis float rather than accuse anyone. My mistake was to have announced I was going to Europe after my birthday. Henry or Ross must have felt compelled to act fast before I got out of range.

Rainy brought in a tray of tea and a soft-boiled egg. David was behind her, his brow furrowed, inquiring about my health. I'd forgotten he was still here.

"Much better, thank you," I replied.

"I've been watching the twins rehearse."

"Good. They need lots of practice."

"Not good. They need you."

"The show must go on. I'll be back onstage by tomorrow."

"I'm glad to hear it."

"And I need to take the train into Portland sometime this week to buy some costumes."

"Do you? Well, now, I just stopped by to tell you that Henry left this afternoon, and I need to get back to my mother. I have someone looking in on her, but I need to be there myself."

"If it's not prying, may I ask what is wrong with her?"

"It's not called prying if you're family; it's called caring. She's got cancer. The doctors say she can't last long, so I'm trying to make what time she has left as comfortable as I can. I owe her that much. I owe her everything. She could have dropped me off at St. Agnes's Baby Home and had an easier life of it, but she didn't."

I understood. I wanted to tell him about my own mother—my real mother. She hadn't abandoned me in an orphanage either. David and I had more in common than he knew, both of us raised alone by unwed mothers who had been disowned by their families and forced to make their way in an unforgiving world.

"If you are feeling up to that shopping trip to Portland, we could travel together tomorrow," he said.

"I'd like that."

David's smile was so broad it put dimples in the creases.

35

"S tart at the beginning," David said, settling back into the first-class cushions. "I want to know everything about your life, and you're trapped on this train with me for at least two hours."

I was so strongly drawn to David that I wanted to blurt out the whole truth. I was certain he'd understand. Of course, I didn't do it, but I wanted to all the same, and that troubled me more than a little. Treating David in a brotherly manner was becoming increasingly difficult as I came to know him better.

But the least I could give him was the truth about his father, and not a word I said about Lawrence Carr was fabricated. Perhaps I was even more honest than a real daughter could have been, divorced as I was from sentimentality. I told him what others had said about Lawrence in his lengthy obituary, and some things I'd heard that did not glow as warmly. No punches pulled.

"Does that agree with what your mother said of him?" I asked at last.

"I was sixteen before I knew who my father was," he said. "She wouldn't have told me then but he died, and the money stopped coming and, well, things got tight, and she had to explain. I quit school to find work. It's funny, I grew up thinking my father was dead. By the time I knew the truth, he was."

It reminded me so much of my own circumstances, I wanted to scream, Yes, yes! I understand exactly! My mother had told me nothing of my father either, and I had always felt cheated.

"You don't seem bitter about that," I said.

"I was. But I was old enough to support my mother." I recognized the streak of independence. I too had worked for a living most of my life. Growing up alone had taught me to do for myself and not count on the other fellow to do for me.

"Your turn," I said. "Same rules."

With half the journey ahead of us, he had no excuse to cut corners. David and his mother had moved to Portland shortly after his birth, he told me, where she bought a small store with the money she inherited from her "late husband." "I was raised a city boy, but I loved horses"—"me too," I said weakly—"and took on any job I could to be around them. A friend knew a man in Texas who needed cowhands, and there I went. Worked ranches in Utah and Wyoming, learned to break horses and shoot up towns on Saturday nights. Shot a few men—just wounded them, but I was headed for a noose until John Black got hold of me. He was a cattleman on a buying trip to Laramie looking to stock his ranch. He took my gun away, pulled me out of the saloon, and threw me in his wagon before the sheriff arrived. When I woke up, I was in Montana getting some sense knocked into me."

He smiled at the recollection. I smiled at his smile. "Everyone called him Black Jack. I came to love that old man. When he got sick, I did my best for him. He left me his ranch."

"But you sold it."

"I hated to do that, but it couldn't be helped. Ma was ill and she couldn't come out to Montana and live in the middle of nowhere."

"So you came back to Portland. Was it very much changed?"

"It's a different city than it was ten years ago, I can vouch for that. Not many people I grew up with are still around. I wanted Ma to move someplace fancier, and I had the money to pay for it, but she wouldn't budge from her friends and her store. I'm going to sell the store. Ma can't work anymore, and that's not my line."

"What is your line?" It occurred to me that I had asked Henry that question on my first night at Cliff House, and received no reply. It was about to happen again.

"Not sure, yet. For the time being, I've got to see to Ma and the store, so I just take odd jobs when I can find them."

"Like your work for Henry?"

He turned scarlet. "Yep. Politics isn't my line either, but when Henry asked me to help with his campaign, I couldn't say no to a cousin. Especially when I'd just found I had one."

"Lucky you," I said sarcastically.

"He couldn't be expected to welcome you home, Jessie. In a way, it's your own doing. If you'd written, if you'd let them know you were still alive, he'd never have come to believe he'd inherit the Carr money in the first place."

"You don't beat around the bush, do you?" I asked archly. He gave me a sheepish grin that made me burst out laughing. No one could stay mad at David when he turned on that wide-eyed innocence.

The train was slowing down for the terminal and I cast about for some way to prolong our time together. "David," I began, "would your mother mind if I came by and paid my respects?"

"No, of course not. Excuse me, but I am surprised you—that is, most people wouldn't care to meet their father's—"

"Where does she live?"

"I'll come to the Benson Hotel and get you. Four o'clock?"

"I'll be waiting."

He was prompt. We rode a streetcar most of the way and walked the last bit into a shabby part of town near the Carroll Market off Yamhill. Some people would prepare a visitor in advance for the surroundings and apologize for their humble home, but David never said a word. I liked that about him.

In truth, the Murray place was much like the rented rooms I had grown up in. I felt quite at home among the faded curtains, threadbare Axminsters, and flag-bottom chairs. There was only one bedroom and I saw no evidence of David's belongings anywhere. He took my arm as we entered his mother's room. In a voice so tender it brought tears to my eyes, he said, "Ma? I've brought Jessie to see you, just like I said."

"Hello, Mrs. Murray," I said, taking her thin hand in mine very gently so the bones wouldn't snap in two. She brought to mind a dead leaf clinging to the tip of a twig, waiting for the next wind to blow it away into the sky. Her cheeks were hollow, her brown eyes dull, and the wisps of her gray hair had been tucked into a hairnet by a pair of large male hands. She looked twice her age.

"Hello, darling Jessie. Come sit by me so I can see you." David dragged over a chair and I sat. "You don't look like him, do you?"

"They say I take after my mother's side of the family."

"I'm sorry he died like that. And your mother too. Poor things. Well, well"—she coughed a little laugh—"whatever his flaws, he managed to father two fine children, didn't he? Perhaps that's enough for any man."

"I brought you some treats, Mrs. Murray. David said you hadn't much appetite, so I thought something special might tempt you to eat." I had fitted a basket full of small jars of preserves, potted meats, some fresh fruit, and soft rolls from a bakery down the street, but she wasn't interested in food. Her eyes never left my face.

"You want to see what David looked like as a child?" she asked, fumbling under her nightgown for a chain. Shaky fingers pulled up a gold locket the size of a quarter but could not open the clasp. I reached over, taking the warm locket in my hands and pressing the pinhead clasp with a fingernail.

"Oh, how sweet," I cooed. "What a beautiful little boy!" It was a double locket, and opposite the photograph of a three-year-old cherub was one of a pretty young woman.

"That's me on the other side, taken the same day."

"You look so happy." I closed the locket and handed it back.

"I've always been happy. I've had a happy life because of my wonderful son. And I'm so grateful you and David have met. I hate to leave him all alone in the world, and now he has a sister."

"Now, Ma, no talk of leaving yet, please. Listen here, Jessie's been in vaudeville for years. Remember how we used to go to the shows? Tell her about those days, Jessie."

So I spent a bittersweet half hour relating lighthearted stories of the stage until her eyelids became so heavy they would not stay open. Finally, footsteps on the stairs turned our heads. A short young woman with a trim figure and raven hair entered the room with the authority of someone who belonged there.

"Company, David?" she asked. "I saw you come home a bit ago."

"You've been watching out the window, haven't you?" David teased, and she blushed prettily. "Jessie, this is Gloreen Whittaker. She lives across the way with her father and brothers and takes great care of Ma when I'm not here. Gloreen, this is Jessie Carr, my half sister."

Her hand flew up to her mouth. "Half sister? I had no idea." Her puzzled frown told me she also had no idea how David, whose father had supposedly died before he was born, could possibly have a younger half sister. It wasn't my problem. "Very pleased to meet you, Miss Carr."

"It is a pleasure to make your acquaintance. How kind you are to help with Mrs. Murray."

She gave David an adoring smile. "David insists on paying me, but I'd do it without payment, out of affection. She's been like a mother to me for the past few years, always helping when I needed it."

I felt like an intruder. "I'd best be going. I've got to get to the theater district and buy some costumes for our little theatrical before those vendors close. No, don't come with me, David, I can make my way to the corner and catch the next streetcar."

"Nonsense," he said. "I'm going with you."

At that, Mrs. Murray lifted her eyelids. "David, did you say you were leaving?"

"Just down the street to put Jessie on a streetcar. I'll be right back."

"You're not going down to *that* part of town again, are you?"

Quietly he said, "Not now, Ma, later." He didn't glance at me and it wasn't my place to ask what she meant.

"I don't like you going down there," she persisted. "It's not respectable."

"I have to go, Ma, to finish a little business. Gloreen will stay with you. I won't be late."

David saw me to the streetcar. After a few blocks I transferred to the theater district for some purchases before making my way through the darkening streets to the Benson Hotel.

36

had been Jessie Carr for so long that it was a bit of a wrench to wrap myself around a different role. But at ten o'clock sharp, Rosie Waters sashayed through the hotel lobby, oblivious to the night manager's disapproving glare. Rosie sent a saucy smile to the bellman and whistled for her own hack. She wore a purple sequined dress cut low where it could have been high and high where it could have been low, a cheap rabbit stole, and red pointy-toed shoes, and she carried a fake ivory cigarette holder between two fingers of her left hand. If the bellman had looked closely, he might have suspected that the dark curly hair was a wig, but he was too busy eyeing the side slit in her dress, hoping for a flash of flesh. Since her stockings were rolled to an inch above her hemline, he got one as she climbed into the backseat of the hack. Rosie Waters was a girl who worked both sides of the street, vaudeville and burlesque. No one would confuse this modern flapper with wholesome Jessie Carr.

The hack deposited me on Union Street near the Egyptian. I paid him and stepped out of the way of the next fare. Gusts of wind swirled through the crowd, lifting crumpled playbills and causing the women to hug themselves inside their wraps. The rabbit stole didn't offer much comfort, but I wasn't going to be outside long. I headed across the street and into the burlesque theater where I had seen Henry and David the week before.

"Evening, fella." I smiled at the young doorman.

"Show's already started."

"I'm looking for a man, not a show."

"I'm a man," he said with a leer.

I laughed. "Sorry, Jack. I'm looking for a Mr. Henry Carr. Do you know him? They say he's a regular here."

The boy shook his head and let me step into the empty lobby. I could hear the audience roar with laughter behind the padded doors. "Hey, Marv!" he called to the bartender. "Lady wants to know do we know Henry Carr?" Marv and another man looked up from behind the bar where they were wiping glasses, preparing for intermission.

"You must know Mr. Carr. A regular. Tall, good-looking, swell dresser, likes Seagram's VO." I nodded toward the bottles of Seagram's behind them. "About twenty-five and a little . . . uh . . ." I patted my belly and they chuckled.

"Yeah, I mighta seen him," the barman said cautiously. The way he said it told me what I wanted to know. I passed him five clams and he remembered. "Not tonight though. A lot of the regulars hang out at Trudell's, a little gin mill around the corner. You might try there."

I thanked the men prettily.

Trudell's didn't usually get going until after the evening shows were over, and only a dozen or so people were downstairs when

I walked in. My dress talked me past the doorman, and I repeated my description of Henry to the bartender. He knew Henry Carr. Hadn't seen him in a few days, but for five dollars, thought I might find him at Dakota's or Markie's. Henry was not at Dakota's, and I was about to head to Markie's when a woman with jet-black hair and a face made up like an American flag crooked a finger at me.

"Hey, hon. Who's looking for Henry Carr?" she asked as she turned away and blew a chest full of smoke into the air.

"My name's Rosie Waters," I said, returning the smoke.

"What do you want with that two-faced sap, a nice girl like you?"

"He owes me."

"A favor?"

"Money."

"Take my advice, hon. Write it off before it comes back to bite you."

"Sounds like the voice of experience."

"Damned right. Don't let them fancy manners fool you. They rub off quick, like silver on a cheap brass ring. And Mr. Big Shot gets a big kick out of using those big fists."

"He beat you up?"

At first she shrugged, as if it mattered not at all, as if she were strong enough to handle rough customers, but then she scanned the room and lowered her voice in a way that proclaimed her fear louder than words. "Wasn't nothing compared to what he did to another girl I know."

"What did he do?"

One question too many. Her breezy manner turned to suspicion, and she clamped her lips together so tight they nearly disappeared.

"Never mind; I understand. And thanks. But I have to find him."

Tossing back the last of her drink, she turned toward the bar.

"Don't say you weren't warned. You'll probably find him at Markie's later tonight. There or Trudell's."

I was running out of fives. "Thanks. Next one's on me."

It was Friday night and Markie's was filling up fast, but I found a good vantage point at a small table against the wall. The room was dark. Candles glowed on each table, and dim electric bulbs gave the bartender just enough light so that he didn't pour the real stuff when rotgut would do. Three colored men with loosened neckties played gentle jazz in the corner. As speakeasies go, it was middling—a dozen tables with tablecloths and a floor swept pretty regularly. I ordered a gin and tonic from the bar— real gin, and yes, I'd pay extra—and noticed the Seagram's VO bottles on the shelves behind the bartender. There had been some at Dakota's too. At the end of the bar, stacked on the floor, were six or eight cases of the stuff. Someone had marked numbers on each box with green chalk, just like the boxes at Cliff House.

No need to wonder any longer what Henry Carr did for a living. Stamping out my cigarette I stood to leave, only to sit down again as Himself came through the door.

He swanned in with six rough-looking men and David Murray in his wake. That gave me a sharp pang of regret. I didn't like being lied to—this from the girl whose very existence was a lie!—and I didn't like seeing David mixed up with Henry's sordid affairs. Campaign work, my foot. David was helping Henry with his bootlegging.

Henry scanned the room, his eyes passing over me without a flicker of recognition, and when he saw that none of the larger tables was empty, he approached the center one and emptied it with a scram motion of his thumb. Henry and his associates called to the bartender for drinks. The guy knew what to bring without being told. Ah, the advantages of regular patronage.

They were loud, but not loud enough for me to make out more than the stray word or two. Curious, I nursed my drink and watched from the wings. Henry sat facing me from the far side of the table, tipping back on his chair legs, smoking one cigarette after another as he tossed off snide remarks that were received with raucous laughter by his minions. David was the only one not laughing. I had a profile view of him as he leaned forward from the edge of his seat, his hands clasped around a mug of ale, staring glumly at the foam.

As I watched, he said something to Henry, who frowned, took out his wallet, and handed him several bills. David pocketed the money and stood up, made a curt farewell, and disappeared up the stairs.

Which, now that I'd gotten what I came for, was exactly what I needed to do. I motioned to the bartender that I was leaving, and fished through my purse for a dollar. Suddenly there was a tough standing over me.

Markie's was obviously not the first bar he'd seen this evening. He swayed a little, and his words were slurred, but he was not yet blotto. I realized with dismay that he was one of Henry's party.

"Ev'ning, dollface. What's a looker like you sitting all alone for? Come join us and I'll buy you a glass of bubbly." His friends were watching, all of them, to see what luck he would have. I wasn't overly concerned. The light was dim and my costume, wig, and makeup were good enough that I would feel comfortable speaking directly to Henry without fear he would recognize me. Still, Shakespeare had it right, discretion is the better part of valor.

"Thank you, but I need to meet my husband at the theater in a few minutes." I folded the dollar under my glass and stood.

"Husband, eh? Well, now, that's one lucky man, that husband." He sneered, grabbing my arm with his rough fingers. "I think he should spread his luck around a little, eh, dollface?" I twisted away from his grasp as I threw what was left of my drink in his face. He sputtered with rage.

I crossed the room toward the stairs, weaving through several patrons. The boozehound shoved them aside as he followed.

Suddenly he crashed to the floor, tripped by an outstretched foot that a gentleman at another table had kindly extended on my behalf. He sprawled messily, and I made my escape into the night.

Markie's was two blocks from the main strip, and the street was quiet. The cold air tasted fresh and clean after the thick smoke in the bar. The corners were dark—no streetlights in this part of town. No place for a girl alone, I thought, heading toward an intersection where a gaslight beckoned. Behind me, the door to Markie's slammed shut. A glance over my shoulder told me my suitor had been down but not out.

Anger at his humiliation trumped inebriation. I bolted for the gaslight but my ridiculous shoes slowed me down, and before I could put any distance between us, he was on me. He snatched at me and got a handful of rabbit stole which I immediately released, but not soon enough to avoid being slung into the gutter, tearing a hole in my dress with my knee. I swung backward hard with my elbow, hoping to hit something vulnerable. My arm hit only air, but oddly enough, I heard him scream.

Someone had lifted the goon off me and a familiar voice drawled, "This man bothering you, lady?"

Without waiting for my reply, David Murray planted a powerful fist in the man's stomach and released him to crumple to the pavement. I had the feeling David wasn't finished, but the door to Markie's swung open just then and a couple of the men from Henry's table came out. "Sammy? That you?" one called. Sammy could only gasp for air.

"Come on," David said, grabbing my wrist. I didn't have to look back to know several dark figures were in pursuit.

37

had no idea where I was going. I didn't need to think about that, only to concentrate on keeping up with David who wasn't wearing flimsy high heels. One heel broke, but I kept on. I had no choice. David would not have let go of my wrist for all the tea in China. I could hear the shouts behind us. "Stop! Thief!" they called, hoping someone would oblige. Fortunately for us, it wasn't a part of town where people minded other people's business.

David knew the city well. He executed several turns, pulled me through a broken fence, doubled back, and cut through an abandoned warehouse until he was certain we'd shaken them. Catching our breaths, we came out on a street near a tired wooden sign that read, MAJESTIC HOTEL. He dragged me into a lobby that mocked the hotel's moniker. A bald man with spectacles perched on the tip of his hawk nose looked up from his newspaper and turned down the radio.

"I'd like a room," said David.

"I got one."

"I'll take it."

"Ain't you gonna ask how much?"

"How much?"

"Two dollar."

"I'll take it." He pulled out his wallet and gave the man five. "Here's a fin. There's another tomorrow if you don't mention we're here."

He came around the desk and took in my broken shoe, bleeding foot, and lopsided wig. "Mum's the word," he said with a leer.

"She's my sister."

"Whatever you say, pal. Number three, top of the stairs." He tossed David a key chained to a block of wood.

The room smelled like urine.

"You knew it was me." I said, pulling off my black wig.

"Not at first."

"How?"

"Your hands. The way you touch your fingertips together." Damnation, I wasn't aware I did that. "I didn't know what you were up to, but I knew you shouldn't be in that part of town alone. So I waited in the alley. I was planning to trail you home without you knowing."

It was the moment for a girl with pluck to mouth off a few lines, but I wasn't feeling too plucky. No telling what would have happened if David hadn't been there to bail me out of the mess I'd blundered into. "Thanks."

"You can thank me by telling me what's going on."

"I don't think I can do that."

"I'm your brother, Jessie. You can trust me."

"You work for Henry."

"Not anymore."

"What did you do for him?"

"I told you. Campaign work."

I threw his words back at him. "I'm your sister, David. You can trust me."

He took a deep breath and ran his fingers through his hair, making it stand on end. "Okay, okay. I'll tell you the truth. Henry runs a bootleg operation. He acts like a big shot, but he's really small potatoes. Fills his boat in Canada, brings it into the coast every few weeks. My job was to distribute the hooch to some Portland speakeasies."

"There's someone bossing him?"

"Sure. You don't work alone in this business, not for long anyway."

"But you're out of it now?"

"Yeah. I wanted out of it after the first job last summer. He told me that was his final run, and I agreed. Turned out there was another final run, and he wanted me to help out again. The money was real tempting. But no more. I'm out."

"He's still bootlegging?"

He nodded. "He's done it for years. The Carr money would have let him give it up. He'd have had plenty of jack to spread around for politics. But you came back, and he had to continue."

"Poor thing. Driven to a life of crime by his cousin's resurrection. What if he fingers you to the police if you don't continue?"

"He won't do that. We've got what we call in Texas a Mexican standoff. I wouldn't go to jail alone, and he has more to lose than I do, with the elections coming up." I looked at him with new respect. David was nobody's patsy. "Now sit down and put your foot up while you tell me your side of the story."

He took a thin towel from a hook by the corner sink and wet it. I peeled off what remained of my stockings and held out my hand for the towel, but he took my foot in his hands and bathed the blood off himself. "This hurt?"

"I'll live."

"Then talk."

I talked. I told him that someone wanted the Carr money bad

enough to kill me for it. I told him about the threat coming up from the beach and about the poison in my sherry. Put those incidents alongside a bootlegger and three strangled girls in the past six years, one of whom was rumored to have been involved in smuggling, and you had motive, opportunity, and ability, all in one person: Henry.

He didn't laugh or brush off my concerns. He stared through me for some moments before he met my eyes. "Tell me about the three girls."

"The Chinese girl was first, killed in October of '18. She was strangled, and some of her hair cut off. The girl in the warehouse was strangled too—sometime late in September of '19, the doctor said. The coroner's report isn't in yet, but I'll bet a hank of hair is gone. And the Indian girl was killed a few weeks ago, as you know, strangled. The tip of one braid was missing."

"What do the police make of this?"

"They brushed off the Indian girl's death as some tribal vendetta, which is not so, and they claim the Chinese girl was a prostitute involved in smuggling and got her just deserts, so to speak. That one's long forgotten. The body they found in the warehouse is in the hands of the state coroner."

"Like as not, at least two of them were killed by the same man. Sounds like a madman on the loose."

I gasped, leaped up off the bed, and gasped again at the pain in my foot. "Oh, my God! I've made a huge mistake."

"What?"

"It couldn't have been Henry."

"Why not?"

"He was hundreds of miles away at college in California in October of '18, and in the fall of '19 too."

Utterly devastated, I sat back down on the smelly bed. Why hadn't I realized that earlier? Henry couldn't be the lock-of-hair murderer after all. He'd not been near Dexter when those girls were killed. He'd been far away at college. David was right. I felt like a fool.

"Well, then," said David, "I guess he can't be in two places at once. Besides, I'll admit Henry's got his mean streak, but he wouldn't harm a woman."

Still, even if he hadn't murdered any of those women, there was his behavior toward me. And there was the woman in Dakota's who'd warned me about Henry's penchant for violence. "You think not? What about my close call at the edge of the cliff?"

"What exactly did he say to you?"

I repeated his words with a visible shudder. "'Don't you know it's dangerous to play around cliffs. You'd not survive a fall from this height.'"

"I don't necessarily hear 'I'm going to throw you off' in that."

"It was there, believe me."

"You may have been mistaken."

I was starting to waver. "What about the poisoned sherry?"

"Maybe the gardener was wrong. He's a gardener, for God's sake, not a doctor. Maybe a bad oyster made you sick. It happens. Maybe the sherry was some bathtub gin with God knows what in it. Look, I don't deny Henry is a pretty unpleasant person—that's why I've broken off with him—but murdering his own cousin?"

"I'm between him and a fortune. You don't believe me, do you?"

"I believe every word you've said. I'm just not sure about your conclusions." Suddenly he stood. "Give me your dress."

"What?"

"You can't leave here in a ripped dress—"

"I came in a ripped dress."

"—and I need to make sure you don't run off before I can rummage up something for you to wear back to the hotel." He picked me up from the bed and unhooked the back of my frock. When the purple dress came off and I was left standing in my step-in, he averted his eyes in a brotherly way. Not feeling sisterly, I grabbed the stinking bedspread. "I'll be back in half an hour with decent clothes, and I'll get you back to the Benson. You get that war paint off, and lock the door behind me. Don't open it unless you're sure it's me." He reached to a pocket inside his topcoat and pulled out the smallest pistol I'd ever seen. "Take this."

"Geez, it looks like a toy."

"It's not. If somebody breaks down the door—"

I nodded. No point telling a cowboy that I was no Annie Oakley. I'd never even held a loaded gun before. I'd used trick guns onstage, though. How different could it be?

Alone in that squalid room with nothing to do but think, I set to the task. So Henry couldn't have killed the Chinese girl or the girl in the warehouse because he was away at school in California. Fair enough. Someone else did, and the same person, given the trademark lock of hair he took from both victims. I'd think some more about that later. And just maybe I had blown out of proportion the menacing remarks Henry had made standing above me on the cliff. But something had sickened me that night at Cliff House, and there had been something in my glass that wasn't sherry. Chen could have been mistaken about what that was. If it had been a bit of soap or residue from some backyard still and a bad oyster was the real culprit, then no one was trying to kill me after all. Dr. Milner thought I had food poisoning. No doubt Chen knew far more than Dr. Milner when it came to roses and rutabaga, but why would I believe a gardener over the respected town doctor when it came to medicine?

Had a lifetime of theater made me too theatrical?

38

Rainy welcomed me on the front steps of Cliff House when I arrived home the next day. "I'll take your coat, miss. And a letter came for you Saturday, just after you left. I put it in your room."

Benny! I hurried upstairs.

Benny wrote like a man, short and to the point. My imagination filled in the details. I pictured him entering Portland's police station on that slow Sunday afternoon, looking official in his good serge suit, and giving the weekend duty officer some excitement. Murder always got people's attention. Benny was good at serious roles; he'd have made a perfect hard-hitting Pinkerton from north of the border, looking for information that might link to a murder in Canada, and the Sunday officer would have spent an hour or more scouring the files to help him.

The gist of it was, there had been four women strangled in Portland since 1916, and all four deaths were unsolved. A common thread could be seen in their station in life: one worked in a bar, one (a Negro) worked in burlesque, and one in a hotel, but she was on record as a prostitute. The fourth was something of an anomaly—she was married and had been killed in her home. I had the sense that her death wasn't connected to the others.

In one of the files, the police had noted that a lock of the young woman's hair had been cut off. The others, said Benny, might have had locks of hair missing, but no one had noticed. It wasn't, I admit, something police or coroners normally looked for, no more than they would note whether the woman's fingernails were light red or dark. The lock-of-hair victim had been killed in February of 1920.

There was no way to link that one to Henry. Once again, he had been away in California studying at Stanford when the death occurred. The other Portland murders had been committed at various times between 1920 and 1924, the last occurring six months ago. Henry might have been in Portland on those dates, but the link with the Dexter murders was missing.

Well, that was that. Henry was certainly an officious prig, but I couldn't make him into a murderer with these facts. In the unlikely event that a bootlegging charge made it as far as the courtroom, a guilty verdict would bring little more than a fine. But what about Ross? He was awfully interested in Indians and dark-haired girls, and he even wore some beaded band around his wrist that was similar to Lizzette's. He would have been living at Cliff House the year the Chinese girl was killed. But he would have been so scrawny and young—just fifteen at the time of her death and sixteen when the one in the warehouse was murdered—that he was hardly a credible murderer. And Buster? He was big and strong and had spent his life in Dexter. I didn't think he was intelligent enough to plan and get away with several murders, but there was that lock of Jessie's hair in the treasure box that couldn't be denied. Beyond that, I was fresh out of suspects.

So much for my mystery-solving career. *Mind your own business*, Mother would have said. From now on, I would. Anyway, I was in this just for the money. Wasn't I?

Only fifteen days until I left for Sacramento.

39

Carr Cousins Extravaganza
Opening Night: Wednesday, September 17
Cliff House Ballroom
9:00 P.M.

Invitations went out Tuesday, hand-delivered to the family, Mrs. Applewhite, Marie, Clyde, and members of the household staff. We were delighted to have David return Wednesday afternoon in time to carry chairs to the ballroom and help finish hanging our painted backdrops. By dinnertime the twins were in such a tizzy they couldn't eat.

Promptly at nine I cranked up a Sousa march on the Victrola and introduced the show in my best emcee imitation.

The first act started stiffly as the girls worked through their dance routine—mostly simple Charleston steps—against a rag-time background with a couple of pauses for jokes. They looked adorable in their matching flapper frocks and headbands. Wild applause gave Val's confidence a lift that carried her through the second act, her dramatic recitation of "The Highwayman" by Al-fred Noyes.

Caro's magic act followed. Dressed in a black cape and turban, she announced that she was going to make a coin disappear. As her assistant, Val, set up a small table and chair, Caro began the patter that was designed to distract. "I'll need to borrow a coin from someone in the audience."

Ross pulled a nickel from his pocket. "Will I get it back?" he teased.

"Now, ladies and gentlemen," she said grandly, as if she were addressing a room of five hundred, "I am setting the nickel here on the tablecloth, as you can see, and covering it with this glass tumbler. Assistant! A sheet of writing paper, please. Thank you. Now watch closely as I cover the glass with this stationery," she said, pressing the paper tightly around the upside down tumbler so that the coin could not be seen and the tumbler was invisible beneath its paper covering. "I'll just tap the table with the glass three times: one, two, three, and say the magic word, Abracadabra, and—oh, dear." She whisked away the paper-covered tumbler and there was Ross's nickel.

"Try again," said Ross helpfully.

Crestfallen, she nodded. "All right, I'll cover the coin like so, and tap the glass three times, one, two, three, and say the magic word, Abracadabra, and—oh."

Caro blinked back crocodile tears. The audience oozed sym-pathy, and I knew we were ready for the finale. "One more time," she said, setting the paper-covered glass over the nickel. "Three taps on the table—one, two, three, Abracadabra—and this time you'd better work!" With that she slammed her hand down on the paper, which flattened entirely as the audience gasped. The glass had vanished. With a triumphant smile, she pulled it from beneath the table where it had magically fallen through to her lap. A masterful bit of misdirection, if I do say so myself. Stunned applause followed.

As we changed the scene, Henry sidled close enough that only I could hear him. "Some trick, eh? But I've got a better one coming. And it ain't a nickel that's going to disappear." I looked past him as if I hadn't heard. As long as I was at Cliff House among family, Henry was powerless.

It was my turn to solo. In a tuxedo costume I had purchased in Portland, I added a little soft-shoe to the song that goes "Nothing could be finer than to be in Carolina," a Tin Pan Alley hit I'd heard William Frawley perform last year to appreciative applause. I sang harmony along with Marion Harris's recording that I had bought for the performance, and, frankly, I thought Marion and I did a pretty good duet. Halfway through the number I realized I was singing directly to David, as if we were alone in that big ballroom, and I immediately moved my attention to Aunt Victoria. I was becoming way too fond of David. Never mind, I told myself sternly. Time will solve that problem. In twelve days I would be leaving Cliff House forever, and David Murray would be ancient history. A sad, but necessary, ending.

Caroline's poem was next, and she recited "Little Orphant Annie" in dialect so perfect anyone would have thought she was an Indiana farm girl. There was a brief pause as she slipped into her kimono and put on her white makeup and wig for the finale, the Carr Cousins performing the *Mikado* favorite "Three Little Maids from School Are We." With our mincing steps, fluttering fans, and twirling parasols, we little maids sang along with the record.

Everything is a source of fun
Nobody's safe, for we care for none
Life is a joke that's just begun
Three little maids from school

Our efforts met with vigorous applause. After many bows, David handed us each a rose and declared he wanted to see the entire show again. Aunt Victoria concurred, but I persuaded the girls that the old vaudeville adage "Leave them wanting more" was sound advice. "We'll do the show again some other time," I told them.

"How about at your birthday party?" asked Val, the last vestiges of shyness having fallen away somewhere between the ragtime and "The Highwayman."

Aunt Victoria's horrified expression suggested this was not socially appropriate. "We'll see," I said vaguely.

I was absurdly proud of my young cousins. I looked over at Caro to my right, shaking her head firmly at Henry, who was trying to worm the secret of the magic trick out of her, and Val on my left, who was showing Mrs. Applewhite how her Japanese kimono costume came together. And there was David standing before me saying quietly, "You are a very talented lady, Jessie Carr, but more important, you're a fine person. I am proud to be your brother."

There were three falsehoods in that statement that I didn't care to dwell on.

40

Aunt Victoria chipped a tooth the next morning and asked if I would drop her at the dentist when I took David to the train station.

"If you don't mind, Jessie dear, Dr. Sandberg can give me a gold crown and afterward I can stop by the drugstore to pick up some more of Ross's asthma medicine."

"Of course I don't mind. I can get Ross's medicine while the dentist is fixing you up good as new," I said, thinking that the police station was just a block from the dentist. I would have time to stop there and see whether any word had come from the coroner—and whether or not I could pry the details out of them. Yes, yes, I'd hit a dead end and given up sleuthing, but this was just tying up loose ends. I was curious to know if the body in the warehouse had been killed by the lock-of-hair madman. If so, it was worth pointing out to the police, wasn't it?

I left Aunt Victoria at Dr. Sandberg's office. Half an hour remained before the eastbound train to Portland left Dexter, so David volunteered to accompany me to the police station.

Officer Wainwright was not on duty today. A cop in his twenties sat at a big oak desk, typing a report one finger at a time. When we entered, he ceased hunting and pecking with a look of relief and approached the counter. The nameplate on his desk read T. CLARKSON. His blue uniform was too big for him and so were his ears, but he looked happy enough to be interrupted by a young lady. I went to work.

"I'm Jessie Carr, Officer, and this is my brother, David Murray," I said with a shy smile that changed to anxiety as the purported reason for my visit emerged. "I'm one of the people who found the Indian girl's body by the road a few weeks ago, and, well, I was wondering whether we could sleep safe in our beds at night yet, knowing her killer had been apprehended."

"No, Miss Carr, I'm terribly sorry. There's been no arrest on that case. I don't think there ever will be. Those Indians just won't talk. But you don't need to worry about your safety. That was just another case of some drunk Indian buck."

"You don't think there's any connection, then, between that killing and the other two murders?"

His jaw dropped. "What other two murders?"

"Why, the Chinese girl back in '18 and the girl they found two weeks ago under the stairs in the warehouse."

"Oh, right, but that girl they found, she died years ago. And I don't know what Chinese girl you're talking about."

"The Chinese girl who was murdered on the docks, strangled, like the others. Some think she was involved in smuggling."

"Oh, I sorta remember now. It was before I joined up. That was when rumrunners were bringing in liquor from Canada on private boats right up to the docks here, bold as brass, and things got a little rough for a time. A couple men got knifed. And a Chinese girl killed, yes, I heard about it. I guess things got too hot for them in Dexter, and they moved on to somewhere else."

Somewhere else where bribes greased the skids. But something didn't fit. "How could there have been rumrunners in Dexter in 1918? Prohibition didn't start until 1920."

"*National* Prohibition started in 1920, Miss Carr. You're not old enough to remember, but Oregon and some other states were dry before that. Oregon's been dry since 1916."

Dumbstruck, I could only stare at him. I had absolutely no idea some states went dry before Prohibition. But then, why would I? I was a youngster then, and perhaps we hadn't toured through any of those states. In any case, wherever we went, there was never any shortage of speakeasies and bars. How would I have known which were legal and which not? They all look alike.

So Henry could have been running illegal liquor as early as 1916. Well, well, there was one mystery solved. That had to be the secret Jessie had discovered. Somehow she'd found out he was mixed up with Canadian bootleggers and had threatened to tell his mother if he didn't start being "nice." How he must have loathed that! A smart-mouthed little rich girl, dangling his crimes over his head.

Finally I found my tongue. "There are several similarities among the murders, as I'm sure you realize." Officer Clarkson did not realize. I explained about the strangling, the age and sex of the victims, and the hair.

"The Indian girl had her hair snipped off too, you say? Let me see . . ." And to my astonishment, he picked a report out of the file box on the desk behind him and began to flip through the pages.

"Is that the coroner's report?"

"Yep. Came in yesterday. I'm looking for whether it says anything about her hair."

"You mind telling us what else it says?"

"Not at all, Miss Carr. Information's headed for the newspaper anyway. Here, you can look for yourself."

With David reading over my shoulder, I flipped through the pages, past what I already knew until I found what I didn't know. Rosita Menendez, her name was. Last known address: Portland. Doc Milner had been right. A Portland woman. What had she been doing in Dexter?

David was frowning. When he saw me looking at him, the frown vanished. "Do you know that address?" I asked.

"I know the street. Near where we were last week."

"In other words, a seedy part of town."

"Could call it that. You see anything in there about her hair?"

"No, nothing."

"That could mean it wasn't cut off. But it could also mean the coroner didn't pay any attention to hair."

"That's so, Mr. Murray, that's so." Officer Clarkson looked approvingly at David. "It also means the same person probably killed those other two, just like you said, Miss Carr. I wonder if the Indian girl was mixed up in rumrunning as well. None of that goes on around here anymore, but then they said she might have been killed somewhere else and dumped here."

We thanked Officer Clarkson and headed toward the train station, engrossed in speculation. "Is the police department clueless about the rumrunning," I asked David, "or is someone being paid to look the other way?"

"I wasn't in it deep enough to get involved in police matters, but it's likely at least a couple of Dexter's officers are on the payroll. Payoffs are kept separate so the police don't know who's involved except for the guy paying them. Look here, I just had an idea. Last week in Portland I ran into an old school chum. He's a policeman now. If you give the word, I'll run him down and ask a few questions about Rosita Menendez. Maybe this is bigger than Dexter."

I'd been down that road with Benny. Still, I found myself saying, "No harm in that."

And then, I looked around. "Oh, dear. We've passed the

drugstore. I have to pick up some medicine for Ross. You go on to the station."

"Train's not in yet. I'll come with you."

According to the information I'd gleaned from Aunt Victoria, Dexter Drugs had stood on the corner of Wickham and Main ever since Benjamin Costello, the owner's father, rode into town in 1884 and hitched his medicine wagon to a post on the empty lot. Within a few weeks he'd bought the lot and built a clapboard store that kept townsfolk in Lydia Pinkham's pills, Ayer's Sarsaparilla, Luden's Throat Drops, Dr. Morse's Indian Root pills, Vicks Vaporub, Jayne's Expectorant, Dr. David's entire line of elixirs, and all manner of toiletries, all the while concocting some of his own potions in a mortar and pestle behind the counter. His son studied medicine for two years at the university in Eugene before coming home to assume the family business.

He was helping a middle-aged woman when we entered. "I'll be with you in a moment," he called from behind the counter, so David and I browsed the shelves for a while. I was not paying attention to their conversation until I overheard the woman say the words "Chinese medicine." My ears stretched toward the counter.

"Our cook gets them at the Chinese market on Sunday," she was saying.

"What did they tell her?" asked the pharmacist.

"That it would help with female problems. Change-of-life symptoms. But I didn't want to, well, try something foreign without asking you."

"Very wise of you." Costello examined the dried substance with a magnifying glass, smelled it, tasted it, and squeezed it between his fingers before making his pronouncement. "This is angelica. Some people candy angelica, so I can't think it could harm you if you want to try it."

"Cook said the local Orientals treat this man like some kind of doctor."

I couldn't help it. "Excuse me. I couldn't help but overhear. This Chinese man, is his name John Chen?"

"Why, yes, it is. Have you purchased medicines from him?"

"Not directly. I'm Jessie Carr, and John Chen is our gardener. He does know a lot about herbs and traditional Chinese medicines. When I was very sick on bad oysters recently, he gave me a boneset drink that cured me at once."

"We don't know much about Chinese medicines," said the pharmacist. "But they are based on herbs, like most medicines, and have been used for thousands of years, so there must be some value in them. This John Chen may be a quack, or he may know something. I'd try the angelica, Mrs. Phipps, and see if it helps. I can promise you that it won't hurt. And let me know what you think."

"I'll do that." She thanked him, and left the store.

"I've come for Ross Carr's medicine," I said when Costello turned to me.

"I'm glad to hear it's helping him. A real miracle drug, that ephedra. Gives asthma sufferers a new lease on life. How did the young man do with that dosage? It was double the strength of the first batch."

"No one said anything about dosage, so I assume he wants more of the same."

Costello pulled out a bottle and began counting white pills into a paper envelope. "It's a new miracle drug. Saved many a life, I'm sure, even in the short time it's been on the shelves. Tell him not to take more than one pill at a time, and to cut that in half if he starts feeling his heart race. Hey, come to think of it, ephedra's from China too."

I was listening for the first sound of David's train and scarcely heard the pharmacist. "How nice." I feigned a polite interest.

"I was reading about it just last week," he said, warming to the subject. He pulled a medical journal from the stack of papers at the end of the counter and laid it before me. A distant whistle announced the train's approach. It would make a ten-minute stop before going on. David hadn't much time, but the station was only a short block from the pharmacy. Costello was rambling again. "The Chinese have used it for centuries. Here, look." He put his finger on the illustration of the plant. I glanced once, blinked twice, then looked again.

I'd seen that plant, and very recently. It was ma huang. The significance came crashing down around my ears.

Oblivious now to the train, I snatched up the journal. "Look, David!" I exclaimed. "It's the same plant that Chen grows."

Our eyes met. There was no need for words. The undissolved white substance in my sherry had been ma huang in pill form, like Chen had said. It was Ross's asthma medicine. Chen would not have known that Ross took medicine; he was never inside the house. Grandmother had been right. It was Ross who had tried to kill me, not Henry. His recent kindness had been a ploy to lull me into complacency. And it had worked, damn him.

"What happens if you take too much of this?"

Costello drew his finger down the page. "Let's see . . . it says here, 'Prolonged use of the drug, which is not recommended, can be the cause of nervousness and insomnia.' No worries there, Miss Carr. Your cousin only takes them on occasion. 'Other side effects include nausea, vomiting, fever, depression, seizures, and headaches. Excessive dose can cause cerebral hemorrhage, cardiac arrest, and death.' Which is why I warn him not to take more than one at a time, and only when he's experiencing severe difficulty breathing."

A man walked into the drugstore with three youngsters in tow. Costello handed me the envelope of Ross's pills and noted the purchase in his ledger before turning to the next customer. I looked at the package with distaste. How many of these little pills had Ross put in my glass of sherry?

"You'd better catch your train," I said to David.

"Forget the train, I'll—"

"No, you go on. I'll be fine. I'll be careful. Now that I know who was responsible." We were outside now. I could see the train pulling into the station. I could see the indecision on David's face as he struggled between conflicting obligations to be with his dying mother and to watch over his sister.

"Gloreen is a real treasure, one in a million. She takes such good care of Ma . . . I don't know how I'll ever repay her, but—"

"But she's not family. Your mother needs her son with her now."

He brushed my cheek with his lips and my heart flipped over. "Take care of yourself. I don't want to lose you too." His long legs reached the train just as it pulled out of the station.

41

The telegram arrived while I was in the ballroom with the twins, hanging lights covered with colorful paper lanterns for my birthday party. For Jessie's birthday party. I was half expecting Jessie to show up. In a perverse way, I was hoping she would.

Of course she would look older now—I always thought of her as she looked in her last photograph, at thirteen—but I'd know her instantly. I'd give her a quick nod, slip out in the confusion, and life would go on the way it was meant to be. Not a bad ending, all in all.

Still flush with success from their stage debut, the girls were putting their newfound skills to use, painting a canvas backdrop with a large Eiffel Tower and a Leaning Tower of Pisa. The words "Bon Voyage" and "Happy Birthday" arced in large letters across the top. Invitations had gone out yesterday, and I expected a near hundred percent turnout. The Carrs had lived in Dexter for ten years, and Aunt Victoria had become a pillar of the community, but I was sure acceptances would be driven more by curiosity over Jessie's reappearance than anything else.

I ripped open the telegram and gave a cry of dismay.

"What is it, Jessie?" asked Caro.

"David's mother died yesterday. The funeral is tomorrow."

"Poor David! How sad."

"He regrets that under the circumstances he will not be able to attend the party."

"What a shame."

Later that day I made up my mind. I told Aunt Victoria and Grandmother, "I'm going to Portland to attend Mrs. Murray's funeral. David doesn't expect it, I know, but I think he will appreciate the sentiment."

"I think it's very sweet of you, Jessie," said my aunt. "A bit unconventional perhaps, but surely no one could criticize such a generous gesture on the part of his closest relation."

And so it was that I found myself on the train to Portland once again, a reluctant passenger this morning, trying to think of some words of consolation to lessen David's pain when I knew from experience such words did not exist.

Mount Hood towered in the distance as I made my way to the brick Methodist church a couple of blocks from the Murray home. It was a simple service. The church was full. Mrs. Murray had been a fixture in the working-class neighborhood for twenty-five years. She had given store credit when people hit hard times, kept an eye on neighborhood children, and even taken in an unwed mother whose family had thrown her out on the street. Loved by many, respected by all, Mrs. Murray would be missed.

David's eyes lit up when he saw me in the back, and nothing would do but that I would sit in the family pew with Gloreen and her father and brothers. I was glad I didn't have to say much. Something about Gloreen rubbed me wrong, like petting a cat's fur against the growth. She was far friendlier to me than I was to her, but she wasn't good enough for David. He seemed to think otherwise.

The sexton had found room in the crowded churchyard for one more grave, and Mrs. Murray's mortal remains were laid to rest beside the low brick wall that circled the cemetery. The cloud cover brought a wintry chill to the late afternoon air, and I shivered in my new fall coat as the expensive-looking casket was laid in the ground. Whatever David's meager finances, he would not skimp on his mother.

David invited the mourners into the parish hall for refreshments. Little sandwiches and several pies and cakes had been laid on a long table, and Gloreen was busy ladling ginger ale punch into cut-glass cups like she owned the place.

"Everything is delicious," I said to David, who kept me close by his side.

"Isn't it? Gloreen is an amazing cook." I felt the unintended criticism—I'd never cooked anything in my life more elaborate than a cheese sandwich. "You don't know what it means to me to have you come to Ma's funeral," he said for the fourth time.

"I'm glad I had the chance to meet her, if only that once." I would always have that connection with David, knowing his mother.

"She really took pleasure in seeing you that day. She spoke of it right up until the end."

It was only then that I noticed what he was wearing. "Oh, you have on her locket!"

"It was her most prized possession. You don't think I did wrong in not burying it with her?"

"Of course not! I'm sure she wanted you to have it, and it will mean as much to you as it did to her. You can remember her that way, young and pretty and happy." He nodded and slipped it inside his shirt against his skin.

I wanted to ask what he intended to do. Sell the store, sure, but then what? It was not the time to talk of future plans. And to be honest, I didn't want to hear anything about his marrying Gloreen. Wasn't it just my miserable luck to find the ideal man, only to have him disqualified by my own lies?

"With all the arrangements for Ma, I haven't had time to run down my friend in the police department."

"Why, of course not. Don't give it another thought."

"I've been giving it a lot of thought, and the more I think, the more I worry about you with Ross around. He put that poison in your glass, and he's bound to try something again."

"Grandmother watches him like a hawk. She's been suspicious of him since the day she arrived. And I'm being careful. I'll be leaving in a few days."

"I'm sorry I won't be able to come to your party."

"It isn't important."

"But I want to see you before you go to Sacramento. Before you leave for Europe."

He sounded as if he really cared for me. Well, of course he does, I told myself harshly. He thinks you're his half sister, for crying out loud. At that moment, one of the older couples, who was waiting for a break in our conversation to offer their condolences, stepped forward and held out their hands to David. I moved tactfully aside. Gloreen sailed by, busy as a hostess at a social gathering. Next she'd be cooking David his dinner every night. All right, I admit it, I was jealous!

Sticking around watching Gloreen play Lady of the Manor was giving me a headache. I curved my lips into my best stage smile and asked her to tell David I had left. I didn't trust myself to carry off a fond farewell when I knew I'd never see him again. "If I say good-bye directly," I told her, "he'll insist on escorting me to the streetcar, and that isn't necessary. I know where it stops, and besides, his place is here. Thank you so much for the spread. Everything was delicious."

"You're welcome, Miss Carr. I'd do anything for David . . . David's mother."

I wanted to slap her.

Returning to the Benson, I paused at reception only long enough to order a bottle of champagne and a light supper sent to my room. Before it could arrive, I walked directly into the dark bathroom and stripped off my clothes, letting them fall to the floor in a heap, turned on the water taps and watched the tub fill around me. My body soaked up the steaming water like a sponge. I lay back, my head on a folded towel, closed my eyes, and tried to let go of my headache. I tried not to think about David. There was no point. He belonged to Gloreen. Instead I concentrated on my next move.

The curtain would soon fall on *She Stoops to Con*. Closing night was so close I could almost smell the roses. The birthday party was two days away. The meeting in Sacramento came three days after that. With any luck Smith and Wade could book passage on an ocean liner out of San Francisco the next day. I had performed to perfection. Applause, applause. Where was the euphoria?

I had to continue as planned. Sure, I wanted to solve Jessie's disappearance and avenge her death, if she were truly dead. Sure, I'd like to finger Henry for bootlegging, and I would do it too, but I could see no way to make anyone believe me. Although he hadn't been anywhere nearby when the cut-hair killings had taken place, I still wondered whether he or Ross had had something to do with Jessie's disappearance. But wondering isn't evidence.

I toyed with the possibilities like final scenes of a play.

I'd walk into the Dexter police station. "Hello, I'm not really Jessie Carr, I'm impersonating her to get her money. The real Jessie Carr was murdered seven years ago and I know who did it. Her cousin Henry."

"Is that so, miss? And what proof do you have? A body?"

"A strong hunch. Henry had a lot to gain from her death, and he once considered pushing me over a cliff."

"Did he now, miss? Step into this cell here while we look into the matter. Mr. Carr, did you murder your cousin seven years ago?"

"Certainly not, Officer, and I want this impostor locked up for the rest of her life."

Try again. I'd walk into Dexter police station. "Hello, my cousin Henry Carr is a notorious bootlegger."

"Is that so, miss? And what proof do you have?"

"Our liquor boxes have green chalk on them and so do boxes in Portland speakeasies."

"Very interesting, miss." Big yawn from the cop. "And how does he acquire his liquor?"

"He probably loads his yacht in Canada, but I can't figure out how he smuggles it in."

"Very well, miss, we'll send a report to our captain, who is on the bootlegger's payroll, and let him handle it."

One more try. I'd walk into the Dexter police station. "Officer, my cousin Ross tried to poison me with his asthma medicine."

"Very interesting, miss. You don't look dead. What did the doctor say to all this?"

"Bad oysters. But our Chinese gardener thinks it was poison."

"There, there, miss. Sit down and relax while we call Doc Milner to see if you're off your rocker."

It was hopeless. Fact of the matter was, I was the only one who would suffer if I tried to rat on Henry or Ross.

It was a Mexican standoff. If only I could talk to David, alone. Even if he didn't know the truth about me, he was the one man in Oregon I could trust. If nothing else, he could fill me in on the distribution part of the smuggling story. If he would talk, that is, which I doubted given his strong sense of loyalty. In any case, I cared about him too much to drag him further into this mess. A bootlegging charge against Henry—if the authorities bothered to pursue it—would immediately expand to his cronies, sweeping up David with the rest of the crooks, and I didn't want that.

I would miss David.

I shook my head firmly. There was no future there, not with my "brother." He thought of me as his sister and was virtually engaged to Gloreen the Wonder Girl, who could cook, tend to the sick, and run a house with one hand tied behind her back. But I couldn't stop thinking about how things might have been.

Room service arrived. I pulled on a robe and let the boy in. Adding more hot water to the tub, I meditated on the hypocrisy of turning someone in for smuggling liquor while sipping bootleg champagne.

Nothing I could do would bring Jessie back. I couldn't bring any of those dead women back to life either, and I was hallucinating to think that Henry had anything to do with them. Talk about circumstantial evidence! Even if, through his smuggling, Henry had been generally involved in their deaths, it couldn't have been direct. He had been far away at college when the Chinese girl and the girl in the warehouse were killed in Dexter. He was in town when Lizzette was killed, true, but that fact hardly mattered without the others. When I had shared my suspicions with David, he'd been dubious. The facts did not fall in my favor. When all was said and done, Henry had not pushed me over the cliff, the white substance in my glass could have been impurities, and Doc Milner had diagnosed oysters.

And Jessie could well be alive and making her way to Sacramento at this very moment to lay claim to her inheritance before her twenty-first birthday—even though my sixth sense was shouting at me otherwise.

There was nothing I could do without proof, and my time here was nearly up. The only choice was to stay the course. Play the charade to the end. Sign the papers and disappear for good into the European countryside.

42

O
h, dear," said Aunt Victoria as she flipped through Friday's mail. It was nearly four o'clock and, after having finished the party decorations, I had joined the twins and Grandmother in the parlor for a few games of Give and Take. Grandmother turned out to be a sharp player—at least her taffy pile was always the biggest. But that could also have been because her false teeth prevented her from eating her winnings like the rest of us. I suspected that in her day she had gone home a few dollars ahead from more than one card game.

Ross was poking up the fire, as men like to do. Ever since I had figured out that he had tried to poison me, I kept a close eye on the lad. Henry slumped in his overstuffed chair, lifting himself out of it only to pour another whiskey and snatch another handful of almonds before returning to his hiding place behind the newspaper. I wasn't sure why he bothered to try to conceal the amount he drank; his mother always pretended not to notice, and none of the rest of us cared. He'd sailed into Dexter Bay a few hours earlier, just as a rare summer storm blew up, talking of rough seas and fussing over some damage to his rigging. I hoped he wouldn't pay attention to our card game. He'd take great pleasure in tattling on us to his mother, although I frankly didn't think she'd mind at this point.

"Oh, dear," Aunt Victoria said again, and we paid attention this second time. "The Reynolds have begged off. Seems Edith is ill. Such a shame. Here's a letter for you, Ross. And you, Jessie."

I ripped open the envelope. "Uncle Oliver sends his regards to all," I said, "and many thanks for the invitation. He will arrive tomorrow, in time for the party, and then return to California with Grandmother and me on Monday." Only three more days. I was going to make it.

"Well, how flattering. He's a busy, busy man, and I hardly expected him to rearrange his schedule to come a day early. What is it, Ross, dear?"

For Ross's face was suddenly contorted with fury. "Damned idiots! Sorry, Mother, but this is insupportable. I have sent in all the correct paperwork for the master of arts degree and stated my intent to continue with the doctor of philosophy in the next term, and here the school morons are saying I haven't met the requirements because I've only attended Stanford for one year!"

The crackle of newspaper drew my eyes to Henry, whose forehead appeared over the edge of the Portland daily. He gave Ross a sharp look, then saw me watching him and lifted the newspaper again. Something was up.

"Oh, dear," said Aunt Victoria. "Never mind, darling. It's just a mix-up. They probably looked up another student's record by mistake. No doubt there are other Carrs who attended Stanford; after all, it's a big school and Carr is hardly an unusual name."

"Like Sacco or Vanzetti," said Caro, proving that Mrs. Applewhite was having some success in teaching current events.

"My thesis has yet to receive final approval, but my adviser suggested I start the paperwork. So I did. And now this!"

"Just write them a letter, darling, and it will all straighten out."

In an act of pure clairvoyance, I knew Henry was going to speak before he opened his mouth, and I knew, more or less, what he was going to say.

"As a matter of fact, I recall a fellow named Robert Carr a couple years older than me. I was glad when he left . . . caused any number of mix-ups."

The truth crashed over me with such force that I was amazed that no one else heard it. Henry was as deep into his own charade as I was into mine. If I was correct, he had not, after all, been far away in California when the girls with the cut hair had been murdered.

Because it was Henry's record the school had mixed up with Ross's. Not some phony Robert Carr who never existed, but Henry Carr, who had only attended Stanford for one year. Henry Carr, who had left Stanford and told no one, not his mother, not the trustees who were paying the fare, no one. Henry Carr, who had pretended to continue at college for two more years while he ran rum from Canada into Oregon and pocketed the tuition money. And I'd wager my entire stash of saltwater taffy that he hadn't left college of his own volition.

Everything depended on my hunch being confirmed.

Excusing myself, I made my way to the house telephone and pulled the pocket doors closed behind me. I reached the operator and asked to be connected to the dean's office at Stanford University in California. Then I hung up and waited for her to call back, my hand on the receiver, hoping I could snatch it up before the ringing alerted the family to an incoming call.

A half hour passed. It felt like a week, but I never moved my hand.

At last the harsh ring came, but as fast as I reacted, it was not fast enough to silence the entire ring.

"I have your party now," intoned the operator, putting me through to someone called a bursar, someone who had something to do with money. The dean's office had closed, but these people would surely have records as to which students had paid tuition, what they had paid and when, records that would indicate the duration of Henry's stay at Stanford. Luckily, the bursar himself was out and an eager underling asked how he could help.

"This is Mrs. Carr," I said, using my lower, older voice, "mother of Ross and Henry Carr, both Stanford students. I'm calling from Oregon, so speak up, young man. We've experienced a mix-up today. A letter came that mistook one son's record for the other's. Might you check your records to see if the dates of attendance for each are correct?"

I drummed my fingers impatiently while the clerk searched for the relevant files.

"Now, for my son Ross, the record should show him attending for three years to earn his bachelor's degree, and another year for his master's, correct?"

"Yes, ma'am. From September 1920 through June 1923, B.A., and the past year, September 1923 through June 1924, on the course work for an M.A."

"And my other son, Henry Carr?"

"Yes, his file is here too. It shows attendance for one year, September 1917 through June 1918, and—oh."

"Yes, just one year, and then there was the unpleasantness," I ad-libbed. "What does your record say about that?"

"Well, Mrs. Carr. It isn't specific, just that he was asked to leave."

"Of course I know all about that. I just want to know what the record states. The exact wording."

"Well, these are never very specific. Most of the time the

dean's note says 'for conduct.' That's all that is written here, so you needn't worry about details getting out."

For conduct. Conduct unbecoming a gentleman? Like cheating at cards, consorting with loose women, drunken brawling?

"Thank you for your help, young man."

Triumph surged through my veins as I set the receiver into its cradle. I had him now!

"Nosy little thing, aren't you?"

I spun around, my heart in my throat. Henry had eased open one of the doors without my noticing and entered the room while my back was turned. He must have heard the brief ring and guessed what I was doing. How much had he heard?

Judging from his twisted face, enough.

My heart thundered, but I hid my alarm. I took a deep breath and told myself I wasn't afraid of Henry Carr. He was dangerous, yes, almost certainly a murderer, but not here, not with the whole family across the hall getting ready to sit down to dinner. I was safe for the time being. I gulped some air and answered with a calm I did not feel.

"I prefer to call it curiosity."

Whiskey glass in hand, he closed the door behind him and leaned unsteadily against it. He was drunk or teetering close to it.

"The sort of curiosity that killed the cat? You should learn to keep your damned nose out of other people's business."

"I generally do, except when I find that other people's business involves me."

"Think you're pretty clever, don't you?"

Time to go on the attack. "You were thrown out of Stanford after one year. What was it, Henry? Cheating at cards? You're not a very accomplished cheater; I noticed it the first time we sat at the same card table. Or was it for fighting? I know you like to beat up women, but I didn't think you fought with men. They're so much more likely to hit back. I figure you found it more profitable to lie about your expulsion; that way you could still collect the money meant for tuition. Too bad Ross had to attend the same university or you could have kept up the swindle another year or two."

"You little bitch. You're as bad as she was."

"That's right, Henry, you *know* I'm not Jessie. How do you *know* that, Henry?" I taunted. If I could make him angry enough, drunk as he was, he might spill the evidence I needed.

"I got rid of Jessie once, and it looks like I'll have to get rid of her again."

"You killed Jessie."

He slurped his whiskey and wagged a finger at me. "Did I? You have no idea how much I hated her."

"And you tried to poison me with Ross's pills."

"That was soooo stupid of me. I panicked when you mentioned leaving the country. A good thing it wasn't fatal. What if the doctor had suspected it was something other than a bad oyster? Blame would have fallen on me or Ross. I won't be that stupid again. No, your death has to be an accident: a fall from a horse, a tumble off the cliff, a drowning at sea . . . Although I would take great pleasure in resolving this personally, it isn't wise. I have friends who do that sort of work for me. A shame, though, to miss the fun."

"I'll go to the police."

"Don't make me laugh. What you think you know and what you can prove are very different things. The police wouldn't believe your accusations—even making them would send you to jail faster than I could press charges. No, you can't go to the police for the same reason I can't go to the police. They wouldn't believe me either—you're remarkably convincing. You've fooled everyone. You would have fooled me too if I hadn't known what really happened to Jessie."

He took a couple of unsteady steps in my direction before remembering where he was. I could read his thoughts as well as if they'd been printed on cue cards. He couldn't hurt me while I was in this house. He would have to wait.

"Almost funny, isn't it?" he continued unevenly. "But I have a way out, and you don't, so I can bide my time. You'll have an accident when I'm well out of the way, and the Carr money will come back to me, where it damn well belongs. My father was cheated out of his share of the inheritance, you know. Cheated. There is one thing I'd really like to know though. How did you do it?"

"I could ask you the same question."

"Well, I have my ideas—as you do, no doubt. It had to be that goddamn governess who fed you all the family details. She knew way too much and figured out the rest. She tried to blackmail me—you were in on that, weren't you? No one does that to Henry Carr and gets away with it. But she met with a little accident of her own on the dangerous streets of San Francisco. It was her own fault. Thought she was so smart. Like you. And greedy too, aren't you? She wanted to squeeze me for some of my money. You want it all."

So Henry had hired someone to run down Miss Lavinia! With a flash of clarity, I understood the rest.

"That car outside the Benson Hotel," I said. "That was no drunk driver; that was your doing!"

"I was here all that day, dear cousin." He smirked. "Ask anyone."

"And the hotel fire. Your man started that."

He just chuckled and took another slurp of whiskey.

The door opened unexpectedly, causing us both to jump. Val peered in. "Oh, there you are. Mother said tell you dinner is served."

"Thanks, Val," I said. "We're coming." She headed toward the dining room as I made to walk past Henry. His breath reeked of whiskey as he said softly, "Enjoy the good life while you can. Keep looking over your shoulder because when you least expect it—" He ran his finger across his throat and snickered.

It was a bad night for sleeping anyway, what with the storm rattling the windows and howling through the trees. I dozed in fits and starts, listening to the surf crash against the cliff and dreaming of Jessie whenever I slipped into sleep. It was the same dream I'd had before, only more vivid now that I knew for certain she was dead. Then I was with her and our feet were wet, and she was trying to tell me something. I tried hard but could never understand her words. I could feel the urgency, though, in my pounding heart. I woke up in a sweat, clutching my Italian beads. Jessie's beads that I wore all the time, even to bed.

When I had taken on this role, I'd adopted more than Jessie's name. I'd taken her family, her money, her past, and her future. I became Jessie Carr. And I owed her something for all that. I owed her the truth. Now that I knew the identity of her killer, I owed her justice, whatever the cost to myself.

But how was I going to repay the debt? Henry would not obligingly repeat his confession in front of a judge, and I had no evidence, no body, and no hope of convincing the authorities that this man had somehow arranged the death of his cousin, their governess, and probably several women who were involved in his smuggling scheme. Nothing I could do would resurrect a single one, but I owed it to them to prevent him from killing again. He hadn't stopped with Jessie; he had started with her. I was to be his next victim, but not his last. He enjoyed killing. He was good at it and even better at getting away with it. And there was no reason for him to stop.

For a fleeting moment, I wondered if telling Oliver about any of this would help me. What would be his reaction to learning that his niece was murdered by her cousin? If the truth about Jessie's death emerged, he'd lose his chance at her fortune. He had never cared a fig about Jessie, and I knew darn well his greed would overcome any scruples he might have. He'd make me continue with the charade, regardless of the risk to myself. No, Oliver was no ally.

I wasn't afraid for myself at this precise moment. Henry was powerless as long as I was at Cliff House, and he had admitted as much. The danger would begin when I left in two days. Death could then come from any direction. I would have to look at every person with suspicion—every waiter, every train conductor, every street vendor—wondering if they were in the pay of Henry Carr. I would have to consider every car a weapon, every meal poisoned, every hotel room a firetrap. I would start by hiring my own Pinkerton bodyguards, although I was not so naïve as to think them immune from Henry's influence either.

It seemed almost funny that I had once figured I could just slip away if things got rough.

I lay awake until the clock chimed six, until I had fashioned a plan that I thought might work.

44

There wasn't time to post a letter. I drove to the Western Union office near the docks and paid fifty cents to send Benny a telegram.

"Same request. Palo Alto. Desperately important. Love from your second-best girl."

It wasn't cost that made me economize with words, it was concern about the damage a gossipy operator could do. Sure, I know they are sworn to be discreet, but I couldn't take the risk. Dexter was a small town, and Henry had lots of friends.

Jack Benny had been on his way to Salem the day after I saw him at the Egyptian, and after that, to San Francisco for a longer run at Pantages Theatre. I hoped he would understand my plea. I hoped it reached him promptly. I hoped he could help me fast. It was a lot to ask. The trip from San Francisco to Palo Alto was long, maybe forty miles, and would consume most of a day. I'd make it up to him somehow.

The rain stopped, but gray skies smothered the bay and strong winds blustered inland from the ocean. My flivver was parked near the first pier, and as I returned to it, I caught sight of the boy from the hardware store crouching at the edge of the water, assembling something in his fishing box. The boy who had rushed to give us the news of the body in the burned warehouse . . . what was his name? Seeing him gave me an idea.

"Hello. You're an early bird. William, isn't it?"

He looked up and pushed back his cap to see my face.

"Yes, ma'am?"

"I'm Miss Carr. We met some weeks ago in your father's store. That your boat?" I pointed to an old wooden boat tied up to the dock beside us, straining at its rope. Someone had painted it a gay blue and yellow and outfitted it with a tiny mast and sail. If it had been any smaller, it would have been a toy.

"Yes, ma'am."

"Do you take it out much?"

"Every chance I get."

"What do you catch?"

"This time of year, chinook mostly."

"Good eating?"

"I sell most of 'em. I'm saving for a bigger boat."

"Do you go outside the bay?"

"Not allowed to. The fishing's usually best in the bay, near the mouth of the river." Where the sailing was best went unsaid.

"It looks pretty rough out there. You're not going fishing today, are you?"

"Ma won't let me."

"I guess you have to be pretty skilled to sail these waters, even on a calm day. The Graveyard of the Pacific and so forth. You must know the coast pretty well, though. Are there any other small bays or harbors along this stretch?"

"Nary a one. Leastways none that I know of. Just cliffs and rocks."

To our left near the canneries, the choppy water bumped the fleet of weatherworn fishing boats against their piers. Out in Dexter Bay a number of fine yachts strained at their buoys, all of them stretched eastward, aligned by the wind and currents. Dexter Bay's marina was popular with the wealthy Portland sailing crowd, located as it was a short train ride from the metropolitan area. One of these boats belonged to Henry, who had sloshed down enough Seagram's last night to keep him in bed at Cliff House till noon. I pointed to the closest yacht. "That's a pretty boat there."

"That's Mr. Sam Walker's. It's new this year."

"You must know a lot about boats. Which is the nicest?"

"Mr. Henry Carr's Herreshoff. Over there."

I followed his finger to a sleek craft tied to a buoy about a hundred yards out. "What a lovely boat! My cousin Henry doesn't fish, does he? I don't remember anything of his on the dinner table recently."

"Naw, he just sails with friends, up north."

"Dexter friends?"

"Big shots from Portland or Salem."

"North to Canada? Picking up hooch, I expect."

"Who doesn't?" His shrug said it all. Everyone winked at the law.

"There sure are a lot of bottles at Cliff House," I said with a confidential laugh. "You know, I heard that a few years back, bootleggers were bold enough to unload their cargo right here in town."

"Pa told me about that. Said the cops scared 'em off." Honest police? I wondered. The cynic in me thought it more likely they demanded too high a cut and drove off the "importers." Was it Henry?

"I guess my cousin Henry is a pretty fair sailor."

It was like turning on an electric light bulb. "He's the best! A real daredevil. I was fishing off the rocks south of here, by your place near the caves, when I seen him come through those giant rocks under power, weaving in and out, then when he was hardly clear of 'em, he hoisted the sails and cut power. He knows where every last reef is. No one else but him would risk that, but he's not afraid of anything."

Ah, hero worship. What a waste. "Golly, I'm sorry I missed seeing that. Was it last week?"

He shook his head. "Couple weeks ago." I remembered. Henry said he had gone sailing with friends for several days up to Puget Sound. The green chalk delivery must have come in then.

"I sure am sorry to see this storm. Henry promised to take me for a ride today. He just came in yesterday—but you know that—and I've never had the chance to see his new boat." I heaved a sighed of profound disappointment as I cast the bait. "And I'm leaving Oregon the day after tomorrow."

"Leaving for good?" he asked with the astonishment of a native who couldn't imagine why anyone would ever want to go anywhere else.

"Leaving on a long trip abroad. I probably won't get back to Oregon for a while." I gave it my most dramatic sigh.

"Well, I could run you out there, quick like, for a close-up look."

"Oh, what a wonderful idea! Would you?"

He dropped into the little vessel and reached up a hand to help me down. I crouched in the damp bottom on top of a coil of rope, and gave up trying to keep my skirt dry. Behind me, William hoisted a tiny sail and shot over to Henry's yacht in seconds.

I had never been in a boat of any kind in my life, and I found the brief ride exhilarating. Young William steered closer to the yacht, within a few feet of the boarding ladder. Standing, he pushed the sail to the side, and the little boat came gently to a stop against the larger vessel. Then he grabbed hold of the ladder and secured his boat with a piece of rope. "Up you go. I'll wait here. Mr. Henry might not want me on his boat without asking."

"I'll just have a peek."

The cabin was locked, and it took only a moment to walk around the deck. Shipshape must be how sailors described boats like Henry's—neat and clean, the deck freshly painted, every bit of rope and rigging in its place. I peered in each window and saw what I expected to see: hundreds of liquor boxes, neatly stacked, waiting for distribution.

Turning him in to the Dexter cops would be a joke. The corrupt police force would only warn Henry to move his boat before making a show of searching for it, and I would lose my one chance to learn how he made his deliveries.

I scrambled back into William's dinghy. "Wow, that's a beauty!"

William didn't reply. His eyes scanned the deserted docks and the road leading to them. His frown told me he was having second thoughts about his impulsive offer. What would Henry Carr have to say when he learned someone had boarded his boat without express permission?

"You know, William, I was just thinking . . . Henry wanted to show his boat to me himself, and maybe he'll be disappointed if he knows I already saw it. If the weather clears tomorrow, he might even be able to take me for that sail after all. I think it would be best if we didn't mention this to him. It could be our little secret. Then if he shows me around the boat, I can act like it was the first time, and he'll be so proud and pleased."

The worry lines disappeared. William yanked up the sail and returned us to the dock in a jiffy. The rough water made it impossible to hold the dinghy steady, but I'm pretty nimble around stage scaffolding and this wasn't much different. William scrambled up to the dock after me without a lick of trouble and tied the little craft up tight. Not a moment too soon—it started raining again.

"Here," I said, pulling a bill from my pocket. "For your trouble."

Astonished, he just stared at my hand. "That was no trouble."

"It was pure kindness, and I can't thank you enough. But I want you to have this to go toward that boat you're saving for. And remember our secret!" I winked broadly.

"Yes, ma'am!"

I dashed for the flivver before the skies opened up. The storm was here to stay. There would be no liquor delivery today.

45

Back at Cliff House I struggled with what I had learned. It didn't make sense—Henry running hooch into the country and unloading it in a waterlogged cave. He'd only have a couple of hours at low tide to reload it and sail somewhere else or the boxes would be ruined by the incoming surge. Caves flooded twice a day with each high tide. Maybe the waves weren't powerful enough to wash away heavy cartons of liquor—or maybe they were, what did I know?—but they would waterlog the cartons and labels at the very least. None of the green-chalked boxes and bottles I had seen showed water damage.

But it was all I had to go on. Young William had seen Henry's yacht darting through the rocks near the Cliff House caves a couple of weeks ago. He had to have been going to the third cave, the one I hadn't explored. Was he meeting another boat inside that cave to transfer the liquor?

Henry had tried twice to have me killed—three times if you count the impulse by the cliff. He had to have an informant working inside the Smith and Wade office, someone who passed on information about my movements so Henry could hire a killer to take care of business. It would have been simple to ask a secretary or even one of the trustees when he could expect his cousin. I no longer thought the trustees had engaged a Pinkerton to search my room or follow me through town. That was Henry's hireling. Each time he had failed, but Henry was getting cleverer about it. He realized how foolish it was to make any further attempts on my life while we shared the same roof. It was simply too risky for him. He was biding his time, waiting for me to leave Cliff House, at which point I'd be fair game. For the time being, I was relatively safe.

I tried to think like a man bent on murder. How would he stage the next accident? Running me over by a car had been the tried-and-true plan—it had worked in San Francisco on the blackmailing governess—but to set it up, he needed to know in advance where I was going to be and when, as he had when I arrived in Portland with Grandmother and Oliver to spend the night at the Benson Hotel before coming to Dexter.

The next place he could intercept me would be at the trustees' office in Sacramento on September 30. Except I wouldn't be there. Then there was the long ocean voyage to Europe, which would present all kinds of opportunities for fatal accidents—falling overboard, food poisoning, random violence—except I wouldn't be there either. I'll bet I could have outsmarted that son of a bitch—double-booked my trip, traveled in disguise on a vessel he knew nothing about, and moved around in Europe like a gypsy until he gave up. Then again, a man of Henry's talents had long arms and the means to pry information out of law offices, telegraph operators, and banks. He would be able to trace me through the money Smith and Wade wired. Henry Carr would give up only when one of us was dead.

He thought he had me cornered. Wouldn't he be surprised?

"There you are, dear. Daydreaming?" Aunt Victoria interrupted my thoughts.

I blinked with confusion and looked around the parlor. "I'm afraid I was dozing . . . I didn't sleep well last night, what with all the excitement."

"Never mind, plenty of time for a nap before the guests arrive."

The tantalizing aromas of roasting meats mingled with baked goods made my stomach rumble. "Mmmmm. Something smells wonderful."

"Doesn't it? Marie hired three cooks to help work her magic. Our guests will feast on gourmet fare tonight!"

"Did you need me for anything?"

"I saw your Ford out front. Are you planning to meet your uncle at the station or shall I telephone Clyde?"

I looked at the clock. Oliver was arriving on the four o'clock train. Avoiding his perceptive eye would be prudent, given my latest intentions.

"I'll let Clyde meet him, if he doesn't mind, Aunt."

"Marie laid a simple luncheon on the sideboard so we can help ourselves whenever we are ready."

I was ready. The twins and Ross were eating warm cookies as we came in.

"Anyone seen Henry today?" Aunt Victoria asked.

"He had a bit to drink last night, Mother," said Ross delicately, "but I think we'll see him soon."

"You're seeing him now," came the gruff voice from the doorway. Henry entered the room, outwardly none the worse for the previous night's bacchanalian excess. I helped myself to creamed chipped beef on toast and a fresh garden salad and sat down at the end. Our glances met, and it's a wonder sparks didn't fly between us.

"Mother, can Sophie and Alice Hartley come early and dress for the party here?" asked Valerie.

"I don't see why not. They're such nice girls."

"Could they spend the night too?" asked Caro, always one to push her luck.

"Well, I suppose so. But they'll have to sleep in your room. Mr. Beckett is returning this afternoon, remember, and will take the green guest room."

"That's okay. Then we can help each other get dressed. Val and I will put up cots so you won't have to worry about a thing, Mother. Jessie, can I borrow your car to go to Dexter and get them?"

Henry gave his sister a nervous look as he dropped into his chair, carelessly slopping his coffee into the saucer and his spoon onto the floor. Leaving the spoon for the servants to pick up, he swore under his breath and reached for another on the sideboard. Evidently black coffee was all he could handle today.

"Of course you can, Caro. It's out front and ready to go. Needs to be moved anyway, before the guests arrive. Put it around back when you get home."

The girls dashed out of the room to get sweaters, nearly running down Grandmother as she entered. I lingered to enjoy her company. I wouldn't see her again—I wouldn't see any of these people again after Monday. Jessie's history had become mine, and I felt I had known them for years. It seemed impossible that I would not know them for the rest of my life, but I would not. We made idle conversation about party preparations, the dinner menu, and how difficult it was to find good cooks these days. Henry stared out the window and groused about the weather. I gathered it seldom rained this time of year. He finished his coffee quickly and left us.

A few moments later the twins clamored down the stairs, chattering like squirrels. I heard them talking to Henry in the hall.

"I'm going to the Grand Ronde reservation with a friend this afternoon," said Ross under his breath, seizing the moment when Aunt Victoria and Grandmother were discussing flower arrangements to bring up the unpleasant subject of the murdered Indian girl. "I don't know if anyone will talk to me, but I thought I'd give it a try. The police have closed the case. Do you want to come? We'll be home in time for the party."

I shook my head. Ross wasn't a bad sort after all. I wish I'd known enough to have trusted him earlier. "Normally I'd jump at the chance, but with party preparations . . . I've promised to help Grandmother with flower arrangements." Weak, but it sufficed. I had a more important investigation of my own in mind.

"Oh, look!" Aunt Victoria said, moving to the window. "Caroline is driving Henry's Packard! He's giving her a lesson. How sweet of him! My, my, and him so fussy about that Packard. What a wonderful big brother he is!"

Ross rolled his eyes. I smiled agreeably and excused myself from the table.

Back in my bedroom, I ransacked the boxes in the closet until I found what I was looking for, a ruled school notebook with blank paper. I could have taken paper from the library desk, where lovely rag stationery of various sizes and gold fountain pens waited for a feminine hand, but I preferred to use—no, I *needed* to use—Jessie's notebook. And I needed to use Jessie's monogrammed Swiss pen and sit in Jessie's chair at Jessie's desk, where she had done her schoolwork . . . or, rather, where she had avoided doing her schoolwork, if I knew Jessie. And I did know Jessie now, very well.

She looked over my shoulder as I wrote. She was in my head, advising me. *List the dates of the deaths first, then where Henry was at those times. Don't forget our governess, poor thing. She wasn't as bad as all that.* But what proof is there? I asked. *Never mind, just write down everything. Let them find the proof. Now put in the part about the bootlegging, and leave Brother David out of it. Put in about the cases of liquor on the boat, and how he couldn't unload them Saturday because of the storm.* But I need to know how he distributes the booze for the accusation to stick, I protested. *He's going to unload them as soon as the weather breaks. We'll find that out later. Now put in the part about killing me. He did, you know.* I know; he admitted it, sort of. "I did and I didn't," he said. But how? I asked. What did that mean? Where are you? How can I prove it? *Let them prove it. Let Father's old trustees earn their money. We'll give them enough to go on, enough to destroy Henry's political career, maybe even enough to send him to prison. They'll do the rest. They don't like Henry either.*

I argued and I thought and I wrote and I rewrote for the better part of the afternoon, so eager was I to present everything to the trustees in the most convincing light, but I knew it wasn't enough. We didn't have much evidence.

"Excuse me, miss." Rainy knocked on the door. "The telephone is for you."

I ran downstairs, anticipating Uncle Oliver on the other end telling me of some delay.

"Hello, doll." Jack Benny's voice came over the wire loud and clear.

"Benny!" I shrieked, not caring who heard. "This is such a surprise!"

"I got your telegram this morning."

"Oh, good! Can you help me out tomorrow?"

"I helped you today."

"What!"

"Can you talk?"

"No, but you can."

"Your telegram arrived early this morning, and I don't have to go on until six, so I borrowed a car and drove to the police station in question."

"You're the best friend a girl ever had, Benny."

"I know. Anyway, like last time, they went for my shtick, showed me what they had, and bingo. March 3, 1918. One strangled girl by the name of Rita Velasquez. Worked in a bar. Some of her hair cut off. No suspects."

"I knew it!" Henry had been enrolled during the 1917–1918 academic year. No one had tied him to the girl's murder, but once again, the victim had dark hair and a foreign appearance.

What happened to these girls? Did they get greedy and demand more money or threaten to expose him? Did they make a nuisance of themselves, pestering for more attention? Did Henry move on to other women and feel he couldn't afford to leave loose ends? Did he just enjoy beating up women and sometimes lose his ability to stop? Or was he so angry about his obvious fascination with the same exotic, dark-haired, foreign-looking women he so despised that he had to atone for his weakness by killing them? Not questions he was likely to answer.

"I know you can't talk, but are you in trouble?"

I drew a deep breath. "Honestly, yes. But I'm working my way out of it now."

"Good girl. Now remember, this Pantages run of mine goes through the middle of October. There's room for you here if you need a place to hide . . . Hello? Are you still there?"

The rush of gratitude blurred my vision and clogged my throat, but I managed to choke out a reply. "I owe you, Benny."

"You sure do, kid. Starting with a full explanation, and I'll collect when I see you next."

I said good-bye and returned to my desk. The addition of a Palo Alto murder that matched the pattern of the others added significantly to the circumstantial evidence against Henry. All I could do was list the facts. Someone else would have to find the proof.

With this new piece of information, I laid out my scribbled notes and began to write an organized report, beginning with my own confession, followed by Henry's statement to me that he had killed Jessie and the governess. I went on to list the times he'd tried to kill me and the murders of the young women in Dexter, Portland, and Palo Alto, showing their similarities and the common hair-cutting trait and how the dates coincided with Henry's whereabouts. I noted his lying about his years in college, and then his bootlegging activities and the little evidence I had. Yes, I was an eyewitness, but I wasn't planning to be around for the trial. By the time this letter reached its destination, the liquor would be off the yacht and into the speakeasies of Portland. I hoped that tomorrow—Sunday—clear skies would permit Henry to continue with his delivery and I could somehow find out how he did it and add that crucial bit to the letters I would mail Monday morning. As backup, I penned copies to send to the governor in Salem and the Portland *Oregonian*, just in case one letter should be intercepted somehow and destroyed. Or in case one of them was on Henry's payroll. I wouldn't underestimate Henry again.

46

T he slam of a car door drew my attention to the front of the house. Uncle Oliver had arrived. Setting down my pen, I hurried to greet him with an affectionate kiss on the cheek. Let him think all was well. Clyde pulled several pieces of new alligator luggage out of the trunk and carried the first up the stairs.

"The green guest room," I directed him, then asked Oliver, "Did you have a good trip, Uncle?"

"Tolerable, my dear, tolerable." He was in a jovial mood. No wonder. In his mind, we were just two days away from the jackpot.

His arrival drew Grandmother from the garden, clippers in hand and a basket of flowers on her arm. She greeted her son with her usual reserve.

"Mother, how fresh you look. Raiding the garden again?"

"Grandmother has taken on the party flowers job," I explained.

She gave a curt nod. "I finished the large arrangements for the entry hall yesterday and the end pieces for the ballroom buffet this morning. These are for the small vases on each table."

Ross rounded the corner of the house from the direction of the garage. "Oh, there you are, Jessie," he said sheepishly. "I'm afraid I— Well, the guests will start to arrive in a couple of hours and your flivver was still in the way—the girls took Henry's Packard into town instead of your car—so I moved it around back and, well, I hit the maple tree next to the garage. I'm sorry. I wasn't going fast, so it isn't too awful, but I'm afraid the fender is well crunched. Oh, hello, Clyde! Could I trouble you to take a look at Jessie's runabout? I've dented the fender but maybe you can pound it out?"

I told Ross not to worry about it, and we rounded the house to see the damage. The kitchen door opened and Aunt Victoria joined us, followed by Henry.

Clyde knelt and examined the fender. "Well, I don't think it's so bad that I couldn't take this over to Bob Clancey's shop and get him to work the metal back in shape. Shouldn't need a new one. But here, what's this?"

Clyde reached under the Ford and picked up a mechanical nut lying on the ground. "Funny, there's no rust. Wonder if it come off your flivver?" He ducked under the car for a few moments and came up scratching his head. "I'll be darned. The adjustment on the service brake is completely loose. The only brakes you got are the hand brakes. If this nut is all the problem, I can put it back on and adjust the brake band in a jiffy. The brake pedal just didn't stop her, did it, Mr. Ross?"

"It seemed all right at first," he said.

"Well, it must've been loose and worked its way off. This beats all, you know that? These babies ain't fancy, but they're built sturdy. You'd think they'd put on a lock washer or something to keep the nut from backing off. Let's see if there's anything else lying on the ground. Where'd you park her?"

I glanced over at Henry, rocking back and forth on his heels, his hands in his pockets, looking like a small boy caught playing hooky. Our eyes met and he raised his eyebrow in the classic "Who me?" gesture. All at once his generosity with the Packard took on new meaning: he had lent his sisters his car so they wouldn't drive my Ford to town. The next person taking the Ford was meant to have a serious accident on the steep road to Dexter when the brakes failed. A fatal one if the car had gone over the edge. That was to have been my fate. Ross's mishap had been minor because the vehicle had been on level ground.

So much for my conclusion that Henry would refrain from further attempts on my life until I'd left Cliff House. Seems I was fair game, awake or asleep. The realization made me more angry than afraid.

"Can you fix it?" asked Ross.

"Sure, nothing to it. I can get the brake fixed right now, but the fender I'll have to take with me to Clancey's. He don't work Sundays, but Monday he'll do it and you can stop in his shop when you're in town and get him to mount it back on." He straightened up and motioned toward the toolshed. "Gotta find my knuckle buster though, or maybe there's a wrench to fit this size nut in there. When I'm done, I'll move her out of the way, how 'bout over there?" He pointed to a flat place out front at the edge of the driveway where the car would not block the incoming guests.

"That would be wonderful, Clyde," said Aunt Victoria. "What would we do without you?" She turned to go back into the house with Henry and Uncle Oliver, and I heard her telling him that the food set out in the dining room was meant to help us last until the ten o'clock buffet.

With Ross still beside us, Grandmother and I could not talk freely, but the sharp look she sent me spoke louder than words. As we watched, Clyde unscrewed the crumpled fender and carried it to his own car to take to Clancey's. Then he disappeared into the toolshed, emerging moments later with a couple of wrenches.

"I don't think I'm much help here," I said as the wind picked up fresh strength and thunder rumbled in the distance, "and I've got some work to finish. Let me know when you're done, Clyde, and what I owe you."

"I'll pay for it, Jessie. It was my fault."

"Thanks, Ross, but anyone who moved that car would have suffered the same consequences or worse, so I'd rather you let me take responsibility. I'm just glad no one was hurt."

"That's so," he said, enlightenment dawning on his face. "It could have been deadly if the next driver had headed to Dexter."

"Quite."

He loped toward the back door as Grandmother and I purposely headed to the front.

"It was Henry," she said. "Henry all along, not Ross."

"Yes."

Looking up into my face, she stopped. "And there have been other things you haven't told me about, haven't there?"

"Yes."

"Tell me now."

So I told her about the phone call to the Stanford bursar. I told her I believed Henry had murdered several women who were connected with his bootlegging, but of course I couldn't tell her that he had also killed her real granddaughter seven years ago. She'd learn about that soon enough.

"I remember thinking that it was a mighty strange coincidence that those cars had been parked to block the hotel entrance just when we were arriving," she said, "and then there was that fast one that nearly ran you down. Surely you have enough to go to the police now?"

"I'll have some hard proof very soon, and then, yes, I'll go to the police after we leave on Monday."

"You dasn't wait that long."

"I have to. Until I get something solid about the smuggling, it's mostly speculation. Things he can explain away or deny outright."

"If you don't stop him, he'll try again and again. He only needs to get lucky once."

"Don't worry."

"Don't worry? I can't help but worry. He'll plant someone on your ship to cause an accident at sea. If you survive the crossing, he'll hire someone to track you in Europe. You'll spend your whole life on the run, like a common criminal, when *he's* the criminal!"

I couldn't explain that I was a criminal too, or that I was going to disappear Monday, or that, with luck, my actions would put Henry behind bars, but I hated to see her so anxious about a future that was never going to exist. To ease her mind, I explained some of the precautions I had considered earlier when I thought I had a future as Jessie Carr, such as signing papers at the hotel in Sacramento rather than at the law office and buying a second ticket on another boat under an assumed name.

Once inside, the old lady laid down her basket and clippers and, with uncharacteristic emotion, took my hands in hers. "You're a sharp girl, Jessie Carr. You'll make it. Remember your middle name. We Becketts are survivors."

I returned to my room to add this latest incident to the litany of Henry's crimes. I stood by my desk, staring uneasily at the papers I had left so carelessly in plain sight. Hadn't I left the finished pages stacked neatly on the right? Hadn't I set the pen down on the top page rather than at the edge of the blotter?

How could I have been so thoughtless—dashing out of the room like that, leaving everything in full view? What was I thinking?

My plan had been to post the letters on Monday from Portland immediately before I hopped the train to Canada. By the time the letters arrived on Tuesday, Severinus Wade would have heard from Oliver and Grandmother that I had disappeared, and Grandmother would have revealed her own suspicions about Henry. The letters would shock everyone, but they would confirm what Grandmother said.

Now that plan had to be revised, and quickly.

It could have been Henry in my room. He'd had plenty of time to come into the house and go up to my room to see what I'd been doing here all day. I reviewed the other possibilities, eliminating the twins, who were still in town with Henry's Packard, and Grandmother, who had been with me. It could have been Oliver, who had been shown to his own room to settle in and might have come looking for me. Ross or Aunt Victoria had had time enough to come to my room and read at least part of what I'd written. Then again, it was possible no one had been here at all. I simply couldn't remember how I had left the papers.

At the end of the four-page epistle, I scrawled a description of Henry's latest attempt on my life. Once again, there was no proof, but it was the best I could do. I hoped Sunday's weather would improve enough for him to attempt to deliver the liquor in his boat, and that I could somehow learn where and how he accomplished it. That would link him firmly to the rum-running and from there to the murders of Lizzette and the other girls. But I dared not wait another day. If necessary, I could write those details in a follow-up from Portland on Monday. I folded the stationery, addressed three envelopes, licked a few two-centers, and went back to my car.

"Finished yet, Clyde?"

The handyman stood up and brushed his hands on his pants. "That's the best I can do for now, Miss Jessie. Couldn't find the right wrench so I put the nut back on but only hand tight. And I looked all over but didn't find those couple of parts that fell off, but I can get 'em first thing Monday morning at Berkeley's, or if he don't have them, I'll take 'em off my own flivver. Don't you worry though, I'll be back Monday morning and fix her good before you leave. Now I'll just push this baby over to the side, out of the way of the party guests."

"Why not just drive it over?"

"I don't want that nut to fall off again and lose it."

He opened the front door and started to push. I went around to the back and helped start it rolling. Once it got going, it was easy to guide the vehicle out of the way.

"I appreciate this, Clyde. How much do I owe you for everything?"

"Three dollars ought to do it. Two for the wrench and parts and one for me."

"Would you do me another favor, please, and take these letters straight to the post office when you get back to town?"

"Well, sure thing, but they ain't going nowhere until Monday morning."

"I know, I know, but it's very important they get there now so they go out first thing Monday."

I felt the load lift from my chest as Clyde drove off. No matter what Henry did to me now, the information I had gathered was safely on its way. At the very least, the exposure would kill his political career, but if all I accomplished was to wash him out of politics, I was in greater danger than when I started. I had to trust that the authorities, pressured by the Carr trustees, would find the necessary evidence.

I walked to the front of the house, pausing at the spot where I remembered leaving my runabout last evening. I could see where gravel had been kicked off to the side and an indentation in the ground from a heel as if someone had been under the car and struggling to get the part loose. If I had time, I bet I could find the missing part within throwing distance.

The hairs on the back of my arms stood up and my neck and

shoulders crawled with goose bumps. I straightened up quickly and scanned the façade of the house. A movement in the upstairs hall window drew my eye. Someone had stepped back from the glass.

47

My dance card was full before the band struck the first downbeat.

"I believe I have the honor," said Uncle Oliver, dapper as a stuffed penguin as he took my gloved hand and escorted me to the center of the floor where no one could overhear us. "At last, my dear, we are alone," he teased. His every word revealed his triumph.

I surveyed the crowded ballroom. Gay paper lanterns glowed overhead and on one wall a painted canvas depicted half a dozen European landmarks I knew now I would never see. The only decoration we lacked was David Murray's mile-wide smile, and that was nowhere to be seen.

I wiggled my fingers at Grandmother sitting at one of the small tables that ringed the room, each covered by a tablecloth strewn with rose petals and decorated with one of her flower arrangements. She acknowledged my wave with a nod, then returned her eyes to Henry, who stood in a corner with several pals, laughing at someone's joke. I had my eye on him too. He had flicked on the charm switch and was playing the amiable host with casual flair. Knowing what I did about him, I found the transformation chilling. It explained a lot: how he could appeal to women, earn their trust and favor, use them, and then when they least expected it, erupt in deadly violence. I wasn't unduly worried about him tonight. The amount of whiskey he was tossing back would soon render him harmless, but Grandmother, bless her heart, was determined to track his every move.

Rain beat hard on the roof but all was warm and dry inside Cliff House. All about us, feminine finery sparkled with sequins and rhinestones against the black-and-white masculine backdrop as everyone waited for the birthday girl and her uncle to finish the first dance. Anticipation hung in the air. Then the band struck up "Look for the Silver Lining," and we started a pretty fox-trot.

"There must be a hundred people here," I began.

"A fitting end to a fine performance."

"After tomorrow, we're home free."

"Have a care; we are not there yet," he warned, but his self-satisfied manner belied his words. Oliver Beckett was a man basking in the glory of success. A man "with expectations," as polite society would have it. And I was about to find out what those expectations were.

"The receiving line went better than I had hoped," I said. "I rather thought people might try to reminisce with me and 'remember when,' but no one in this town knew Jessie beyond her bank book. You will be amused to learn how popular I am. Every dance is spoken for, and the unlucky ones are walking about with grim faces, determined to cut in. I am Princess Charming at the royal ball with all the bachelors vying for her hand."

Oliver chuckled.

"What a good dancer you are!" I exclaimed. But of course he

was. Being an amiable guest was Oliver's stock-in-trade. A single man who danced with wallflowers was an asset at any gathering, so much the better if he had a sincere gaze, a gentle wit, and a flirtatious manner. I wondered . . . with all the money he expected to rake in, did he plan to abandon his career as a professional guest for a more permanent way of life? He was in for a rough landing. On Monday he would learn he'd been double-crossed. I did not want to be within a hundred miles of Oliver Beckett when he found I'd done a flit.

"We have some business to discuss, my dear, and there's no time like the present. On Monday, we'll separate at the Portland train station, you to Sacramento, Mother and I home to San Francisco to await your arrival. Once you've accomplished the legalities, you'll tell Mr. Wade about your voyage and ask him to book a first-class stateroom for you to Cherbourg. That's the port nearest Paris where you want to start your grand tour. Then ask for ten thousand dollars to be deposited in the Crocker National Bank for—"

I gasped. "He'll never—"

"Yes he will, and without batting an eyelash. Not with lumber fetching ten times the price it did when I was your age and forests so thick they'll never run out. Tell him you will need ten thousand for a new wardrobe, shopping in Paris, and a suite at the Ritz. Then you will come directly to San Francisco to wait for your ship to sail, withdraw the cash, and give it to me."

"All of it?"

"Never fear, you will have plenty yourself. You and I will visit the steamship line's office and rebook your passage to a second-class cabin, and the difference is yours. It will be enough to cover a respectable hotel and your expenses for some time."

Ingenious. And how did he expect to get future installments with me in Europe and himself gadding about the U. S. of A.? I did not need to ask.

"October and November are rather disagreeable in Paris; I

think you will be happier traveling south to the warmer climate along the Mediterranean. Whenever you are ready, you must cable Smith and Wade that you have found property to buy, something expensive, and ask for funds to be wired into a local bank. Of course, you will not buy anything extravagant, although you may eventually want to purchase a modest villa on the sea. Every so often you will pretend that you require a large sum of money to buy property or a painting or a new automobile, when in reality you'll be wiring most of that money back home to me."

So that was how it was to work. Uncle Oliver had never been plotting to do me in. He needed me around for years to come if his scheme was to work. I nodded my understanding as the music stopped and polite applause fluttered through the room. "How much money?"

"I told you once that I was not a greedy man, and I am not. I will require only twenty thousand dollars every year. How you get it is your business. Oh, and another thing. You will suggest to Mr. Wade that your trusted uncle be placed on the Carr Industries board at the earliest opportunity."

Clever Oliver. That way he could monitor my withdrawals to make sure I didn't kill the goose that laid the golden egg.

"I believe I have this dance, Miss Carr?" I turned to see an eager young man with a thin face and too many teeth.

"Why yes, Mr. er"—I checked my dance card—"Jackson! Excuse us, Uncle Oliver." Jackson, Jackson . . . the banker, if I remembered correctly. Jessie certainly attracted men whose primary interest was money. The band struck up "Ain't We Got Fun," and the older set ceded the floor to the youngsters and their lively Charleston.

"You look lovely this evening," Mr. Jackson said rather loudly.

"Thank you," I replied. He was definitely not a hoofer, and I had to tone down my steps to match his.

"Your green gown is very pretty."

"Thank you. It's shockingly heavy, you know. Feels like I'm

wearing a suit of armor." It was one of the ritzy frocks I had bought in Portland, the dark green calf-length silk with a million clear glass bugle beads sewn onto it, making me sparkle at the slightest shimmy. "With all these beads weighing me down, I can hardly dance!"

Mr. Jackson's toothy smile soured when someone tapped him on the shoulder to cut in. Next came Mr. Lowe, a local attorney with more hair on his lip than his head. He wasn't the sort to let a little thing like a full dance card keep him from his shot at the heiress.

"Where have you been all my life?" he asked by way of an introduction, and without waiting for an answer, "You are a vision of loveliness, Miss Carr. That dress brings out the green in your eyes."

"Thank you, Mr. Lowe. It's shockingly heavy, you know. All these beads weigh me down like a suit of armor." Same scene, same lines. Another fox-trot.

I watched as Ross, an empty glass in each hand, headed for the west wing "gentleman's room" at the end of the corridor. For those who wanted hooch in their punch—which was most of the crowd—a discreet table of gin, whiskey, and rum had been set up in one of the small rooms, allowing everyone to maintain the polite fiction that men heading down the corridor were going to straighten their ties. In a moment Ross returned and handed one of the glasses to Captain Henderson, the police chief, who could not, of course, be seen getting his own.

My next partner, the son of the Dexter Cannery owner, was tall and dark, but his best friend could not have called him handsome. The unattractive first impression vanished the moment he spoke.

"Care for a glass of punch, milady?" he asked in a delicious baritone tailor-made for radio.

"Mmm, yes, please, Mr. Scarpetta."

"With or without rum?"

"With."

"That will be this one," he said, handing me the cup in his left hand. "I brought one of each, to be sure of getting it right."

"But what about you? You're left with hoochless punch."

"No sacrifice is too great to win the favor of the birthday girl. Besides, my next glass will be punchless hooch to make up for this one." He looked me up and down in silence.

"What's the matter?" I asked finally. "Aren't you going to tell me how pretty my frock is?"

"Like everyone else? You can't need that many compliments. I'll tell you that your shoes are delightful, but I'll wager your feet will be killing you by dinner. How can you dance in such high heels?"

The band began playing "Way Down Yonder in New Orleans."

"Oh, that is one of my favorite jazz tunes!" I said.

"Hmm, yes. Sadly, this is not a jazz band, and I'm afraid poor Hank Creamer wouldn't recognize his own song if he were here tonight."

I laughed. "You're right, this is awful. Let's sit." We moved to the nearest table and I couldn't resist saying, "As a matter of fact, I know Hank. He's written a number of popular songs and is a talented song-and-dance man himself."

"He's a *friend* of yours?"

"I haven't run into him in a while, but yes, we've shared billing a few times."

"But I—but I thought he was colored?"

"He is."

"Oh, my God," he said, clearly horrified. "How very . . . interesting."

Seemed Mr. Scarpetta and Henry had bigotry in common. It was funny how quickly he turned ugly again.

Precisely at ten Aunt Victoria directed the parade of servants who carried in platter after platter of scrumptious fare. The band took a breather. By now, some of the guests were pretty gassed.

Ahead of the game, Henry stood at the other end of the room, encircled by admirers and carrying on like a populist, railing against Bolsheviks and aliens. I suspected Mr. Scarpetta was an avid supporter. Dear Henry . . . little did he know I'd already scotched his precious political career.

"It's going well, don't you think?" asked Aunt Victoria, misinterpreting my smile.

"Everything is magnificent, Aunt. The food is divine."

"You look lovely tonight, Jessie darling. Your dear mother would be so proud of you. I see you are wearing her pearls."

My breasts were bound tight for a boyish profile and the pearls lay flat on my chest. Even doubled, the rope reached to my waist. I was wearing Blanche's gold bracelet as well, but none of it made Blanche any more real to me. When I wore Jessie's glass beads, I felt Jessie's presence. No one who knew me would have believed it, but I much preferred Jessie's Venetian beads to all of Blanche's finery.

At eleven, servants carried a large cake into the room and I blew out twenty-one candles to the accompaniment of "For She's a Jolly Good Fellow." I saw Val whispering to the bandleader, and moments later the musicians cranked up the Charleston number from the Carr Cousins vaudeville show. Before Aunt Victoria could object, the twins and the Hartley sisters performed the catchy routine to enthusiastic applause. So that's what those four were doing this afternoon, shut away in their room! They were so cute even Aunt Victoria had to applaud.

"I wish David Murray could be here to see us," said Caro wistfully after the fuss had died down.

"People don't go to parties the same week they bury their mothers." Henry sneered, swaying on his feet.

"I just meant that he wanted to see us do our act again. He said so! But he's coming tomorrow to say good-bye to Jessie, and maybe we can do it then, if Alice and Sophie are still here."

The band started up again. I was claimed by Mayor Franklin,

a clumsy dancer who had governed Dexter since the Flood, and we began an awkward turn around the floor until, mercifully, someone tapped his shoulder. I caught my breath when I saw who was cutting in.

"You looked so pathetic trying not to step on his feet that I took pity on you. You should thank me for rescuing you," Ross said as he steered me into the stream.

"The conversation was scintillating too."

"Let me guess—plans to pave the planked street? The cost of the new fire engine? Fortunately he's a first-rate mayor, so his other qualities can be overlooked."

"You're a first-rate dancer, Ross."

"Don't act so surprised. I'd return the compliment but you already know you're the best dancer in the room. Oh, I just recognized the song they're playing—'A Good Man Is Hard to Find,' isn't it? This band manages to make every number sound like a nursery song."

"Do you know Mae West's version?" I asked wickedly. "'A Hard Man Is Good to Find'?"

His sharp laugh turned heads. "So you're off on the Grand Tour, are you, cousin? When do you leave?"

"Next week. I'll let Mr. Wade book the stateroom on the next ship to sail, or whichever one he thinks best."

"How long do you figure to travel?"

"I'm not sure. Until I see enough of what I want to see."

"While you're gone, I'll not be idle. I plan to solve the murder mystery." With nothing to do but wait for Stanford to accept his thesis, our bored scholar had turned detective.

"A new research project for you? Good luck. Did you learn anything at the reservation this afternoon?"

"Everyone was pretty tight-lipped. But I've only begun to sleuth! I'm a bloodhound on the trail. A regular Tom Swift. Right after I heard about the coroner's report, I contacted him and asked him about hair cutting. The body hadn't been buried, so he had another look and, lo and behold, there was a lock of hair missing, just like the other two."

Too late now to add that to my letter to Smith and Wade, but they would find that fact for themselves. I thought how refreshingly normal Ross seemed when he wasn't trying to impress with big words.

"You can bet the coroner was pretty interested and wondered how I'd known to ask about hair. Probably thought I did her in—except I would have been all of sixteen at the time. So I told him about the others, and he said that because the girl was from Portland, it made him wonder whether there were similar deaths in that city. He's looking through the police files to see." I wondered whether anyone would tell the coroner that someone else had been asking the same questions a few days earlier.

Henry returned to the ballroom, a full glass in hand and Grandmother on his tail. He sat down heavily beside Mr. Scarpetta. Heads together, they talked without sharing a single smile while Ross and I took several turns around the dance floor. Delivery problems? An uncooperative weather forecast? How was Henry going to unload all those cases of Canadian hooch with seas too rough to leave the harbor? Was Scarpetta in on it?

One person who was definitely not in on it was dancing with me. "Next week I'll nose around the Indian reservation again," he was saying, "and try to learn what that girl was doing in Dexter. And there has to be some Indian in town who knew what she was mixed up with. The same for the Chinese neighborhood, although I don't have any connections there, except maybe Chen. And it's been years, but maybe I can find someone in Portland who remembers that girl who was killed in the warehouse. Something—or someone—brought her to Dexter, and I aim to find out who."

The low rumble of thunder could be heard over the music while rain lashed against the shutters. I looked at Grandmother, who was watching Henry through half-shut eyes. Henry was standing at the window—raging at the weather, I was sure.

The hall clock struck two as the last of the lively set was saying its farewells. Rainy met me in my room to help me undress.

I handed her Blanche's pearls. "Here, these go in the velvet pouch. Where are my Venetian beads?"

"Right here, miss. I wonder why pearls cost more than glass beads," she said, holding Jessie's beads in the light. "Pearls are pretty, but they're plain white. These you can look at for a long time and see different colors, swirls, and shapes. There!" She fastened the clasp and stepped back. "Is there anything else you need before I go upstairs?"

"What? Aren't you going to bed?"

"No, miss. We all got orders to report to the ballroom to help clean up. Mrs. Carr wants the house back to normal by morning."

I was exhausted, and I hadn't been working since daybreak. Aghast, I considered countermanding Aunt Victoria's orders, then backed off. Let her run the house, I thought, she knows more about servants than you do. I could, however, give one order. "Well, then, Rainy, tomorrow morning you must sleep as late as you like. I don't want to see you before noon, you understand? And I don't care what anyone else tells you."

She smiled. "Yes, miss. Sleep well."

I fell asleep at once but could not take her advice. My sleep was interrupted by flashes of dark dreams that culminated in the now-familiar Jessie dream. She was in some dark place; she was frightened; Venetian beads sparkled all around her. Her feet were cold and wet. Then my feet were cold and wet and I was Jessie, trying to move away, trying to call for help. Calling to hurry. No one heard our voice.

48

Just before noon I put on a plaid wool day dress and comfortable shoes and went downstairs to appease the growling beast in my stomach. The house was weirdly quiet; the ticking of the grandfather clock seemed as loud as it did at midnight. It was Sunday—my last full day at Cliff House. Gray skies and soggy ground were the only reminders of last night's storm. I found Caroline in the dining room hunched over a plate of eggs and toast.

"Good morning," I said. "Where is everyone?"

"Sophie and Alice left," she said morosely. Postparty melancholia had settled in. "Their father came by to fetch them for church."

The buffet table was set with late breakfast as if it were any normal Sunday. I marveled at Marie's stamina . . . did the woman never rest?

"Your dance last night was quite the hit!" I said, joining Caro at the table.

She brightened a little. "Yes, it was, wasn't it?"

"You killed 'em. However did you and Val teach the Hartley girls all those steps, and so quickly?"

"We practiced all afternoon in secret. I did my magic trick, too."

"No! Really? Where?"

"In one of the spare bedrooms, the one next to the bar. I was careful to do just as you said—never show anyone the same trick twice or they will figure it out. I made sure that different people were in the room each time I did it."

"You're quite the entertainer. I'm so proud!" She didn't notice the catch in my throat when I said it.

At that moment, Ross came into the dining room looking none the worse for wear. "Where is everyone?" he asked.

"The Hartleys just left," said Caro, resuming her long face. "Val's upstairs."

"My grandmother and Uncle Oliver had breakfast in their rooms," I added, "and I haven't seen your mother, but I'm sure she's up. It's astonishing how the house looks—you would never think there had been a hundred people here for a party last night!"

"Yes, Mother is indefatigable. I saw her from my window with the gardener earlier this morning. Henry was up early too."

"Oh?" I asked, keeping my voice light. "When was that? I thought he'd be sleeping it off this morning."

"So did I, considering what he poured into himself, but I heard him in the bathroom a couple of hours ago. He and Scarpetta had a sailing date yesterday that they couldn't keep, so now that the weather has cleared, it's anchors aweigh."

Ambushed by overconfidence! I was so sure he'd have a hangover and not appear until the afternoon, I hadn't even considered getting up earlier. Swallowing a last bite, I excused myself from the table and went into the kitchen where I slipped out the back door, circled around the garden, and picked up the path to the cliff edge.

Once there, I shaded my eyes with my hand and squinted out to sea. I had no idea how long it took a sailboat to travel from one place to another, but I was betting that Henry would repeat his trip of a few weeks ago—the one the boy William had described—sailing south along the coast to the rocky area by the third cave. That had to be the way he made his deliveries, although for the life of me, I couldn't figure out how, unless it was a transfer at sea. A strong wind from the south blew into my face as I scanned the empty ocean.

Dejected, I sat on the grass beside a copse of scraggly bushes, heedless of the damp. How long did it take to navigate out of the harbor, turn south, and sail several miles along the coast? An hour? Three hours? Had he left yet? All I could do was wait and watch.

Shockingly, there was his boat, right in front of me, emerging from behind one of the massive rock formations that stood a half mile out in the sea. It skimmed across the water, sails full of wind, bobbing like a painted horse on a merry-go-round in a way that would surely have made me sick if I'd been aboard. It was heading south into the wind in a zigzag pattern with sails that shifted back and forth, something that puzzled me because it would have been faster to go straight, but I am not a sailor and know nothing about these things. Young William had been right—Henry was headed for the waters off the caves. As I watched, I estimated the amount of time it was taking him to go the distance down the coast.

I could see a figure walk from one end of the boat to the other, pick something up, and walk back. If I could see him, could he see me? I made myself smaller and waited for the boat to disappear behind another rock sentinel so I could hide behind the bushes. I considered walking south to the lower headlands nearer the third cave to get a better look, but the terrain there was exposed and treeless—I would stand out like a soloist on an empty stage.

It was midday. Low tide came at two. Would the third cave be dry at low tide, or would there be enough water in it to get a sailboat inside? And why would a sailboat go inside a cave to unload cargo a few hours before high tide? As soon as I saw Henry's boat returning to harbor, I was going to climb down the path to the beach and find out.

"What are you doing?"

I nearly jumped out of my skin. So much for my instincts about being watched. I had been so intent on Henry's boat that I'd ignored everything else.

"Val! You scared the daylights out of me!" I stalled for time, trying to think of an innocent reason to be sitting here spying on her brother. Meanwhile, there she stood beside me, big as life, in full view of the occupants of the boat.

"I was just enjoying the view and watching that pretty sailboat go by."

"That's Henry's boat." She stepped forward and waved both arms vigorously, trying to catch someone's attention. I saw two figures on board now, then a third and fourth. My heart sank.

"Is it, indeed? What a coincidence! It's a lovely boat, isn't it?"

"I'm glad they got out today. He was mad that they didn't get to sail Thursday or Friday because the sea was too rough, even for him."

I had to assume they had a spyglass and could identify us. It was time to walk conspicuously away as if we had just strolled along the headlands for a breath of fresh air and were returning to the house.

"Mother's looking for you."

"Is she? Well, let's go back. You were marvelous last night, by the way. That dance routine killed 'em . . ."

Aunt Victoria met me in the library, a ledger book open on the table. Because I was leaving for some months, she felt duty bound to review the household expenditures with me to make sure I approved of everything.

"That really isn't necessary, Aunt. I think you do a fine job managing the house and consider myself blessed to have you living here."

Nothing would do but to examine the last seven years of expenditures—the garage and shed additions, the tennis court, the garden, all the servants and what each was paid, the regular maintenance on the house, food bills, clothing for all five of the family and servants' uniforms, donations to church and charity, and tuition for the boys. She had not purchased new draperies but the ones in the parlor were looking faded . . . did I think she should? I thought I'd scream with frustration.

"Whatever you think best, Aunt, I have complete confidence in your judgment."

Fidgeting did me no good. Aunt Victoria was relentless in her review. When I edged toward the door, she restrained me with her hand on my arm. The trustees had paid for the boys' tuition at Stanford, but she did not want me to think they had also funded their living expenses away from home. Rather, she had taken that money from a small sum she had inherited from her father. I wanted to shout, "I don't care! I don't care! I've got to go back and check on Henry's boat!"

At last I escaped the library only to be caught by Rainy, who had been hovering at the door. "Excuse me, miss, but I should be starting the packing. Did you want to give some instructions?"

I most certainly did. I would need to travel light and wanted to choose from among my more practical outfits. But at the moment, I was desperate to return to my lookout point, afraid I would miss seeing Henry's boat on its way back to Dexter Bay.

"We'll pack together this evening, Rainy. I'm off for a walk now." And I left her, no doubt wondering what on earth was so important about a walk.

I reached the cliff moments before Henry's sailboat came into view. Pushed north by the wind and farther out at sea than it had been on its southerly voyage, the sleek vessel clipped along prettily. Calculating approximately how long it had taken for the boat to sail the distance south, I figured Henry would not arrive back in Dexter Bay for a good two hours. The coast was clear for a visit to the third cave.

I was not so idiotic as to go alone. I didn't know what I would find, if anything, and there was always the chance that someone from the boat had remained behind in the cave. I ran back to the house where I found Caro slumped in an overstuffed chair, scowling at the pages of a fashion magazine.

"Do you know what I've wanted to do ever since I arrived?" I asked her.

"What?"

"Explore the caves. Would you like to come with me?"

"Oh, we've done that. So have you."

"Well, that's true, I went inside the closer ones, but I want to hike over the rocks to that far cave and take a look at it."

"It looks like the others. They're boring. There's nothing inside but slime."

"It's low tide, and there probably will be a lot of agates on the beach after yesterday's storm."

"Oh, all right. Why not? There's nothing else to do around this stupid place."

49

The moment her foot touched the beach Caro exclaimed, "Oh, phooey! We forgot to bring a bucket! And I'm not climbing all the way back up there to get one!"

"Never mind," I said. "My handkerchief is large enough to knot the corners and make a pouch."

The pace I set was rather fast for rock hunting, but Caroline was sulking and didn't notice. "Are you still planning to do your routine for David Murray when he comes this afternoon?" I asked, trying to find a happy subject.

"I guess." She kicked at a piece of driftwood.

"Who was that nice-looking young man I saw you dancing with so many times last night?"

She reddened. "Oh, nobody."

"Well, Mr. Nobody looked quite taken with you."

"He's not. He's sweet on Sophie. All I heard was 'Sophie, Sophie, Sophie,' until I thought I'd throw up."

So that was it. For effect I reached for a purple agate and dropped it in my handkerchief. "Hmm. How old is he?"

"Eighteen."

"Just wait a bit. When I was your age there was a boy of eighteen who swore his undying devotion and a week later fell madly in love with the youngest singer in a sister act he met the day before. Boys that age are as changeable as hemlines."

"But he goes to high school with Sophie and sees her every day. I hate studying with Mrs. Applewhite! I'll never meet anybody cooped up here!"

Privately I agreed but didn't see any sense in saying so. We walked a while, passing the first cave, then the second.

"I hate it here! Oh, it hasn't been so bad this past month, with Ross and Henry home and you coming back, and the show and the party and the shopping trip, but now you are all leaving! You're leaving tomorrow. Ross is leaving as soon as his thesis is accepted. Henry won't be home again after he wins the election. Rainy season starts soon and the most exciting thing to happen in this stupid place will be church on Sunday. It will be so boring, I'll go screwy!"

"I didn't realize you were so unhappy."

"Why would you? You have an exciting life. You ran away to vaudeville, and now you're getting away again and going to Europe and we're stuck here like . . . like criminals in prison. If it weren't for our visit to you in Europe, I'd jump off that cliff! When do you think that will be? Christmas?"

Lying to people I care for has always been hard. I should have tried harder. I should have just said, "You're coming in January," and been done with the topic, but a foolish surge of conscience caused me to hedge. "Well . . . I don't know really . . . I'm not entirely sure where I'm going or when, so it will be difficult to plan . . ."

"You're going to London and France and Italy. That's what you said. You said we could come too."

"Yes, I know. I know I said that, and I meant, well, it will be winter when I arrive and not too pleasant in those countries, so, well, I'll probably go someplace like Greece or Spain first, for the winter, I mean, and then, once I have a place to stay, I'll write and we can see what the circumstances are—"

She pulled up and glared at me through narrowed eyes. "You're lying. You don't want us to visit you at all."

"That's not true." It was exactly true, or at least it used to be, but by tomorrow she and the whole family would learn the extent of my deception, and a missed trip to Europe would be low on their list of concerns.

Caroline would not be calmed. She was already worked up about Mr. Nobody and this topped her off. She started to cry. "It isn't fair! You're leaving and we're staying and I hate it here!" And she threw down her agates, turned, and ran back toward the path.

"Caro! Wait! That's not true!" I took three steps after her, then stopped. I didn't have time to chase after her, nurse her back to good humor, and still explore the far cave before Henry got back. *Don't go there alone!* said a voice in my head. I knew that. There might be someone there, left behind in the cave. But there might also be the one bit of evidence I needed to make my case against Henry stick.

By my reckoning, I had at least an hour and a half, almost certainly more, and if I hurried, that would be plenty of time to climb the rocks and take a quick peek in the far cave.

I took off running along the strand. Its width was narrowing; the tide had turned. Was it my imagination that the noise of the waves sounded louder? Even at low tide a person couldn't get around the outcropping without getting wet up to the waist, so I scrambled over the boulders, ignoring the scrapes on my legs and hands as I struggled to maintain my balance. When I finally jumped down to the cove on the other side, I twisted my ankle. Without pausing to rub the pain, I pushed on.

I knew I had plenty of time but I was nervous nonetheless. Being caught alone by Henry would be fatal. I tried to calm myself with the fact that it had taken him at least two hours to sail the distance from Dexter Bay south to the caves. He couldn't be back before five o'clock and it wasn't yet four. *Don't go there alone!* I have enough time, I replied. And it was my last chance.

The far cave was different from the other two, taller and narrower, with permanent access to the sea. I crept up to its mouth and peeked around the corner, listening for anything unnatural, looking for any movement. After a period of silence, I picked up a rock, threw it far into the cave. No reaction. I rounded the corner and went inside.

It looked like Nature had built herself one of those pointed-arch cathedrals I had seen in Oliver's travel books and decorated its wet walls with frescoes of colored algae, red and white barnacles, and starfish. A narrow ledge, smooth from centuries of erosion and slippery with strands of green slime, skirted the north side of the cave all the way to the back. A few feet below, the rising sea churned like boiling water, even on a relatively calm day like today. The waves broke against the cave's mouth and sloshed noisily inside, each one bringing the water level closer to covering my walkway. I had arrived just in time. It wouldn't be long before the ledge was submerged. I wondered whether high tide regularly filled the cave, and one glance at the barnacles stuck high on the walls answered the question.

I had expected to see something. Boxes perhaps, or rope or a gangplank. Some sort of residue that would tell me Henry's boat had been here and unloaded its cargo. But there was nothing. The cave was completely empty.

Had his boat actually entered the cave? Would it even fit? Right now, its mast would probably scrape the ceiling, but there could have been room for a sailboat at low tide when the water was several feet below this. It could have motored inside and tied up on any of the jagged rocks that spiked the ledge. It could have unloaded those liquor boxes right here. Another boat could have followed it in and loaded up. But I hadn't seen any other boats. And because the cave was not visible from the promontory by the house, I hadn't actually seen Henry's boat here, only headed in this direction.

Why had I been so certain that the smuggling occurred in this cave? I had placed too much stock in the dreams about Jessie. Henry's boat hadn't been here. He had probably sailed farther south to drop off the Canadian hooch, perhaps to a tiny harbor that no one knew. Water dripped on me from the ceiling. I wiped my face on my sleeve.

A loud noise behind me spun me around and sent my heart into my throat. A shower of rocks the size of my head had fallen from the ceiling and tumbled down the slope of the ledge until they plopped into the water. Was this the day it all collapsed? Chiding myself for overwrought nerves, I continued.

In less than a minute, I had picked my way to the back of the cave. It seemed lighter back here, and I thought my eyes had become accustomed to the dark until I looked up and saw a streak of dark blue sky some thirty feet above me.

With that, I understood everything.

To my left a long-ago avalanche created when the earth split apart now filled part of the fissure with a rockslide that sloped halfway up toward the light. I could see at a glance that the liquor had not gone that way—no one could climb up that rock pile carrying boxes, even if it did put them closer to the opening. No, the smugglers had come here, to the back of the cave where I was standing, and hoisted the boxes straight up through the crevice to a waiting truck.

Mystery solved. I'd already mailed my letters, but I would find the time to send another round with this added information. Henry was finished now.

I felt his eyes on me before I saw him. I knew who it was before I spun around, even though it defied all logic. It should have been impossible for anyone to get here that quickly. Ahead of me at the mouth of the cave, backlit by the daylight, stood a familiar silhouette brandishing a club in one hand.

50

"Don't be stupid, Henry," I said, keeping my voice carefully neutral to disguise the terror that seized me. Like all bullies, Henry's pleasure came from tormenting weaker beings, and instinct told me the slightest whiff of fear from me would excite him beyond control. "Caroline knows where I am."

He stepped inside the cave and started purposefully in my direction. "Indeed she does. She is the one who told me. And she thinks I'm in my room right now," he said, his voice buoyant with the sort of self-satisfaction that comes after a hard-won contest of chess. The cave floor was slippery with strands of seaweed caught like hair on the jagged rocks, but he was sure-footed.

"It's too late, Henry. The game's over. There are already three letters in the mail to the authorities, exposing you as a bootlegger and—"

"Liar! You just figured it out yourself five minutes ago. And you won't be telling anyone."

"*And* as the murderer of four girls in Dexter, at least two in Portland, and one in California."

That caught him like a blow to the face. He was still a good distance away but I could see his lips tighten and his eyes squint with hate. My only chance was to convince him to flee.

"You think you're so smart, but you're really a dumb Dora. You don't know a thing about those girls. They deserved everything they got. They asked for it. Like Jessie asked for it. Besides, you can't prove a thing."

"The information I gave the authorities will let them prove it. Face it, Henry, we're finished. Both of us. I admitted in those letters that I'm not Jessie. I'm leaving tomorrow, and no one will ever hear from me again. If you leave right now," I continued in a tone of friendly advice, "you can get clean away too. You have until tomorrow to put as much distance as possible between yourself and Oregon."

"You'll be dead by tomorrow, you interfering little bitch!"

"If you kill me now, suspicion will fall on you at once, and you won't be able to get away."

"You are just like her. Goddamnit!" he screamed, years of pent-up torment bursting out of its confines. "I hated her! And I hate you even more. I waited so long for that money—Jesus Christ, seven years they said I had to wait until they could legally declare her dead. Seven years! Do you have any idea how long that is? And then you come in at the last goddamn minute and try to steal everything. It's *mine!*"

Like a slavering beast with its mouth open and its eyes glittering wet, Henry panted heavily. The madman had lost all control, and I thought this was the moment to make a break for it, to push past him on the ledge, to escape while his rage consumed him. But his was a cunning madness that sensed my thoughts before I could act on them. A sly look came over his face. His chest began to heave as he calmed himself with great gulps of the cool, moist air, and as I watched, he harnessed his demons, calling them back from pointless ranting for the promise of a greater pleasure—killing.

Slapping his palm again and again with a driftwood club as large as his arm, he came closer, now a canny predator toying with his prey. I couldn't back up any farther. The only place for me to go was into the roiling sea where a girl who didn't swim well even in a still pond stood no chance. I'd be dashed against the rocks before I had time to drown.

Henry was only a few yards away. I played my last card.

"David Murray is coming. He's probably here now, looking for me."

That brought some flicker of thought through his mind, and he said, not too convincingly, "Murray? That dumb mick? I'll take care of him when it's time. Right now, it's time for you. You wanted to be Jessie, I'm gonna help you be Jessie. You look like Jessie. You sure as hell act like Jessie. Well, I'm gonna help you die like Jessie."

For a big man, he moved fast. With his powerful forehand, the club struck my legs out from under me and I collapsed to the floor. The force was so great that the driftwood cracked. Then I saw my leg and realized it wasn't the club that had snapped. Yet I felt nothing at all. Confused, I looked at my leg for what seemed like hours, until an agonizing pain exploded at the point of contact and spread to every pore in my body. I cried out in anguish.

Seconds later came the second blow, aimed squarely at my head. I managed to take the brunt of it with my arm. Head ringing, I fell back, blinded by the searing pain, and braced for the blow that would crush my skull and end the suffering.

Henry chuckled with glee. "That should hold you for now. What, did you think I was going to kill you myself? Hell, no, I'm not going to kill you. I didn't kill Jessie. That surprises you, doesn't it? But I've always been smarter than you thought I was. When they find your body, the ruling will be accidental death by drowning. You're going to drown here, like she did. Nobody's ever gonna blame me. Your broken body will wash up on shore with water in your lungs, and the only possible conclusion will be that you were caught in the caves at high tide and drowned. Unless your body washes straight out to sea like Jessie's did, damn her to hell. That cost me a seven-year wait for my money! I need your body, so this time, I'll be watching for it when the tide turns in a couple hours. This time, I'll make damn sure the body's retrieved."

He tossed the club aside and looked behind him at the vanishing ledge. "I'd love to stay and watch, but I've got to go before I get trapped in here too. Wouldn't want that to happen, would we?"

He started away, then turned back, a foolish grin on his face. I heard a metallic click as he came toward me, a pocketknife in his hand. Reaching down, he pulled up a hank of hair from the side of my head and roughly sawed it off. Taking a white handkerchief out of his pocket, he placed my hair tenderly in its folds, then turned to go. He didn't say another word. He didn't look back. No need to. Jessie Carr was as good as dead, a second time.

51

The water didn't come slowly and gently, lapping at my feet, as it did in my dreams. One frigid surge poured over the ledge and drenched me head to toe, and a second one followed.

The pain was so severe, I threw up. Gagging and spitting, I dragged myself with my good right arm toward the rockslide where the ledge was still dry. The floor acted like a cheese grater, shredding first my dress and then my flesh like so much cheddar, but I kept at it until I was a few feet higher, out of the water's reach.

My left leg was useless. My shoes had vanished. Shivering violently, I licked the salt from my lips and watched as ocean swells surged through the mouth of the cave, increasingly violent as they became trapped in the confined space. High tide was only a couple of hours away. Even if I could have walked, the ledge between me and the entrance was under water. There was no way out now.

The tide showed no mercy. Another surge rolled me over. Like a sodden rag doll, I pulled myself closer to the rockslide. In minutes the entire floor would be covered.

I looked up through the crevice at the slit of sky feeling as if I'd fallen to the bottom of a well. Here, I thought, the men stood as they hauled the boxes up like buckets of water with that pulley I'd stumbled over when I first took a walk in this area. What did it matter now? Everything is irrelevant when you are looking squarely at death.

The water came at me again, not in regular waves from the sea but from all directions now, sloshing over me and throwing my body to and fro as I hung on to a rock. I didn't consciously decide to climb higher on the rockslide; it was the instinct for survival that forced me up, inch by inch.

There was no ceiling above me. This part of the cave opened to the sky some thirty feet up. I didn't fool myself that I could get out that way—even with all limbs intact, it would have been impossible for anyone to climb up the sheer walls of that great gash in the earth. I was simply trying to escape the relentless sea. Teeth chattering, I got up on one bleeding knee and began to claw my way up, dragging my broken leg behind me, wondering why I wasn't dead already from the pain.

Several times I gave up and fell on my back, exhausted and throbbing, but every time the water rose and lapped at my feet the dream came back and I could hear Jessie urging me on. *Keep going. Try harder. Don't give up. Not much farther.*

Inside the crevice I had almost reached the level of the cave ceiling. The sea had nearly filled the cave behind me completely. My time was running out. As I made a final effort to wrench my body a foot higher, my fingers touched some powdery dirt. Even in my current state I realized that water would wash away loose dirt. I had reached a place the water could not reach, the top of the rockslide. I could go no higher.

I lay there on that bed of nails for what seemed like eternity, sweating from the exertion even as I shook from the cold and wet, until I noticed a flat space to my left. Gathering my strength with several deep breaths, I hoisted myself up and over to a narrow shelf that protruded from the wall and rolled onto its smooth floor with relief.

My right hand brushed against something soft. Unable to see in the fading light from high above, I could only feel. It felt like a sack of sticks. I pushed it back out of the way a bit, and my shaking fingers closed around something small, round, smooth, and hard . . . a string of beads. Even in the dark I knew what they were—my Venetian beads.

Except that *my* Venetian beads were still around my throat.

I had found Jessie.

52

More than anything in the world I wanted to go to sleep. Sinking into warm oblivion where everything was soft and dry seemed immeasurably better than the black hell of pain that engulfed me. Death would feel good. But Jessie would not let me go.

I've waited for you for so long. You can't leave yet.

I couldn't stop shivering. My clothes, my skin, my hair, every part of me was wet. Every part of me hurt except my leg, which was already dead. The rest of me wanted to stop hurting too. Some things are worse than dying. Sleep was the escape.

I just want to go to sleep and be warm again, I told her. I want my mother. Let me go.

Teach me a song.

What?

Teach me a song. One you used to sing on stage.

"Three Little Maids from School Are We"?
Yes, that one. Sing it.
I can't. I'm too cold.
Sing it.
I can't!
Sing it.

Three little maids from school are we
Pert as a school-girl well can be
Filled to the brim with girlish glee
Three little maids from school.

Louder.

Everything is a source of fun
Nobody's safe, for we care for none
Life is a joke that's just begun
Three little maids from school.

I like that. Now teach me the dance that goes with it. The one your mother taught you.
I can't. I can't move.
I've waited so long.
All right, all right. Here's how it goes. On eight beats, tiny mincing steps: one, two, three, four, five, six, seven, eight. Stop, bow right; stop, bow left. Eight again in a circle. Repeat, opposite direction.
Oh, this is fun! Let's do it again!
I can't.
I want to do the dance!
We don't have a third.
Yes we do. Here's your mother.
Mother? No, you're dead. My mother's dead, Jessie. She died when I was twelve.

I was orphaned at eleven. Same thing. Come on now, sing the words while we all dance! From the top.

Three little maids from school are we
Pert as a school-girl well can be.
Filled to the brim with girlish glee
Three little maids from school.

Now the chorus. It should be louder. Sing louder.

Three little maids who, all unwary
Come from a ladies' seminary—

Why did you stop?
My throat hurts! I can't do it. Leave me alone! I just want to go to sleep.
Don't you dare die now! Stay awake! I've waited for you all these years. Keep singing.

Freed from its genius tutelary
Three little maids from school.

Louder! You sound like a raspy whisper.

Three little maids from school!

You skipped a line. Let's start over. Louder.

Life is a joke that's just begun
Three little maids from school.

Oh, I like that one! Shhh. Listen! Do you hear that?
What?
Someone's calling Jessie! Do you hear? Up high.

No, I didn't. Yes, now I heard. She was right. Someone was calling for Jessie. Someone was looking for us. David Murray? Had David come to the house and found me missing?

Down here! I called. We're down here. The words rang clear and loud in my head—like the songs I'd been singing—but Jessie was having none of it.

They can't hear that. Louder.

Here! Down here, I rasped.

They're going away. Louder!

Help! Help!

It's no good. They can't hear you. Whistle.

What?

The unholy whistle. Quick.

I took a few shallow breaths to put some air in my lungs, fitted my tongue against my teeth, and let fly the shrillest notes on a sliding scale that I could manage.

"Jessie? Jessie?" I heard them calling from very far off. To save my life I couldn't reply.

A flurry of unintelligible orders followed, then scrapes, clanks, and squeaks. I heard a string of mumbled profanity as the person lowered into the crevice realized he had missed the shelf where I lay.

"I see her! Shit, she's too far away," Ross shouted. "Haul me up, quick! We need to move about six yards over."

In moments he was back. Climbing out of the sling that brought him down, he set an oil lantern on the shelf. "Jessie! Jessie! Thank God you're alive!" He leaned back and shouted, "I got her." He continued, more gently, "We've got the doctor on his way. Can you get over here—no, never mind, I'll pick you up and try not to hurt you. Damnit, you feel like ice!" He gathered me clumsily in his arms and shifted me into the canvas sling.

"Get Jessie."

"What? Yes, yes, I've got you."

"No, get Jessie. I'm not Jessie. Jessie's there." Only then did he notice the remains. He lifted the lantern. "That's Jessie," I croaked. "Henry killed her. He tried to kill me the same way. You can't leave her here."

The weak light shone on the crumpled remains and I saw what was left of Jessie for the first time—little more than bones, matted hair, and some scraps of clothing had survived seven years on the inaccessible underground shelf. And her Venetian beads.

"Okay, David, haul her up!" he shouted.

"No! Get Jessie! Don't leave her!"

Creaking and groaning under the weight, the bootleg pulley strained to lift me.

"Get Jessie! Don't leave Jessie!" No one listened.

Strong arms lifted me out of the sling. "You're safe now. I have you," David said as he yanked off his topcoat and wrapped it around me. It felt like an oven, all warm and soft, and smelled of leather and pipes and men. He held me tight as Chen and Buster dropped the sling down into the crevice again for Ross.

"Make him get Jessie. David, please. Make him get Jessie."

He frowned at me, no doubt thinking that I was hallucinating. "You're safe now, you're right here."

"I'm not Jessie! Jessie's still down there, dead. Henry killed her, like he tried to kill me. Seven years she's been waiting."

"You're not Jessie?"

"No . . . an impersonator."

"You're not my sister?"

"No."

"Thank God!" And he kissed me gently on my icy lips. "I knew I couldn't feel this way about my own sister! Hold on a second, I've got to help Buster pull up Ross."

In less than a minute the two men had raised him to the top.

"Jessie . . ." I whispered, too weak to cry.

"I got her," Ross said tersely as he climbed out of the sling. He paused long enough for Buster and Chen to see what he'd brought up, then he folded the corners together in a bundle and picked it up.

"Let's go home," he said.

We headed toward Cliff House, me in David's arms, my head on his shoulder, warm and safe and alive and happy enough almost to forget the pain in my leg. Behind us, Buster, the only person who had truly loved Jessie, dropped to his knees on the ground, sank his head in his hands, and let out a one-note wail that hung in the air until the wind carried it out to sea.

We reached the house just as Doc Milner's sedan pulled up and Val bounded down the front steps calling, "Here's the doctor!" Henry was right behind her, his face white as a plaster bust.

"Is she—" he croaked, no doubt praying I was as dead as I looked.

"She's alive," said David, his voice sharp as a steel blade, "but she's hurt pretty bad. Jessie's dead, but I figure you knew that. We found her too. Her bones have been in that cave since the day you killed her seven years ago. Listen up, Henry Carr, because I'm telling you a fact. If this girl dies, I will kill you with my own two hands, before the hangman can get to you."

"Jessie's here, Henry," said Ross, laying the bundle on the ground and opening it so everyone could see the pitiful skull and remains.

Val screamed, then dropped to the grass in a faint. Aunt Victoria rushed down the steps, and froze at the bottom, paralyzed with confusion over whether to tend to me or her daughter. "Henry? Henry?" she kept saying. "What happened?"

Caro ran up. "What do you mean, she isn't Jessie?" Everyone started babbling at once.

"Arrest Henry," I tried to say, but no one heard my feeble attempts to speak. And who was there to arrest him?

Doc Milner broke into the mayhem. "All right, all right, the dead are dead, and no one can help them. I've got to look to the living. Get this girl to her bed right now. Get that one some smelling salts."

David carried me into the house as if I weighed no more than a doll. Doc Milner began issuing orders to Rainy as we entered the hall.

"I'll need hot water and clean towels—"

"I already got those in her room," said Rainy. "I heard Miss Valerie telephone for you and I figured you'd want that. And some mercurochrome. And I put a clean sheet over her bed."

"Good girl. Get me every hot water bottle you have, filled with hot water, not boiling." Aunt Victoria sprang back to life and darted toward the kitchen with a set to her jaw that said she would wait to ask questions after the crisis had passed. "You, girl, what's your name?"

"Lorraine, sir. I'm Miss Jessie's maid."

"Get some brandy or whiskey and come with me, Lorraine. You've got sense."

Grandmother was waiting for us at the top of the stairs, her face like stone as she followed David into my room and stood by the bed as he laid me gingerly on the sheet. The commotion had alerted Uncle Oliver, who appeared at the threshold, pale as flour paste, with Grandmother on his arm. The old lady insisted on taking the chair closest to the bed, closest to me, so he stood behind her, his pudgy hands gripping the chair back. I must have looked a horrible sight because a collective gasp went up as the doctor unwrapped David's topcoat.

Rainy came in with a bottle of brandy, followed by Chen carrying several hot water bottles.

"Give her a couple swigs of that," the doctor said.

It gagged me a good bit along the way, but the effect was liquid fire slithering down my throat and pulsing through my veins.

Without being told Rainy began washing the blood off my face, exposing the wounds as the doctor put his stethoscope to my chest. The room was as silent as an empty church. "Someone get me some scissors," he snapped. "I'll have to cut these clothes off."

Ross rummaged through my desk until he found some shears. Doc Milner began cutting away the wet, shredded fabric that clung to my skin, peeling it off in pieces just as Aunt Victoria came in with more hot water bottles. He covered me with a blanket and put the rubber bottles on top of my chest so the warmth could seep into my skin.

"Leg's broken. I'm not sure about the arm. What do you think?" He looked at Chen.

Looking startled to be asked his opinion, Chen stepped forward. His fingers worked methodically up my left arm from the frozen fingers to the bloody shoulder before he said in a quiet voice, "I think, not broken. Cracked perhaps. I think set it anyway."

Doc Milner nodded. Without another word the two began making preparations to set my arm and leg. Rainy continued washing my scrapes and dabbing them with mercurochrome. My skin was so numb I barely felt the sting.

"I . . . I don't understand," began Aunt Victoria as she searched the faces in the room for an explanation. "How can you say she's not Jessie? She must be Jessie. She— You look just like Jessie. Just like Blanche."

Ross replied for me from the corner of the room. "Says here her name is Leah Randall. Her mother was not Aunt Blanche, but some vaudeville singer named Chloë Randall."

A low cry escaped Grandmother's lips. Ross's soft eyes hardened into polished jet as he read aloud from the notes in his hands. The notes I'd compiled on Henry's crimes.

"She's an impostor," he said, and he packed the word with venom enough to kill.

I found my voice. My throat was on fire and every word scratched its way out like cactus past raw flesh. "Henry knew it all along. But he couldn't say how he knew because he had killed the real Jessie. He beat her senseless in that cave where he delivers his whiskey, and he left her to drown so he could get the Carr inheritance."

Aunt Victoria's hand flew to her mouth and she moaned, "No, no, no," in disbelief, over and over as I continued.

"The idea was for her body to wash ashore with water in the lungs so her death would be ruled an accidental drowning, and no one could blame him. But her body didn't wash up because, before she died, she managed to crawl above the waterline to a dry shelf. I only found her because he did the same thing to me. I'd be there still if you hadn't come. Dead by now." I looked at David, standing beside the bed. "How did you find me? Did you know about the bootleg deliveries?"

Grandmother made her way out of the room as David took my hand and explained what had happened.

"When I got here, no one knew where you were. Caroline told me she'd left you on the beach, heading for the cave, but the beach was already covered with water. I thought you might have been trapped and I knew Henry used one of the caves to bring up his shipments every few weeks, but I'd never seen the place. I grabbed Ross and a couple servants, and we found the hole pretty quick when we saw the pulley nearby. I was never so glad of anything in my life as when I heard you whistle. Valerie was with us. She ran back to the house to call Doc here."

"Where's Henry?"

"Getting the hell out of here if he has an ounce of sense."

"I don't believe this." Aunt Victoria spoke up in frightened denial. "What are you saying? Henry would never hurt anyone. Why, he was just a child himself when Jessie disappeared! I'm going to go find him so he can clear this all up."

Ross indicated the notes in his hand. "This is a matter for the police."

"No! Not the police!" said Aunt Victoria. "You'll ruin his reputation right before the election!"

"I've already done that," I told Ross, ignoring Aunt Victoria. "I wrote a long letter to Smith and Wade, confessing everything and giving them all the information you have in your hands. I sent another to the governor's office and one to the newspaper for good measure, in case Henry was bribing the police. Clyde mailed them for me yesterday. I can't prove everything, but it's enough for them to start their own investigation into the other murders I believe Henry committed."

"Other murders?" Ross asked.

I lacked the strength to explain further. "It's all in there."

"You'll go to prison for your part," said Ross.

"That wasn't part of my plan," I said weakly. "I was going to leave tomorrow morning and disappear for good."

"You're not going anywhere anytime soon, young lady," said the doctor.

Aunt Victoria couldn't make sense of anything. "I don't believe any of this. You are Jessie. You must be Jessie! You knew things only Jessie would know."

"She's an actress, Mother. An impersonator and a damned good one. Who set you up? Who fed you all that information?"

I could feel Oliver tense, but I knew better than to look in his direction. "Your governess, the late Miss Lavinia. She had the goods on Henry and was trying to blackmail him. He hired someone to run her down in San Francisco. He tried that on me too, in Portland the day we arrived. He had someone waiting in a car at the Benson. At the time I thought it was a liquored-up driver. It was meant to look that way. But Henry boasted about it to me Friday night. He knew I couldn't tell anyone without exposing myself. Like you once said, David, we had a Mexican standoff."

David nodded absently, his mind obviously miles away.

"Henry tried to kill me two other times: with a heavy dose of your asthma medicine, Ross—that's why you ran out of your medicine unexpectedly—and by ruining the brakes on my Ford. When those didn't work, he told me he'd track me down in Europe and make it look like an accident. He was going to get the Carr money, no matter what. I couldn't let him do that. And I couldn't let him go on killing." I was talking to Oliver now, trying to make him understand. "I had to find out what had happened to Jessie, who killed her."

Grandmother sat back in her chair. I hadn't noticed her return. I was looking up at Ross. "I'm truly sorry for what I did," I said as tears began welling up in my eyes. I blinked hard but they overflowed and made my voice crack. At that, David, who had been stroking the back of my hand with his fingers, lifted my hand to his lips and kissed it, right in front of everyone. I don't know what they were thinking, but I thought it was wonderful. Everyone hated me, but not David. At least I still had David. I took a deep breath and pressed on.

"It seemed pretty harmless when I started, just a way to divert some of the Carr money in my direction. I didn't mean to hurt anyone. I did it for the money, sure, but then I came to care about your family. You're a really nice family, and I loved being one of you, even if it was just for a few weeks. Being Jessie Carr was the best role I ever had."

Aunt Victoria shook her head with disbelief. "But you look just like Blanche! Just like Jessie! The freckles, the hair . . ."

"I believe I can explain that." All eyes turned to Grandmother. "This is from my son Clarence," she said as she slowly unfolded a piece of paper. "It was the last letter I ever had from him." Without

looking at it, she began to recite what she had long ago committed to memory.

> *Dear Mother,*
>   *Our ship docked yesterday. The crossing was smooth*
> *water and sunshine all the way to England. I met up with*
> *my partners in London. We're staying at the YMCA near*
> *St. Paul's until our deal gets under way. As soon as I have*
> *the money, I'm sending to New York for Miss Randall and*
> *we're going to get married. I know what you said, but Chloë's*
> *not that sort of actress; she's sweet, beautiful, and I love her,*
> *and we're going to get married as soon as I can support us.*
> *I'm sorry you don't approve. You will change your mind*
> *when you meet her.*
>   *Your loving son,*
>   *Clarence G. Beckett.*

She paused as she refolded the letter, then looked directly at
me with eyes that would pierce anyone's defenses.

"When were you born?"

"April 25, 1899."

She nodded. It was the answer she expected. "He wrote this in
October of 1898. It was delivered to me along with a letter from a
nurse at the London Hospital telling me of his death from meningitis. She had found this letter in his pocket, addressed but not
yet posted. She said the disease came on quickly, and he did not
suffer."

Everyone in the room looked from Grandmother to me and
counted the months in their heads. Even Doc Milner stopped
mixing the plaster and stared. Ross's nervous cough broke the silence. "You don't . . . ah, you don't look twenty-five," he said uselessly.

"My mother never talked about my father. Not his name, not
anything, except that he left her with promises he never intended

to keep. And a baby. She was very bitter. I suppose she thought someone would have notified her in the event of his death." I aimed a questioning look at Grandmother, who was staring at the wall without a particle of emotion in her face.

"I could have done so," she said, finally. "Clarence had mentioned her in a previous letter and I knew where she was working. But his father and I were angry that he would waste himself on an actress, and we saw no reason to have any further contact with her after he was gone. A couple of months later she wrote to Clarence at our San Francisco address. I never opened the letter. I marked it 'Addressee Unknown, Return to Sender.' I never considered the possibility of a child. And that is why you look like Blanche. Clarence and Blanche were five years apart but as alike as twins."

Chen held a teacup of a foul-tasting potion to my lips. "This will help you sleep and take the pain away."

"What is it?" I croaked, not that it mattered. I'd have slurped mud if Chen gave it to me. Part of my brain heard him answer, but the rest of me was asleep before I could close my eyes.

54

The remainder of that night was a jumble of disconnected impressions: Rainy applying a cool compress, then hot water bottles, Chen brewing warm drinks, Doc Milner's stethoscope pressing on my chest. David telling me that I had to get well, that he couldn't bear losing me now—words that warmed me more than any wool blanket ever could. And Grandmother sitting in the chair by my bed in a silent vigil the whole night long.

She was still there when I finally woke up. I knew it before I opened my eyes; I could smell her lavender scent. At first I thought it was just the beginning of another day at Cliff House, then my fingers touched the Venetian beads still at my neck, and everything that had happened blew back into my head like a gust of wind. I could see a bit of gray sky through the window, but the light was low. I could not tell if it was morning or evening. I tried to ask about the time, but no sound came out of my mouth for several minutes. After sipping some water, I managed to whisper the question.

"Three o'clock," replied Grandmother. Rainy brought the clock from my desk to the table beside the bed so I could see for myself.

"The doctor said he'd be by again before dinner," Rainy told me. "He'll be so gratified you're awake at last. You've been delirious. You had us real worried there for a while, but the fever broke. It looks like you're going to pull through now. Do you think you can swallow these?" She handed me two Bayer aspirin tablets.

A polite rap on the open door turned my head. Chen was there with another cup of his hot drink. "How do you feel today?"

Groggy. Numb. Alive. Afraid to move lest the slightest shift wake up the pain. "Not too bad," I said, my spirits rising as I realized it was true. Chen held my head up and put the teacup to my lips. In a few minutes I had finished it. The now familiar taste was no longer as unpleasant as it once was. "What is that?" I asked him.

"Comfrey for the bones to knit faster; valerian to ease the pain and help you sleep."

"Is David here?"

"Mr. Murray left on Monday," said Rainy.

"Monday? What do you mean, Monday? What day is this?"

"Thursday, miss."

"What! I've been unconscious for four days?"

"Not all the time unconscious. Sometimes you were talking."

"The fever was talking," Grandmother corrected her. "You have been very ill, Jessie. You are not out of danger yet. You must lie quietly and try to sleep while your body mends."

She called me Jessie.

"If I brought you some chicken broth, miss, do you think you could drink it?"

But before it came, I was asleep.

When I next awoke, Ross was standing over me. He was

dressed in a traveling suit that made him look a dozen years older. Or maybe he had aged over the past few days. Nodding at Grandmother, who had all but put down roots beside my bed, he dragged over the desk chair and settled in for the long haul. At last I was aware of the world beyond my bedroom, and there were so many questions I needed answered.

"I wanted to talk to you before we left," he began, but I wouldn't let him take his time.

"Where's Henry?"

"Henry's dead." He said it in the matter-of-fact way of a man quoting the stock market, all the while looking at some papers in his hands.

"What? Oh, no! Oh, my God, no, David—"

"David didn't kill him. He killed himself. While we were all in here with you on Sunday night, Henry took off—for his boat, I presume. He couldn't take his own car—Doc Milner had blocked it when he pulled up in front—so he took your Ford that was sitting off to the side, out of the way. He didn't know that Clyde hadn't finished fixing the brakes. He drove straight into a tree rounding a curve. We buried him Wednesday. We buried Jessie that day too."

I was not sure how I felt. Sorrow didn't quite fit, nor did joy seem appropriate. A curious mixture of satisfaction and regret came to the fore. "I'm sorry," I said untruthfully—I could be nothing but relieved that Henry was no longer running loose trying to kill me—but decency requires some expression of sadness when speaking to a brother of the deceased. And I was glad the real Jessie was buried properly at long last. She deserved a decent burial.

"I am too. But to be honest, it was the best possible solution. If he'd been captured and arrested, we all would have had to endure a long trial and publicity that would have stretched everyone's agony across many months. And then a hanging. Mother couldn't have withstood the strain."

His mention of Aunt Victoria made me realize I hadn't seen her since Sunday.

"Henry's death brought in the police on Monday before your letters had reached their destinations. By the time the letters arrived, they were irrelevant. I had your notes, after all, and everything you said was proved true. Mother refused to believe any of it until a police search of Henry's yacht turned up a collection of hair he had taken from his nine victims which, conveniently for the police, he had labeled. Jessie's was number one. Yours was still in his pocket. We're all to blame. We should have known something was wrong. We *did* know, down deep. But like Mother, we turned a blind eye and refused to face the truth. Henry was always a bully boy who loved nothing better than causing pain. We found excuses. We told ourselves he'd grown out of it, or that we were overreacting. And sometimes, he seemed so, well, normal. At least you stood up to him."

"It's hard to see people clearly when we love them."

"Maybe. Anyway, Mother and I are leaving in an hour for California. Severinus Wade took the first train north when I telephoned him Monday. He brought papers to sign, and sat in the library with me for hours until I understood the ramifications. And so I've made some decisions. I decided to sell this house at once and move Mother and the twins to Palo Alto with me while I work on my doctoral degree. The agent that Mr. Wade engaged to find us a house produced two that fit the bill. Mother and I are going there now so she can choose. It will be far better for the family to be at Stanford with me than here. Cliff House was never meant to be a permanent residence, and it doesn't suit us at all."

It sounded like a good idea. The twins would have a social life; Aunt Victoria would not be surrounded by memories of the deaths at every step she took. Grandmother was nodding her approval.

Ross continued. "The girls might want to study at Stanford—the school is very progressive and accepts female students—or, if not, they will at least have the opportunity to meet people.

Anyway, Mother and I will not be home for several days. I wondered . . . that is, I was wondering what your plans were. After
your recovery, of course."

My plans? My plans were to lie still until the police came to
arrest me for fraud. "I'll plead guilty to all charges, so you needn't
worry about the embarrassing publicity a trial would bring. I hope
the police will wait a few days before taking me in—"

Ross shook his head. "We're not pressing charges. We're
calling it all an unfortunate mistake. When all is said and done,
you're still family. You are Jessie's cousin. We can't hush it up
entirely, of course, but the newspapers are far more interested
in Henry's death and the murders than in you. That's why I
need to get Mother and the girls away from here as soon as
possible. Movers will be here Monday to start packing up the
household."

An awkward silence hung in the air between us. "Oh, I almost
forgot," he said, noticing the papers in his hand. "David Murray
left this note for you." It was a single sheet of paper, creased. Anyone could have read it. I assumed everyone had.

> *Dear Jessie,*
>   *They assured me you were going to get well or I would*
> *never have left your side. Unexpected business reversals mean*
> *I need to travel for a while. I hope we will meet again one day.*
>   *Yours,*
>   *David.*

I burst into tears. That was it? That was all? I may have been
muddled and half frozen, but I clearly remember him kissing me
and saying, Thank God I wasn't his sister. Didn't I remember him
holding my hand as I lay in bed, willing me well, telling me he
couldn't bear to lose me? This note didn't read like a man in love.
I didn't know if I was in love with David—I hadn't allowed myself
to consider it, under the circumstances—but I sure as heck wanted

the chance to find out. And now he'd disappeared. On business? What was that about, for crying out loud?

"Where did he go? I don't understand," I said, wiping my eyes on my nightgown sleeve.

"No, I expect you don't. None of us did, except Henry, of course. David Murray had to leave the moment the police came into the picture. Turns out he is the bootleg boss of Oregon—or was, until you dragged the governor and the newspapers into the middle of his operation. Even the people he was bribing to look the other way couldn't ignore it after your letter linked the boot-leggers to all those murdered women."

I must have looked like a fish with its mouth open for bugs. "But—but—" I sputtered. I looked to Grandmother for a denial, but she only nodded. "But he worked for Henry!"

"Henry worked for him. For many years. And David said he didn't know about the murdered girls, although he was aware of Henry's reputation around town for beating up women. I think I believe him about that. The police, however, might be harder to persuade. Most of those girls were involved in Henry's smuggling, hired to keep the police happy. David said they weren't profes-sional prostitutes, just poor working girls who needed money. And since they were mostly Indian or Mexican, there was little interest in their deaths. Henry must have figured they knew too much about the smuggling operation to just let them walk away."

Or he simply liked killing, I wanted to add, but didn't.

"But David just returned to Portland a few months ago. He was a cowboy . . ." I trailed off with the sinking realization that I had been had.

David was as much cowboy as I was heiress. It had been an act, a fairy tale calculated to distract from his criminal activities. The story about selling the Montana ranch gave him an expla-nation for the money in his pockets; the cowboy image must have played well with women. Had his mother known? I thought not. Damn him—how could he do this to me?

"The only part of his story that was true is the part about being Lawrence Carr's illegitimate son. He must have known for years who Henry was and that they were cousins, but for whatever reason, he kept it to himself. Anyway, it came out last spring, and Mother confirmed it when Henry asked."

And all the time I was spinning my tales to him, he was spinning to me. It really was a good joke all around. So why wasn't I laughing?

So that's what it felt like being swindled by someone you cared for and trusted. Betrayal hurt. A whole lot. It shamed me that I had caused more hurt than anyone.

"David couldn't say much in his note. He was afraid the police would get hold of it and use it against him."

Yes, that explained the stiff tone, the lack of any personal message. I felt a little better as I reasoned it out. The wonder was that he didn't hate me for having destroyed his entire operation by tying it all to Henry's crimes. He had to flee the state—maybe the country—and lie low while the heat cooled. If he had professed his undying love and written that he would come to me later, the police would know that they had only to watch me and wait for him to reappear. Still . . .

"But the police didn't get hold of it," I observed.

"No."

"Thanks."

Ross stood up. He turned to Grandmother and asked, "Did you tell her about Oliver?" She shook her head. "Your uncle left right after Jessie's funeral. He had some business in New York to attend to. He said to give you this."

He tossed a large sealed envelope on my bed. I recognized it at once and my heart leaped into my throat. It was the envelope I had left in Randolph Stouffer's desk drawer back in Cleveland, the one with the photos and playbills of Mother and me. My most precious possessions, bar none. I didn't bother to ask myself how

Oliver had found them—he must have been watching me more closely during those days than I realized. It was enough that he had found them, realized their value to me, and taken them to use as collateral, in case I stepped out of line.

Well, the swindle was over, and we had lost any chance at the Carr fortune. It wasn't my fault. He couldn't blame me. I had done my best. I hadn't counted on Henry turning into Jack the Ripper and trying to add my hair to his gruesome collection. And I had shielded Oliver as best I could with the lie about Miss Lavinia. Surely he was grateful for that!

All this went through my head in a flash, and my undamaged hand shook as I reached for the envelope. No matter how hard I tried to convince myself otherwise, I knew Oliver blamed me. My impersonation was to have been the feast after his lifelong famine, his one chance to reach the Big Time. My failure doomed him to Small Time scrimping for the rest of his life, genteel panhandling from his wealthy friends. And I had known from the start that Oliver Beckett was not a nice man.

My one good hand fumbled with the clasp. I pretended for a few more seconds that I didn't know what I would find.

I lifted the flap. Inside the envelope was my childhood, torn to shreds. It felt like my mother had died all over again.

Uncle Oliver had had his revenge.

I fought back the tears. Grandmother was talking to Ross about my future.

"As soon as Jessie is able to travel, she'll come to San Francisco with me," she was saying. She called me Jessie. I hadn't imagined it yesterday. "She will have time there to recuperate and decide what direction to take her life. Is that acceptable, Jessie?"

Why not? Where else did I have to go? I remembered that Jack Benny was still in Frisco playing at Pantages. I owed him thanks and an explanation. And he'd be good for some advice on getting a job. Maybe he'd know of some act that needed a girl who could do a little of everything . . . maybe other performers there would know of something. After all, San Francisco was a big town with lots of theaters and circuits. But instead of buoying my spirits, the thought of returning to vaudeville's gypsy life only dragged them down. I had left that life behind when I came to Cliff House. I was no longer eager to return.

Maybe I'd continue south, to Hollywood, that town at the edge of Los Angeles where all the moviemakers had gathered after the Great War. I'd heard that life was glamorous in Hollywood, and the weather was always lovely. Everyone knew that Mary Pickford and her husband, Douglas Fairbanks, lived in Hollywood in a grand mansion with its own swimming pool— imagine that! Mary Pickford had been my idol forever. She and her husband had started their own film company, United Artists. Maybe I could get some sort of job with them. Any sort of job—I wasn't too proud to sweep floors. And I had friends, vaudeville performers who had gone over to moving pictures, who might be able to point me toward work.

"Jessie? Did you hear me?"

After all that had happened she still called me Jessie. A lifetime of borrowed stage names had left me indifferent to what I was called. No one used my given name. Without a father, I had no real family name, and my first names had always mirrored the parts I played. No longer. I knew who I was now and how I fitted in. I had found a name that belonged to me, the one that kept my cousin Jessie close to me, and I would keep it, if my grandmother had no objection.

"Oh, I beg your pardon, Grandmother. I was thinking."

"I said, you should come home with me until you are restored to health. I hope you will, child. It will give me the chance to show you some pictures of Clarence—your father—and to tell you what he was like as a child and a young man."

"Of course, Grandmother. That would mean a lot to me."

"I failed both my granddaughters. I should have done more for

Jessie, but I thought she was better off living with a family than a crotchety old lady. I didn't take her unhappiness seriously. And I failed you. If I had not allowed excessive pride to keep us from writing to your mother, I would have learned about Clarence's daughter. I am not a wealthy woman, but I could have provided you and your mother a decent home. Perhaps I still can, for you, at least."

When all was said and done, I didn't get Jessie's money, but I did get her family. The Beckett half, anyway. Knowing that my father had loved my mother so much he intended to go against his parents' wishes to marry her erased some of the bitterness toward men that I had carried around all my life. Knowing something about my parents, grandparents, aunts and uncles, and cousins, living and dead, gave me a sense of belonging I had never before experienced, a definite place in the great scheme of things. For the first time in my life, I felt part of something larger than myself. It felt good.

Just then Rainy came into the room carrying a tray of soup and crackers, and my stomach growled in appreciation. As she helped me sit up against the pillows, I shifted my shoulders and felt something hard and warm fall to one side against my breast. Dumbfounded, I groped for the object and pulled it from beneath my nightgown. A gold locket, just like the one David's mother wore. I pressed the pinhead spring and it popped open to reveal the photographs of young David and his mother. It *was* David's locket. What on earth was it doing—

Then it came to me like a great wind blowing up the coast. David's mother had valued her locket more than any other object she'd owned, and it served as his messenger, conveying the words he couldn't write down or pass along through anyone else. He must have slipped it around my neck while no one was watching. He trusted me to understand what it meant, that in leaving me with his mother's necklace he was making a promise: *I will see you again. I will find you somehow and reclaim my mother's locket.*

But Grandmother was waiting for my reply. I put the locket back beneath my clothes against my breast before someone could ask about it. "Thank you, Grandmother. I'd be grateful for a place to stay while I mend. And Rainy—I'm sorry my leaving puts you out of a job. I wish I could take you with me."

"Never mind that, miss. Mr. Ross offered all us who wanted to go to California a job but . . ." She looked shyly at Ross. "But . . . well, Doc Milner said he could use a quick girl like me to help him with his patients, and, well, I'd rather stay in Dexter where my family is than go to California."

"Oh, Rainy, that's wonderful! You'll make an excellent nurse."

Pink with pride, she fussed. "Now, there, let me put this extra pillow behind you, miss, so you can sit up a little and eat."

Ross got to his feet. "If you leave before Mother and I return, I'd like to say . . ." Whatever it was, he couldn't say it. "Well . . . good-bye." His Valentino eyes held mine for an awkward moment, then we both looked away, embarrassed.

He got as far as the hall before turning around. "Oh, I almost forgot . . . the storm that blew through the night of the party? It was brief but violent. A day or two later—we're not sure which day—a large section of the weak south cliff collapsed into the sea."

I didn't have to ask which section.

Jessie had known. *Hurry! Don't leave me.* Time was short and she hadn't wanted to be lost forever when the crevice that opened into the cave finally split off and that giant slab of rock crumbled into the churning sea.

POSTSCRIPT

How much of *The Impersonator* is true? The short answer is: a lot. Of course, the story is fiction and the main characters—Jessie, the Carr family, and David Murray—are products of my imagination. However, most of the vaudeville references are historical fact. The Kanazawa Japs, the Seven Little Foys, Cats and Rats, Baby Silvia, Houdini, Bill "Bojangles" Robinson, W. C. Fields, the Venetian Masqueraders, and so forth were acts that played the Big Time circuits in 1924. Some of the names are familiar today, especially to movie buffs, because most early radio and film personalities started in vaudeville—people like Milton Berle, Mae West, the Marx Brothers, and Jack Benny left vaudeville for long careers in radio, film, and television.

And while the little town of Dexter is fictional, the other locations mentioned are real and their descriptions as accurate to the time period as I could make them. The hotels are genuine (the Benson is still one of Portland's finest hotels and the Black-stone in Omaha has been rehabbed into an office building), as are the theaters, although, sadly, many were casualties of urban renewal.

Almost no one alive today has been to a vaudeville show. While minstrel shows, circuses, and other sorts of variety performances existed before the Civil War, vaudeville is usually considered to have started in the 1870s. The genre peaked in the 1920s and declined in the early 1930s, usurped by radio and the movies. To see what real vaudeville, and its risqué cousin, burlesque, looked like, check into some of the short features on www.youtube .com, including some of my favorites:

www.youtube.com/watch?v=vZo4imTt4Og
www.youtube.com/watch?v=PsVQ9e8nWx0
www.youtube.com/watch?v=jQ6Zh6UbQ-I
www.youtube.com/watch?v=SA6wYvVnq4g
www.youtube.com/watch?v=49B3ZnxibTQ&feature=related

I hope you enjoyed reading *The Impersonator* as much as I enjoyed writing it. If you'd like to see what Jessie's world of vaudeville and the Oregon coast looks like, visit her Pinterest page at www.pinterest.com/mmtheobald/jessies-world-the-impersonator/.

If you have any questions or comments about *The Impersonator* or suggestions for future books in this series, contact me through my Web site, www.marymileytheobald.com; my Facebook page, www.facebook.com/pages/Mary-Miley/303906933020831; or my Roaring Twenties blog, marymiley.wordpress.com. I'd be happy to let you know when the next book comes out.

ACKNOWLEDGMENTS

Particular thanks go to my mentor, Donna Sheppard, who taught me how to write better than any English teacher ever could, to Tom Fuhrman of my critique group who provided technical know-how when it came to sabotaging antique cars, to Dr. Mark Pugh, a pharmacist who listened to my questions about how to murder people with drugs and deadly herbs and did not alert the police, to Erica Gilliam, a master gardener who made sure I got the horticulture right, to my critique group (Marilyn Mattys, Vivian Lawry, Kathleen Mix, Sandie Warwick, Susan Campbell, Linda Thornburg, Josh Cane, and Libby Hall), and especially to my editors at Minotaur, Kelley Ragland and Elizabeth Lacks, and their awesome copy editor, Ragnhild Hagen, whose sharp eye saved me from several embarrassing mistakes.

I have always been intrigued by stories that involved memory loss, impersonation, and look-alikes. My favorites include

Josephine Tey's *Brat Farrar* (1949), the novel that served as the inspiration for this story, as well as Mary Stewart's *The Ivy Tree* (1962), Joy Fielding's *See Jane Run* (1991), and Sebastien Japrisot's *A Trap for Cinderella* (1963).

IS YOUR BOOK CLUB READING *THE IMPERSONATOR*?
CONSIDER POSING THESE QUESTIONS

1. Did you hear stories from your grandparents about the Roaring Twenties? Prohibition? Women's rights?

2. What parallels do you find between Prohibition of alcohol in the 1920s and today's prohibiting of recreational drugs? Do you think the government should prohibit or regulate alcohol, recreational drugs, medicine, cigarettes, or other items?

3. Some historians believe the women's movement made its greatest advances in the 1920s. What evidence for this did you find in *The Impersonator*? What examples of limitations on women did you notice in the story? What could Jessie do or not do back then that we take for granted today?

4. The Twenties brought new freedoms to young American women that older ones never had. How was Grandmother's life constrained by her times? Aunt Victoria's life?

5. Vaudeville began in the 1880s and reached its height in the 1920s when this story takes place. It declined in the 1930s and was gone by the 1940s. Why do you think this popular form of family entertainment disappeared? What replaced it?

6. What does Jessie want in the beginning of the story? Does she achieve it at the end? What price does she pay for her role in the scam?

7. The Roaring Twenties was a virulently racist era, the height of the Ku Klux Klan in both northern and southern states, and a time when anti-black, anti-Catholic, anti-immigrant, anti-Semitic, anti-Asian, and anti-gay sentiments were universal. Why do you think Jessie is more open-minded than was typical in this time period?

8. Is there more than one impersonator in the story? What themes about impersonation did you notice throughout the novel?

9. Whom did you first suspect? When did you begin to suspect the real culprit?

10. How did you anticipate that the strong resemblance between the heiress and the imposter might be explained?

11. What did you find most or least appealing about the historical setting? In what ways might the historical setting have affected the mystery plotline? What do you think a historical setting offers a mystery writer that a modern setting might not?

12. Do you support Leah's decision to adopt Jessie's name? Or Grandmother's intentional decision to continue using it? What significance does a name have for the main character?

13. Which of Leah's skills as a performer overlap with detective skills? How much of the solution depended on luck or coincidence?

14. How might Jessie become tangled in another crime-solving opportunity? What other characters do you hope to find in future books?

15. If a movie were made of *The Impersonator*, who could you see playing the role of Jessie? David? Any other characters?